maybe, one day

Anna Beukema

Copyright © 2021 Anna Beukema

All rights reserved.

ISBN: 979-8-7635-3159-6

For Nina.

CONTENTS

	Acknowledgments	i
1		1
2		Pg 14
3		Pg 33
4		Pg 46
5		Pg 64
6		Pg 85
7		Pg 98
8		Pg 110
9		Pg 129
10		Pg 145
11		Pg 163
12		Pg 183
13		Pg 202
14		Pg 220
15		Pg 262

I'd like to thank all my readers for supporting me throughout the journey that has gotten me so far to finally write my first book.

I'd also like to thank Nina, who has supported me through this all, who has given me that final push towards actually publishing this work.

It has been a dream of mine to publish a book, but I never thought I would be good enough to do it. But with everything that has happened in the past year, I couldn't hide it from the world anymore.

So, a huge thanks to all of them. I will always be grateful for the support.

1

Divorce is a cruel thing.
Nobody should ever have to deal with it all, really.
It's harsh, it's painful, especially when one realizes that their entire marriage has just… failed. That perhaps, it was never right in the first place.
It stings, cuts deep into Riley's heart as she sits at the law firm, waiting for her future ex-wife to show up so they can sign the fucking papers and just get it over with.
Everything else has been dealt with – her wife has moved out; Riley will keep the apartment and the furniture.
No matter how much she tried to convince her wife to just take half of it, or at least let Riley pay, she had stubbornly refused.
Her wife just chose to move on, not wanting any of their things, probably to leave it all behind to start over, start fresh.
If Riley is honest with herself, she wishes she could start over. But the feeling in her heart will not change if she does, so she doesn't think it'll matter much if she stays in her current home or not.
She simply doesn't want to go and find a new house, she loves the view she has from her current home, she loves the atmosphere and the location.
She taps her fingers on her thigh impatiently, perhaps even nervously.
She doesn't even know if she can do it.
She doesn't even know if she'll be able to pick up the pen and sign her name, ending something that has lasted for years. Ending something that she once cherished so deeply.
She sighs, though, annoyance seeping through when she checks the watch on her thin wrist for the umpteenth time.
She has always hated it that her wife tends to come late to everything.
It's just cruel to think that one can be cheated on, not just once, not twice or three times.
No, counting it would probably not even help. All that she knows is that

her wife has been seeing someone else for two fucking years.
Two years, and she was too blind to see.
Two years of her life turn out to be nothing more than a lie and she cannot believe it, still.
She can't believe it, not even after walking in on her wife doing it with another woman. The image is just burned into her mind.
How could she ever forgive her wife? How could she ever forgive herself for being so oblivious?
She asks herself these questions, but she knows she has yet to ask herself the biggest one.
How could she forgive herself, knowing it was her own fault all along?
They loved each other once. Riley is so sure of it.
She knows it for sure, that there was a moment where she thought; I want to grow old with this woman.
Oh, how things can change.
Riley feels bitter when she rises from the uncomfortable leather seat, her pencil skirt tightly wrapped around her legs when she moves to stand in front of the window.
She crosses her arms in front of her chest, fisting the satin fabric of her fancy button up into her hand.
It's cliché, really, when she finds herself staring into the city. She wonders how many people have been in this office, feeling the exact same way she's feeling, now.
Hopeless. Void. Like their entire life is based on a fucking lie. Like they wasted so many years on something that turned out to be fake.
Her view is amazing, but she can't enjoy it, no matter how much she tries.
She wants to be able to kick off her ridiculously high heels. She wants to be far away from here, somewhere tucked safely in a bed and cry.
It's all she wants.
But she is standing here, waiting for her wife to show up, waiting to get divorced so she can move on with her life.
She smooths out the blouse she's wearing. She tucks her loose curls behind her ears.
She bounces on her heels impatiently, clasping her hands behind her back while she stares into nothing.
Her lawyer is wise enough not to speak right now, knowing just how cold she can be.
She needs the silence. She needs to think things through, she just needs to find herself again, if that's even possible.
If she's being completely honest with herself, she doesn't even know who she is anymore.
She thought she knew.
She thought she had it all figured out, she thought she had her life planned

out for herself.

Her chuckle is hollow when she shakes her head to herself, realizing how much she's been lying to herself, too.

Who is she, really? She thought she knew what she wanted, but if she's honest with herself, she doesn't have a clue.

How can she call herself the real her when she has done nothing but live a complete and utter lie, only caring about what others might think of her?

She doesn't know the answers and until she does, she has to leave this all behind her.

They've been together for far too long, she knows.

She should've known that they weren't meant to be.

But how could she when she pushed her true feelings as far away as possible? When she didn't really see her, but only saw what could be?

Her career, her money, her reputation, it all seems to fade, it all seems like it doesn't matter, and she knows it's true.

She purses her lips the moment she hears the glass door to the conference room open. She doesn't bother turning around, already knowing who stepped in.

"You're late." There is a sour bitterness in her voice when she speaks.

"You're early." An equal tone rolls from her wife's lips.

Riley clenches her jaw when she turns around, meeting angry blue eyes.

She doesn't bother saying more, sitting down next to her lawyer, who has the papers prepared and ready to be signed.

"Just one signature and you won't have to be annoyed by that anymore."

The lawyers' cheeks turn red the moment he realizes what he is saying.

Riley rolls her eyes, automatically pushing imaginal hair behind her ear. She sends her lawyer a glare, satisfied when he seems to crumble further back into himself.

"Can't wait." Her wife grumbles under her breath.

For a moment, Riley's green eyes find blue.

For a moment, Riley remembers why she once cared about her.

It's strange, really, to think that they have gotten here.

To think that they are on opposite sides of the table.

"Mrs. Dunn, I have your papers. Please, sign every page. Take your time to go through them." He hands her wife the papers.

"Please, call me Ms. Fitzgerald."

"You're still Mrs. Dunn." Riley mutters, hoping that Camilla doesn't hear, but she does.

"Like you care." She snaps, snatching the papers from the lawyer's hands.

Riley feels her nostrils flare when she looks up, meeting an equally frustrated expression.

Camilla has been nothing but angry with her and Riley feels like she deserves it.

She feels like she deserves it and yet she can't do anything with her frustration. It should be pointed at herself and yet she is throwing it all on Camilla.
Riley's gaze softens when she realizes that it is still her fault.
She is the one who started to neglect their relationship in the first place by working late and never really caring about what Camilla did anymore.
It didn't just happen. It didn't just come out of nowhere, no. It started even before they got married.
It started slowly when Riley finished law school. It started when she got hired at one of the best firms in New York and she cared more for her career than for her fiancée.
It slipped in.
It slipped in and at some point, she didn't even know the person she was living with anymore.
At some point, she didn't even know herself anymore either and she did not even realize that.
She knows that she is to blame for that. She is to blame for that and yet, she cannot stop her heart from aching when she thinks of the moment she truly realized it was over.
Camilla is looking at her, that similar pain in her eyes when she must be thinking the same thing.
Her blue eyes are sad, her lips pursed, a permanent crease folded between her eyebrows.
She's still beautiful.
She's still gorgeous. Her long, dyed dark hair falls in natural curls around her face.
Riley always thought she looked a bit like… Margot Robbie. Margot Robbie mixed with perhaps Julianne Hough, but then more graceful and with darker hair.
The way she sits in her chair, wearing that suit, it still leaves Riley breathless, and she hates herself for it.
Riley can feel the fight drain from her body. It leaves with a single breath as she picks up the pen that seems heavier than it should be.
She doesn't read a single word on the papers, but she signs anyway.
This is really it.
The end of nearly twelve years together. The end of an incredible friendship that turned into love.
Except that it may not have been that kind of love.
The kind of love that makes you feel like you're living on cloud nine. The kind of love that makes you think that nothing better could ever happen to you.
She's never felt that way and she wonders if it even exists. If it does, she sure as hell didn't have that with Camilla.

It breaks her heart all the more, though.

It doesn't feel like a relief when everything is signed. It doesn't feel like it's real at all.

But it is. The lawyer says something, but she doesn't hear a word. She just rises from her seat, straightening her skirt before moving out the room, taking her fancy coat in the process.

She wants to flee. She wants to run, but people here know who she is. It's not her firm, her firm doesn't handle these kind of cases, but still.

In these several years she's been working as a criminal lawyer, she's been well-known among the local law firms.

They know who she is and she has a reputation to uphold. So she walks, with her chin high, chest lifted.

She walks, as if nothing has happened, using her stoic, lawyer poker face while she moves to the elevators.

She glances at her left hand.

She never took off the ring.

Not once in her marriage, she took off that ring.

Now that her marriage is over, it still feels wrong to remove it. It still doesn't feel like it is really happening.

"You can't take it off, can you?" Camilla's voice is surprisingly soft next to her.

Riley doesn't bother looking up.

She simply doesn't know what to say.

She used to be able to ramble about anything and everything to Camilla, even after things had gotten bad. She has always been good with words in her career.

This must be the very first time in her life she can't find the words.

"I am sorry, Riley." Her voice is sincere when she manages to choke out the words and for the first time in months, Riley is able to look her in the eyes without feeling so angry, so lost.

Camilla tries to smile, but it falters. Her eyes are filled with tears and all Riley wants to do is take her in her arms, but she doesn't.

"Don't be." Riley murmurs, waiting for the elevator to arrive. "Don't be, Cam. Don't be sorry for something that isn't on you."

"But it is, Riley." She shakes her head. "It is my fault. It's both our faults. You pulled back from me, maybe, but I let you. I let you slip away when I should've fought for you."

Riley's heart just breaks. "Should we have fought, though? Should we have? Were we really meant to be, Cam? Because I don't believe that anymore."

"I used to." She looks like she's on the brink of crying. "I used to believe that we were."

"Me, too." Riley's smile is painfully filled with sadness.

"I loved you, Riley." Her eyes are heavy, her voice raw. "I loved you, but I

don't think we should've gotten married in the first place."
"Yeah." She shakes her head, her voice barely a whisper. "We were blinded. Maybe we shouldn't have gotten married, but I shouldn't have pulled away the way I did. I... I have learned from that, now. I know that it was something wrong, that I should have been there for you when I wasn't."
The elevator dings, the doors slide open. They silently step into it, grateful when nobody else joins them.
"Can we... do you think we can forgive each other? For hurting each other the way we did?" Camilla reaches for Riley's hand, and she lets her take it.
It feels foreign and familiar at the same time.
"I already did, Cam." Riley's green eyes flash between blue. "It's myself I can't forgive."
"You should." Camilla encourages her. "All this anger... all my anger, it isn't pointed towards you, Riley. It's because I allowed us to get into this mess."
The way Camilla treats her now, Riley would have never expected this to happen. She would have never expected that this conversation would happen, that Camilla would come to her and talk.
Talk like they used to.
Talk like they should've done all along. Maybe they could've made it if they had just communicated.
"I know what you're thinking." Her laugh is quiet and empty. "I know you're thinking that if we would've fought, if we would've just talked... that we would still be together."
"I don't know anything, Camilla." Riley shakes her head, still aware of her hand in Camilla's. "All I know is that... I forgive you. You broke my trust, you broke my heart, but part of me knows that it was my fault. I just..."
The elevator announces it presence on the ground floor.
They step out, their hands still entangled.
Riley takes a breath while they hover in the lobby, quietly standing together, not quite ready to say goodbye.
"I want us to be okay." Riley continues. She realizes how that sounds, so she quickly continues. "I want us to part... okay. Not that we remain friends, but that... we go our separate ways not hating each other. That we can remember the good things that we did together."
Camilla is softly crying, now. Riley is, too. She doesn't care about who sees, not anymore.
"We were great once." She recalls, squeezing Riley's hand. She lifts it up, softly caressing her palm.
She then moves, very slowly, very delicately in order for Riley to pull back if she wants to.
She doesn't. She allows her now ex-wife to remove her wedding ring.
She allows her ex-wife to kiss her hand, to pull her into a hug.

"I will always love you in a way, Riley." She mumbles, trying to hold herself together.

She doesn't respond when Camilla pulls back, taking her hand to place the ring in.

Camilla moves to wrap Riley's own fingers around the ring, her fingers gently tapping Riley's hand.

"I hope you will find that love, Riley. You deserve that."

"So do you." Riley bites her lips. "I am so sorry I couldn't be that for you."

"Don't apologize, okay? You have nothing left to apologize for." Camilla moves to cup Riley's cheeks, wiping away a few tears.

The touch is bittersweet.

Riley hates how heavy the wedding ring in her hand feels. She hates how it seems to burn through her hand, leaving a gaping hole that she can feel aching in her chest.

"You will find it." Her ex-wife reminds her. "Love. Someone, who will love you better than I did. Someone, who will be able to keep you without having to try because you love her so much, too."

"Maybe, one day." Riley mumbles.

"Goodbye, Riley."

It's the final goodbye that Riley always feared. It stings, it hurts, and she hates that it has to happen.

They can't be friends. Too much has happened for them to stay in each other's lives.

She has no idea if she will ever see Camilla again and it hurts. It hurts so fucking much.

"Goodbye, Cam." She cries silently. She feels a soft pair of lips on her cheek, before it disappears and Camilla leaves with it.

It only leaves her heart aching worse.

Her apartment is empty. The apartment that used to be theirs. Their large loft that seems way too big for just her alone now, even though Camilla has left her months ago.

Camilla insisted on taking it those years ago because it offered a view on Central Park.

At first, Riley didn't like it. It was too big, too cold.

She has grown to love it, though.

With their salaries, with their careers, it was easy to afford, really.

She knows that one day, she will move away from here, but not until she has found the courage to do so.

Somehow, it's one thing of the past she still has, something she can't let go just yet.

She notices that she still has the wedding band pressed in her palm. It's burned into her skin, almost too heavy for her to carry any longer.

MAYBE, ONE DAY

The flickering lights of the city are mesmerizing as she stares, a glass of red wine in her free hand, the wedding band in the other.
She hasn't eaten and she knows that drinking on an empty stomach is a little too reckless, even for her.
She usually thinks things through before actually doing it, but right about now, she can't find it in herself to care.
Now that she thinks of it, she doesn't really have anybody else left in her life.
It's always been Camilla. Always.
Riley's parents were never in the picture after she came out to them.
They hated her for what she was. She left them and she never looked back.
She hates how she still cares. She despises how she wonders if they have followed her career, and if they are secretly maybe proud of her.
She wonders if they are even still alive.
She wonders if they know what a mess her life has become.
There is only really one person she can call. Only one person she trusts. A person she hasn't spoken to in a long time because she never had the time (that is what she's telling herself).
She wants to call him. She wants to be able to call him and tell him what has happened to her, but she can't.
She neglected him, as simple as that. She left him just as much as she left everyone else in her life, not bothering to check in regularly.
She left him behind when she should've been there for him. She doesn't even know how he is doing now.
She just never called, she never met him. He had stopped trying eventually and she didn't even notice.
She can't do it now. Not when she realizes how wrong she has been about everything.
Not when she realizes she has been prioritizing all the wrong things in her life. She can't.
She can't call him.
The loneliness really dawns upon her when she glances at the big city at her feet.
She has it all, people think.
She has money, career. People look up to her. She has a ruthless reputation around the city and people have always envied her.
She had the most beautiful woman in the world as her wife. She had a powerful career, an expensive loft.
She had it all, except that it now means absolutely nothing.
She stares and stares, her heart bleeding, aching so much that it leaves her wondering if it'll ever be able to heal.
Millions of people pass the streets here every day.
She shares the city with millions of other people, so many stories, so many

feelings.
So much pain and suffering and a lot of that comes from own choices.
Like hers.
She moves to her kitchen island.
She places her empty glass of wine on the dark marble with a small clink, before moving to put her coat back on.
It's a cold day. On her heels, she moves to the elevator. She goes up.
As far as she can go.
She moves out of the elevator, up the stairs that guide her to the roof. She opens it with a key she once found in the door, and they never bothered to change the locks.
Nobody knows she has been coming up here for years. Nobody knows that this is the only place on earth where she gets to be herself.
Hours, days, maybe even weeks she has spent on this rooftop, thinking.
Feeling like she actually mattered. Because in some way, she never felt like that.
She never felt like she mattered, especially not after what happened with her parents, after Camilla did, what Riley herself did.
She tried to fill the emptiness with her career, the satisfaction of winning cases, of people fearing her in court.
It never worked, not fully.
The only place she could ever feel free, has been right here on the rooftop.
Staring out over the city, seeing the ocean in the distance, feeling like she is on top of the world.
When she would think about everything, all those stories, all those people who went through something similar… it gives her some kind of comfort.
She tried to forgive herself. She tried to become herself.
She tried to find out who she was, and she had no idea.
But being on this rooftop, being able to feel so alone, so aware of her surroundings has always given her strength to keep going, to keep going until she will know who she is.
It's always been her moment to breathe the moment she got on top, standing near the edge, clutching onto the railing, aware of the incredible height.
Aware of just feeling everything, all at once.
The wind is harsh in her face, just like reality.
It is even raining, but she doesn't care that it soaks her to the skin. She stopped caring a long time ago.
She clamps onto the ring in her hand, her long hair flying uncontrollably around her head in the wind.
The darkness of the sky gives her a strange kind of comfort while she hears the traffic, far, far down.
Sirens, tires screeching. The wind blowing roughly in her ears, partly

deafening her.
Birds up in the sky, the cold wind cutting her in the skin.
The rain cooling her off.
She looks down at her hand, bringing it up to open it for the first time ever since Camilla placed the ring there.
She sobs.
She sobs when she realizes just how broken she is.
She sobs when she realizes how she wasted years of her life to her career, to an empty marriage, only to have it all end up meaningless.
She keeps looking at the ring she has been wearing for years.
It's engraved into her, almost.
But, as she stands there, almost blowing away in the strong wind, she throws it away as far as she can, her shoulder hurting with the force she uses.
She doesn't see where it goes, she doesn't see if it comes any far, but it's gone.
Part of her life goes with it.
Twelve years, to be exact.
Twelve years fall down a skyscraper in the middle of New York, only to be crushed onto the ground.
Crushed until there's nothing left.

It takes her a good two hours before she moves back down to her apartment, taking the stairs.
She is trembling on her legs; from the numbness the cold gave her. Her hair dripping with icy rain, she shivers when she makes her way down.
She is just trying to tuck the key into her lock when she hears a soft voice.
"Everything okay?"
Riley snaps up her eyes, only to meet the bluest eyes she has ever seen.
Blue eyes that belong to the neighbor that moved into the only other loft on her floor a while ago.
"Yes." Riley just purses her lips, running a hand through her hair, wondering why her neighbor is looking at her with such… softness.
It feels inappropriate and it makes her uncomfortable. The blonde hair of her neighbor contrasts with the dark walls of the hallway.
Her smile is too bright for this time of the evening, and she is wearing scrubs, looking like she just returned from her job.
Her neighbor that Riley doesn't even know the name of. Her neighbor, a beautiful woman with a certain mystery over her that intrigues her more than it should.
"Are you sure?" the blonde raises an eyebrow in curiosity, but drops the subject when Riley doesn't speak, instead returning to try and get her numb fingers to move.

The moment Riley manages to turn the lock, opening the door and step inside, she glances across the hall, where the blonde has already disappeared.
She sighs, taking off her coat when she closes the door with a loud thump. She doesn't bother hanging it up, she just drops it to the floor, kicking off her heels to make her way to her bathroom.
She steps under her spacious shower, turning the water as hot as her skin can take, trying to wash it all off.
Trying to cleanse the pain of the past, but nothing seems to help. The water screams down her body, but it doesn't change anything.
She still feels the same way and she feels silly for thinking that a hot shower could help her any.
She hates this.

She calls him anyway.
She cries when she hears his voice for the first time in months and he exactly knows who she is without even speaking.
She cries her heart out when he stays.
He stays on the phone, and he comforts her, and he accepts her like she has done nothing wrong.
He tells her that he is on his way over and in that moment, she realizes that he doesn't live all too far from her.
She realizes that she has been so wrong all her life.
He hangs up the phone, telling her to stay put.
She doesn't deserve him.
She doesn't deserve her brother, not after what she did.
She half expects him not to show up, but when her doorbell rings, she feels the need to vomit.
She is nauseated to the core, her legs want to give out, but she manages to buzz him into the building.
It takes a few minutes for him to knock on the door. She barely registers herself walking to open it, her bare feet cold on the expensive granite floor.
Her eyes widen when she sees him.
Austin.
Her adopted younger brother. The one who stayed with her parents after she left because of their homophobia.
The one she never called because she always assumed he agreed with them.
The brother who admitted he never did and left, too, showing her his loyalty. And still, she managed to fuck it up.
Still, she prioritized her career, not having time for him at all.
She is ashamed, so deeply ashamed when she sees him.
She can't really move when she sees him hovering in the entrance. She cannot believe it only took a single phone call to have him here.

She can't believe that he came in the first place without hesitation.
His dark brown eyes are still the same, just like she remembers, containing admiration and a certain warmth she hasn't seen in anyone else's eyes lately. They look at her the same way as they always did – with that sweetness Austin had only reserved for her.
His sad smile hasn't changed, either. He always had this mysterious look over him that makes him seem pained.
Here he is, tall, muscled and the way his hair is shaved into the shortest tomahawk she's ever seen makes her wonder why he didn't do that sooner. It suits him so perfectly well.
He stands there, waiting patiently for her to let him in. Waiting for her to say something.
He looks incredibly good. He wears a white turtleneck, a thick leather jacket and jeans.
His style has changed subtly over the past months. He has changed and yet he is still her brother. He is still the person he always was.
She tries to speak, but the words don't come out of her mouth.
"I..." she chokes, right before falling apart completely. There are so many regrets that she has.
The biggest one on her list is definitely that she hasn't been there for him.
He catches her when she falls. He catches her and carries her into her apartment, settling her on the couch while she clutches onto him for dear life.
"I should have called." She cries. She is tipsy, she is emotional, but she means every word. "I should have called. You are my brother."
He doesn't speak when he holds her. He doesn't speak when she messes up his light turtleneck with her smudged make up.
He lets her cry, and she thinks he is crying, too.
"I don't even know why I didn't... why I wasn't there for you, Aus." She moves to sit up, trying to compose herself while she feels like her entire life is crumbling down.
"Because you were hurt. Because you've seen so much shit." He states, as a matter of fact. His big hands cup her cheeks gently, his thumbs brushing away those tears, that unnecessary pain. "Because you had reason to. You needed to be alone. You were always on your own."
She shakes her head, her fingers wrapping around his wrists. He looks like they never parted at all. "I have been selfish. I have been focused on myself and days became weeks and weeks became months and before I knew it I never... I never called anymore, and I thought it was too late."
"It's never too late." He says, sternly.
He may be two years younger than she is, but he is wiser. He always has been, and she knows that she needs him.
She has needed him all along.

Even if they don't share blood, even if they aren't biological siblings, he is closer to her than anybody has ever been
Not even her parents could compare when things were still good.
"I can't forgive myself for what I did to you." her eyes are focused on his, her hands still around his. "I cannot express how... how sorry I am."
"Riley, look at me." He says firmly. He takes her chin between his thumb and index finger to make her look into his eyes. He's always had a way of just knowing. "We all hurt. Of all people that I know, you hurt the most. You had reason to leave, and you had reason not to contact me. Even though it... may not have been necessary, I understood. You're my family."
"I don't deserve you." she chokes again, barely able to contain her feelings.
"You're drunk, Riley." He shakes his head. "You are drunk, and you are emotional, and I don't know what happened at all, but one day you'll understand."
"Understand what?"
"What unconditional love is."

2

He stayed. He stays.
She can feel the guilt gnawing inside of her, but she never shows him that. She holds it back, makes sure that she puts on a mask whenever she feels emotional.
She tries to hold back her feelings, her thoughts when she thinks about it all. She just wishes that she could get rid of the culpability, that she could move on from the past but she's noticed it isn't easy, at all.
But he never even seems angry, or frustrated.
She knows how he feels about it all. She can tell in the way he looks at her, that he's only happy that she is back into his life.
She can tell that he's grateful, that he has missed her. She has missed him just as much, but she realises that only now.
But he stays. He texts her. He calls.
And Riley answers. She texts him back.
She stays, too.
She vows to herself to put her brother first, because that is exactly what he deserves.
It is something she should've done years ago, really.
She spends a few days alone in her large loft, drinking and sleeping and working out, mostly.
She takes just a few days off work, but only because her boss insisted.
She goes to the roof every day. She stands there for a few hours, trying to figure out what to do with herself.
Trying to figure out what she should do, trying to figure out who she is.

Struggling to move on.
She has no idea how, though.
There's a gaping hole in her heart that she can't get rid of.
She misses Camilla.
She misses the idea of Camilla, of what they could've been, of what they were before it all went wrong.
She misses her touches, her soft voice and just… she misses having her around. It may be lonelier than she's ever felt before and it stings, really.
But she goes on.
She does yoga, creates a routine for herself like she used to do – before she sacrificed all that for her career.
She starts running again, too.
She runs a few miles every day, wearing headphones that blast upbeat music into her ears for her to be able to distract herself.
Today is no different from that.
Her mind never stops spinning, with what ifs, with what she should've done in the past, the wrong choices she's made.
She has been trying to understand herself, why she did the things she did, but she never really gets an answer.
She keeps thinking about Camilla's words.
I don't think we should've gotten married in the first place.
It lingers in her mind.
Riley was the one to propose. She had been sure of it, she knew it.
She knew she wanted to spend the rest of her life with Camilla and yet, they fell apart, worse than she could've ever imagined.
She knows that people change, but she always thought that the two of them would find a way to grow together, instead of growing apart.
And she can't stop thinking about the fact that perhaps she is the one who caused it all.
No matter how much it hurt to see Camilla in bed with another woman, no matter how angry Riley has been at her for that, she knows it was her own fault.
She understands that she is the one who started pulling back and she wonders how she should've done things differently.
What she questions the most, is if things would have been different if only they had communicated.
If only.

A part of her wants to believe that. A part of her wants to believe that they would have been great together.
But she knows it's a lie. She knows that they were too different.
Riley is closed up and introverted in a way not many people are. She is hard to read and she likes to be alone from time to time.
Camilla never understood. Camilla always tried to change her and maybe that was her mistake.
And perhaps it was a mistake that Riley let her do that.
Perhaps, Riley didn't bother telling her that she didn't want to change that way, that she couldn't change that way because that was simply who she was.
She goes over their relationship, over and over again, tracing each step, every decision she's made.
She hates how she couldn't see then what she sees now.
That their love was not genuine. It wasn't based on true love, it was based on the fantasy of what could be.
The importance of career and money had taken over and Riley knows it.
She knows that she made a mistake by letting Camilla into her life this much, but she has been naïve in the past.
She has been naïve to think that they could've been something.

"It's... closed." Riley huffs in amusement while she tucks herself further into her jacket in the cold wind that blows through the concrete jungle. Austin is standing next to her, wiggling his eyebrows when he pulls out a set of keys from his pocket, opening the doors to the luxurious restaurant that Riley has never been to.
"You work here?" she quirks a curious brow as they step inside.
The moment she looks around, she is stunned. It's modern as much as it's warm, the interior a dark shade of brown mixed with black.
It's classic and ageless at the same time.
There are light marble pillars every now and then, offering a contrast in the dark, cosy restaurant.
"I do, but... I own it, too." He shrugs, as if it is nothing, quickly moving behind the bar on the left to take off his jacket.
"You own it?" she is just about to drop her jaw, but she quickly shuts it.
"I opened it two months ago. You're not the only one who's been quite successful." He grins, moving around the bar, going to the back, only to

return in a black chef's jacket, with an equally black apron wrapped around his waist.

He is still busy tucking his head in a black bandana when she starts smiling like a goofy idiot, sitting down on a stool.

"So, since you expected lunch from me, I'll cook for you. I have been meaning to try a few new recipes and I know for a fact that you have a good taste so… I'll use you as my personal tester." He laughs when he sees the surprise still written on Riley's features.

"How?" Riley asks him, still looking around a little too flabbergasted. "I mean, this is amazing, Aus, but… how?"

"I met River during college, I think you met him once or twice a while ago. We worked together for a long time until we saved enough to start our own restaurant." His dark eyes sparkle while he leans his hands on the bar.

"River?" Riley eyes her brother curiously.

"Hmm, yes. He's my best friend."

"Best friend?" she sends him a teasing wink, only to chuckle at his bright laughter. She knows full well how straight her brother is.

"Yes, Riley. Just a best friend. He on the other hand, he's just as much of a useless gay as you are."

She lets out something that's a mix between a huff and a scoff. "I am not a useless gay."

"Didn't it take like three years for you to see that Camilla was into you?" he grins, but it falters the moment he realises what he just said, his eyes widening slightly.

She already shakes her head. "You don't have to walk around on eggshells around me, Austin. It's fine, really. But well, perhaps I would've noticed sooner if she hadn't been experimenting with… men."

Another laugh bubbles from Austin's throat, despite him trying to hold back and it comes across as an ugly hyena cry, making Riley laugh, shaking her head in amusement.

"I'm happy for you, Austin." She smiles then, loving how he just looks at her with a happy grin stretching his lips. "I'm proud of you, I just… I'm sorry, okay?"

He instantly holds up his hands, motioning for her to stop talking. "You have nothing to apologize for, Riley. Really. I thought we talked this through?"

"I won't stop regretting the way I handled things." She explains, leaning her elbows down to be able to look into her brothers dark eyes. "I should've been there for you and I wasn't and… I think I fucked up more than I ever thought I could."

His soft smile is meant to be comforting, but it only makes her feel more guilty.

"Okay so… how about we just leave it in the past, Riley?" he offers then, reaching for her hand with one arm. She takes it, still surprised at how wise he can be. "There is nothing we can do about it now except… move on."

She knows he's right. He always is.

She nods silently, trying to smile, but it's hard for her. It's hard for her, because she feels like her whole life she's been making the wrong decisions. She knows she won't be able to let it go as easily as he can, but for now she wants to drop the subject. She wants to focus on the good things between them.

Austin just smiles at her, before pouring her a drink.

He slides a martini right in front of her, making her snap out of her daze. "Drink."

"It's two in the afternoon." She raises an eyebrow, but slides the glass closer by its foot.

"Something tells me you need it." He grins, winking while he disappears back into the kitchen, leaving her alone with her thoughts.

She knows she should leave it in the past. Like he said – there is nothing she can do about it now except… making it up.

Except proving she won't make the same mistakes again. She just has too much to make up for.

She left her brother. She just left him behind, too focused on her own little life to be bothered by him.

She has no idea what had come over her. She has no idea why she ever thought that was a good idea.

She knew he loved her. She knew he supported her.

And yet, she didn't call. She didn't contact him.

Before she knew it, days turned into weeks and weeks into months and it became harder and harder to even think about calling him.

She hates it took her divorce for her to contact him. She just hates a lot of herself right now and she has no idea how to fix it.

She doesn't know how she can make up for everything, but perhaps being here, supporting her brother could be a start.

Baby steps.
But she thinks that, no matter how much she'll be there for him from now on, that she won't be able to forgive herself for what she's done.
She cups the glass, brings the edge to her mouth. For a brief moment she winces when the cool glass touches her lips, but then, she eagerly takes a sip.
She's always loved martini's.
She has no idea how Austin even remembered. He seems to just… still know her, even though they barely did things together the past years. Even though she's changed, he knows her and it is scary.
She is so deep in thought, toying with the glass in her hand that she barely notices Austin coming back from the kitchen to hand her a plate of food.
"Pasta?" she grins, smiling when she watches the tagliatelle.
"Yes." He grins. "Smell?"
She dips her head, smelling the plate of freshly cooked pasta. "Truffle and… cheese?"
"Pecorino, obviously. It's salty and fresh, a perfect contrast to the truffle. We import from Europe." He laughs, leaning back on the bar, waiting for Riley to start eating.
"So, you're going to eat with me or..?" her mouth already starts to water when she smells the exquisite combination of melted Italian cheese and good quality black truffle.
"Oh, no. I'll just have a sandwich." He hands her cutlery and she instantly digs in, wrapping the tagliatelle around her fork.
It is fucking delicious. She moans when she tastes it on her tongue, loving the simple, but elegant flavour of the combined ingredients.
She chews, not realising she closed her eyes when she hears a chuckle from her brother.
"Aus… this is…" she swallows the bite. "This is really good. Italian, though?"
"Yes." He smiles. "I have travelled through Europe years ago, remember? Stayed when I discovered the Italian kitchen."
"You went with River?" she smiles, taking another bite. This is truly one of the best things she's ever had.
"Yes. He has an Italian grandparent, so all of this is inspired by his long, lost family." Nodding, he moves around the bar with a towel thrown over his shoulder. He takes her empty martini glass, only to grab a fresh wine

glass.

He pours her red wine. "Taste. The wine should really fit with the food."

She stops eating for a moment, taking the glass. She wants to take a sip, but he stops her before she can.

He takes the glass from her, swirling it. He holds it up for her to look at. "Look. It's not bright red like the fruity wines, it's a little brownish."

"Hmm." She smiles, loving how he is so seriously invested in explaining to her what she's having. He seems passionate about it and she remembers the time he would stand in the kitchen in their childhood home, cooking delicious food, even for a teenager.

"Here, have a try. Swirl, smell." He hands her the glass back and she follows his example, swirling the glass around, only to stick her nose in and smell...

"Brunello?" she guesses, making him grin from ear to ear.

"You're good."

"I'm rich. I've had more wines than I can count, Austin. I know which ones I like." She smiles when she remembers the giant wine cooler she has in her kitchen.

"Taste." He still urges her, and she does.

She takes a small sip, enjoying the taste while she slurps a bit of oxygen to be able to taste it better. She nods instantly. "So good."

"I know right? Brunello di Montalcino Riserva, from twenty-fifteen. I mean, I could've let it age a bit, but still... it's good, right?"

"It is." She grins. "How about you come over to my place sometime? Take River with you and we just... cook?"

"How about River and I will do the cooking and you arrange the wine and desert?" he winks at her.

"It's a deal."

She decides to get back to work, but something about it just doesn't sit well with her.

But as a criminal lawyer at Harrison & Hale, she has obligations.

She can't just stay away for weeks and expect everything will be okay, she knows she's important to the firm.

So, she returns to work, working probably more hours than she ever has before.

She doesn't work to reach more, she doesn't work to earn more and gain experience, like she used to.

She works more because she feels the need to escape reality.

Her own reality.

And it works, for a while.

She prepares several cases for court, has meetings with clients and works harder than ever before.

She does remind herself to take enough time to get to know her brother again. It is not that she is forcing herself to spend time with him, no. She thoroughly enjoys his presence. She enjoys his nerdy jokes about food and wine and loves how obsessed he is with cooking and his restaurant. She can tell how much he loves his work, how he enjoys every single moment of what he's doing and she can't help but envy him.

She is proud of him. Of what he has reached so far in life, that he has managed to get this far and make a living out of his hobby, out of his passion.

It has been good between them, even though they're slowly rebuilding their friendship. Their bond was never truly broken, but the fact that Riley has done more things she isn't proud of, she can just feel it between them.

She knows he would never blame her, but the guilt is eating at her. It still bothers her. She's afraid she's going to do it again.

She is afraid that she can't change who she is and that she'll be alone for the rest of her life, that she won't be able to show even her brother how much she cares about him.

And so, she works. She tries to bury those thoughts, that empty feeling in her chest.

It is late on a Friday night as she works through her main case, trying to prepare for court for the next week.

Her client is guilty, she knows this and yet, she is going to fight for his innocence, defending him.

It bothers her more than it should.

It bothers her that she isn't fighting for the right side of this.

The stupid part is that she's never had problems with it before. She just did her job, cared about winning and that's it.

She has no idea what changed. She bites the end of her pen in annoyance, a bad habit she's picked up the past weeks after her separation.

There is a knock on the glass door of her office, just when she thought she was the only one left on the floor.

She lifts her head to smile when one of the two managing partners Michael Hale walks in, a kind smile hugging his lips.
He's been out of the office the past weeks and she hasn't seen him when she returned after her short leave.
"Riley. Good to see you back." His voice is friendly, as always.
Sometimes it still surprises her that he is one of the best lawyers this city has ever seen, because he is always way too friendly, way too kind.
But, he fights for what he believes in, though, that is probably what makes him so good.
She rises from her seat politely, straightening her suit.
"Michael. It is good to be back." She lies.
"Did you take enough time for yourself?" he lingers somewhere in the middle of the office, as if he's doubting if he should sit down or leave.
She leans against her desk, smiling when she nods. "Yes."
"You know you could always take more time off." He continues, his dark eyes friendly. Of all people at the office, Michael is probably the only one who actually likes her. "I know what divorce can do to a person. I know it could be healthy to take some time. I doubt those few days you were gone did any good."
"I have had more than enough time." She insists. "There's nothing for me at home, anyway."
He smiles then, crossing his arms in front of his chest. His suit is shiny in the dim light of her office. "Well, I figured you'd still be here today. I wanted to talk to you about something."
"Oh? You can sit down if you want to." She motions one hand to one of the leather chairs, grabbing a glass of water for the managing partner.
"We're hiring." He then says, grinning when he moves to take the glass and sits down in the chair.
She joins him on the other seat. "You are?"
"We're a growing firm. We get more clients every week, as you are probably aware." He takes a sip as he mysteriously hides his smile behind the glass.
"You're one of the best we've seen so far, Riley. You may be cold and stoic, but that is what makes you so ruthless. You remind me of Deborah when she was younger."
At a complete loss for words, she looks at him with wide eyes. She patiently waits for him to continue.
"We are happy to announce that you will be the next junior partner at our

firm, should you choose to accept."

"What?" she asks stupidly. She had expected to get promoted, she just didn't see it coming that it would happen so soon already. Perhaps in a year or two, but not now. "Do you think I am ready for that?"

"I think you've been ready the moment you set foot into this building the first time, Riley." The smile is truly genuine as he plucks his neatly trimmed beard. "You can hire your own associate if you want to. We will go over the details on Monday, okay? When Deborah has the time."

"Yes, absolutely. Thank you, Michael." She rises from her seat, smiling subtly when she looks at her boss.

He extends his hand when he stands as well. "You've earned it. With everything that you've put into your work, you really deserve it."

"Thank you."

"And now, go home, Riley. It's late. Enjoy your weekend. And think about it." He smiles, winking when he turns around.

"I have to finish something first before I go."

"Don't stay too long, okay?" he hovers near the door, before quickly disappearing into the hallway, to his own office probably.

Flabbergasted, she drops herself in the chair behind her desk. If she's being honest with herself, she doesn't think she deserves this.

Sure, she is good at what she is doing, in court, with her clients. Excellent even.

But she doesn't think that she deserves it, not at her young age.

She's only thirty-four after all. She's been working here for nearly eight years, but she doesn't think that that is enough.

She doesn't even know if she wants it.

She sighs, not quite able to let her work go for the day.

She will just take her cases home to go through, placing them in her briefcase. She grabs one last cup of coffee from the lobby, before returning to retrieve her coat and bag.

She hovers near her desk, leaning on it while she stares out the window. Her view here is almost better than it is from her home.

Almost.

She can even see her apartment building from here, not too far away.

The city is dark now, raindrops sliding down the window.

The buildings she can see are lit partly, she can't help but feel that certain solitude falling over her once again.

She sips on her coffee absentmindedly, suddenly doubting if this is truly what she wants to do. She knows she's often defending criminals.

She knows she is able to set most of them free, while she is fully aware that nobody is actually innocent.

She doesn't know if this is what she wants. She doesn't know if this is what she has been imagining when she started law school.

Criminal law is intense, but she doesn't think she loves it as much as she should.

She loves the firm, she loves working for Michael and Deborah, but there is just something bubbling inside of her that she can't shake.

She has always tended to want to get into civil litigation, but she has been thrown into criminal law instead.

She is wondering what she should do. Though she is so thoroughly honoured by the fact that they want her as junior partner at this firm, she has been doubting if this is her true calling.

Perhaps she should think about it before she even… says yes. To be junior partner requires more dedication, more devotion to the firm and she doesn't know if she can bring that up, not anymore.

She sighs when she puts on her navy coat, taking her leather briefcase while she walks to the elevators.

She releases her hair from the usual bun at the nape of her neck when she steps in, running a hand through her curls.

She takes a cab home. She barely registers herself making her way into her apartment building, trying to shield herself from the pouring rain.

Usually, at this hour of the night, she's alone in the lobby. But now she is accompanied by a familiar blonde.

The woman is standing, waiting for the elevator to come down. She is wearing blue scrubs, her long blonde curls in a messy bun, looking exhausted.

Riley decides to be civil for once when she steps in front of the elevator, scraping her throat to subtly announce her presence.

"Hi." The blonde sounds just as tired as she looks.

"Hello." Riley glances next to her, smiling shortly. "Long day at work?"

"You could say that." The woman chuckles, rubbing her hand in her neck, her jacket thrown over her other arm.

"What do you do?" Riley can't help herself when she asks the question, preferring small talk over awkward silence.

"I'm a surgeon."

"Impressive." Her smile is genuine, she finds. When she glances aside, the woman's blue gaze is fixated on Riley's face.

"What about you?"

"I practice law." She just says vaguely, looking up to the small screen atop the elevator to see which floor it's on.

"Impressive." The woman chuckles shortly. "We live on the same floor." Quirking a brow, Riley shifts slightly so she won't have to turn her head each time the blonde is talking.

"My husband and I moved in a few months ago. I saw you a few times, but you never really said anything." She doesn't seem to judge Riley by any means, but there is a certain curiosity that gives Riley the feeling she has to explain herself.

"I'm quite busy." She offers loosely.

"I figured." The smile is faint and blue eyes dart away from Riley's face.

"Sorry about that. I'm Riley Dunn. A little delayed, but welcome to the building." She offers her hand, smiling softly when the blonde slides her own hand in Riley's.

"Jules Gibson. So, you're married right? I think I spoke to your wife a few times when we just moved in."

"Ah, uh…" Riley doesn't like explaining what happened. "It's complicated."

"It always is." Jules grimaces vaguely when she stares at the closed metal doors.

"Is it?" the words roll off her tongue before she can stop herself.

The blonde looks up at her in surprise. "Relationships can be… tough."

Riley just nods. She doesn't really know what to say, something that doesn't happen to her often.

A brief silence falls between the two waiting women.

"We got divorced." She suddenly blurts out.

"Oh. I'm sorry to hear that."

"Like you said, relationship are tough." She just shrugs, tapping her foot on the floor impatiently while the elevator finally seems to arrive.

She lets Jules in first before entering after, watching the blonde smile gently. Her blue eyes are a deep shade of blue that Riley doesn't recall ever seeing before.

There is a sadness haunting them that has her attention, but she won't pry.

They don't even know each other.
Jules's smile is genuine, though. Despite that sadness, despite the hesitance in her stance, she seems sincere.
Her nose scrunches up when she smiles, her chin dimpled in a cute way.
"Hey, uhm… I know that we don't know each other, but we're neighbours. Would you like to come over and share dinner?" Jules then speaks unexpectedly, her voice so soft, it comes across as shy.
"Dinner? Now? At ten-thirty in the evening?" Riley is amused and flattered at the same time.
"Oh, right. I forgot about the time." The blonde grimaces as she pushes on the button for the eighteenth floor.
"It's no problem. Perhaps another time." She offers weakly.
Right now, she's tired. She's tired and she wishes to be alone.
However, when she sees the subtle disappointed look on the other woman's face, there is just something inside of the brunette that makes her think that perhaps, this woman might be just as lonely as Riley is.
She changes her mind. "Actually, I now remember that I haven't eaten yet, either."
Riley watches how sad blue eyes turn hopeful.
It is so childlike, so honest and pure that it's almost painful to see. It settles strangely in Riley's stomach.
Whatever grief Jules is carrying with her, Riley can almost feel it.
"Really?"
"Yes, really." A smile curls Riley's lips when she watches the blonde light up.
There is just something about it that Riley can't resist. She has no idea what it is, but she somehow doesn't mind not being alone anymore.
Maybe they could be friends.
Maybe it's something Riley needs, just a friend, someone who doesn't know all the stains of her past.
When they arrive on their floor, Riley speaks up again. "How about I meet you in ten minutes? Allow me to change in to something easier."
"Sure. I'll leave the door unlocked, just walk in whenever you like." Jules responds before they part ways, both fiddling with the keys to their respective doors.
Riley regrets saying yes the moment she steps into her apartment, longing to just drop herself onto her bed, just so mentally exhausted of the past

weeks trying to ignore her feelings, trying to fix things with her brother. But she is not the type to not be true to her word, so she just makes her way to her walk in closet, changing into a simple black turtleneck and matching comfortable slacks.

She puts her hair in a messy ponytail, her hair curly due to the rain, not bothering to check if her make up is still intact from the day.

She takes a bottle of red wine when she takes her keys, moving out of her apartment, to across the hall.

Even though Jules mentioned leaving the door open, she knocks anyway. It feels inappropriate to just walk in.

Jules opens the door before Riley has time to breathe. She has changed into a simple black hoodie, wearing glasses and leggings.

It's… different.

Her eyes roam down Riley's body with amusement. "This is what you call… something easier?"

Glancing down, Riley feels a smile creep up her face. "I don't really own anything… relaxed."

An amused huff leaves Jules's lips, but she steps back while she lets Riley into her apartment.

The layout of the space is mirrored from her own, but it looks so, so much different. It is homey, colourful in an artsy way and the furniture doesn't match at all.

"Wow, your apartment looks amazing. I love what you've done with it." Riley smiles when she follows the blonde to her kitchen. She sets the bottle of wine on the counter.

"Thanks." The blonde smiles, reaching into her fridge. "Do you like reheated lasagna?"

"Yes, I do." Riley awkwardly leans against the counter, realising that she hasn't done anything like this in… years.

She never had many friends and the friends she did have, had always kind of been there. She's never felt the need to make new friends.

"Good." Jules places the platter into the preheated oven, grabbing two wine glasses from the cupboard. "You didn't have to bring any wine."

"I didn't want to show up empty handed." The brunette just shrugs, crossing her arms in front of her chest, quietly checking the watch on her wrist.

This might be the first time in years that she's eating dinner this late at night, sharing it with someone.

"If you don't mind me asking…" Riley begins, watching how Jules grabs a bottle opener, her blue eyes curious when she glances into green. "…but where is your husband?"

At the mention of her husband, Jules's face seems to fall just slightly, but it's gone before Riley is even sure it was there in the first place.

"He has a nightshift at the hospital." The blonde explains, struggling to place the screw in the cork.

Riley just smiles, hovering near her, her arms up as a silent offer to try instead. Jules seems grateful when she hands the brunette the corkscrew and the bottle.

Riley opens the bottle with ease. "Is your husband also a surgeon?"

"Yeah, we met in med school."

"Hm, power couple." Riley grins, pouring wine into the glasses. She feels free enough to sit down at one of the barstools at the kitchen island, watching Jules mirroring her.

"So they say." This time, the smile never reaches blue eyes. "So how long have you lived here?"

Riley realises that she is staring at the blonde. She isn't sure why, but she is fast to avert her gaze.

"Just over four years now." She keeps smiling politely, taking a sip of the wine. "How are you liking it here so far?"

"Only thing I can complain about is the elevator. They should've made two instead." She seems to light up again when Riley chuckles.

"Yes, it's always been a disaster. I leave fifteen minutes early every morning, just in case." Even though it isn't funny at all, they burst in a fit of giggles, and Riley feels like the child she never could be.

It breaks the ice and Riley is grateful for it. She's never been good with socializing.

It's just easy being around Jules. She seems nice.

"I've never done this before." Riley motions around the apartment.

"Trusting your new neighbour into not killing you?" the blonde jokes, taking a sip of her wine with a sparkle in her eyes.

"Something like that." Riley's lips stretch further. "I don't usually have much time to… well, make friends."

"You want to be friends?"

"Well, we're neighbours. I'm pretty sure we'll bump into each other occasionally, so why not?" she is smooth when she leans one elbow on the counter, her hand dangling over the edge, the wine glass still in her other hand.

"That is true. I think I'd like that."

"Bumping into me?" Riley rolls her eyes at herself, at her lame joke. "Forget I said that. Must be exhaustion taking over."

The blonde lets out a small chuckle, hiding behind her glass while a grin remains. "So, are you a native New Yorker?"

"No. I'm from DC." The lawyer smiles, feeling a little more at ease. "I attended NYU, and after that I kind of stuck around. You?"

"My family is from Baltimore, but I moved to the Big Apple with my parents when I was seventeen." Jules smiles at the memory. "Always loved New York."

"It has its charms." Riley agrees, smiling when she can smell the lasagna from the oven. Her stomach rumbles loudly enough for both of them to hear. "Never skipping dinner again."

She laughs, but suddenly yelps when she feels something furry at her ankle. She almost drops her glass when she immediately lifts up her feet in a hurry. "What the fuck was that?" her eyes widen as she looks down, but she sees nothing. She quickly sets the wine glass on the counter while she watches Jules laugh, the blonde's throat bobbing while doing so. "This is not funny."

The surgeon's laugh is bright and happy and Riley can't help but chuckle along, but she safely takes off her shoes, crossing her ankles on her seat. In this moment, she's grateful that she's flexible and watches around the room, to whatever furry thing could've touched her.

"That was Scooter." The blonde finally manages to catch her breath, a fresh blush on her cheeks and a few strands of wild, blonde hair in her face.

Quirking a brow, Riley looks around, but she still sees nothing. "Scooter?"

"Our cat. You're not allergic, are you?" Jules grins, still amused by the way Riley reacted.

It's not like Riley is accustomed to cats. "No, no, I am not. I just never had a pet before, so he just scared the living shit out of me."

"I noticed." Jules's eyebrows shoot up in amusement again, but she hides her smile when she rises from her seat to check on the lasagna. "He likes you, though."

"Scooter?"

"He never shows when we have visitors, usually." The surgeon explains. Riley takes a sip from her wine before tucking up the sleeves of her turtleneck. She redoes her messy bun, tucking it tighter in the hair tie. She doesn't notice Jules is watching her until she's finished. It is an uncomfortable moment, but they are both saved by Scooter, who jumps up on the counter.

"Oh, hello there." Riley smiles, watching a grey cat moving to her. He has big orange eyes, his fur is thick and he might just be a tad overweight. He purrs when he moves to Riley to lick her fingers. "…and that is very, very unsanitary."

He keeps licking her fingers. The brunette smiles, letting him lick her fingers before she moves up to tickle him under his chubby chin. He lets out the cutest little meow.

"He isn't allowed on the counter. He tries to jump up sometimes, but usually he falls off." Jules laughs, crossing her arms while she leans against the sink.

"Clumsy little thing then, are you?" Riley coos with a small smile, loving how soft he is. His tail is up and high and the lawyer thinks it's a good sign. "He really likes you."

"Well, I think I like him right back. Can I pick him up?" the brunette throws a glance at Jules, who only nods and smiles, watching the whole thing.

Riley rises from her seat, reaching for the cat with both hands. She lets out a little oof when she holds him, realising that he's heavier than he looks. He instantly purrs more, gently pushing his little head against Riley's cheek, his paws over her shoulder.

"Ouch. Fuck, his nails." Riley can feel sharp nails dig into her shoulder, but she doesn't move.

"Yeah, sorry about that. We have to cut them. Scoot, let her go."

"Sorry, I usually don't swear this much." Riley grimaces when the nails dig further into her skin. Her turtleneck is going to be ruined, but somehow she doesn't care. "Come on, boy. Let me go."

When Scooter doesn't bother to move, only purring and licking Riley's face, Jules steps in.

She's close when she wraps her hands around his little torso, removing the cat from Riley's chest. The brunette quickly moves to wash her hands before sitting back down.

There is something… oddly refreshing about Jules. The way her blue eyes connect with Riley's, the way her smile remains while she holds the cat, petting it briefly before putting it on the ground.
Riley moves to see if her sweater is still intact, but she thinks there are a few tiny holes in her shoulder.
"I can pay you for that."
"Don't worry about it." The lawyer insists. She grabs her glass again, watching how Jules removes the food from the oven.
The blonde winces when she holds the heavy platter, but smiles when she places the food on their plates.
She spends at least another hour at Jules's place. She sees pictures of the blonde and her husband. The guy looks familiar and Riley vaguely remembers spotting him in the lobby a while ago.
The two look very happy in the pictures and Riley smiles sadly at that. She just wishes she could've been that happy with Camilla. There aren't really any pictures of Riley and her ex-wife, looking at each other so happily. They never even took the time to just… enjoy their lives together.
They were always separate, living apart but under the same roof.
But Riley tries not to dwell on that, she tries to focus on her neighbour instead.
They talk, both avoiding heavily loaded topics and Riley can't seriously remember the last time she's had such a light hearted chat with someone. Lately it was either all business or loaded with emotions, so this is very welcomed. Jules seems to enjoy it just as much, laughing in between, smiling and telling small stories.
It feels natural. Riley feels like they could be friends and honestly, she likes the thought.
It feels good to be able to connect with someone else, instead of the people she already knows.
It feels good that she's still able to come across as an actual nice person. It's all very… overwhelming, in a good way.
So, she talks lightly. She makes terrible jokes, smiling each time Jules laughs at them.
They share a few college stories, realising they went to the same school around the same time.
Jules is just about a year younger than Riley is and it's nice to have someone like her to talk to.

It just feels like they've known each other for a long time, but Riley is careful.
She's careful with sharing things about herself, because she's never been comfortable with who she is.
She's always felt like she couldn't entirely be herself, that people would judge her for it.
It's a stupid fear that she's built over the years, a fear she doesn't know where it comes from.
But she doesn't share, also because they just really met.
Still, she enjoys the time they spend together. She enjoys the way Jules's nose crinkles when she laughs, she enjoys the way Jules gestures enthusiastically when she tells a story.
She enjoys the sound of Jules's naturally low voice.
She just enjoys having a new friend.
The moment Riley returns to her own place, she smiles, for a moment reality forgotten in the back of her head.

3

"I don't think I can do it."
It's the first thing Riley says when she steps into Deborah's office Monday morning.
The older woman sends her a stunned look, but doesn't speak. Deborah never speaks when she doesn't have to.
"Riley?" Michael Hale stands right beside Deborah Harrison, looking faintly puzzled.
They are two founders of the firm, those people whose names are on the wall, on the building. The two most powerful people that Riley has ever had the pleasure of meeting and working with.
"I've been thinking about it, becoming junior partner." Her hands are shaking. She's never spoken up like this before. "I don't think I can do it."
"And why is that?" there is a small smile tugging on Deborah's lips and Riley hates that the woman doesn't reveal any other emotion rather than being amused.
"Because this is not how I imagined my future."
It is true.
She has been thinking about it over the weekend. After dinner with her neighbor, she hadn't been able to sleep.
She'd been staring out her bedroom window most of the time.
She'd been googling about her options; about what she could do with the degrees she has.
She has been doing a lot of research and she doesn't want this. As much as she loves working for Deborah and Michael, it doesn't make her happy to be in this field of work.
She knows that she's put everything in this career, in this firm. But she can't do it anymore.
She can't go to work and not love it as much as she should. She just can't think about the people she's keeping out of jail while they should belong behind bars.

It's done for her. She really doesn't understand why it took so long for her to see, why it took Camilla cheating on her to open her eyes about it all.
She doesn't know why she's never really chosen what she loves. None of the things she did in the past ever made her happy and she can feel it draining her vitality.
She is choosing her own happiness now.
She is choosing to move on, and she doesn't feel like she can while she's here. She needs something new, something that will give her the energy she has been lacking the past years.
"I don't think I belong here, not anymore." She just says, sucking her lips between her teeth while she awaits their reaction.
Deborah's smile only grows, while Hale seems thoroughly confused, glancing between the two women.
"Can I ask where you think you belong, then?" his voice is not unkind, he simply seems sincerely interested.
"I've always thought that when I'd become a lawyer, that I could be a voice for the people who don't have the strength, the resources to stand up for themselves." She begins slowly.
When her bosses don't speak, she folds her hands behind her back, trying not to show that she's actually nervous about telling them.
"I have found a position I'd like to apply for. And it's not here." She admits then, her green eyes flickering between the two managers.
"And where may that be?" Deborah leans against her hardwood desk, her suit tight, her chin high and Riley has never been more intimidated.
"At the American Civil Liberties Union." She speaks, smiling when she remembers what she has found. "They have a position for their LGBT projects here in New York."
"You want to defend people from the LGBT community?" Deborah seems surprised.
"Well, yes."
"That's…" Hale scratches the back of his neck, but smiles when he meets Riley's eyes. "…different."
"It's beautiful, Riley. I am happy for you. Have you applied yet?" Deborah says, making Riley shoot up her eyebrows in surprise. She had no idea how her managers would respond.
"No, I have not. I don't know what my chances are."
"We would happily keep you until you find something else, okay?" Hale then says after exchanging a look with Deborah. "Just keep us posted."
"Uhm, really?" she glances between the two managing partners, who look at her with smiles on their faces.
"You have put so much time and effort in this firm, Riley. We know what you're capable of and we are grateful that you have been working for us. But if it's time for you to move on, then it's time. There is nothing much

we can do about that." Michael smiles.

"I've always had a feeling you wouldn't stay here. You lasted longer than I expected you would." Deborah grins now, and it's the widest smile Riley has ever seen on her.

Riley smiles, grateful for the fast that they are accepting her choice to leave. "But if you knew I wouldn't stay, why would you offer me the position of junior partner?"

"Despite the fact that I knew you wouldn't stay, that you didn't belong here, I think you're still one of the best attorneys we've seen so far." Deborah explains and Hale nods in agreement. "You've won many cases, and you've worked more hours than I did when I was your age. You work hard, Riley. That is why we wanted you to become junior partner. We saw a bright future for you here."

"Thank you. Really, thank you. I appreciate the opportunity and I would've taken it if I didn't belong somewhere else." She says, from the bottom of her heart. "I have loved working for you."

"That is always good to hear. Take your time, Riley. Keep us updated about your applications." Hale nods.

Riley steps forward to shake their hands, smiling when she turns to leave the office.

That went so much better than expected. It's step. It's a small step, perhaps, but she needs it.

She needs something new. She needs to feel like she's actually doing something good.

It may not pay as much as at the firm, but she couldn't care less. She has plenty of savings, she can easily afford her rent on her own.

It is no problem at all.

For the first time in a very long time, Riley actually feels excited.

She feels like there is hope, after all.

It only takes a few days for her to get a response from the American Civil Liberties Union. They invite her over for an interview and she doesn't think she's ever been this anxious.

She straightens her pencil skirt out of habit when she walks into the building, watching several people wander around the foyer. She walks to the reception, quickly introducing herself.

She's being sent to the fourth floor, where she gets to sit down in the hall, waiting for Sean Walker, the man who will be her boss if she gets hired.

She only sits for a minute when she gets called in by him. He has grey eyes, doesn't look amused and barely takes the time to shake her hand when he guides her into his disgustingly old-fashioned office.

"Please, sit." He sits behind his desk, not bothering to grab her file.

She feels uncomfortable under his dark gaze, but she doesn't show. She takes off her coat and sits down, trying to smile.

"Criminal law is something else entirely from what you will be practicing here." He starts, his voice low and cold.

"Yes, it is."

"Care to explain why you would like to transfer to ACLU?" he seems bored when he taps his fingers on his desk.

"I would love to work for an organization that truly holds my passion, sir. Criminal law is not my passion."

"You're thirty-four. Why did it take you so long to find what you truly want?" his eyes bore into hers and she doesn't think this is the regular interview.

He's almost... offensive.

"Because I've always been focused on the things that didn't matter, instead of where my heart lies. In law school I have been focusing on every type of law I could get into, simply to explore my options. I always preferred civil litigation, but I got a huge opportunity in criminal law I couldn't deny myself. I was searching at the time, and now I feel like it is time to start what I have always subconsciously wanted to do." Her words form hesitantly. "I have struggled with many things, personally. I just wish to help where I can, help people I feel a personal connection to."

"Why would you feel a personal connection to the people of the LGBT community?"

"Because I am one of them. I have experienced what it is like in this world to not be what society wishes you to be. I have experienced homophobia from the people I trusted the most and I cannot believe that in this world today, we still have to fight the way we fight to let our voices be heard." She swallows when she remembers her parents. She pushes the thought away, trying to focus on Sean.

She doesn't like him, but she doesn't care. She only cares about the job, about the people she feels connected to.

She wonders why it never occurred to her that this could actually be her calling.

"I have experienced clients who wanted nothing to do with me because I am gay. They refused to be represented by me, only because I love who I love. I wish that to nobody. I want to help when I can. With my license, I can practice law and with that I want to actually make a change."

Sean doesn't seem impressed, but at least his gaze never moved away from her own. At least, it's something.

"You know what this position means, right? You'll be writing pleads, briefs, handling hearings and trials, both in state and federal court. You will be working closely with the entire department, the legal and non-legal program staff, work with fundraising professionals." He scrapes his throat. "You will have to develop strong co-counsel relationships with other public interest

lawyers and ACLU volunteers. We want you to be able to travel for litigations, legislative and policy advocacy, conferences and we want you to be open to public speaking to represent us for the media."
"Yes."
"You only have experience in criminal law. Why do you think you're suited for this job?" he averts his eyes, observing his nails and she knows what he's trying to do.
He's trying to break her, but she won't have it.
"Like I said before, I always wanted to get into civil litigation. Criminal law has prepared me for this. Criminal law is one of the most intense things there is, and I know that I can do this. My specialty isn't necessarily criminal law, sir. It's winning." She swallows deeply.
"You said you're one of them. How will you expect to be able to separate your personal life from your professional life?"
Riley can only smile. "Just because I will be able to empathize more with clients, doesn't mean I can't separate my feelings from my duties. I am more than capable of doing so, as I have experienced before. I see it as a strength, that I will be able to understand what our clients go through, what we are fighting for."
He remains silent for a moment, straightening his tie. He seems to think for a moment, his eyebrows furrowing.
"Tell me one thing, Miss Dunn." He leans forward, his elbows on the edge of his desk, his fingers folding together. His grey eyes are more serious than she has seen so far, his lips pursing. "I have seen your records. I have seen your ratings. You have won over 93 percent of your cases."
"That is about accurate, yes." She has no idea where he is going with this.
"This is incredibly high for a lawyer your age." He states, finally looking down at a file on his desk. "We would be lucky to have someone like you in our legal department. But I don't think you'd be ready for the job."
"How so?" she isn't even offended. She just knows that Sean is the type of guy to just look and look for something to hit her with until he finds it.
"You're stoically cocky." He just says, as a matter of fact. She almost laughs.
"In our line of work, that is necessary, Mr. Walker. If you show yourself as someone who has a weak spot, they will tear you down." She knows this. She doesn't understand why being arrogant would be an issue. "It is better to be able to show no signs of weakness, something I have experienced myself."
He nods thoughtfully. "Your statistics don't lie. On record, you are an amazing lawyer. I will take this conversation into consideration. To be honest, I've had more candidates for this position than I expected. My assistant will call you within a few days to let you know if we would like to offer you the job."
He actually smiles when he rises from his seat, leaning over his desk to offer

her his hand.
This shake lasts longer than the first one and she smiles back, not really sure how he feels about her, but she says her goodbyes politely before returning to her own office.
She just can't wipe the smile off her face.
Even if she won't get the job, she knows she wants something like this.
And she would fight forever to be able to do it.

She is grateful when she makes her way home Friday afternoon.
She doesn't think she's ever left the office this early, but she simply doesn't have more to do for the day.
So, the sun is setting when she makes her way into her building, grateful that she can spend the weekend relaxing and just… thinking.
She's been thinking a lot lately. Thinking, reading. Her mind has been busy and even when she sleeps, she feels like her head keeps spinning.
But she smiles when she steps into her apartment.
Her brother and his friend will be over soon, and because she's invited them over to teach her how to cook properly.
She likes River the moment he sets foot in her apartment. She remembers seeing him before, but they've never really spoken much.
He looks about the same age, his blue eyes sparkling. He has a long beard, is even bigger than Austin, and she can barely imagine the two of them in a kitchen.
They make simple hamburgers so delicious she considers taking permanent cooking classes from them.
They move around her kitchen with ease, making small talk. They talk about how Austin and River met, how they instantly hit off as friends.
How people thought they were a couple, but Austin started dating a girl.
How they went to Europe to party.
She enjoys every silly story they share.
"Oh my God." She moans when they're sitting at the dining table in her large kitchen, River laughing with happiness when he finds out that Riley loves the hamburgers so, so much. "This is so fucking good. I mean, fuck."
Austin grins, clearly enjoying his sister enjoying the food and the company.
"It's very easy, really." River just shrugs with a grin on his face. He watches the woman.
"I'm just surprised you can eat a hamburger so gracefully, Riley." Austin chuckles, when another piece of tomato falls on his own plate.
"Years of practice." The brunette grins then, making River laugh behind his glass.
It is good, to have Austin here like this. It's good to meet his friend.
Riley gets along with River surprisingly well, chatting happily while Austin is mostly just watching them get to know each other like a proud dad, a

typical smile toying his lips constantly.
Riley can't believe on all the things she's missed out on.
But Austin accepts her.
It is like no time has passed and yet, Riley feels like the gap between them might never be fixed.
She feels the guilt, still.
She can tell by the look in Austin's face that he just knows. She's grateful that he doesn't mention it, glad that he seems to understand that it'll take time.
Her thoughts already drain down when she can feel emotions taking over. She hates it, tries to listen to their stories, but they notice.
"Are you alright?" River suddenly asks, his light eyes worried. He runs a hand through his short hair, looking between her and her brother hesitantly.
"Yeah, yeah, I am good." The brunette tries to shrug it off, but it's just hard to see past her mistakes now that she is thinking about it. "Just thinking."
She puts it away, focusing on her brother and his best friend, when her phone rings. It's only seven in the evening, but she wonders who it could be. She has a vague idea, but she isn't sure.
"Uhm, excuse me, I have to take this." She shoots them an apologetic look but they just shrug, continuing to eat.
"Riley Dunn."
"Miss Dunn, I'm Chloe Teles from ACLU, I'm calling regarding the job position Staff Attorney for the LGBT projects." A voice sounds.
"Ah, yes, I was expecting your call."
"I would like to congratulate you. We want you for the job."
She's perplexed. She had no idea what she expected, really. Not even a second interview is apparently necessary.
She had expected to be turned down; she had expected that Sean would've hated her.
"Really?"
"Yes. Mr. Walker has only forgotten to ask when you will be able to start."
"I have a two weeks' notice." Riley grins when she walks into her bedroom for some privacy.
She glances out the window, watching the dark city glow in all its glory.
"That should be no problem. We will send you the details per email, as you requested when you applied for the job."
Riley can't wipe the smirk from her face when she finished up the call, moving back to her kitchen where she's met with two pairs of curious eyes.
"I have some news." She grins.
"Oh yeah? You're getting married?" Austin jokes, but River elbows him in the ribs, making Riley chuckle behind her hand when her brother chokes on air.
She grins when she sits back down, glancing between the two men at her

table.

"No. I have been hired at ACLU. I am now going to be defending people from the LGBT community." She grins proudly.

A wide smile forms on River's lips and Austin just seems surprised.

"I didn't even know you applied for that job. Congratulations, Riley!" He then holds up his fist, wanting her to bump it but she shakes her head in mocking disgust, a smile tugging at the corner of her lips.

River bumps it instead, while Riley explains the whole thing. How she wants to choose for herself, what she wants instead of what offers her the most money.

How she wants to find her passion, what she'd really like to achieve in her life.

River opens up about being gay, about how it affected his life just about as bad as it affected Riley's life.

He tells the lawyer that he is truly surprised to hear she would fight for people who don't always have a say in this world.

"It is just strange, how society nowadays still believe in the old tales of the Bible." River says when Austin briefly mentions that their parents were religious. "How can we ever compare our life now to the way it used to be?"

"We can't." Riley shakes her head, playing with her wine glass. "I still don't know why even now, in the twenty-first century, people are so closed-minded. They don't realize that Jesus just cared about love, about respecting each other and leave people in their own value. It is not like being gay, or bi, or transgender or anything in that matter is a sin. It's not like we have a choice."

"Yeah, exactly." Austin nods. "Even if it were a sin, which it definitely isn't, who are they to judge? Who are they to judge others in the way they live? Like you said, Riley, it's about respect and leaving people in their own value. I don't get it."

"Yeah, me neither. But it only makes me proud to hear that you're going to fight for that, Riley." River's grey eyes sparkle when he raises his glass, clinking it with Riley's.

"I am, too, Riley. Really. I've experienced a lot of shit, even though I'm not gay." Her brother shakes his head in disbelief. "Can you believe the amount of people that were disgusted, just because River and I went to Europe together? How they made assumptions about us?"

"What did they say?" Riley's eyes move between the two best friends.

"That River was going to make me a faggot, too. That he was in love with me and that he was only trying to get me in a sexual way." Austin grins when he sees the roll of River's eyes.

Riley rolls her eyes with him. "Yeah, because gay guys can't be friends with straight guys."

They have a conversation about it all for more than an hour. About religion, about opinions and society, when Austin opts that he and River go home, since it's been a long week for them all.
"I'll walk you downstairs." Riley smiles when she insists on taking them downstairs, always hating it to just dump them in the elevator.
They take the old metal box down, walking into the foyer for Riley to let them out.
"Thank you for cooking that delicious meal." She grins, pulling her brother in for a hug. He's much taller than she is, but she doesn't care when she nuzzles her head under his chin.
It feels... good. It feels right to be able to do this and she has missed him so much.
When she pulls back, she watches how River offers a hand to shake.
Now, usually, Riley isn't the type to hug, but she can't help but open her arms for the bigger guy.
River grins when he wraps his arms around Riley, holding her shortly for pulling back.
"Thank you for tonight, guys." Riley's green eyes dart between the two hovering near the glass exit. "We should do it again soon."
"How about you cook for us next time?" Austin smirks when he teases her, earning him a small smack on the arm.
"I'll make sure to burn your house down, then." The lawyer teases back.
"It was great really meeting you, Riley. Was about time." River smiles, his blue eyes lighting up when they meet Riley's.
"Yes, it was." She agrees. "Get home safely, okay?"
"Will do. Thanks for having us." Austin throws a wink her way, before the two turn around to disappear from Riley's vision.
Smiling, she turns around to move to the elevator. She rolls her eyes when she notices that somebody has probably taken it up when she presses the button.
Her smile fades, though. She is going back up to an empty apartment.
An empty bed. She has to admit to herself that it has taken her a long time to get used to the fact she's sleeping alone.
Sure, things had been distant with Camilla for a long time, but there was just something different about not sleeping together anymore.
It is strange when Riley remembers the last time she and Camilla had sex. It wasn't too long before she walked in on her wife having sex with somebody else and Riley wonders how much that person has ever meant to her.
She wonders if she loved the girl she cheated with. Surely, if she did, she wouldn't have wanted sex with Riley, right?
There is just no logic, it doesn't make much sense. Even though Riley has made mistakes, she would never, ever cheat.
She just... she can't do it. She couldn't. There had been several

opportunities for her to do so and she chose not to.

She starts wondering what drove Camilla to do it when a gentle voice startles her.

"Riley."

Riley glances aside, spotting Jules in her usual scrubs.

Her voice is soft, but quieter than before.

"Jules." Riley gives a polite nod, offering a small smile.

She watches Jules shortly, noticing how flustered and exhausted the blonde really looks. As if she hasn't slept in weeks.

She has dark circles under her eyes, her cheeks hallow. She seems to have lost weight, too.

But beside that, she notices that Jules has a small bruise on her cheekbone. Instant worry flushes her chest. She takes a step closer. "Are you alright?"

A surprised look shows on Jules's face, but she quickly recovers. The blonde's hand flies up to gently feel the bruise on her cheek, as if Riley has only been referring to that. "Yeah, uh, got attacked at work today by a patient. He... he panicked when he realized where he was."

A frown shadows Riley's face as she studies the blonde, but Jules clearly doesn't feel comfortable, so she averts her eyes.

"That sounds horrible. Are you sure you're alright?"

The blonde looks like she wants to take the stairs by now, which leaves Riley quite a bit puzzled.

"Jules?" Riley narrows her eyes, not wanting to overstep, but she softly nudges Jules's elbow.

The blonde instantly flinches away from her, and Riley doesn't blame her. She just got fucking assaulted and Riley should've thought about the consequences before acting.

"I'm sorry, Jules."

"Don't be." The blonde shakes her head, her bottom lip trembling as if she's about to cry. She seems shaken up about it all and the lawyer doesn't blame her.

Riley wants to ask. She wants to offer... something.

But it's awkward and distant and she shuts up when the elevator shows. They make their way in silently.

"If there's anything I can do, will you let me know?" Riley cringes at her own words, but she doesn't know what else to say.

She just wants to offer her friendship to the blonde.

"I will, thank you." the blonde's voice is flat, but she smiles anyway.

It doesn't reach her eyes, but after everything the surgeon went through, Riley knows it isn't directed towards her. At least, probably not.

The moment they reach their floor, Riley shoots the blonde a sympathetic smile. "Goodnight, Jules."

"Goodnight, Riley."

Jules disappears before Riley can say more.

She notices the husband the next day. He seems to be coming home from a night shift when she waits for the elevator to show so she can take out the trash.
Riley gives him a smile when she notices he looks equally as tired as Jules does after a long shift at the hospital.
She tries to avoid him by going back to her apartment, but he already notices her.
"Hey, Riley, right?" he steps out, but his hand prevents the doors from sliding closed as she steps in.
"Yes, I am."
"I'm Liam. Jules has told me about you, sorry I haven't been able to introduce myself before." the smile on his face is tired, but it seems genuine.
His brown hair is a little too long to be practical for a surgeon and his brown eyes are kind.
"Riley." She offers her free hand to shake. "I'm sorry for not introducing myself earlier either, I know you two moved in a while ago."
He waves it off with a small smile. "No worries. Jules has mentioned that you had dinner with her a while back. Would you like to join us some time? I'm sure she'd like that."
She flashes him her professional smile, ignoring the fact that Jules has been different to her today. "But of course, I'd love to. If it's not too much trouble."
"Oh, it's not a problem, really. Jules loves to cook, and I am pretty sure she would like for you to come over." His brown eyes linger a bit too low for Riley's liking, but she lets it slide since she isn't even wearing a bra, not expecting to bump into someone on her way out.
"Sure."
"How about tomorrow night at seven?" he proposes, taking off his jacket that he wore over his scrubs.
"Sounds good, I'll see you then." She watches how he pulls back so the elevator closes before he can speak.
Great.

She takes a bottle of wine again. She has no idea what to do with herself when she knocks on the familiar door, not quite sure why Liam has invited her.
They are neighbors, sure, but this is New York. New Yorkers often tend to just be on their own.
Besides that, Liam absolutely doesn't look like the type of guy Riley would befriend, and she is pretty sure that Liam feels the same way about her so it

leaves her wondering.

She doesn't want to go, but she can't cancel. She hates cancelling plans, so she finds herself in front of their door, knocking subtly.

"Riley!" Liam opens the door, looking much better than he did the day before. "Come on in."

Riley offers a kind but distant smile, nodding at him when she steps into the apartment, but it feels so much more strained and forced than it did when she was just with Jules.

She notices the blonde in the kitchen, preparing a meal.

"Hey." Jules offers, smiling lightly. Her bruise is still there and Riley wonders how much the assault bothers her.

She can only imagine what it must be like to be attacked by a patient.

"How are you doing?" Riley asks politely to nobody in particular, handing the bottle over to Liam, who motions for her to sit down at their dining table.

"Good." Liam smiles, sitting down beside her. He isn't pushy, he is charming but Riley still can't manage to bring herself into small talk.

An awkward silence falls between them and it's then that Riley notices the music in the background.

She grins when she feels familiar fur at her ankles. "Scooter."

"Ah, I see you've made a friend." Liam's voice is cheery, crinkles beside his eyes when he smiles.

She smiles at him, showing her best side while she strokes the grey cat. Scooter instantly starts licking her hand, making her smile.

"Does he always do that?"

"With us he does. It's his way of showing people he likes them." Jules smiles while she puts a bowl of salad on the table, standing between Riley and Liam, her hand on Riley's chair for support while she leans forward.

Riley watches Liam's gaze darken, but it's gone so fast she isn't sure it was even there in the first place.

The blonde moves back to the kitchen.

"Hmm, well I like him right back." Riley smiles her prettiest smile at Liam, trying to ignore the awkward tension in the air.

"He's a good cat." The man laughs softly. "Jules, can I help you with something?"

"No, I'm good." The blonde waves off with a smile.

Another awkward silence falls between them, and Riley is grateful for Scooter as he jumps into her lap.

She came prepared – she put on an older pair of slacks and an older sweater. She cradles the little cat, loving how he is just a bit chubby, his fur soft against her skin as she presses a kiss atop his head.

"He really likes you." Liam looks surprised. "Anyway, Jules told me you are a lawyer?"

Another polite smile toys on Riley's lips. "I am, actually."
"What kind of work do you do?"
"Oh, actually I am between jobs now. I start next week at the ACLU."
"The union?" the surgeon narrows his eyes slightly.
"Yes. I'll be representing civil litigation cases, mostly in the LGBT community." She's proud of it.
She really is, but a moment of insecurity falls over her when she watches Liam narrow his eyes a bit, before it disappears, and a fake smile takes place on his thin lips.
"That sounds amazing. Are you part of the community as well?"
"I'm gay, yes." Riley admits then, before moving her gaze back to the guy.
He falls silent for a bit. There's just the tiniest homophobic vibe about him before he smiles again, nodding in understanding.
"Ah, I see. Well, it's beautiful what you do." He keeps the smile plastered to his face, but it is so obviously fake.
Riley instantly feels uncomfortable, and she wonders what he thinks. She has never kept her sexuality a secret, not even to strangers.
But she's always been careful with it. And judging by the way that Liam looks at her now, she is almost sure that he's at least the tiniest bit homophobic.
She can feel something tug at her gut when she sees the look on his face change into something kinder.
She knows it's a façade, she knows that it's feigned, but she's simply grateful when he starts talking again.
If he truly were to be homophobic, he doesn't tell her and she's grateful for that. But she knows that she will never want to have dinner with him again.
It's too forced, to strained. She doesn't like the unsettling feeling pool in her stomach whenever his gaze locks with hers.
She hates it when he smiles his fake smile, but how his gaze softens the moment he looks at his wife.
She decides to go with it. She makes small talk with Liam. They wait until Jules finishes dinner.
There is just something uneasy about it all and Riley wants nothing than to flee home, making a mental note to never have dinner here again, at least not when Liam is around.
There is something peculiar about this and she hates how uncomfortable she feels in their presence.
She goes home as quickly as possible, completely ignoring Jules's curious gazes.

4

She stands in front of the ACLU building for the second time in three weeks, her leather briefcase clasped to her side as she finds the courage to get inside.
It's her first day and she wonders if she has made the right choice.
Usually, she thinks things through, but applying here has been… impulsive, especially for her. She just decided to apply on a whim, and she hopes it's been the right decision to accept the job.
She loves the fact what she gets to do, but she wonders if it's the right organization. She wonders how it'll be, working for Sean Walker.
She sucks in a breath as she finally moves inside, only to be met by an Asian woman with an incredibly arrogant stance.
Her navy suit is draped around her body with such perfection and Riley wonders if she's had it handmade.
It would make Riley smile if it weren't her first day. Instead, the woman walks up to her, not amused at all when she extends her hand.
"Tessa Jensen. I'm the Senior Staff Attorney, I will be guiding you through your first weeks. After that, you'll report to me." The woman has hazel eyes, her lips are pursed, and Riley doesn't think she's ever seen anyone with higher cheekbones than this woman.
"Riley Dunn. Pleasure to meet you." she just says, taking the offered hand in her own.
There's a slight twitch on the corner of the Senior Attorney's mouth, leaving Riley wondering if she's just playing.
But the woman already moves to the elevators, being spoken to by many people. She must be well known around the organization as they make their way to the fifth floor.
Riley follows Tessa, until she's being guided into a small office and a file is being pressed in her hands.
"Get ready. We have court next week, meet up with our client. Prepare the

case." Tessa just says, about to leave.

"We?" Riley glances at Tessa with curiosity when the older woman is about to leave.

"We will go to court together. I will see how you're doing. I have faith that you'll have no problem in court, given your… statistics. However, I still like to get to know my staff, so yes, we." Tessa looks around Riley's office, as if she's thinking about other things to say. "If you have any further questions, my office is at the end of the hall. Chloe will meet up with you, she'll walk you through everything."

"Okay." Riley smiles, taking off her coat to put it on the rack.

"Password and stuff is on the note on your desk." With that, Tessa leaves the small office, closing the door behind her.

Riley lets out an amused huff while she takes her briefcase and the file and sits down behind her pc, that looks too old to even function properly.

Her office is small, and it looks like it hasn't been used in a while.

She smiles though, turning on the pc and she focuses on the case she has. She reads the deposition they've had a while ago.

Her client has had a dishonorable discharge, which makes it impossible for her to find a proper job. The woman believes it's because she's an out transgender woman.

She's suing her employer for firing her based on discrimination and Riley instantly knows that this is what she wants to do. She wants to fight for these kind of people, so she digs in.

She digs in, barely noticing that time is passing. She meets up with the client, like Tessa told her to, so she can hear the story for herself.

Riley builds her case after that, listening to the recorded deposition, finding witnesses, other people that may have been fired for the same sort of reason to build a stronger case.

She works, enjoying every minute of it. She works until there is a knock on her door.

She mumbles a vague yes, before looking up to meet Sean' grey eyes.

"Mr. Walker." She instantly rises from her seat to offer him a handshake.

He takes it with a small smile.

"Ms. Dunn. I see you've settled in quite well." He nods, sitting down in one of the chairs across her desk. "Though I admire your enthusiasm, at this office we go home before seven in the evening."

She looks at her watch. It's after nine in the evening. "I lost track of time."

"It's a good trait, really." He encourages her. She has no idea what has shifted his mood, but he seems actually… nice. "It's admirable that you are devoted to your job. Go home, though. I am sure that you will have more than enough time during the normal office hours to figure things out. Working late is highly unnecessary."

Riley just nods with a smile. "I will go home."

"Also, no file leaves this office. Work is work, home is personal. Don't mix it." He warns, rising from his seat with a subtle sparkle in his eyes. "I am sure you will do many good things here, Ms. Dunn. We are happy to have you."

"Thank you, sir." she throws him a polite smile. He nods once again, before leaving the office.

She grins, leaning back in her chair. This is not at all what she is used to. She is going to have get used to the fact that they actually find personal time important here.

She doesn't think she minds. She needs that. She needs time for herself, she needs to work less and perhaps go out more.

Meet her brother, maybe.

She shoots him a quick text if he's up for meeting in the coming weekend. He instantly replies with a thumb's up emoji.

She gets ready to go home, hating how the weather is turning colder and colder in the fall.

She takes a cab, watching how it's starting to rain when she exits her cab, hurrying inside.

She almost rolls her eyes when she notices someone familiar waiting for the elevator.

It's as if the universe is toying with her.

Usually, she'd rarely bump into people at the elevator but ever since she's gotten acquainted with Jules, she's been bumping into her often.

"Riley." Blue eyes are surprised.

"Jules." Riley remains stoic, still not sure what to do with the mixed feeling she has about her neighbors.

"I'm sorry about the other day." The blonde immediately speaks, probably referring to the dinner they've had with Liam.

"Nothing to be sorry for." Riley waves it off, not sure if she's in the mood to talk about this stuff, but Jules continues.

"No, it was... awkward. I'm sorry."

"It's no problem, Jules." Riley still doesn't feel easy about it all, but it had nothing to do with Jules. It was all Liam and she knows it.

"I'm sorry about dinner, really." The surgeon doesn't stop. "Liam can be a bit... intense."

The brunette grimaces, silently ordering the elevator to hurry the fuck up. "So I've noticed."

"He's not homophobic, you know."

Riley finally glances beside her, hating how she is smiling at the vulnerable looking blonde next to her.

Jules looks like she always does – tired, just in her scrubs, her hair messy. Still, she's gorgeous.

So even Jules must have noticed the way her husband behaved.

Riley can't find it in herself to not smile.
"I thought he was." She replies then.
"He's just… he has strong opinions, but he never… he would never judge." Jules smiles sadly, and there is just something about it that makes Riley's heart sting.
She just quirks a curious brow, not wanting to pry. Jules's face tells a different story from her words and Riley wonders why the blonde is trying to defend her husband.
She wonders what they really think.
The blonde seems to think if she should elaborate for a moment. "We really aren't homophobic; I hope you know you're always welcome at our place."
"Okay."
They silently step into the elevator, a strange tension between them as it goes up to their floor.
"Have you had dinner yet?" Jules asks then, her voice softer than it was before.
Sighing, Riley's eyes meet hers. "Look, Jules, you don't have to do that. If you don't want to be friends, then sure, we won't be friends."
"I want to."
Riley raises her eyebrow again, challenging the blonde.
Jules's face is determined, though. "I meant when I said I wanted to be friends, Riley."
"Okay." She just says again. She has no idea what else to say, really.
"So, will you have dinner with me?"
"Sure."

It isn't awkward.
Riley invites Jules over instead of going to the blonde's apartment. She makes some pasta with tomato sauce, a simple recipe that Austin recommended.
It's her first time to try it and she smiles when Jules joins her in her kitchen to help.
"So, uhm… I hope that I haven't ruined things. I like you." Jules suddenly speaks, catching Riley off guard.
The brunette glances beside her, watching how the blonde stirs the sauce.
"You haven't ruined things, Jules." Even though Riley isn't sure it's the truth, she wants it to be. But then again, it wasn't Jules who had given her the idea that she wouldn't be okay with Riley's sexuality.
"Well, I think we've might have crossed a line. I really hope you know that I don't want that to happen again." The surgeon glances at the stove on the kitchen island.
Just when Riley opens her mouth to speak, there's a loud knock on the door, startling the both of them.

She quickly makes her way to open the door.
She gasps when she sees who it is. The person she hasn't seen in weeks.
She blinks a few times, wondering if this is real.
Camilla is standing right there, tears in her deep blue eyes.
"Cam?" Riley's voice turns incredibly soft when she sees her ex-wife for the first time since their divorce.
Camilla looks like she's drunk, hurt when she glances over Riley's shoulder to see Jules standing in the kitchen.
A sarcastic chuckle bubbles from Camilla's throat.
"What are you doing here?" the lawyer doesn't feel at ease.
"I was… in the neighborhood." She stumbles over her own words. "But you already have company so I'll just… go."
Riley is just thoroughly confused. "How did you get into the building? Why are you here?"
"Because I miss you!" Camilla just blurts out, her eyes bloodshot, her lips pursed, and she seems pained.
"You have been drinking." Riley pushes her ex-wife further into the hallway softly, closing the door behind them to offer them some privacy.
"I know, I know, okay?" she rolls her eyes, her hair messy.
Riley is careful when she takes Camilla's face between her hands, her green eyes looking intently into blue.
"Why are you truly here?" she murmurs.
"I… I don't know."
"You don't miss me, Cam." Riley shakes her head, her thumbs softly caressing Camilla's cheeks. "You are drunk, and I have a feeling that right about now you're thinking that perhaps, we should get back together, even if it would just be temporarily."
"I hate how you still know me." Camilla's laugh is void and it touches Riley's soul.
Pressing a kiss on her forehead, Riley takes her in her arms.
"Already moving on? With Jules? She's pretty." Camilla mumbles in the lawyer's shoulder, grasping onto her ex-wife for dear life.
Riley ignores the comment, trying to comfort the woman she once loved. It would've been awkward if Camilla hadn't been drunk, but the brunette is pretty sure that if Camilla wakes up tomorrow, she won't remember a thing.
"Cam, go home. Take a cab." Riley just murmurs in her hair, closing her eyes for a moment.
She inhales the smell of Camilla's shampoo, a scent that was once so comforting.
Now, it's just vaguely familiar.
She softly nudges Camilla to let her go, pushing her towards the elevator gently.
"Go home, okay? Don't walk, just take a cab or order an Uber." She

presses the button, watching how Camilla sobs into her hands.
"We fucked up, didn't we?" she cries quietly, her body trembling.
"We did." Riley's heart breaks seeing her like this.
She thought that… perhaps Camilla didn't care as much as Riley did, but seeing her like this… it shows the lawyer that her ex-wife is hurting, too.
It shows her that perhaps, their life together wasn't all a lie. They once cared, they once loved each other.
They enjoyed each other's company; they were good together.
"Cam?" Riley speaks when the elevator dings.
When her piercing blue eyes meet green, Riley scrapes her throat. "I… I don't think it would be good if you stopped by again, okay? I need… I need to not see you. I need to move on. I can't move on when I find you crying on my doorstep."
Camilla nods, not speaking much as she attempts to contain her tears.
"Take care of yourself, okay?" Riley just nods as Camilla steps into the elevator.
She watches how the doors close, and neither woman tries to stop it.
Riley hovers for a few seconds after the elevator hums quietly and her ex-wife disappears once again.
She lets out a sigh she didn't know she was holding, trying to compose herself when she remembers that Jules is in her apartment.
Shaking her head, she hopes she won't be too emotional.
Jules is still in the exact same spot, moving around quietly to finish dinner.
For some strange reason, Riley's heart only aches more when she watches the blonde.
Jules is beautiful. Her long blonde hair is in natural curls, falling around her shoulders angelically.
She's wearing a dark Henley, dark jeans and her figure is just… beautiful.
Her smile is sad when she turns around, noticing that Riley stepped back in. The brunette silently makes her way to the kitchen, grabbing two plates to put on the dining table.
"Are you okay?" Jules's voice is gentle and careful and Riley appreciates that she doesn't pressure too much.
"I will be." She breathes, trying to smile, but she can't help herself. Her heart is aching.
She misses Camilla, she misses it all and she feels like a failure. Her heart is aching, and she doesn't know how to make it stop.
She can push it away, she can put on a mask and keep going, but it'll only make things worse.
She leans back against the counter, not quite sure what to do with herself.
Jules shuffles towards her with questioning eyes and it is only then that Riley finds herself crying softly.
She tries to hide it, she wants to walk away from the blonde, but Jules is

sweet when she slowly reaches for Riley.

Riley lets herself being hugged by the surgeon. She allows herself to cry into her shoulder, her own arms slipping around a slim waist, only to cling onto it desperately.

The warmth of Jules's body against her own somewhat manages to calm her racing heart, but she can't stop the tears from falling.

She can't stop the sobs escaping her throat when Jules holds her close, their bodies flush.

Riley has no idea how long they stand there. She has no idea how long she's unable to compose herself, but when she pulls back, Jules seems to snap out of a certain daze.

Her blue eyes are kind and worried when she retracts her arms from around Riley. "Do you want to talk about it?"

Shaking her head, Riley wipes the tears from her face. "No, let's go eat. Must be cold by now."

They silently move to the dining table. A comfortable silence falls between them, and they both seem to have enough to think about.

They both are lost in thought as they eat, quietly enjoying the others' company.

But then, Jules speaks up. "So, your new job must have started by now. How is that going?"

"It's going well, actually. Just had my first day." Riley smiles, grateful for the distraction.

The smile Jules sends her way is reassuring and Riley doesn't know why she needs that so much.

She doesn't know why the hug had been so incredibly comforting, something she actually needed.

Maybe she has just been craving human touch, since it's been so long since she's touched a woman.

She doesn't know.

The only thing she knows is that Jules is an enigma.

She's a mystery and Riley wants to unravel her.

She gets through her first week without much trouble. It's challenging, it's different from the firm, but she loves it.

She likes the people. Sean is actually a really nice man, he reminds her of the silly dad type, the type who would just make jokes and laugh about them loudly, while everyone else would try and understand the joke.

Tessa has been kind, too. Even though she seems stoic, the moment they are alone the façade seems to fade slightly.

It's nice.

Chloe has been nice, too, but she's already back to assist Sean on his cases and it's just Riley and Tessa now.

But they work together well. They've been going over their case, preparing for court next week.

Tessa barely has to say anything as Riley takes the lead, as they discuss the case they've built, the arguments and witnesses.

Riley is pretty sure that court will be no problem next week. She only looks forward to being back there.

And so, the weekend passes quickly. Riley tries to relax, she works out.

She meets with Austin in his restaurant and tastes more recipes he wanted to try. She enjoys every moment with him. He's funny, he's smart and still, she has no idea why she backed out on their relationship.

She tries to comprehend what has happened to her that makes her want to pull back from people.

There's a reason why she started working so much. There's a reason why she barely communicated with Camilla, and it wasn't because she didn't care.

She pulled back from Austin, despite the fact that they were once so close, despite the fact that things were well between them.

She needs to know why. She needs to know why she has this desperate feeling of pulling back as soon as she gets close to someone.

She doesn't want that. It's ruining more than it's doing good.

She notices that she still doesn't tell Austin everything. She just can't.

She keeps him at an arm's length, not letting him in and she wonders if there was ever a point in her life where she would let someone in completely.

She can't think of one. She can't think of one single person she has let in. None.

It scares her. She just seems incapable of opening up and she always thought it was because she was so introverted.

But as she's reviewing herself, she knows it isn't just that. She doesn't trust Austin completely.

She didn't trust Camilla completely.

She doesn't trust anyone with the things that make her, her. She just can't.

No matter how much she tries with Austin, no matter how much she goes back to her relationship with Camilla, she can't figure out why it went wrong, because they have never given her a reason not to trust them.

Not until Camilla cheated on her, anyway.

Perhaps she should seek help. She doesn't want to; she has always hated any kind of therapy. But if she can't figure this out herself, she needs help.

If she is ever to love again, if she's ever going to meet someone, she wants it. She doesn't want to be alone for the rest of her life.

She can't do that.

She just can't.

She spends her weekend finding a therapist online, applying for an intake.

She wonders what she should do with herself.

She goes up to the roof, even though it is freezing cold. She'd rather bury herself in her coat, her scarf than remaining inside.

The fresh air gives her a sense of reality. It gives her the idea that she… she's actually alive.

As if it's waking her up from her constant daze.

But the weekend passes.

She spends a few days in court, only to win her case. They celebrate, Friday night.

Chloe and Tessa, even Sean strolls along as they make their way to the bar just a block away from the office.

"To Riley and the many cases she'll win!" Sean smiles while he holds up his beer. The four of them clink their glasses together.

"To Riley!" Tessa has a lopsided grin on her face that amuses Riley to no end. The woman is anything but talkative, but the moment she speaks, it's always witty or clever.

Chloe is quiet. She's observing more, still looking like she's not sure about Riley's presence, but she goes along anyway.

Riley finds herself actually having a good time as they sip on their beers, talking through the case that wasn't all too complicated.

"I've always wanted to see you in action." Tessa then laughs after one beer.

"Oh?"

"Yes. After I looked you up when you applied, you almost seemed too good to be true. But now that I've seen you in action, your numbers did not exaggerate."

A certain pride fills Riley's chest when she hears the words. It's not often that people actually compliment her on her job.

"It's my only talent, really." She jokes humbly, smiling when Tessa sends her a smirk.

"We are really happy to have you, Riley." Sean smiles then, his grey eyes genuinely kind. "You're a great addition to the team."

"Thank you, sir."

"Oh, please, just call me Sean." He waves it off.

A comfortable silence falls between the four of them, but Riley scrapes her throat. "So, do you celebrate after every win?"

"Mostly." Chloe then grins. "Need an excuse to drink."

Tessa laughs shortly, leaving Riley to grin like a goof. These people, they are actually not at all like Riley expected them to be.

Once they warmed up to her, they are kind and funny and Riley wonders why she ever thought they would be cold-hearted people when they do what they do – fight for people like her.

There's just an unspoken agreement between them four – they keep things fun, on a professional level. They don't talk too much about personal things

and Riley is grateful for that.
She doesn't feel the need to talk about herself to complete strangers.
She actually has fun, as they sit in their fancy suits, completely out of place in the bar, but they don't care.
She enjoys spending her time with them, hearing stories of the special cases they've had, how terrible it is that still, in the twenty-first century, people can be so discriminated for who they really are.
It's a heavy topic, but they all agree on one thing – that they will fight for these people until they can't no more.
Riley admires them all. Chloe turns out to be a paralegal, but she's actually in law school to be able to do the same thing as Tessa and Riley are doing right now.
Riley offers to help her study if it's necessary – knowing how much and how hard you have to work to get through it all. There's a small smile tugging on Tessa's lips when Chloe greedily accepts.
Sean smiles when they all fall into light conversation, realizing that it's late and that they should go home to celebrate the weekend.
Before Riley has a chance, Tessa drops money on the table and they make their way out of the bar, only to realize it has started to snow.
Riley grumbles something under her breath. She fucking hates snow. She hates the darker seasons and she's hurtfully reminded that her birthday and the holiday season are coming up faster than she could've anticipated.
Sean stops a cab for Riley, but she insists that he takes it. She can wait.
Eventually, it's just Riley and Tessa waiting for a cab to show, shielding themselves under the lean-to from the bar.
"So, I know that Sean knows your motivations from starting to work here, but I don't." Tessa casually starts the conversation. "Why do you want to fight for the LGBT community?"
The brunette feels uncomfortable, and Tessa instantly notices, her hazel eyes softer than Riley has seen so far, a genuine smile on her lips.
"I'll go first then." The other lawyer takes a deep breath, vapor slipping through her lips with each exhale. The darkness of the city falls over them both as they stare into nothing, buried in their fancy coats. "I used to have a brother. We were close – I looked up to him like I did to nobody else. He was the only one capable of… making me feel understood."
Riley nods, smiling softly when Tessa seems insecure about telling her story.
"He… he came out to me when he was sixteen, I was twelve. At the time I didn't really know what it meant, but in the years that followed, I discovered truly what it meant to be queer." She grimaces, pursing her lips and she looks like she regrets starting. "I'm bi. He was the first to know and he was so proud of me. But one day, when he had gone to college and I was still in high school, we had police on our doorsteps. I just… I knew that something had happened. He had been beaten to death."

"Wow." Riley breathes, her eyes wide. She can just... she knows it happens. She knows that people get abused for who they are. She knows the world can be cruel, but murder...

"Yeah. All because he was gay." The hurtful smile on Tessa's face is enough for Riley to admire the woman for her strength.

"You dedicated your career to him." The brunette murmurs, watching the other woman nod.

"After he died, I started finding ways to fight for us. For people from the LGBT community. Even though the world changed, even though same-sex marriage is legal, we all... get so much shit. Homophobes are real, still to this day and I just... it makes me sick." The blonde shakes her head in disgust.

"I know." Riley hesitates for a moment. She wants to share her story, especially after what Tessa just told her, but she still hesitates.

"It's okay, you don't have to tell me." The blonde smiles softly.

"My parents were... religious. They were stern and my whole youth I've just known that I was gay." She sniffs a few times, her nose cold due to the weather, but she doesn't care.

"I was so afraid to come out to them, that I never really did. I went to college, I lived in the dorms there and at some point, I just didn't want to hide who I was from them, not anymore. I thought I'd be safe, you know, living in the dorms, maintaining a safe distance. I went home one weekend and I planned on coming out. I am still not sure if that has been the right decision to make."

A silence falls between them as the brunette buries her hands deep into her pockets.

"What happened?" Tessa is soft and sweet, and it surprises Riley.

"They were furious. They threw things at me, they almost sent me to the hospital right then and there if my brother hadn't stepped up to calm them down. They called me many things, words that even I had never heard before. They made sure to tell me what they thought of me, that I was an abomination, a disgrace, a stain on the family name." she falls quiet. She never even told Camilla the details about it all.

"They went to my room and threw my things out the window. They tore all the pictures from the wall, and they told me to leave and to never come back." Riley can still feel exactly what she felt in that moment.

She can still feel how powerless, how hurt she was.

"You know, they were supposed to be the people I could trust. And they threw everything away just because I am the way I am."

"Fuck them." Tessa spits.

"I still love them, you know." Riley's voice is soft and filled with grief as she speaks. "The worst thing about it all is that they made me feel guilty. They made me feel bad for who I was and to this day, I still believe that I was in the wrong. That I am in the wrong."

"They brainwashed you, Riley." Tessa moves to stand in front of the brunette. "You come across as a strong person. You know what you want, you fight for it, and I think that... I think that you'll come a long way fighting for people. But I hope you know you shouldn't forget to fight for yourself, too."

Riley has to swallow away the lump in her throat.

"I'm right, aren't I?" Tessa smiles then, placing her hands on Riley's shoulders. "Look, I am not prying into your private life, okay? Just... don't let people walk all over you just because you love who you love."

A sad huff leaves Riley's lips as she avoids looking into Tessa's eyes.

"And just... if you ever need to talk, my office is always open. We're not as professional, as distant as the life at the fancy firms you're used to. We are people, not assets." The blonde reminds the other lawyer.

"Yeah. Thank you, Tessa." Riley just smiles back, finally looking up to meet caring eyes.

It's truly the last thing she ever expected to see. Tessa always seems so stoic, so distant and guarded, so this is a true surprise. A pleasant one, but a surprise nonetheless.

"Even though we have a small LGBT department, we are close. I hope you know you can tell us everything if you ever need to."

"I think I do, now." Riley admits quietly.

"Good. Now, let's go home. I am freezing and I would really like to warm up." Tessa grins, removing her hands from Riley's shoulders.

Tessa silently stops a cab, motioning for Riley to take it.

"Thank you, Tessa. Have a good weekend." She means every word when she lowers herself into her cab, knowing that she has an entire weekend to think about Tessa's words.

She uses her lunchbreak the next Monday to go to the therapist she found online.

She regrets it the moment she sees it's the cliché shrink set-up – a couch where she is allowed to sit or lie on. An older man in his sixties with a terrible shirt and a jumper, glasses on the tip of his nose.

It's cliché, but somehow the man seems kind and comfortable enough for her to talk to, even though she has no idea what to say to him.

The only reason she picked him is because he is well known to be friendly to LGBT people.

She doesn't trust anyone these days, not anymore.

"James Paulson." The man has piercing blue eyes, but he smiles sweetly at her as she sits down on the leather couch. "Can you tell me why you've applied?"

She opens her mouth to speak, but no words come out. She shakes her head.

"You wrote that you recently got divorced. Do you need help to get through that?"

"No." she is determined that that isn't it. "I think I am here because… every time someone gets close to me I… I push them away as far as I can, and it has ruined too much for me at this point."

"Your marriage?" he smiles, putting his notebook aside, crossing his knees.

"Among other things."

"What else?" his tone is even, but still friendly.

"The relationship with my brother. We… we were always close, but the past years I've done nothing but push him away." she speaks quietly. She hates this.

She feels vulnerable, she feels the need to cry, and she isn't sure if pushing people away is a legit reason to see a fucking therapist.

"Why?"

"Why what?" green eyes find those intense blue ones. Even though James seems like a stern person, she feels at ease with him.

"Why did you push your brother away? Why did you push your spouse away?"

"Am I not here for you to answer that? To unearth these things?" she shakes her head at herself, hating that she refuses to just open up for once.

His chuckle surprises her. "I am here to talk with you, Riley. I am here so we can discuss what is going on with you, I can help you with the way you think, with the way you feel. So, why do you think that you pushed them away?"

"Because it scares me shitless when people get close." She blurts out.

"I know you probably hate the question, but I need you to elaborate on that. Why does it scare you?" He still smiles.

She has to think about this for a moment. She has never really thought about all the why's.

"I think… because I don't trust them."

"You said you have always been close to your brother. What makes you not trust him?"

She sighs for a moment. It's exhausting to think about.

She tries to trace back everything she's ever done. She started working hard, needing time for herself to just think.

She pushed Austin away, she pushed Camilla away because she never fully trusted them and the why is also a big question for herself.

She wants to trust Austin. She knows that he is trustworthy and that her distrust is misplaced.

So why can't she just… trust him completely?

James must notice her hesitation. "Can you tell me something about your childhood? Your parents perhaps?"

"Uhm, my parents were religious."

"Were?" he raises an eyebrow in surprise.

"I am pretty sure they still are today, but I haven't seen them in over a decade." She shrugs it off, but the sting in her heart hurts.

"Why is that?"

"Because they threw me out the moment they found out that I was gay." She grimaces once again, hating how opening up is just so fucking painful.

She knows it must be done to get somewhere. She has to know how she can work on herself, so it doesn't happen again.

So that history doesn't repeat itself because it is too painful. She's hurt so many people, including herself and she can't live with herself if it happens again.

She needs Austin in her life, and she wants to trust him, she wants to be able to build a relationship that doesn't scare the living shit out of her.

"How were your parents before you came out?"

"Stern. They pushed me into becoming my best self." She thinks about it.

"How did that make you feel?"

Another silence falls between them as Riley thinks of her answer. "I think it made me insecure. Nothing was ever good enough for them and they blamed me for it. I tried my best, always, but nothing I ever did was enough for them."

James nods quietly, his gaze friendly as if he understands. "So, would you say that your childhood has been rough on you?"

She lets out a tiny chuckle. "I wasn't abused, or anything. They wanted the best for me, so they encouraged me to do my best, to become better."

"Is that true, though? Did they want the best for you or is that what they have been telling you?"

The question cuts into her soul. Her eyes widen as she glances at her therapist. He's… direct.

"I-… I don't know." she doesn't really know anything at this point.

"Let me rephrase the question. Did you have the feeling that your parents truly loved you?"

"No." it rolls off her tongue before she even realizes it.

James smiles knowingly, nodding quietly before grabbing his notepad. "Riley, pushing people away doesn't just happen without reason. The fact that you want to hide your true self, that you never open up, it says a lot about what has happened to you when you were younger."

"Already diagnosing me?" she smiles, not minding when he chuckles softly.

"I can't say for sure yet, Riley, because we haven't spoken all that much yet. Could you perhaps give me an example of something your parents made you do? Something that you failed and what happened after?"

She tries to think about it. "I can only think of the simple things; as a kid I always had a… bad concentration level. My brother was two years younger, but he always excelled at everything in school, straight A's, he was the perfect student. But I could never focus long enough to get that and my parents... they told me that if Austin could do it, I could do it to. But I couldn't. I usually got only B's or a C+. When I got a B+ once, I was so happy that I showed it to them. But they got angry with me, telling me that I could do better than that. They told me that I should become the best version of myself and that they believed I was smarter than that."

"Did they call you stupid?"

"Not directly." She shakes her head.

"Are there other things like that?"

"I don't remember, but they compared me to Austin constantly. He always did everything right and I had to be like he was – a sweet, calm child, whom everyone loved. It wasn't that bad, I mean…"

"Don't sugarcoat it, Riley." James shakes his head. "How often did they make you feel like you weren't enough?"

"All the time." She mumbles, trying to smile, but she can't bring it up to curl her lips.

She can't bring it up to pretend that everything is okay.

"Can you tell me other things that made you feel… unworthy?"

She remains silent for a moment. "I think that… when I was thirteen, I started getting my own opinions on things. Like, on the world, on what I wanted to be. Every time I'd fight my mother on something she thought was right and I thought was wrong, she'd throw a Bible verse into my face, telling me I should read the Bible and see what Jesus would want us to do. What Jesus would think about a certain matter."

"She didn't give you the option to have an opinion?"

"I suppose so." She just nods, shivering when she remembers her mother being angry with her.

"So your mother used the Bible against you?"

"Yes." There was no doubt about that. She had been thinking about it for a long time. "I think she had her own opinions, used whatever verse she could find that was similar and just… use it against me, use it to silence me."

"That's… interesting." James smiles. He glances at the clock then, scribbling something down on his notepad. "From what you've told me so far, I think that… you said that you've never been abused."

"Yes. They never laid a hand on me." She shakes her head determinedly.

"Are you familiar with emotional abuse?" he then speaks carefully.

She looks at him, trying to find the words, but she just can't. She shakes her head then, fiddling with her fingers in her lap, her thumb and index-finger toying with her imaginal wedding band.

"Verbal abuse can have psychological consequences, just like physical abuse, Riley." He speaks, still a careful tone in his voice. "From what you have told me so far, I think that perhaps, you've been through more than you think you have. Pushing people away because you don't trust them – it's not nothing. I think it comes from the fact that you have never been able to be yourself in your childhood, that you've always felt so insecure about who you really were, and that you were never allowed to have your own opinion, that you don't trust people into being actually… acceptant. You don't trust people to allow you to have your own opinions, to have your own feelings and that can come forth from having parents like you did, Riley."

She just stares at him.

"I hope you don't get me wrong here, but you have probably how such a low self-esteem that you don't bother trying to prove yourself to others, emotionally speaking. You don't open up, because you don't think your own feelings are worth anything, that your opinion actually matters." He never tears away his gaze.

It feels like she's being punched in the gut. Almost an hour with this man and he is more right than she has ever been about herself in the thirty-four years she's been on this planet.

"I…" she doesn't have the words.

He smiles in an encouraging way.

"Are you saying that I ruined my marriage because I've been… mentally abused?" she can't believe it.

He instantly shakes his head. "Riley, I don't know what happened between you and your spouse. I don't kn-"

"I pushed her away. I pushed her away as far as I could and just stopped caring along the way." She admits it to herself.

"How did she react?"

"She let me. We grew apart. We did nothing together, we only slept in the same bed, had occasional boring sex and that was it. We never talked. She told me I should talk more, but every time we would have an argument I'd just… pull back. I couldn't ever find the words. And then she stopped trying."

"You grew apart?"

"We grew apart. I worked a lot and she… she let me. She let me." She realizes it. "She let us pull apart. She didn't correct me when I was wrong and I didn't see, not until it was too late."

"Then Riley, I don't think that the fact that you have trouble connecting with people, that that is what ended your marriage."

"You don't?" she needs to know.

"I don't think so." He shakes his head. "But be careful, Riley. What I tell you doesn't necessarily have to be your truth. I don't know exactly what happened, I was never there. I can only help you see things more clearly, deal with your emotions, your thoughts."

She just nods. She's exhausted. She has too much to think about right now and all she wants to do is flee.

She wants to run, and she wants to never look back. She never wants to attach to people again because all it causes is pain.

"Our time is up, here." James then speaks. "We've talked about a lot. Let it sink in, okay? And I think it would be wise for you to come back next week."

She nods. "Okay."

They make another appointment, for the next week on Friday night. She thinks that will be better, since now she still has to return to work, and she knows she'll be distracted.

She feels numb when she steps out of the building. She thought that going to a therapist would give her a moment of clarity, but all it did was make things a lot more complicated than she thought it would.

She knows he's right, though. Deep down, she knows he is.

She knows what her parents did, she knows how it affects her personal life today. She knows she has problems.

She hates being grown up. She hates being responsible for her own feelings, her own thoughts and she hates how it is draining her.

She's grateful that the moment she steps into the office, she is able to push it aside. She will have plenty of time to think about it when she gets home tonight, but now she has to focus on her job.

The day goes by quickly, really. She and Tessa work on a case together and Riley loves how good of a team they make.

Tessa doesn't mention the heavy conversation outside the bar the other night and Riley is grateful for it.

She's so, so tired the moment she steps out of the cab, on her way to her apartment building.

The city is covered in snow and Riley only realizes now that Thanksgiving is in three days.

She is just going to spend it alone, she knows. She hates holidays. She hates how forced it all is, really.

She stands on the pavement, not quite ready to enter the building just yet.

She glances up, still stunned with how small a building can make her feel. She has no idea how long she stands in the darkness of the evening, soft snow falling down.

"Uhm, you do know that there's a heater inside, right?" Jules's voice is playful, but it startles her.

She glances aside, smiling instantly when she sees the blonde with a red nose, buried in her dark scarf, wearing a knitted beanie.

She looks adorable and Riley feels a pang in her chest.

She has no idea why.

"I know." she offers a tiny smile.

"Are you going to come inside or are you standing here all night?" the blonde motions her head towards the glass entry to the building.

"No, I'm going inside." She shakes off her daze as she follows the surgeon inside.

"Rough day?" Jules then speaks as they stand in front of the elevator once again.

"Something like that." The brunette hums, not quite sure what to say.

She has too much on her mind.

"Are you celebrating Thanksgiving?"

"I have to work." She uses as an excuse. She knows full well that she won't spend the entire night at the office.

"Too bad. Liam is working then too; I was hoping that maybe we could share dinner." The blonde smiles a beautiful smile, her blue eyes light and sparkling. She has a few snowflakes in her lashes and Riley hates herself for noticing.

"I'm sorry, I don't have the time." She shakes her head, letting Jules step into the elevator first when it arrives.

"It's fine, Riley. Is everything okay?" Jules's voice is filled with worry.

"Uhm yeah, why wouldn't it be?"

"Because you look like you're about to lose your mind."

Riley scoffs. "I don't look like that."

"You kind of do." Jules smiles carefully. The brunette doesn't like how the blonde is able to read her like that.

"I've just had a rough time. I'm fine." She insists right back.

Jules nods, in a way that tells Riley she understands that the brunette doesn't want to talk about it.

"If you ever need to… you know, get something off your chest, you know where to find me."

The moment green eyes meet blue, Riley can't stop herself from smiling sadly. "Thank you, Jules. The same goes for you, you know."

She carefully nudges the blonde in her shoulder, hoping she's getting the message that Riley means it.

"Thank you."

They part silently when they arrive on their floor.

Riley takes a long, hot shower, going over her conversation with James.

She finished, puts her long hair in a high bun. She instantly climbs into bed, not bothering to have dinner.

She sleeps instantly, so emotionally drained that she has no energy to do anything else.

5

She works late on Thanksgiving. Everybody is already gone and she's the only one left at the office.
She has a set of keys, so she just grabs the files of her active cases, puts them in her bag and goes through the entire building to make sure that indeed everybody is gone.
Then, she moves to lock it up, activating the alarm before leaving.
She buries herself in her jacket when she makes her way outside, the wind icy in her face.
She feels alone if she's being completely honest with herself. Austin has invited her to spend the evening, but she can't.
She just doesn't want to. She has to be alone, she has to be able to think, to breathe and somehow, she feels like she can't lately.
It's just too much, too overwhelming. Things seem to go at such fast pace, and she just needs to take it slow, take baby steps instead of giant leaps.
Her heels click on the pavement when she makes her way to the street to stop a cab.
It takes a few minutes before she actually gets one and shivers when she steps in, giving her address.
It's just funny how she can feel so lonely while she's surrounded by millions of people in this city, how she can feel so void even when her relationship with Austin is growing.
It's like a piece of her is missing. A piece that was perhaps never there in the first place, but now that she's aware of it, she can't ignore it anymore.
That gaping hole in her heart only just seems to grow.
It hurts more than she thought it would. She has been thinking about her parents, about why they are the way they are, why they treated her so differently from Austin. She wonders how they are.
For years, she has pushed the thought of contacting them as far away as

humanly possible, but she has started to think about it ever since she started going to James.

She just feels like she has never been able to close her past. Never been able to let it go, accept it for the way it is.

She remembers the fury in her parents' eyes when she told them about it. She remembers their outbursts, the way they made her leave before she even got a chance to fight them properly.

She wonders why they would hurt her so much.

Why on earth they would hate their own biological child.

She can't comprehend it, she just can't. If she were ever to have a child, the only thing she would want is for them to be as happy as possible in this fucked up world.

She just doesn't get it, and the longer she thinks about it, the crazier it gets in her eyes.

So she pushes it away again, for now. Maybe she will be able to deal with it later.

When she arrives at her building, she doesn't care that she accidentally throws a hundred dollar bill to the cab driver, leaving before he can even say a thing.

She makes her way inside, going up to her apartment. She doesn't bother changing into something easier, instead she grabs her MacBook and sits down at her dining table, her pencil skirt tight, the sleeves of her blouse tucked up a bit.

She grabs the files, puts on her glasses and continues working. As long as she doesn't have to feel, she'll be okay tonight.

She just can't take it to think about everything that's happened to her, so she throws herself into her work.

She forgets to eat dinner.

Instead, she just puts on some music on her home cinema set and grabs a glass of wine before returning to work.

She absentmindedly hums along to the songs in the background, starting to work on the details of her cases.

She highlights the most important things, printed depositions, the cap of the highlighter between her teeth as she works.

She sighs then, taking the cap from her mouth to lean back in her chair. She undoes her hair from her professional updo, instead tucking it in a messy ponytail.

She stretches, groaning when she can feel her back crack.

She's been pulled out of her concentration when there's a quiet knock on the door. Arching her brow, she rises from her seat.

Her heels click on her floor as she moves to open the door.

An instant smile is on her face when she sees her neighbor in front of her.

"Jules." Riley is amused when she looks down on the blonde, a slight blush

on Jules's cheeks when she sees the brunette's professional wear.
"Really? Even at home, you're wearing that?" the surgeon shakes her head in amusement.
"Well, technically I'm still working." Riley toys with the highlighter in her hand. "What can I do for you, Jules?"
"I heard the music coming from your apartment and you told me you were going to work today. I just uhm…" Jules tucks her loose blonde hair behind her ears, the sleeves of her dark hoodie too large for her. "…I came because I wanted to make sure that you've eaten."
"I haven't actually, but I have some important cases to work on." Riley can't help but melt when she sees the blonde subtly bounce on her heels, as if she's nervous.
"Are you going to eat, though?" blue eyes are curious when they look into Riley's.
The brunette checks the watch on her thin wrist. Eight-thirty and she hasn't eaten yet.
Her stomach betrays her, starting to rumble.
Riley sighs, rolling her eyes when Jules chuckles softly.
"Look, Riley, you don't have to have dinner with me. I just wanted to check up on you." Jules's face falls slightly.
"I would love to have dinner with you, but I still have to finish my work." Riley pushes her glasses up in her hair, hesitating.
She wanted to spend Thanksgiving alone, but she thinks that it's Jules who doesn't want to spend it alone.
She wonders why the blonde wouldn't go to a friend or family instead of knocking on Riley's door.
They barely know each other.
Jules clasps her hands behind her back, her lips pursing in disappointment.
"Okay. Uhm, well, enjoy your evening, Riley." She tries to smile, but Riley can see right through it.
A soft sigh escapes her lips. "Jules, wait. Just… okay. I can't promise I'll be talkative because I really have to finish some things."
"I don't want to intrude." The blonde already makes her way back to her own apartment.
"Jules. We can order pizza if you want?" the brunette offers then, observing how the surgeon stops in her movements, only to turn around.
"You don't have to do this." Jules smiles then, but her blue eyes are sadder than they were before.
"Jules, we'll order pizza, okay? We're friends. I'd hate to think that you would have to eat alone tonight." Riley motions for the blonde to come into her apartment.
When Jules still doesn't move, Riley takes a step back to open her door further, raising her eyebrows expectantly.

"Fine." The blonde's lips curl subtly. Riley can just tell that she's holding back a bigger smile and she wishes that Jules wouldn't hold back.

Riley just grins subtly when the blonde walks past her into her apartment. She closes the door to make her way back to the table.

She grabs a glass of wine for Jules and sits down behind her laptop.

"What pizza do you want?" Riley grabs her phone then, already pulling up the app for pizza delivery.

"Hmm, just a margarita please." The blonde smiles, instantly taking a sip from her glass while Riley orders for the two of them.

"I have to finish up some things." Riley motions to the papers sprawled over the table.

"It's okay." Jules smiles, while Riley quickly gets back to work.

She works quietly, trying to be quick.

She gets lost, however. She is so focused on her work, that she barely notices Jules observing her while she goes through every page, taking in all the information, coming up with strategies for court.

"You really love your job, don't you?" the low voice of the blonde startles her.

She looks up, meeting a smile and bright blue eyes. "I do."

"I can tell."

Riley puts down her pen, her glasses on the table. "So much that I even work on Thanksgiving."

A chuckle escapes beautifully shapes lips. "Usually I work too, but this year they gave me time off."

"Without your husband?" Riley's lips curl as she decides to be done with her work. She shouldn't be working when she has someone over.

"Yeah, it's cruel, isn't it?" Jules grins, taking a sip of her wine.

"Hmm, well, at least I have some company now, so lucky me." she sends a genuine smile Jules's way, making sure it's received properly.

A comfortable silence falls between them. While Riley cleans the table, she rises from her chair to put the files in her bag.

"I'm just gonna go change. Be right back." She smiles at the blonde sitting at her table, quick to move into her room to change into comfortable slacks and a simple turtleneck.

Barefoot, she makes her way back into her living area when the intercom rings. She lets the deliverer in and waits at her door.

She accepts the pizza and makes her way back to settle near the blonde at the table.

"So, tell me about your job. You're a surgeon, but what is your specialty?"

"I do trauma surgery. People who come in after accidents. I mostly handle the ER." The blonde smiles then.

"Oh. That must be intense." Riley raises her eyebrows when she hands the blonde her own pizza.

They start eating.
"I love it." Blue eyes sparkle.
"I could never do that. I can't handle blood." Riley grins, taking a bite of her pizza. "Once, as a kid, my brother had fallen badly and there was a lot of blood. I remember waking up to people laughing at me because I fainted."
A small laugh escapes Jules's throat. "It's definitely not for everyone."
"What about Liam? What's his specialty?"
"Ortho. He fixes bones." Jules shakes her head in amusement. "We sometimes have surgery together."
"What's it like to work with your husband?" Riley can't imagine working with her partner.
"It's good, actually. Because we know each other, we work together well." The blonde smiles softly, but for some reason it doesn't reach her eyes.
Riley nods thoughtfully. "I don't think that I could work with my spouse."
A curious gaze goes her way. "Why?"
"I think in my field of work it'd be... disturbing." The brunette tries to imagine herself working with Camilla.
Camilla had also been working in law, but they always agreed to never work at the same firm.
They knew they would never go against each other in court since Camilla specialized in corporate law and Riley had always been working as a criminal lawyer.
But still, the thought of working with your spouse is quite unsettling to Riley. She lets out a small giggle. "If Camilla and I were to work together, I think we would've drove each other mad."
An amused huff comes from Jules. "It's different at the hospital."
"Well, the only thing I imagine is Grey's Anatomy scenes. Have sex in on-call rooms, stealing other people's surgeries and getting involved with your colleagues." Riley can't help the small laugh that she lets out.
The blonde has an amused twinkle in her eyes when she finishes her pizza. "It's nothing like that."
"Too bad. I love the drama." Riley grins, but she falls silent when she takes a last bite of her pizza.
"I've been thinking about transferring to another hospital, because I'm working with Liam, but I'm not sure."
"Why is that?"
"I don't know. I don't think Liam would be happy with that and like I said, we work together well."
Green eyes meet blue. "But?"
"But I see him all the time. It would be nice to come home and talk about our days, instead of having lunch together at the hospital and seeing each other in OR's."

"Hmm, well, if you want to transfer, I think you should." Riley tries to show her support.
She still wonders what Liam is thinking. She still wonders if he is as genuine as his wife, but she doesn't think so.
That unsettling feeling in her stomach has never really left.
"I'm thinking about it." Jules smiles then, leaning back in her chair. "I forgot, but uhm... happy Thanksgiving, Riley."
"Happy Thanksgiving, Jules."
The smiles the two women exchange are soft and Riley loses herself in blue eyes for a brief moment, before realizing she's sharing a holiday with a married woman.
She doesn't know why she let Jules in. She doesn't know why she agreed on doing this.
There's just a strange, unspoken connection between them that Riley can't quite put her finger on.
Maybe it's just because Riley is physically attracted to the other woman - she is really beautiful after all.
Her long, blonde hair curly and messy when she runs her hand through them. Her blue eyes big, bright, and emotional most of the time.
Her smile filled with something Riley thinks might be sadness, but she isn't sure.
She doesn't mind her company.
She doesn't mind spending the holiday she was supposed to be spending alone, with Jules.
Even though they are distant, even though they don't share too much about themselves, Riley doesn't mind.
There is just something about Jules.
She knows she shouldn't think that way. She knows that Jules is married and that Riley will never get to know her like her husband does, but still.
She wants to know.
She wants to know it all.

She didn't celebrate her birthday in early December. She only met with Austin before that to talk.
To explain why she needs the time to herself.
Instead, she buries herself in work. She desperately needs the distraction, because she feels like she's about to break down and she doesn't want that.
She just wishes she wouldn't feel at all, this month.
Seeing families preparing for Christmas, the entire city decorated with lights and Christmas trees is just too painful for her. It only reminds her of what she can't have - the family she has lost.
She's grieving.
So, she tries to avoid everybody during the entire December month.

She spends Christmas alone. Austin has tried to get her into celebrating with him and his friends after she spent Thanksgiving and her birthday alone.

She has been visiting James once since the intake conversation that has been more revealing than she expected it to be.

It's been good as much as it has been confronting her in the most painful ways. It is exactly why she needs the time alone, to process.

James had been proud when she told him that for the first time in her life, she chose a path in her career that she actually wanted to do.

He had been so understanding and encouraging and it is nice to have someone like him, even though he is just her therapist.

They get along quite well. He's been reminding her of her worth, that she can be whoever she wants to be without being stained by what others might think of her.

It's been hard accepting that she may be damaged, in a way that she'll always be.

James has been reminding her to carefully rebuild her relationship with her brother.

Her therapist encouraged her to talk to her brother, to tell him what she's going through if she wants him in her life.

So, she has. The day before her birthday in early December, they had sat down and talked. For hours.

How Austin has always felt guilty for the way Riley has been treated by their parents, that he's always felt the need to fix things, but how he held back when he realized that the more he cared about Riley, the more she pulled back.

They've come to an understanding, though.

They have agreed that they would take it slow, that they would talk if something would bother them. And Austin has been understanding, so understanding.

He's been there for her when she had an emotional breakdown, just holding her and telling her that everything would be okay.

But she knows the guilt hasn't left. It isn't something she can let go of in the blink of an eye. No, it stings.

It stings, it stays, and it bothers her.

She just can't believe how all these years she has been able to keep it inside of her.

How she's been able to hide all those feelings from everyone and mostly herself, is a mystery.

The divorce hits her harder than she expected it to. It has toppled her over the edge, making her realize that something was off about herself.

That something needed to change. It's been good as much as it's been breaking her heart, over and over when she recalls putting her signature on that piece of paper.

It's been hard on her because she has to find herself, not only on her own, but in her work, with the people around her. And she misses it.

She misses Camilla, in a way. She misses the friendship they used to have before they even got married. They had been genuinely close, and she wonders how she has been able to let it slip away from her, something so precious.

Something that could've been so beautiful. It's all gone now, and it seems to crash down on Riley as the Holidays arrive.

She's grateful for her new job, though. It's such a welcomed distraction, something that has been keeping her together the past weeks.

She has grown closer to Tessa over the past week. They've worked together, travelled together and Riley feels like Tessa is becoming someone she can trust.

She has the same thing with Austin. She isn't all too afraid anymore to put her heart on the line, despite her need to be alone now. It's different now.

Of course, she is frightened and careful, but she knows deep down that Austin would never hurt her. He would never put her in a position where she'd doubt herself again, she knows this.

And so, she intends to step out of her comfort zone more the moment she feels like she'd be ready, after things might calm down a bit.

She's always hidden her feelings, just so she wouldn't have to show them, so that people wouldn't think she'd be weak, so that people wouldn't have an opinion on them.

She knows it is a process to let that go, but she wants to. She wants to fight for it.

A quiet knock on the door gets Riley out of her daze, out of her train of thoughts when she's staring into the city from her bedroom window, once again thinking deeply about everything she's been through.

She lifts an eyebrow in surprise, not quite sure who it is knocking at her door in the middle of the night, on a day between Christmas and New Year's Eve.

She shuffles on her socks, placing her glass of Campari on the kitchen counter on her way.

The moment she opens the door, someone with a lot of blonde hair tumbles forward, straight into Riley's arms.

She is fast when she catches Jules, who seems to be… intoxicated. The scent of tequila hits Riley's nostrils as she tries to steady the two of them.

Two hands grip on the sleeves of her Henley.

Jules winces in pain, pulling back quickly.

"Wow, easy there." Riley's eyes grow wide when she sees a crying woman in front of her, looking so disheveled that it makes the lawyer wonder where the hell she's been. "What's wrong?"

"I don't want to be alone." Jules's voice cracks, her eyes fixated on the floor as she wobbles on her feet.

Riley instantly reaches out to steady her again. "Is something wrong with your husband?"

A meaningless chuckle escapes the blonde's throat, so empty that it makes Riley uncomfortable. She feels the urge to reach out to Jules, but the blonde seems just… confused.

"No, god no. He's fine, he has a night shift at the hospital." Jules finally looks up.

There is so much pain in those blue eyes that Riley has to swallow away something.

She runs a hand through her loose curls, waiting for Jules to elaborate as to why she's here, but it occurs to her that perhaps the blonde doesn't want to tell her.

"Come in, Jules."

She watches how the surgeon opens drunk, teary eyes wide in surprise, clearly not expecting Riley to let her in.

The blonde seems hesitant as to what she should do once she's in Riley's apartment.

The brunette quickly closes the door, reaching out to give Jules a subtle push towards her living room, but the moment her hand is on Jules's arm, the blonde finches away as if Riley has hit her.

It gives the brunette a nauseating feeling in her stomach. It's not usual for someone to flinch… from such a small touch, right? Does the assault from a while ago still bother her? Did Riley cross a line?

"I'm sorry, I just…" Jules manages to crack out, her voice trembling as she visibly tries not to burst to tears. "…I don't know why I came here."

Riley moves to face her, watches how the blonde protectively crosses her arms in front of her chest.

"Are you afraid of heights?"

Blue eyes snap up in utter surprise. "Uh, no?"

"Can I show you something?" Riley doesn't understand why she's even doing this.

For some reason, Jules decided to come here, even though she might be drunk.

Riley has a strange feeling that perhaps the blonde doesn't really have anybody else, and she decides not to ask about what is going on. She doesn't want to push the surgeon into saying or doing anything.

"Sure."

The brunette moves to her coatrack near her front door, grabbing one thick coat for Jules and one for herself.

"Where are we going?" the blonde seems a bit more held together when Riley hands her the jacket.

"You'll see." She smiles, still not quite sure why she's even doing this.

Jules hesitantly puts on the black coat, glancing down in insecurity as if she doesn't know if she should be wearing it in the first place.

Riley smiles when she sees how the blonde fits into her jacket with ease. "Do you trust me?"

"I suppose?" blue orbs are just so fucking intriguing, so helpless and Riley just knows that she has to be there for Jules.

For a moment, Riley can't move when she sees the emotions in blue eyes, as if Jules is silently trying to tell her that she's not okay.

As if she's quietly trying to give Riley a message, but the brunette isn't entirely sure.

"Okay. Come on." Riley tucks a scarf around her neck, opening her front door. She quickly grabs her keys when she lets Jules step out first, urging her silently to move to the elevator.

Jules seems confused when Riley presses the button for the top floor, but smiles when Riley looks at her.

The lawyer just can't figure the woman out. She can't figure out what is going on and it annoys her.

She observes how Jules anxiously toys with the wedding ring on her finger.

She watches how the surgeon winces when she notices Riley looking.

On the top floor, the lawyer goes first, moving to the stairs that she knows will take them up the roof. She opens the door with the key, walking first without looking back to see if Jules is following her.

She is grateful it isn't raining, but the cold air tells her that they might not be able to stay out long.

The wind is icy, the night dark, but she smiles instantly when she sees that there is barely a cloud up, a few shy starts trying to shine their way down the sky.

"Wow." Jules's eyes widen when Riley moves to the edge of the building, offering the best view of the city.

Somehow, Riley can't take her eyes off Jules when the blonde moves next to her, her eyes wide in anticipation, a small smile curling the sharp bow of her lips.

Somehow, Riley can't hold back the smile when she watches Jules close her eyes, inhaling deeply, taking in the evening air.

"Yeah, got to love the smog." The lawyers smile grows when the blonde lets out a chuckle without opening her eyes.

Riley stays close enough to the blonde because she still seems a bit wobbly on her feet.

But the smile on Jules's face grows when her eyes flutter back open, taking in the city before them.

"This is…"

"…breath-taking." Riley finishes for her. "Right?"

"It is. How did you manage to get a key?" the moment blue eyes meet green, Riley feels the need to pull Jules into a hug, but she doesn't. With the way Jules has recoiled from her touches before, she isn't sure what she can and cannot do around her. "I found it in the door years ago. They didn't seem to miss it and never changed locks."

"Wow." The blonde breathes again, looking stunning when she smiles, her blonde hair waving around her head in the icy wind. The tip of her nose is red, her hands buried in the warm pockets of Riley's coat.

They remain silent for a moment. "Why did you come to me, Jules?"

"Because I didn't know where else to go." She replies without hesitation, glancing back at Riley, who has been looking at her the entire time. "Liam is working and just… I'm sorry."

"Don't be." Riley shakes her head. "Don't be sorry. I told you the other day that I would be here. I meant that."

"It's the tenth anniversary of my father's death." The blonde's gaze moves back over the city, roaming over the skyscrapers.

"It doesn't get easier, does it?" Riley then murmurs, finally averting her gaze from the other woman. Side by side, they watch over the city, buried in their coats, alone with their thoughts.

"Can I ask you something?" Jules's voice seems to have calmed down.

"Of course."

"Why did you let me in? Why are you showing me this?"

Riley doesn't meet Jules's curious eyes. "Because you looked like you needed it."

"You don't know me."

"Does that matter?" Riley sniffs a few times, always getting a runny nose from the harsh wind on top of the building.

"No, but… you didn't have to do this."

"I know." Riley smiles then, not even knowing the answer herself. Perhaps she just… perhaps she needed it, too.

A comfortable silence falls between them and Riley isn't sure if she's imagining Jules shuffling closer to her, but at some point, their shoulders press together gently.

Riley finds comfort in the small touch. She finds herself leaning in, somehow desperate for human contact.

"I'm sorry about your father, Jules." Riley doesn't really know what else to say.

"It's okay."

"It isn't, based on how you showed up at my door." She continues, not knowing what possesses her to speak this way.

She wants to keep her distance, but things with Jules seem to go just naturally.

She feels that yearning when she's around Jules, a certain trust that she feels even though the blonde has that mystery over her that settles badly in Riley's stomach.

She has no idea why she's feeling so conflicted, but she wants to give Jules the benefit of the doubt.

The blonde purses her lips and Riley wonders if she has crossed a line.

"It's just… Liam thinks I'm overreacting. He doesn't seem to understand that perhaps the pain doesn't lessen over time." Her lips bend down, her gaze darkens.

Riley tries to hide her surprise. So much for a supporting husband. "I hope you know it's okay to feel the way you feel, regardless of what your husband might think."

Blue eyes dart to meet green. There is a surprised look on Jules's face as she parts her lips, ready to speak, but no words ever come.

There's a silence when both their gazes move to look over the city.

"We should get back."

Oh.

Perhaps she overstepped.

Perhaps Jules didn't want to hear this. Riley wonders why it is that the blonde comes across as so guarded and mysterious, yet she came knocking on Riley's door drunk.

She's a riddle.

"We should." Riley just agrees, already making her way back to the door, when a hand on her arm stops her.

"I'm sorry to have bothered you with this, Riley." Her voice is soft an apologetic.

"You really don't have to apologize, Jules. Like I said before, I meant it when I said that I'm here for you." Riley wants to move back inside, but Jules hovers near the edge, staring over the city.

Riley waits, patiently so.

She stands somewhere behind the blonde, watching her shoulders hunched, hearing the quiet sobs that manage to escape her lips.

They stare over the city, the vapor of their small breaths mingling when Riley steps closer again.

"Do you need a hug, Jules?"

Blue eyes are still so bright in the soft light of the moon. Jules nods, looking so defenseless that Riley fears she might break her if she holds her too tightly.

But she leans forward, snaking her arms around Jules's shoulders to hold her.

She can feel Jules's arms settle around her waist; the blonde's face pressed into Riley's bare neck.

She honestly doesn't care. It's warm and the tears fall into her shirt, but she doesn't care. She holds Jules as if her life depends on it, realizing too late that she's crying, too.

She has no idea why she's okay with exposing herself in front of the blonde like this. She has no idea why Jules seems to feel the same way as they stand on the rooftop, fighting their feelings quietly, holding each other tightly.

Riley just presses herself closer, her nose buried in blonde hair that vaguely smells like coconut shampoo.

She likes how Jules seems to radiate a certain warmth that settles in Riley's heart.

She knows that there is more to her neighbor than meets the eye. She has a feeling that they just silently understand each other, and Riley doesn't think she's ever had that kind of connection with someone before.

It scares her.

But she pushes it aside, holding Jules because she needs it. She's grieving over her father, a man that has died a decade ago and the blonde is still so, so hurt over it.

Jules only seems to cry harder when Riley pulls her impossibly close. She seems to fall apart when Riley feels her weight shifting, barely able to catch her.

"I'm taking you inside, okay?" Riley mumbles in her ear, feeling the blonde nod. She supports her all the way down, into Riley's apartment.

She settles Jules on her couch, making a cup of hot cocoa. She grabs a blanket, only to drape it around the blonde carefully.

She hands the mug, hesitant of where she should sit herself.

"You could join me." Jules sniffs, wiping the tears away from her face. Her eyes are bluer than ever when she finally looks up to meet Riley's questioning gaze.

The blonde pats the empty space on the couch beside her and Riley carefully drops herself, smiling when Jules lifts the blanket for Riley to settle under.

"Do you want to watch a movie?" Riley smiles, taking the cup from Jules as the blonde tries to settle into the couch further, handing it back when the blonde lets out a long sigh.

"Yeah."

Riley tries not to stare. Jules's make up has faded and she looks... so, so beautiful. Her blue eyes are so bright, despite the pain pooling in them.

Her lips pressed into a thin line, she looks like a cute version of grumpy cat, making Riley smile to herself when she grabs the remote.

"Disney?"

"Aren't we too old for that?" Jules lets out an amused huff, her voice raw with emotions.

Riley scoffs. "You're never too old for Disney, Jules."

"Okay then." The smile on the surgeon's face is worth it. She looks puffy, but Riley finds her stunning.

She smiles when she plays Coco, her favorite Disney film.
She realizes it may not have been the best choice for Jules, because the movie is about death and the afterlife, but the moment she glances aside, the blonde is smiling.
She's smiling and Riley gets lost for a moment. Her heart flutters.
The moment she realizes she's been staring she tears her gaze to the screen.
She can feel her eyelids starting to droop.
She can feel herself falling into a slumber, and she lets herself.

She wakes up with a sore neck. When she opens her eyes, all she can see is the ceiling.
She realizes her head has dropped back on the rest of the couch. She groans quietly when she stretches her muscles.
It is then, that she notices Jules. The blonde has fallen asleep on the couch as well. She's tucked under the blanket she has stolen from Riley completely, her feet propped against Riley's thigh, her head on the armrest.
Her hands are propped under her chin, and she looks peaceful. Riley almost doesn't have the heart to wake her.
She just… looks. She watches Jules sleep quietly, she admires the woman.
Jules just seems to have been through a lot. Like she's carrying so much with her, refusing to bother other people with her burdens.
But even the best of us fall, Riley thinks to herself. Even the best of us, the strongest of people sometimes need comfort.
So, she lets Jules sleep. She has no idea what time Liam will be home, but she just can't wake Jules.
She can't do it, she doesn't have the heart, not when Jules is constantly looking so tired, not when Riley has the feeling this might be the first time in a long time that Jules is actually sleeping.
She, however, is wide awake. She moves quietly around her living room, grabbing her half-empty glass of Campari when she moves back to stare over the dark city.
Clouds have taken over the sky and snow is softly whirling down. It's charming, from here.
The flickering lights, the snowflakes, the city that never sleeps.
Taking a sip of the red liquid, she can feel the bitter taste linger on her tongue.
She is so deep in thought that she doesn't notice Jules stirring on the couch.
"What time is it?" Jules's sleepy voice startles her.
She quickly checks her watch. "A little after five."
Panic flashes over Jules's features, but it disappears quickly.
"I, uh… should get home." The blonde sits up, stretching lightly. "Thank you for last night, Riley."
"You're welcome, Jules." The smile on her face is genuine when she slowly

steps closer, helping Jules unwrap herself from the blanket.
There's a moment, where Riley realizes that Jules is staring at her as she moves around the couch. Blue eyes watch carefully and Riley wonders what is going through the blonde's head.
Her blue gaze is lingering and intent, making Riley wonder what the hell she's trying to communicate.
But Jules never speaks. She stands up, sending a grateful smile towards Riley, moving to her front door.
She hesitates before she leaves.
"Riley?"
"Yes?" Riley watches her as she walks closer slowly, not quite sure what to do.
"I... thank you. Really."
"I haven't done much, Jules." The smile twitches on the corner of Riley's lips.
"You've done more than you think you have." Her smile is painful.
"Okay." She just nods, trying not to late her gaze linger on Jules too long.
"Can I... give you a hug?" blue eyes force Riley to look at them.
"Yes." She says it way more determinedly than she actually feels.
She lets Jules reach, she lets the blonde snake her arms around Riley's waist, as if they've been doing it for years.
Her own arms pull the blonde closer by her neck, tightly around her shoulders. She has the feeling that this won't be their last hug.
She has the feeling that they need each other, even though they have no idea what is going on in the others' lives.
She sinks into Jules's embrace, nuzzling her face into the blonde's shoulder. She can't shake the feeling, the soft familiarity this hug brings. She loses herself in it.
She loses herself in Jules as they stand, front against front, their hips attached, their arms tightly around the other as if they are both trying to communicate what words can't.
And Riley has no idea how to feel about it. It feels good to be able to let go. They stand longer than they should, probably.
But Riley knows, oh she knows that they both need it, so much more than she ever though she needed someone to hold onto.
It's just strange that it's Jules.
It doesn't feel awkward, or forced, it's not foreign but rather something that seems they've both been secretly longing for.
Or at least, that's what Riley thinks. She thinks that Jules feels the same way, considering how she's holding the brunette.
Ever since they started hugging, Jules's hands have mindlessly traced patterns on Riley's back, over and over, a comforting feeling that the brunette is welcoming.

And Riley has done nothing but let her hands wander over the blonde's shoulder blades, as if she doesn't know where or how to hold her.
She can hear a quiet hum from Jules's throat as the blonde pulls back and Riley instantly misses her warmth.
She instantly misses the feeling of the blonde's body pressed against her own, realizing it has been a long time since she's felt so content.
She hates how she has to snap back into reality when Jules smiles softly, her hand on the doorknob.
"I'll see you, Riley."
"Yeah. And Jules?"
She could get lost in those blue eyes.
"Thank you, too."

She doesn't celebrate New Year's Eve either. She hides on the roof, locking the door behind her as she stands around midnight.
She will be able to watch the ball drop from here. She can hear the crowd on Times Square reverberate between the buildings, echoing through the city.
It's lively and Riley couldn't feel emptier inside.
She watches the lit ball from the distance, realizing that this is the first time that she's alone on New Year's. Usually, she'd celebrate with Camilla.
Or she'd be working alongside the other workaholics.
But now, she's alone on the rooftop of her building, staring over the city and wondering where the hell her life just went to shit.
She wonders what Camilla is doing right now. She wonders how her ex-wife is spending the Holidays.
She thinks that Camilla is probably having a better time than she's having right now.
She glances at her watch. Just a minute left.
She looks at the ball, watching it lower slowly as they count down the last minute of the year.
Every second that passes, she just feels more void.
She has ignored Austin's requests to spend the night at his place with his friends and he hadn't pushed her, knowing she needs time.
She can't socialize now. She can't bring herself to being nice to complete strangers and pretend nothing is wrong.
She's just too tired. Too tired to pretend, too tired to get out there.
Exhausted and mentally drained.
She just wishes she knew how to make it stop.
She notices the last ten seconds, burying herself deeper into her jacket as the cold wind cuts its way into her skin.
She knows the moment the year has ended the second the fireworks start.
She smiles. It's beautiful.

It's breath-taking, really. The city is being lit by the colors in the sky, people are cheering in the distance.
She can't take her eyes off the view. Over the entire city, fireworks display, and she thoroughly enjoys it, despite hating New Year's Eve.
It's an overrated holiday and she has never liked it. But on her own, standing on the rooftop, she feels untouchable.
Lonely, but untouchable. It's a feeling she can't quite describe much more, but it has settled in her stomach, and it bothers her just as much as it comforts her.
She is not depending on anyone else, it's just her and she wishes she could overcome her past.
She hates how her mind has been so occupied with her personal issues.
She hates how it bothers her, all of it. She hates how it takes so incredibly long to just... recover.
To give her mind some peace.
But as she's standing there, feeling the strong wind wrapping around her body, her hair waving around her.
Her eyes watering as she stares over the city, the loneliness she's feeling is also... comforting.
It is like a warm blanket around her, that nobody can hurt her, nobody can get to her, nobody can touch her.
It is strange. Perhaps she is feeling more because she has been drinking. Perhaps she is just emotional because everyone around her seems to be together and she's just alone.
Alone on the rooftop, without a wife. Without friends or family.
Maybe she's meant to be alone.
She doesn't know. She can't take it anymore.
She just can't. She bursts out into tears when she watches the beautiful fireworks over the big city, the cold seeping through her jacket, into her sleeves.
She lets the tears fall like never before - nobody is here to see them anyway.
So she cries her heart out, the wind blowing the tears in her ears as she tries to wipe them away. She smiles through her sobs, because deep down she can still enjoy the view she has.
Deep down, she knows things will be okay, that this is her low point.
Her voice trembles with each exhaled sob. Her throat aches more and more, but she can't stop her tears from flowing, she can't stop her vision becoming blurry, the fireworks in the distance only vague sparkly colors for her now.
She's in fucking pain. That loneliness is haunting her, and she wishes she knew how to fix herself. She wishes she could just be better in the blink of an eye, nothing to worry about.
But it can't be like that, so the void settles in her stomach as she cries. She

still can't stop, but she hasn't been trying to stop either.

She lets them flow freely, she lets herself feel everything that is bubbling up from her chest right now and no matter how much it hurts, she knows it will be a relief.

The fireworks lessen at some point. A new year has started. Perhaps she can start over, too. Perhaps this year will bring her something better than the past year has brought her.

She can only hope for something better.

She glances at the watch tucked around her wrist - it's time for her to go back inside. To get to sleep and ignore her feelings again like she always does.

She smiles sadly when she turns around to step back inside, going down to her floor, only to find Liam and Jules standing in the hallway, clearly trying to get to their apartment.

They are obviously tipsy, sharing a few kisses. It hurts.

It hurts and she knows it's because she realizes that she's just... alone.

"Riley!" Liam exclaims drunkenly when she steps out the elevator, grinning when he leans in to hug her.

She clumsily catches him, smiling softly when he presses a kiss against her cheek. "Happy New Year!"

"Happy New Year, Liam." She smiles at him as he pulls back, watching how Jules moves to lean in and hug her.

"Happy New Year, Riley." She whispers, holding the brunette tightly. Riley needs it.

She hates it that she does, but she needs it. She loves how Jules holds her so closely, so delicately.

She loves how Jules presses a gentle kiss against her cheek before pulling back and move back to her husband's side.

"We are going to play some games." Liam wiggles his eyebrows. In that moment, Riley realizes that they are really drunk, but she doesn't mind. "Want to join?"

She thinks about it for a brief moment, watching how Jules clings onto her husband with a hopeful smile plastered to her face. Liam seems... relaxed. Sweet, even.

She then shakes her head. "No thanks, I'm just going to sleep."

"Are you sure?" Liam raises a worried eyebrow and all the annoyance she's felt about him before falls away slightly.

"Yes, but thank you for the offer." She grabs the keys from her pocket, running a hand through her hair as she watches Liam press a kiss to Jules's cheek.

"Okay." Jules nods and Riley watches how her arm is wrapped around Liam's waist.

"Happy New Year." Riley smiles faintly, before quickly disappearing into her own apartment.

With a relieved sigh, she hangs up her coat and disappears into her kitchen. She grabs the most expensive bottle of red wine she owns, opening it up to pour herself a glass.

She doesn't bother actually going to bed. She might be exhausted, but she knows she won't be able to sleep with her mind constantly running over things, over past decisions she's made and how she's feeling about it all.

So instead, she turns on soft music, standing in front of the giant window in her living room to continue to stare over the city, watching the fireworks in the distance while she tries to ignore her own reflection.

She looks old. Worried. A permanent crease between her eyebrows, her green eyes are sad, dark circles underneath them.

Her cheeks are hollow, and she knows she has lost weight. She knows she hasn't been eating well, but she can't find it in herself to care.

Her hair is long and untamed, and she should really get to a hairdresser. She should get a new haircut.

Sipping on her glass, staring into nothing, her phone rings.

She answers without bothering to see who it is calling her.

"Riley! Happy New Year!" Austin's voice sounds drunkenly on the other end of the line, causing Riley to smile instantly.

"Happy New Year, Aus." She replies softly, imagining her brother at a party somewhere, given the loud music and voices in the background.

"Next year, you celebrate with us, okay?" he yells.

"I will, I promise." She can feel the guilt already building in her chest, the guilt of turning down his invitations for this year.

"How about we go for a drink tomorrow night?" she proposes then. She can hear a surprised squeal.

"Yes! Text me the details. I love you!"

"I love you too, Austin." She flutters her eyes closed, meaning every word, trying to hold back a sob when she realizes just how good of a man he is.

After everything she's done, he still loves her the same. After everything, he gave her a second chance and she knows that he would give her a million more if he had to.

"Bye, Riley." He hangs up before she has a chance to say more.

She feels angry. With herself. For being so incredibly oblivious as to what is truly important.

She can't forgive herself. She can't forgive herself for ruining her marriage, she can't forgive herself for what she's done to the people she cared about the most.

She doesn't care that she's had a hard childhood, she is the one who ruined things. She has made the decision of pulling back, not her parents.

It is all on her.

The guilt is filling her heart, her head. She can't find it in herself to enjoy the wine anymore.

She turns off the music, just ready to get to bed, when there's a soft knock on the door. It's barely audible and Riley almost doesn't hear it.

Curious, she makes her way over, opening the door.

"Jules?" she raises an eyebrow in surprise.

"I knew you weren't going to sleep yet." The blonde smiles softly, buried in a comfortable hoodie.

"I thought you and Liam were going to play some games."

"He fell asleep." Jules rolls her eyes with a playfulness to it.

"Men." Riley snorts for a moment, before her face falls. "What are you doing here, Jules?"

"I was worried about you. I have this feeling that you spent New Year's alone."

Riley closes her eyes for a moment, not quite sure what to say. She lets out a quiet sigh when she opens her eyes and meets such a soft, blue gaze that she feels just about ready to fall apart once again.

"I did. I have a lot to... think about." She admits then, making no move, no indication to let Jules into her apartment.

"I hope you remember that my offer still stands. I'm here if you ever need to talk. Just a door away." The smile is meant to cheer Riley up, but it's not very helpful.

"Thank you." She nods, genuinely. "But I just... I have to go through this alone."

"You don't have to do everything on your own, you know." The blonde raises a brow.

"I know."

An amused huff leaves Jules's lips. "Do you?"

Riley lets out a small chuckle, crossing her arms in front of her chest. "I do. I just... I don't like talking."

"Hm, I figured." Blue eyes sparkle and Riley can't look away.

"How so?"

"You never reveal too much about yourself."

"I could say the same about you, Jules." Riley does smile by now, grateful that the blonde is able to distract her, even though it's just for a split second.

"I suppose we're both mysterious then. Anyway, I'll get out of your hair. Just... let me know if you need anything."

Jules looks like she wants to turn around, but Riley's fingers wrap around the blonde's wrist gently before she can leave.

Riley hesitates, biting her bottom lip, not quite sure what to say.

Jules smiles. "Do you need a hug?"

Sometimes, Riley wonders how Jules just seems to know.

Even though Riley never responds to the question, Jules already opens up her arms.

The lawyer falls into them smoothly, hating how much she is depending on these hugs lately. Hating how much she needs them, how she's started to depend on them.

It's warm and strong. Jules's arms are around her shoulders, her own around the blonde's waist to keep her close.

She sinks into it, leaning against the surgeon heavier than she intends to, but she just... she lacks strength.

She lacks a lot of things right now. Self-control, composure, strength. It's not like her to just hug a stranger and actually feel good about it.

It's not like her to fall apart in front of someone she barely knows, let alone someone she doesn't trust.

But is it, though? Is Jules someone she doesn't trust? Because lately, they've been having a lot of moments that Riley never thought she would ever have with anyone.

It feels strange to have a friend like this. A friend, where no talk is needed and actions are just so much stronger than words.

And Riley craves that. She can't put into words how she's feeling, she can't put into words what she wants, or who she wants to be. She just can't.

So, this is very welcomed.

She doesn't cry, she doesn't move, she just lets herself be held. She lets herself be vulnerable in front of this beautiful stranger.

She lets herself being comforted by the warmth that fills her heart.

She allows herself to enjoy it, and she can feel how it gives her some sense of hope.

Hope that things might just work out if she's strong and patient enough.

Hope for a better future.

6

"Happy New Year, Riley!" Austin looks hungover, but his smile is so bright that Riley can't help but smile herself.
"Hey, Happy New Year!" Riley opens her arms for her brother as they meet in front of the bar that Riley proposed they'd go to.
He instantly scoops her up in his big arms, twirling her around a few times before setting her back down on the snowy pavement.
"Let's get inside, it's fucking freezing." Riley laughs as she opens the door, waiting for her brother to follow her.
She wipes fresh snowflakes from her hair, that she tucked into a tight ponytail.
She shivers when she takes off her jacket, taking a seat at the bar while her brother follows.
"You sounded like you had fun last night." Riley grins then, ordering herself a martini, dirty.
Austin orders a whiskey as they shift in their seats, their knees almost touching as they look at each other.
Her brother grins. "Hm, oh yes I did. Such a shame you weren't there to witness River's drunken state."
"River's? I think I would've had much more fun watching you." She laughs quietly. "Because I remember very well that one time when I was in college… when we were both drunk and you thought it was a good idea to hit on a mannequin."
Cringing, Austin shakes his head in disgust. "I was hoping that you had forgotten about that one."
"Never." Riley chuckles, nodding at the bartender as he slides a glass her way. She instantly takes it between her fingers to take a sip.
"How are you? It's been a few weeks since I've seen you." Brown eyes are worried when they look into green.

"I've been… busy. I needed the time." She tries to smile when she remembers the last month.

"You spent much time alone, didn't you?" he asks, his voice softer than it usually is.

"I did."

"I hope you know that I won't pressure you into doing anything you don't want to." He bites his lip in insecurity.

"You don't, Austin. I know that I have a lot to make up for, and I am willing to fight for that." Her green gaze is boring into his eyes. She needs him to know. "You don't pressure me. I want to be here. I want to spend time with my little brother."

"Did it ever bother you that I was the favorite kid?" he changes the subject suddenly, taking a sip of his whiskey.

"Of course, it did, but I never blamed you for that. You were way too cute, so I get it." She teases, loving how his brown eyes start to sparkle.

"I don't get it, though. You're so much smarter than I am."

"I think mom and dad have always felt that I was different, Austin. It's not about who's smarter. They knew I was different, and they didn't like what they saw." She shakes her head.

"Do you really see me as your brother?" he seems hesitant, fiddling with the coaster under his glass. He avoids her gaze.

"Austin, you're more family to me than our parents ever will be. It's not about blood." She is determined. "Do you really see me as your sister?"

"Yes." He nods seriously then, a tiny, reassuring smile on his lips. "Which is why… I want you to know that they have tried to reach out to me."

Her eyes widen in shock. "What? What did they say?"

"It was several weeks ago, after you divorced from Camilla. I think they knew." He shakes his head. "They called."

"Did you answer?"

"No."

"Austin, just because I've had trouble with them, doesn't mean that you are not allowed to have your own relationship with them. They adopted you. They loved you and I am pretty sure that they still do." She purses her lips when she realizes the bitter truth in her words – that they will always care about Austin, but they never… they never cared for her.

They never told her that they loved her. They never said that she was enough, they never showed their pride.

Austin shakes his head. "I saw what they did to you. I will be forever grateful that they took me in, but I can't… I am so angry with them, Riley. They ruined so much good, they ruined us, they ruined you."

"Nothing is ruined, Austin. It's never too late, isn't that what you said?" she bounces his words back.

"I can't forgive them. You didn't know how they were after you left. You don't know what they said, you don't know how much they hated you. Every single conversation was about you, Riley. They kept saying how happy they were that I was a normal kid, that they loved me for it and I just... they hated you." He looks like he's about to cry, but he holds back, his nostrils flaring as he speaks.

She just purses her lips, unable to picture her parents so... angry. Sure, they had been angry often, but hate? She has never noticed that, pure, plain hate. The way Austin portrays it tells her that they hid a lot from her and she's grateful that she hasn't noticed all of their despise.

"They never knew the true meaning of family like I do, Riley." There is now a single tear in his eye.

"How can you call me family, when I left you, too?" she chokes on the words. She feels that pang in her chest, the regret of acting the way she did.

"You didn't leave me because of me, Riley. I saw that. You have never... you never judged me, you've always accepted me for who I am and even though you have been distant I knew you loved me. Every conversation we did have, you would ask how I was doing. You would make sure that I was okay before you would hang up." His features are sad. "I have missed you, but I knew I could come to you if I ever needed you. You always let me know, Riley. You always had my back, whether you believe that or not."

"But I didn't call you for months." She reaches out for him, their hands gripping on each other's forearms.

"But the last time we called, Riley, you told me to call you if I ever needed you. You told me that you were busy, that you had a hard time, and I respected your distance. I know you. I know you need time for yourself when heavy things are happening, just like now. I would never blame you for taking all the time that you need."

"But I-"

"Stop, Riley. Stop." He shakes his head determinedly, an unexpected smile hugging his lips. "This guilt you're feeling? It isn't necessary. You're you, okay? You tend to just pull back when you feel too many things. You don't talk about them. You've always needed more time to process. So please, please, let that guilt go. I have never blamed you. I have missed you and sometimes I wondered how you were doing, but Riley, I love you. You're my family, okay?"

"Stop." She cries softly. "You've already made me cry."

"I tend to do that." He jokes and they both laugh through their tears, their hands still gripping each other's arms.

He pulls her closer, into a tight, brief hug.

"Please? We have absolutely no obligations towards each other. There isn't a book or a rule that says you have to call every week, or every month. There aren't rules regarding us, okay? You don't have to text me every day. Just... take your time and just remember that I'm here if you need anything." He mumbles into her hair.

"You're too good for this world, Austin." She pulls back, wiping away the tears from her cheeks. She holds him by his biceps, making sure he's looking into her eyes when she continues. "I love you. You are my family too and I want to prove that I care."

"Stubborn." He shakes his head with a smile, before sitting back down in his seat. "Now, how about we go to a club tonight? I feel like we need to blow off some steam after this conversation."

"Sounds good."

"But not too long, because I have an appointment in the morning!"

They dance. They get drunk and they dance, and they twirl around each other as they used to do when Riley first went to college. He would visit her during weekends, and they would go out.

Riley would buy the alcohol and smuggle him into nightclubs even though he was too young.

Those are the times she misses, but now that she's here, with him dancing clumsily, she knows that they will be okay.

They are both so wasted, and she doesn't think she's had this much fun in… years.

Austin invites River somewhere along the night and River takes one of his friends, too. They dance until deep into the night, drinking around and acting like they don't have to worry about anything in the world and she loves it.

She needs it.

Austin insists on taking her home somewhere in the middle of the night, taking her all the way up to her apartment, where they both drunkenly stumble into Riley's neighbor.

She looks like she's just been climbing the stairs, but it barely registers with drunk Riley.

"Jules!" she slurs, laughing when she throws her arm around Austin's neck to steady herself, but she has to stand on her toes to reach him. "My brother Austin. Austin, my neighbor Jules."

"Gooood to meet you." Austin laughs just as drunken as Riley as he extends his hand.

Jules takes it with an amused grin.

"Did you work?" Riley lets her eyes roam over the blonde's body, noticing she's wearing her usual blue scrubs.

"Yes."

"Did you save many lives?" Riley grins, trying to find her keys in her pocket.

"Just a few. Take care, Riley." There's a softness to Jules that Riley doesn't know is real or not since she is too drunk to function like a proper human being.

"You, too." She smiles widely, watching how the blonde moves into her apartment.

Austin then guides her to her apartment where they struggle to open the door.

"So, Jules huh?" Austin wiggles his eyebrows the moment they set foot inside.

"What about her?" Riley clumsily moves to her kitchen, laughing when she tries to grab a glass to fill it with water.

"You like her."

"She's married."

"Oops." Austin's eyes grow wide, and he bursts into laughter.

Riley laughs with him, but soon forgets what they were even discussing in the first place. "You can crash here if you want."

"Oh, that would be great, honestly." He slurs, grinning when he drags himself to the couch, only to drop on it and fall asleep instantly.

She grins widely when she grabs a fluffy blanket, giggling to herself when she throws it over him completely, his entire head also covered.

Still chuckling to herself because she's so darn funny, she makes her way to her bedroom, only to drop on her bed without even changing.

She falls asleep before she notices.

The moment she wakes up, she can just... feel her head spinning. She groans deeply, her stomach protesting when she turns and she's just really... cold.

She shoots up, realizing that she is still fully clothed lying on her bed instead of buried under the blankets.

Nausea washes over her as she moves, quickly trying to escape to the bathroom.

She stumbles over her own feet as she runs, almost laughing at herself when she heaves into the toilet.

It's been years since she has been this hungover. Though, could she be hungover if she's still drunk?

She has been drinking so much she wonders if she'll ever be sober again. The thought makes her laugh out loud, while she clings onto the toilet bowl, disgusted by the entire situation.

But her world is spinning, her stomach hurting as she throws up in the bowl, feeling miserable but amused at the same time.

She groans to herself when she can feel her ribcage contract in a painful way, hating how she can't hold down the insides of her stomach.

She tries to, but she loses the fight as most of the booze from last night goes lost.

She breathes, finally done when she flushes the toilet. She makes her way to the sink to brush her teeth. She steadies herself by leaning against it, still quite wobbly on her legs.

She snorts when she sees herself. Her make up is smudged all over her face, her hair is a bigger mess than she's ever seen and her clothes... she looks like she half attempted to undress but stopped somewhere along the way.

Her eyes are red-ish and she looks like she hasn't been sleeping in weeks.

She feels weak when she finishes to brush her teeth, quickly trying to clean her face and put her hair up in a bun, changing into something easier.

She finds a long, lost NYU hoodie at the bottom of her closet, some yoga leggings she bought recently while she makes her way to her kitchen silently, trying to hold back a laugh when she sees Austin on her couch.

He's sleeping on his stomach, drooling over a pillow. The blanket is pooling on the ground and his arm and leg are thrown over the edge.

It would take one, tiny push to let him drop to the floor, but she won't give him that shit.

He's probably just as hungover as she is.

She silently moves around the kitchen, trying to gather some breakfast. She makes bacon, grabs a glass to put some water in for her to drink.

But somehow, her grip is weak, and she drops the glass on the floor. It breaks into a thousand pieces and Austin is up in no time, nearly dropping to the floor when his dizziness takes over.

"What the fuck?" he looks around, dropping back on the couch.

"Sorry!" Riley yells as she bends down to pick up the pieces, but she's too drunk and she loses her balance.

She slips on the water, her hand first on the floor, right into a piece of glass. She lets out a hurtful yell. She is never, ever this clumsy, this uncoordinated.

"Fuck, Aus? There's... there is a lot..." she gags when she sees her own blood seeping down the floor, a small pool forming when she tries to get up, but she feels incredibly lightheaded.

"Blood?" Austin is by her side instantly, guiding her to sit on one of her barstools. "Do you have a first aid kit?"

"Neighbors." Riley mumbles, watching how a large piece of glass is sticking out of her left palm.

"What?"

"They're surgeons. Maybe they can fix me up. I need..." She rolls her eyes back into her head when she watches the blood.

Austin desperately tries to wrap a towel around her hand, hitting the glass, hurting her more.

She hisses under her breath. "I just need to lie down. Just... ring their bell, please? Find them or take me to a bloody fucking hospital."

"Okay, okay." Austin's brown eyes are just as red as Riley's, telling the brunette that he's probably still intoxicated as well.

But he guides her to the couch, making her lie on it before he disappears into the hallway.

It doesn't take long for him to return with a sleepy looking Jules. The blonde looks like she just managed to put on some clothes, her hair in a bun high on her head as if she's been sleeping with it.

She's wearing a bag and hurries to the couch when she sees the lawyer lying there, her face pale.

"What the hell happened?" Jules sounds worried when she sees all the blood.

"It's just a scratch." Riley shakes her head when she tries to sit up, dizzy in her head, feeling the desperate need to empty her stomach again.

"This is not a scratch." Jules shakes her head, carefully sitting down beside the brunette.

They don't even notice how Austin has started to clean up the mess in the kitchen.

All Riley knows is Jules's soft hands working around her hand, slowly unwrapping the towel.

"It's deep." The surgeon just mumbles, her blue eyes focus on Riley's hand. The brunette tries to ignore the close proximity. She tries to ignore how Jules's scent registers, how the warmth of the blonde's hands radiates to Riley's own.

"I'm drunk." Riley just grins, making Jules huff in amusement.

"I figured you wouldn't do something this stupid while you're sober." She replies, but her gaze never moves from the piece of glass in Riley's hand.

"What does that mean?"

"It means you're usually really… quite elegant." A chuckle escapes Jules's throat when she finally looks up to meet green eyes.

She's close. Riley loves the color of her eyes.

She loves that light blue, that mystery, as if the blonde contains the deepest secrets of the universe.

It's intriguing and Riley hates how she wants to reach out and tuck a lost strand of hair behind Jules's small ear.

She hates how she can't take her eyes off the blonde's makeup less face, how beautiful she is, how she's mapping her entire face, the shapes, the colors, each curve, each wrinkle, wanting to remember it all.

She sees the subtle freckles on Jules's nose, two tiny birthmarks – one above her lip and one above her eyebrow.

It is adorable.

She wants to run her thumb down Jules's jaw, feel her dimpled chin and just lean in and…

"I'm going to take it out now." The surgeons low voice warns. "It's going to hurt."

Nodding, Riley prepares by closing her eyes, hissing through clenched jaw when she averts her face, scrunching up her nose.

She isn't really prepared when Jules moves, a sudden pain flashing in her hand.
"What the fuck!" she wants to scream, but she holds back. The blonde is fast when she wraps the towel back around, ordering the brunette to hold tightly.
"I'm going to stitch it up."
"Without some kind of anesthetic?" Riley's eyes grow wide. She is in pain. She can't handle much more.
"I can give you some local anesthesia." Jules grins then, clearly amused by the whole thing.
"Couldn't you have used that before you took it out?" rolling her eyes, Riley grunts something else under her breath.
The blonde shakes her head, showing a small syringe.
"Oh god." Riley feels the need to vomit.
She can hear Austin's laughter from the kitchen.
"It's not funny!"
"Careful there, Jules. She might barf all over you." The tall man makes his way over to the couch with a preventive bowl for Riley to vomit in. "She's never been good with… blood."
"I have to…" she rips her hand away from the blonde, holding it close to her when she flees to the bathroom.
She heaves into the toilet for the second time within half an hour, feeling so crappy that she thinks she might need two weeks to fucking recover.
She hovers for a moment, not quite sure if there's more on the way.
She feels a hand running soothing circles over her back. It's warm and comforting and she doesn't have to turn around to know to who it belongs.
"Jules? I might die today." Riley groans, clutching one hand to her stomach. She tries to ignore the pain in her injured palm, tries to ignore the unexpected waves of nausea.
"You'll be fine, Riley." Jules's voice is not amused, not judging. It is gentle and soft, and it is everything that the brunette needs.
"I'm drunk as fuck." Riley can still feel her world spinning when she sits up, feeling how Jules hands her a piece of paper to wipe off her chin.
"I can tell." The smile the blonde sends her way is almost enough to distract Riley from the stupid situation she's in.
"I just wanted to make breakfast." She pouts, feeling the sudden need to cry. "I just wanted to make breakfast and I dropped the glass and Austin was sleeping and I didn't want to wake him because he was sleeping so peacefully, and it's been years since he's been here like that and I just… I wanted to make him some nice breakfast because I haven't been there for him in a long time, but I care, Jules. I care about him." She rambles drunkenly.
She feels the warm liquid stream down her cheeks, and she hates herself for

being so fragile in front of Jules.
It is like a piece of her allows her only to be like this with the blonde. She knows for sure it isn't even the alcohol talking. Perhaps it makes it easier, but still she knows she wouldn't have behaved the way she does in front of anybody else.
She hates it.
"I know you do." The blonde just mumbles.
She falls apart and she doesn't know why. She has been falling apart so many times recently that she thought she wouldn't have to go through that again, but here she is.
She can't get rid of it; she can't forgive herself for the things she's done. Or rather, the things she didn't do.
"Hey, hey, look at me." Jules's voice is soft, it's comforting, and Riley wants nothing more than to lean in, but the only thing she notices is two hands wrapping around her wrists carefully.
Riley tries to hold back her sobs, her vision blurry with her tears when she looks up to meet the softest blue eyes she's ever seen.
She could just... drown in them. She could look at them all day, trying to figure out what is going on behind those orbs.
"I fucked up, Jules."
"Isn't he here? Doesn't that say something?" the blonde murmurs softly, still holding Riley's wrists.
There's blood seeping down, but neither of them notices.
"He's here because he's loyal."
"He's here because he cares. He's here because you care."
Scoffing, Riley rolls her eyes. "He's here because he would feel guilty if he didn't forgive me."
"That's not true, you know." His voice suddenly sounds. It's soft and just about as hurtful as Riley is feeling in this moment.
Green eyes snap up. She looks at her brother, hovering in the door.
"You think you fucked up, Riley. You think you've done something so terrible that you can't be forgiven, but you should stop beating yourself up for it." He shakes his head, his lips pursed into a thin line. "Nobody is blaming you."
"I'm blaming me." They ignore the blonde in the room, who has now tried to focus on Riley's wound.
"And you shouldn't."
"I ruined my marriage. I ruined your trust." She shakes her head, only now seeing how Jules's is gently dabbing the wound clean, but the blood seeping out is too much.
"Riley. Stop it." His voice is louder than Riley expects it to be. "You keep punishing yourself for everything. You've always blamed yourself for things that were simply out of your control, and it has to stop. I love you; I care

about you and there is nothing to forgive."
"There is."
"Stop." He snaps. "Stop! Just stop! Why are you even doing this to yourself? Why can't you forgive yourself for something that isn't even your fault?"
"Who else should I blame then?" she snarls, shaking her head. "Should I blame you for me not calling you? Should I blame Camilla for the fact our marriage was ruined because I was the one that pulled away?"
"Relationships go two ways, Riley. Wake the fuck up!" he kneels down by now, ignoring Jules completely. "Wake up! We all make mistakes, we all forget things, we all try to hide from the feelings that make us sick to our stomachs because yes, things hurt. We sometimes do need time for ourselves to process all that shit that's happening around us. Yes, we feel fucked up sometimes, but that is life, Riley. As for us, I could've called. I shouldn't have given up on you and I did! Camilla gave up on you, mom and dad gave up on you. We all left you fucking alone."
Riley can just feel the fight drain from her veins the moment Austin cups her cheeks, clumsily sitting on the ground before her.
"Riley, I love you. You've done more for me than anybody else has ever done, okay? I know that you love me. I know that you care, but I also know that you're damaged, we all are. So please, for fucks sake, can we just… leave this behind us? Can we move on? Can we trust each other and just… be?" he's mumbling by now, his brown eyes filled with tears.
He sends an apologetic smile towards Jules, but the blonde smiles reassuringly.
Riley parts her lips to speak, but the only thing escaping her mouth is a soft sigh.
She knows he's right. "I'm sorry."
"Don't be." He presses a kiss on her forehead. "You're just a bit messed up. A lot has happened."
"I'm wondering how many motivational speeches you have to give me before I finally get it." She grumbles to herself. She watches Jules, how the blonde's lips twitch in a secret grin.
She watches Austin's eyes roll in amusement. She lets out an exhausted huff and an eyeroll, before starting to chuckle at the ridiculousness of this entire situation.
The moment she lets out a giggle, Austin can't help but snort as well. He laughs quietly, leaning one hand on Riley's shoulder as he squeezes comfortingly.
No matter what happens from now on, he has always been right – this love, friendship between them, it's unconditional.
Riley realizes that now. She has never expected anything from him, and he has never expected anything from her. They accept each other for who they

are, and it is so good.
She just hates it that she hasn't been able to see that before.
"Well, how about I stitch this up now?" Jules smiles, glancing between the siblings with a playful gaze in her blue eyes.
Riley finds her beautiful. She admires her, she has no idea why, but she just does. She handles this entire situation with grace and Riley is so grateful that things aren't awkward.
Austin just nods, standing up to leave.
"Let me help you up." The blonde mumbles, leaning down to throw Riley's healthy arm around her shoulder.
They stumble up.
"I'm sorry you had to see that, Jules." Riley breathes, hating how she's allowing herself to be such a mess.
"It's okay to fall apart sometimes, Riley."
Their noses almost touch when they glance at each other. Riley hovers longer than she should, smiling sadly.
"I have been falling apart quite often, lately." She admits, finally able to tear her gaze away as they walk into the living room.
Jules just smiles, helping Riley to sit back on the couch. "I think people should fall apart more."
"Why is that?" Riley eyes her curiously.
"Because it gives us something to think about. If we bottle it up, nothing is ever helpful." The blonde grimaces, ignoring Riley's worried gaze.
"Hey, uhm… how long do you think that'll take you?" Austin suddenly cuts in.
"I don't know. Half an hour, tops?" Jules looks up at him, smiling politely.
"Riley, I wish nothing more than to stay, but I have an appointment with a local supplier." He groans, rubbing his face. "I regret making that appointment."
"I was going to make you breakfast." She pouts, making Austin grin from ear to ear.
"You? Breakfast?"
"I can cook." She defends weakly, wincing when Jules works on her hand with a small syringe.
"Sure you can." He laughs, leaning down to give her a kiss on the cheek. "Please don't forget what I told you this morning, okay?"
"I'll try." She smiles up at him, tucking on his shirt.
"Good to meet you, Jules." He grins then. "Sorry about this mess of a sister of mine."
"It's fine. She's not that bad." Jules teases with a gorgeous smile, looking up to the tall man to silently nod goodbye.
"Goodluck with that." He seems pale the moment he looks at the blood and Riley's hand. "I will call you."

"You do that. Goodluck with your meeting." She waves him off, smiling when she watches him leave.

The moment the door closes behind him, her smile falters.

"I'm really sorry about that."

"Hey, don't worry about it, okay?" blue eyes look up briefly, before focusing back on Riley's hand. "We all have our shit to deal with."

"I just wish you didn't have to see that."

"Even though I know you're drunk, I admire you for showing those kind of feelings, Riley. It's important." The blonde almost urges her.

Riley watches in disgust how the gaping cut in her hand is being sewed by Jules's skilled left hand.

"You're a lefty." She says dumbly, hearing a tiny chuckle coming from the blonde's mouth.

"I am." Jules works on the stitches silently, while Riley just can't seem to take her eyes off the other woman.

Riley hates it. She hates how attracted she is to Jules. She hates how badly she wants to get to know her, to be able to perhaps hug her a little more often.

"You said it's okay for people to fall apart." The brunette scrapes her throat.

"I did." The surgeon hums.

"If you ever need to, I'm right here."

Jules stops in her movements, the needle between her fingers. She hesitates when she looks up.

There's something in her eyes that Riley hasn't really seen before, something she can't explain.

A certain... desperation, hurt and it's all mixed with the impossibility of letting go. Of giving in.

Jules's holding back and Riley doesn't think she'll ever let go, whatever it is that makes her so fucking guarded.

The sadness that radiates from Jules's features - Riley can almost feel it herself.

She watches how the blonde bites her lip in order to keep her feelings contained. She watches how Jules seems to be seriously contemplating if she should let go.

If she should fall apart.

But she doesn't. Instead, Jules swallows away a lump in her throat, lowering her gaze back to Riley's hand.

The gentleness Jules uses to treat Riley just hits her right in the gut.

The way those blue eyes snap back down settles in the brunette's stomach.

It's like Jules wants to fall apart, but she can't. Something is stopping her, and Riley wants to know what it is, but she knows better than to push.

"I'm here for you." She just reminds her neighbor.

"Stop saying things like that." The blonde shakes her head rather aggressively.

"Why?"

"Because if you keep going, I might fall apart and I can't."

Riley bites her lips, watching how the blonde is holding back her pain. She looks like she's carrying the weight of the world on her shoulders and she's choosing to bear it all alone.

Instead of saying more, Riley leans forward in the slightest bit, her free hand reaching up to rest on the blonde's shoulder.

Jules flinches for a moment, but relaxes when she looks up to meet Riley's eyes.

"I'm not pushing you, Jules. I just hope you know that I mean what I say." She flickers her eyes between blue.

"I know. I… thank you. You're all done here." The blonde looks down, finishing up the last stitch, wrapping a bandage around it. "Just keep it clean and I'll check up on you in a few days. I wouldn't really let it get wet under the shower."

"Okay." Riley retreats her hand, watching the blonde clean up the mess they made. "Thank you for… patching me up."

"It's my job."

"Should I pay you then?" a grin forms on Riley's full lips when she watches Jules rise from the couch, placing the stuff in her bag.

"No, it's fine. You're my friend."

Even though Riley still might be drunk, she quickly rises from her couch as well to guide Jules out. "Thank you, really. You didn't have to do that."

"Saves you a lot of trouble in the ER. Don't worry about it." Jules smiles faintly, already her hand on the doorknob.

Before she can go, Riley carefully pulls her closer, though. She pulls Jules into a hug and by the way the blonde instantly clings onto her, Riley isn't sure who needs it more at this point.

The surgeon has dropped her bag when she buries her face in Riley's shoulder, not ashamed, the two of them just holding each other.

Their bodies melt together, their arms tightly wrapped around the other.

Riley tries to ignore how it makes her feel. She just wishes that Jules would talk to her. She just wishes they could be real friends, and not held-back and distant as they have been.

But Jules pulls back. She grabs a pen from her pocket, taking Riley's healthy hand. She writes down a phone number.

"In case you need me for the stitches." She smiles. Her eyes are red trimmed, her smile doesn't seem to reach her eyes.

She looks like she's hurting, and Riley just hopes that there is somebody she can talk to.

"Thank you." The brunette whispers, watching how Jules turns then to

open the door and disappears without another word.
Riley remains in an empty apartment.
She's   alone   and   she   wishes   she   weren't.

7

"I was a disaster." Riley complains the moment she lets her brother into her apartment.
It's been a week since her breakdown, a day since Liam has taken out the stitches in her hand.
She hasn't really spoken to her brother, but she knows that they both have had a lot to think about.
"You weren't." his dark eyes sparkle when he places the groceries on her kitchen island.
"I was. I was out of line. I... I'm sorry for behaving the way I did." She shakes her head, softly closing the door behind him.
She leans her back and her palms flat against it, not really able to look him in the eye just yet. Biting her bottom lip, she glances down at her white button up, the shiny grey slacks and her bare feet underneath.
She wiggles her toes, not quite sure what else to do.
River should be here too, soon, but he had to finish up his shift at the restaurant before he could make it.
"I think you needed that." His voice is suddenly closer.
A finger under her chin, lifting it up to meet his dark brown eyes and his mischievous smile.
"You needed that, Riley. You're fine. We're fine. Yeah?" his eyes search her face.
She watches him, wondering what the hell she did to deserve a brother like him. Really, all this time she has been the older sister, but the roles have been reversed.
He has been the protective big brother the moment she came out of the closet with her parents. He has been looking out for her more than she has been for him, and she wants to go back to the way they were.
She wants to be able to be there for him too, instead of being focused on

her own shit. It's something that she's been talking about with James.
Her brother deserves more than a sister that keeps falling apart. And so, she smiles at him.
It's small, toying on the corner of her lips, but she can see the instant sparkle in Austin's eyes the moment he notices.
She leans forward, tucking her head beneath his chin, her arms wrapping around his muscled waist.
No words are needed, really. She can feel his big arms around her small shoulders.
It is strange how safe it makes her feel, especially when he places a kiss atop her head. He doesn't speak – he's never been one with many words.
But when he speaks, his words just… hit her. They have an impact on her and she knows how smart he is.
But now, no words could ever describe what it is they are feeling. It's like they are coming to terms with what has happened, that they finally feel like they can move on from the gaps in their past.
It is exhilarating for the brunette as she sighs deeply, clinging onto him.
He is, and always will be, her family. He is the only reason she even knows what true family is.
Family supports.
Family loves unconditionally, no expectations, no reservations, just real love, genuine care for each other and she knows it.
She knows that that is what she wants with him. She wants him in her life, she wants to make sure he's okay, that he's happy and she wants to be there for him when things might not go well.
She wants to make sure that he'll be alright.
"What is on your mind?" his voice is soft, gentle and she smiles when she pulls back, but her arms remain around his middle.
His smile is wider than hers.
"I think your last speech has been of great help." She nods, a crooked smile on her face when she thinks about it. "I've been coming to a point where I think I can accept the past? I don't know, it doesn't feel like as big a burden as it used to."
His grin is wide when he nudges her shoulder. "I'm glad."
"I needed you to tell me what you did last week. I needed to hear that so badly." Her smile turns into a grimace when she can feel sudden tears occupy her eyes, streaming down her cheeks.
She can't help herself when she laughs through her tears, watching Austin's face crinkle in worry before he smiles softly.
"Fucking hormones." She mutters then, pulling back from her brother completely.
The snort Austin lets out is amusing her, making her chuckle at herself.
She has been foolish. She has been oblivious, and it has taken its toll on her.

But she can only move forward, and she wants nothing more than that. She wants to live.

"I'm happy, okay?" his laughter fades. "I am happy to have you in my life and I am happy to see you grow."

She opens her mouth to speak, but a knock on her door startles her.

It must be River.

Austin grins the moment the door opens, watching his best friend step into the apartment.

"Rilesie!" River winks at her, before scooping her up into his arms.

It's like she's a ten-year-old all over again, being spun around before he puts her back to the ground, grinning when he pecks her cheek.

"Hello to you too." She laughs, shaking her head in amusement when she sees River do the same to Austin. She bursts out in laughter when her brother groans, trying to fight his way out of his best friends' arms.

"I can feel the love." She giggles, making her way to her kitchen, unpacking the brown paper bags with the ingredients of tonight's dinner; lemon chicken out of the oven, baked potatoes, and an Italian salad to finish it.

She grins when she sees the amount of chicken Austin brought, instantly placing it in her fridge.

"Hmm, lemon chicken?" River's light eyes sparkle when he shrugs off his coat, rolling up the sleeves of his hoodie.

He makes his way through her kitchen, grabbing his apron.

"Yeah, I figured you would like that." Austin instantly joins him, taking his own apron.

"What should I do?" Riley feels a little helpless when she watches Austin and River move through her kitchen like a well-oiled machine.

"Grab us some wine, will ya?" River winks happily, his beard bouncing when he chuckles at the roll of Riley's eyes.

"White or red?" she hums to herself when she walks to her fridge.

"Depends on which you have."

"The best Italians, obviously." Another roll of her eyes has Austin giggle, too.

"I think white goes best with lemon chicken." Her brother then speaks.

"I've got… Chardonnay IGT Monteverro. From 2011." She glances at one of her most expensive wines.

She feels like celebrating, grinning, but it falters when she watches River's eyes widen in horror.

"That wine is over a hundred bucks, Riley. We can't just drink that now!"

"Why not? You two are the best cooks I've ever encountered. Should I drink it alone otherwise?" she smiles widely, watching him relax a little more.

"I think Chardonnay would go excellent with this. Maybe you have a cheaper one to start with?" Austin winks, calming his best friend.

"Of course, I do." She laughs when she takes a cheaper version of Italian Chardonnay, grabbing three glasses of wine while River and Austin work on the kitchen and preheating the oven.
She pours them the glasses, placing it on a safe spot on the counter.
She is about to ask how their week has been, when there's another knock on the door. Raising an eyebrow in surprise, she makes her way over on her bare feet, opening the door.
"Jules." Riley's smile is on her face instantly when she watches the blonde hover in her doorway, a shy smile on sharp lips.
Blonde hair is tucked in a loose ponytail. She wears a simple hoodie and leggings, smiling when she notices that Riley has company.
"Oh, sorry, I didn't mean to disturb you."
"It's fine, Jules. What can I do for you?" Riley leans against her door, quite happy to see her again.
It's been a week after all, and she hasn't bumped into her at all.
"Uhm, I was about to ask if you wanted to have dinner together, but you already have plans." She motions to Riley's kitchen with a sparkle in her blue eyes.
"You should join us!" Austin calls out then, before Riley can even open her mouth.
"Oh, no, I wouldn't want to intrude."
"Jules." Riley lets out a small chuckle. "You never intrude. We have enough food to feed the entire building."
The blonde glances into the kitchen, watching the two men move around each other before looking back at Riley.
"On one condition." Her grin is mischievous.
Arching a brow, Riley awaits in amusement.
"You wear something relaxed as well instead of… that." A hand motions to Riley's outfit, making her look down.
"There is nothing wrong with my outfit. It's comfy, Jules." She bites her bottom lip, hearing a laugh from River in the kitchen.
"Just grab a pair of sweats and you'll change your mind." The blonde speaks up, laughing when Riley lets her in with a scowl.
"She doesn't even own sweats." Austin's grins now, too. "Hello, Jules."
"Austin."
"I'm River." River laughs when he walks closer, shaking hands with the blonde.
"Jules. I live across the hall."
River wiggles his eyebrows, then. "You've come at the right time. We are making some lemon chicken and Riley was about to pull open a bottle of wine."
"That sounds really good, actually."
Riley just chuckles to herself, making her way to the kitchen island where

she pours Jules a glass of wine as well.
"Please, sit down." Riley smiles.
She watches the blonde for a moment. She notices how blue eyes sparkle in a way she hasn't really seen before.
A constant smile hugging Jules's lips, she looks... happy.
There's something in Riley's chest that makes her feel warm when she notices. It may be sheer content, relief to see that Jules can actually look like she doesn't carry a heavy burden with her constantly.
It's refreshing to see how Jules instantly makes conversation with River and Austin.
She doesn't even notice that the conversation is about her, not until three pairs of eyes are looking at her expectably.
"What?"
"I have a pair of sweats in my apartment. And an oversized hoodie." Jules laughs then.
"Good... for you." Riley raises her eyebrows, hearing Austin's low laugh and River's high chuckle.
Rolling her blue eyes, Jules smiles widely while sipping her wine. "They are yours, if you want to."
"I'm perfectly comfortable in my own clothing, Jules, but thank you." She laughs.
"No, really. It feels like this is a business transaction." Austin quips then.
Riley scoffs, taking a sip of her wine, looking at River to await his support for her choice of outfit.
She watches him hesitate.
"There is nothing wrong with a woman and a good wardrobe but... I'd have to agree with them." River offers his fist to bump it with Jules's.
"If you came here just to plot against me..." she threatens them, watching them fall into a chuckle together.
It's... strange. It's light-hearted and unexpected and the way her heart swells tells her that she might care about these moments than she initially thought she did.
And Jules being here just... completes things.
She just doesn't see it yet.
After some encouragement of Austin and River, Jules jumps from her chair to retrieve the comfortable outfit she had been speaking about.
"Seriously?" she shakes her head when Jules leaves the front door open. She grimaces at her brother and his best friend.
"She's right, though. You always look like you came straight from the office." Austin laughs, starting to prepare the potatoes while River finishes up spicing the chicken.
"There's nothing wrong with my outfit!"
"Always wearing contacts, too. Where did those glasses go?" her brother

keeps teasing her.

"I wear them… sometimes." She fights weakly.

She grins when she watches Jules re-enter the apartment with the outfit in her hands.

She quickly moves closer, shoving them in Riley's arms.

"You can change in the bedroom." River jokes.

"Oh, really?" sarcasm drips from her voice when she rolls her eyes.

But the smile, it never leaves her face.

"Just… don't break anything while I'm gone." She feigns a deep sigh, glancing between the two men as if they are her sons.

"I wouldn't dare." Austin raises his hands, laughing when Riley flips her hair over her shoulder arrogantly before disappearing into the bedroom.

She still laughs to herself when she watches the hoodie, and the sweatpants Jules has brought her.

Seriously, nothing is wrong with her current outfit. It's comfortable.

She takes off her clothes, quickly changing into the soft sweatpants and hoodie and it's…

"Whoa." She tucks herself further into the hoodie, smiling secretly when she inhales Jules's subtle scent that radiates from the fabric.

And the sweatpants? They are… heavenly.

Softer than any pants or slacks Riley has ever worn, and she wonders why she hasn't thought of it before.

She tucks her hair in a messy bun, before returning to her living area.

She smiles instantly when she watches the three people in her kitchen, moving around like they own the place.

They are laughing and chuckling to each other, as if they're sharing secrets Riley isn't allowed in on.

She scrapes her throat then, shuffling back to her seat at the island. River and Austin laugh loudly.

"What is so funny?" she throws them a look.

"This is just… a first." Austin laughs, his gaze warm when he meets Riley's.

She glances down at the hoodie that's at least four sizes too large for her. She's drowning in it.

But her heart skips a beat the moment her green eyes meet blue. There's a playfulness to that blue gaze that makes her smile like an idiot.

A certain warmth, care that Riley hasn't seen before.

The entire night, Riley is the quiet one. She just simply observes, laughing at River's crazy antics, at Austin's sarcastic jokes.

She enjoys Jules's company, too.

Somehow, Riley feels like she's met Jules before. Like they've met in another lifetime, everything is familiar.

From Jules's silly jokes to the way she throws her head back in drunken laughter after the fourth bottle of wine they've opened.

From proposing to play games to the way she pouts when Austin and River suggest they'd better get home.

It is just too beautiful. Riley knows she won't be able to stop smiling, not even after she and Jules will say goodnight.

Seeing the blonde bloom like this, beaming like she belongs, it is something she wants to remember forever.

But something still doesn't sit right with her.

She wonders if Jules has her own friends. She wonders, why Jules still has that sadness over her when she doesn't think anyone is looking her way.

Her happiness is genuine, but the grief is, too.

It is why she makes sure that her brother and his best friend leave first.

They are drunk, but happily so and River is amazing when he takes Jules in his arms to hug her tightly.

As if he can feel her loneliness as well. And Austin, he's had this knowing smile on his lips the entire night and Riley isn't quite sure what it means. She refuses to ask, though.

They say goodbye in front of the elevator, with River giving both Riley and Jules a big kiss on their cheeks.

Austin just gives them a subtle nod, but his eyes sparkle and his grin is sweet.

There's a silence washing over them the moment the two men disappear downstairs, the elevator softly humming.

"I uh... I should give you these clothes back." Riley buries her hands in the pouch of the dark hoodie, smiling because it still smells like Jules.

"Oh no, they're yours. Now that you've had a taste of heaven, I don't think you'd be able to live without them." There's a teasing shimmer in those blue orbs while they stand in the hallway, just the two of them.

"Hmm, they are pretty comfy." Riley bounces on her heels, smiling when she sees the fluffy socks she got somewhere along the night, socks that make her feet look giant.

"It's cute."

An instant blush creeps on Riley's cheeks when she hears Jules's shy voice. "Only because you haven't seen me like this before. But I can wash and return them, it's no problem really."

"No, no, keep them." Jules smiles then, so, so beautiful.

Her hair is tangled in a lower bun now, but it almost falls out. She has a healthy blush on her cheeks, that smile that makes the corners of her eyes crinkle is stunning on her.

"Thank you, then."

"Hey, uhm... I wanted to thank you. I know that you didn't invite me in, but I had fun."

"I wanted you there, Jules." Riley's closed-mouth smile is only growing. She's unable to stop. "And I had fun, too. If they come by sometime again,

I'll make sure to invite you. And Liam if he's home."

An instant shadow falls on Jules's features and this time, it certainly doesn't go unnoticed by Riley.

She arches a curious brow, but the blonde's fake smile is supposed to comfort her.

Except it doesn't.

"Jules." She wants to reach out, but she can't push her either. She has been wanting to ask, for so long.

There is something going on with Jules and her marriage, something that is too much to talk about.

"No, it's fine. I'm looking forward to the invitation."

"Jules?" Riley asks then, biting her lips, clasping her hands behind her back while she glances at the curious look on Jules's face. "I… don't want you to go home yet. I enjoy your company."

Jules's eyebrows shoot up in surprise. Her smile is genuine again and that worry that she had before, it seems to fade.

Did she cross a line?

"I…" Jules's lips remain parted as she searches the words.

She doesn't find them.

Instead, she falls forward, stumbling drunkenly into Riley's arms. The brunette has trouble steadying them but once she does, she can feel a breath tickling her neck.

She can feel a face pressed into her bare neck, some kind of warm liquid seeping into her hoodie.

"Jules?" she asks softly, her arms snaking around the other woman to hold her.

The familiarity of hugging Jules is something Riley wants to get lost in. She closes her eyes, pressing her nose in soft, blonde hair.

The warmth coming from the blonde gives her the energy to softly guide them back to her apartment.

What she doesn't realize, is that they are drunk. They are drunk, vulnerable and both longing for something more, but neither realizes.

Riley murmurs things in Jules's hair while the blonde allows herself to fall apart completely.

She sobs, her body shaking with them, but Riley is strong.

They make their way into Riley's apartment and collapse on her couch, holding onto each other tightly.

And Riley allows her to fall apart. She is there, holding Jules as she trembles, hiding her face in Riley's hoodie, in her neck or shoulder.

Riley's heart is aching. She is aching, because in the soft cries Jules lets out, she can hear the pain.

The pain that someone has been carrying with them for years. This isn't nothing. This is a lifetime of suffering, a lifetime of not being able to truly feel.

And every cry, every sob, it is tearing through Riley, cutting like tiny knives right into her heart.

She has no idea why these cries break her fucking heart. She has no idea why she cares so much she almost can't hold back her own tears.

It's like Jules is communicating all her pain to Riley, and yet, she is holding back.

She doesn't speak, she just cries.

She sniffles, she hides her face from the brunette while they lie on the couch, clinging onto each other.

"I have a decision to make." Jules's voice is raw, sore from the shed tears.

Riley just nods, holding her tightly. She tries to ignore the way her body responds to the proximity.

She just wants to be here for Jules, like she promised she would.

"Is it an important one?"

"Very." The blonde pulls back slightly, tucked between Riley and the back of the couch. Her eyes red-trimmed, bluer than ever.

Her cheeks wet, Riley cups them carefully, trying to clean them as well as she can, not noticing the way Jules is looking at her.

Riley smiles sadly. "I think you'll make the right decision."

"But what is the right decision?" Jules instantly asks her, almost desperate to search some kind of answer that she doesn't have to struggle with herself.

"Jules, I don't know what it is about." Riley starts, looking down at the blonde, who looks up at her in almost child-like expectation. As if the brunette has all the answers. "All I can tell you is that… you should choose for you. You shouldn't decide out of what you think might be right according to the world. You shouldn't decide out of fear. You should choose yourself. Does it make you happy?"

"What if I lose people because of it?" Jules's voice is small and fragile as she speaks.

"Then perhaps those aren't meant to be in your life. I don't know what is going on, Jules. But I hope you know it is really important in life to choose yourself, sometimes. Your heart matters." The brunette mumbles, her grip around Jules tightening without her even noticing. "Your heart is beautiful, Jules. If you lose yourself because you think you make the right decision, is it really worth it?"

A silence falls between them while Riley starts studying the ceiling. If she looks at Jules right now, she isn't sure if she can handle it.

She is drunk, she knows she'll regret looking at her.

"Whatever will happen to you, Jules, I hope you know that you can always knock on my door." Riley promises quietly then, making the mistake to look into ocean blue eyes.

She swallows away a lot of feelings when she watches Jules's vulnerable stare.
Emotions twirling behind her eyes, worry lines creasing her forehead.
Riley can't help herself when she reaches with her hand, slowly tracing Jules's jaw.
She can feel the blonde lean into the touch. She can hear the soft, relieving sigh escaping Jules's parted lips.
In that moment, she knows she crossed a line.
She wakes from her drunken daze, realizing just what she did.
Jules is fucking married.
She can't be touching her in ways that are too intimate for friends.
She smiles at the blonde, but groans when she sits up, using a backache as an excuse to untangle herself from the surgeon.
She instantly misses Jules's touches, the way they fit together when she sits up.
"I think you know what to do, Jules." Riley smiles softly then, watching how Jules sits up too, struggling to put her hair back into a bun.
The blonde purses her lips in a way that tells Riley she still might be struggling with whatever it is she has to do.
"I'm here for you." A gentle reminder.
"Yeah." Jules grimaces, but her eyes are soft when she wipes at them. Her wedding ring around her finger, Riley averts her gaze.
It feels wrong to even look at her.
It is wrong to have Jules in her apartment like this and she knows she has to be careful.
She knows that there is a weird attraction between them, perhaps only from Riley's side, but it's not very helpful.
She just wants to be a friend. She wants to make sure that Jules has someone to fall back on if things might ever escalate.
She has the feeling that Jules needs it. Needs her.
With the way she's been falling apart tonight, with the way she has held on to Riley before, the brunette is almost sure that Jules needs her more than she needs Jules.
"I should go home." The blonde rises from the couch, leaving the empty spot beside Riley cold.
"Yeah." Riley stretches as she stands up, too, following the blonde to the front door. "I was going to ask if you were going to text me when you get home, but…"
Jules lets out a small chuckle. "You do know you have a terrible sense of humor, right?"
"It still makes you laugh, though, so I think it's more than worth it." She flashes a smile at the blonde, loving how she instantly reciprocates.
She hates how she can't stop herself once again when her hands fly up,

softly drying the remaining tears from Jules's cheeks.

She feels fingers wrap around her wrists, holding her in place as they stand, their eyes connecting.

Green meeting blue, as if they've done it a million times before. As if they can read each other without speaking.

And Jules is so fucking soft, her hands comfortable around Riley's.

Her thumbs caressing fragile, pale cheekbones. Their noses almost touching, Riley's heart is aching for more.

She doesn't know what it is. That strange connection, that odd sense of trust she has when she's with Jules.

The ring of the blonde's phone snaps them out of their daze, Jules quickly answering the phone.

"Hey, baby." Her voice is soft when she talks into the phone. "An emergency surgery? When will you be home?"

Another silence while Riley vaguely hears a heavy voice on the other side of the line.

"Yeah, I'm about to get into bed." Blue eyes refuse to meet green. "No, I had a good night. Yeah, I love you, too."

With that, she ends the call.

Reality crashes down on Riley, harder than she expects it to. Jules loves her husband.

Jules is going to bed, waiting for her husband to come back from his heavy job as a surgeon.

Jules isn't hers to hold.

It makes her crumble into herself, the realization stinging in her chest.

"You should get home, into bed." Riley tries to smile, but she can feel it isn't reaching her eyes.

"Yeah, I should." Jules nods in agreement, but she isn't making any indication of her going back to her apartment.

"I hope that you'll make the right decision." Whatever decision she has to make, Riley means her words.

She wants Jules to be happy.

"Me, too." With that, the blonde leans in to press a soft kiss on Riley's cheek.

She burns with it. She burns with Jules's touch, her skin on fire, her body itching to reach out, but she doesn't.

Instead, she can feel the blonde lingering longer than she should. She can smell the soft coconut that is mixed with something that is only Jules.

She feels her heart breaking the moment Jules steps back without looking at her.

She watches the blonde leave to her own apartment, unlocking the door hesitantly.

"Goodnight, Jules." She whispers.

"Goodnight, Riley."

The moment Riley steps back into her empty apartment, she knows what she has to do.
She can't stay here any longer. She can't be here, knowing who is living next door.
She can't stay and knowing that she'll let herself care.
She knows this.
She is putting her heart in danger, she is putting Jules's marriage in danger.
She can't be living here; she needs the distance.
She doesn't go to sleep. Instead, she pours herself a glass of Campari, moving to stand in front of her window.
She sips on the bitter, red liquid, deep in thought.
She already knows what she has to do.
Staying here won't do her any good. Staying here will break hearts, it'll destroy things.
She has to be able to be herself, on her own, without being distracted by others. And yes, she wants to be there for Jules, she wants the blonde to be happy, but she can't… she can't put her heart out on the line, not when she knows another marriage is involved, not when she knows that her own heart is still healing from her previous heartbreak.
It is too much.
It is overwhelming, in a bad way and she knows something has to change.
For too long has she been thinking about Jules.
For too long, has she been worrying about the blonde's wellbeing while it is not up to her, and it scares her.
She grabs her laptop, sitting at her kitchen island.
She opens Google.
Searches for a new place.
A new home.
Where she can start over.
A place that isn't stained by the past, or by feelings. Some place where she can grow into becoming her own self before she distracts herself with others.
She   knows   exactly   what   to   do.

8

She's tired. She's had court all fucking week and it has been exhausting her. It's been a long time since she's had a big case like she has now. But, in spite her exhaustion, she loves every minute of it.
Work has been good for her. Sean, Tessa, and Chloe have been treating her well and she finds herself mostly enjoying Tessa's company.
They have lunch together almost every day, at that little café just around the corner of the office, if neither of them has court. It's been good.
But now, she's happy that the week is over when she changes into the hoodie and the sweatpants Jules gifted her.
It's been two weeks since she's last seen her neighbor.
She's been busy preparing her cases, finding a new home.
And she has seen a few potential apartments not all too far away from here, but closer to the office. Apartments that aren't as large as this one, but then again she doesn't need all that space.
The only thing she wants is an extra room she can use as an office, since she's been secretly taking her work home, much to Tessa's dismay.
But she enjoys it. She does it because she wants to, not because she has to.
She's just sitting on her couch, MacBook tucked in her lap, searching a few websites for more apartments.
Something scratches at her front door. She quirks a brow, thinking that she might has misheard, but the scratching continues.
She puts her laptop aside, making her way to the door.
The moment she opens it, a furry thing hurries its way into her apartment.
"Scooter? Is that you?" she instantly closes the door after finding the hallway empty, grinning when she hears a few soft meows coming from her couch.
She chuckles to herself when she finds Scooter, big orange eyes, lying on her couch, right in the spot she just occupied.
"You mean little thing. Why are you even here? Did they lock you out?" she

grins at him, sitting down carefully.

He turns to lie on his back, meowing softly. She is careful when she starts to scratch his fluffy, chubby tummy, making him purr heavily.

"Shall we get you back then?" she murmurs, trying to turn him around. She then grabs him, tucking him over her shoulder.

He purrs even harder in satisfaction when he settles in her neck. She doesn't even need to hold him.

She reaches her arm back when she scratches his little head, feeling his nails digging into her skin, but she doesn't mind.

She takes her keys, carefully making her way to the apartment across the hall. He remains in her neck, like a warm, fluffy scarf and she doesn't mind it at all.

She knocks on the door, but nobody opens.

"Well, looks like I'm babysitting you tonight." She smiles, turning on her heels to move back to her own apartment.

She shoots Jules a quick text to let her know that she's having Scooter, but she doesn't get an immediate reply.

She settles back on the couch, trying to scoot him out of her neck, but he manages to lie down, half in the hood, half in her neck, softly licking the skin of her cheek when she tries to glance at him.

"Only because I like you. But this is very unsanitary, yeah? Your parents should've raised you better, boy." She grins, grabbing her laptop again, careful not to move too much.

The rest of the night is spent with a sleeping Scooter in her neck and her watching apartments.

She responds to a few, trying to get an appointment with the realtor. She absentmindedly rubs Scooters back, hearing his small, satisfied meows.

"Maybe I should get a cat when I move. Just one like you." She keeps talking to him, jutting her lips as she speaks. "Or you could come with me. I think you like me better than your own parents. I'm so much more fun. Yes, I am. Yes, I know you feel it too."

She giggles to herself when she smoothly slides to the kitchen on her socks, Scooter purring louder and louder.

She tries to get him off, getting him to drink or eat something, but he refuses to remove himself from her.

She really doesn't mind it. She grabs herself some Campari with ice cubes before settling back on her couch.

All this time, she hasn't been able to stop thinking about Jules, not really.

She hasn't been able to stop trying to figure out what it is that makes the blonde hurt so much that she can't talk about it.

But it's not her place to ask, Riley knows this.

Though, it doesn't stop her from worrying.

Somewhere along the way, somewhere these past days, she has forgotten to worry about her own problems.

She has focused on Jules instead and she cannot figure out why she wants to know. She can't figure out why she cares so much.

If it were to be anyone else, as Riley thinks back, she never would've started caring so much as she did for Jules. It's disturbing.

And she's been thinking about their last interactions for way too much.

She's never liked to intervene in other people's lives personally, but the way Jules had broken down in her arms those two weeks ago dawdles in her mind.

How hurt Jules had been.

Her blue eyes had been so filled with emotions, with anguish and Riley knows she couldn't talk about it.

What could it be? Why couldn't Jules let go? What is it that she has to decide? Has she decided yet?

She moves to stand in her favorite spot in her apartment – the place that offers her the best view of the darkening city. Rain is softly tickling against the windows, making her view somewhat blurry.

But there's beauty to it. Scooter happily watches with her, his paws digging into her shoulder when he pushes his little head against her ear. She leans back into him softly, smiling when she can feel him licking her.

The glimmering lights are something she will never grow tired of as she stares, deep in thought while sipping her drink every once in a while.

She knows that she and Jules are strange friends, they share these odd little moments, not sharing too much.

But lately, Jules has become a persistent fixture in Riley's life and she wishes the blonde would let her be there for her.

Not just as an emotional outlet, but someone she can talk to.

But the surgeon has kept her distance. Riley misses the hugs that they shared and she despises herself for growing close to somebody she doesn't even know.

So, finding a new place to live is something she thinks might help. She just wants to be able to stop worrying about Jules, stop thinking about her in ways that are far beyond appropriate.

Somewhere around midnight, her phone buzzes and lights up with a text message from Jules.

Asking if Riley is still awake, if she can come by to grab Scooter on her way home.

She quickly shoots back a text, letting the blonde know she's still awake.

It's about ten minutes later that there's a knock on the door and Riley makes her way over, Scooter still tucked comfortably in her neck.

Jules looks stunning. Even in her blue scrubs, exhausted from a long shift at the hospital, her eyes light up, her smile hugging her face in the prettiest of ways.

The moment Jules spots them, she lets out a snort. "Scoot, what are you doing?"

Smiling, Riley tries not to stare at the blonde in blue scrubs, visibly tired but blue eyes sparkling the moment she sees her car.

"And I see you've changed your mind about comfy clothes. I am so proud, Riley." Jules chuckles.

It's light-hearted, adorable, and Riley wants to hear it more.

"How about we get Scooter home, shall we?" she tries to take him out of her neck, but he protests by digging his nails further into her skin.

She hisses under her breath, trying to ignore the way Jules holds back a laugh.

"It's not funny, Jules."

"It kinda is." The blonde laughs, opening the door to her own apartment before moving back to Riley to help the cat.

"It's not. He's hurting me."

"I think he has missed having you around." Jules laughs, but it falters slightly when Riley's green eyes look at her.

A soft smile hugs Riley's lips then. "I have missed him, too."

A comfortable silence falls between them as they try to get Scooter out of Riley's neck. She smiles when he keeps protesting, but Jules manages to get him off.

He is instantly standing by the brunette's legs, his front paws up against her knees, as if he's begging her to be picked up.

"I think he loves me more." Riley teases the blonde, hearing a small chuckle.

"I am afraid that Liam and I have failed as parents. Perhaps we should get him a friend, so he won't get lonely." Jules smiles when Riley looks at her.

That smile can light up an entire village. Really.

Riley can feel that warmth in her chest, something tugging at her heart when she realizes just how close Jules is standing next to her.

She can vaguely smell coconut mixed with hospital. She watches how Jules untangles her blonde hair from her bun, letting it fall in wild curls around her shoulders.

The silence between them is comforting, both women seeming a bit lost in thought.

"Would you mind… going to the roof?" the blonde speaks suddenly.

Surprise shapes Riley's features, but she nods with a soft smile. "It's raining, but… we can go."

She wonders what Jules is thinking. She wonders what is going on in that mind of hers, as Riley sees her biting her lip in nervous anticipation, or at least, that is what the brunette thinks.

She isn't sure.

But they get dressed, as they move to the top floor, taking the stairs to the door that leads them straight to the roof.

The air is colder up here, instant vapor escaping their mouths.

The rain is thankfully not as bad as Riley thought it'd be.

The traffic in the distance, some birds flying over.

A sigh escapes Jules's lips and Riley can tell that she needed the escape.

The brunette doesn't really wait for Jules to follow – she has the feeling that the blonde needs some time to herself.

So, Riley moves to the edge that offers her a view of the west of the city, watching over Central Park.

They stand for several minutes, neither women minding the low temperature. The sky is slowly clearing up, grey clouds disappearing up north, taking the rain with them.

The sky is now dark, but clear, the stars seem just a little closer than usual and the dim light the moon gives off is stunning, really.

The subtle scent of petrichor enters Riley's nostrils and she happily inhales, enjoying every minute up here.

She always has.

There hasn't been a single moment where she hasn't enjoyed either the view, the fresh air, or the person she's currently up here with.

A small, random chuckle sounds beside her as Jules appears. Riley just raises an amused brow, her lips twitching slightly.

"What's so funny?" she asks when the blonde doesn't speak.

"I was just remembering one of the most embarrassing moments of my life."

Riley's smile grows when she watches the sparkle in blue eyes. "Which is?"

"Me and my friends used to go to Central Park often. It was in the early summer when I heard a lady call out; 'Anyone who wants ice cream, get over here!'"

The blonde chuckles to herself again, gazing to the park that isn't too far away from them. "So, me and my friends practically ran over, waiting for the lady to give us some ice cream. There were a lot of kids, and a few adults. But it just turned out to be a giant family and they looked at us like we were insane when we stepped closer."

A small snort is Riley's response. Despite all the seriousness she has experienced with Jules, the scene she just described somehow doesn't surprise her at all.

"You didn't." a laugh bubbles from Riley's throat before she can stop herself.

A bright giggle comes from Jules, the sound filling the cold air and Riley wants to remember this.

She wants to see this happy side more, she knows. It makes the blonde so, so beautiful.

Jules's grin is wide when she glances at the brunette.

All Riley knows is blue, blue, blue.
Those bright, sky-blue eyes that she knows will linger in her mind forever.
After their laughs fade a bit, Riley tries to remember the last time she's embarrassed herself, in a funny way.
"Austin and I went on a road trip a long time ago, when I graduated high school. We made a stop at a Walmart to stuff our car with unhealthy food and drinks. We didn't realize that someone had parked the exact same car next to mine. So, we placed all our stuff in the trunk and stepped into it, but Austin was like; 'this feels different.' I tried to get the car to start, but it just wouldn't. When we got out, a guy was just stepping out of my car, and we all burst into laughter when we realized that none of us had locked our cars and we were about to take the wrong one." Riley can't stop her giggles when she watches Jules try to hold back.
But the blonde can't. She tries to hide it behind her hand, but she can't hold back, her laugh louder than before.
"And you laugh at me for wanting ice cream."
"I never forgot to lock my car again." Riley snickers. She can't remember the last time she has shared that story with anyone.
"That is priceless." Jules's laugh fades, but the smile on her face remains and it looks amazing on her.
Nodding, Riley agrees silently. She figures that Jules doesn't want to talk about anything serious.
If she's being honest with herself, neither does she. It feels good to talk about things that just seem to make the world a better place.
"My brother can be an idiot." Riley grins then, watching Jules's eyes look up at her in expectation. "We went out clubbing years ago and when we left, he thought it'd be a good idea to hit on a mannequin. Took him two minutes and me lying on the ground laughing to realize that it wasn't a human."
A bark of laughter sounds. Riley scrunches up her nose when she grins, laughing quietly. Only now does she notice that the blonde has moved a bit closer to stand beside her.
"Drunk stories are always the best." Jules laughs, her shoulder bumping with Riley's.
"Sometimes." Riley smiles, running a hand through her hair in order to save it from the wind.
A silence falls between them. There may be a lot of silences between them, but Riley enjoys them. She finds herself appreciating the fact they don't have to talk, that they don't have to fill that quietness.
"Can I ask you something?" the blonde's shoulder is still against Riley's.
"Go for it." Riley smiles.
"What would you do if I'd fall apart again right now?"
The question is loaded, it's expectant and Riley's eyes instantly snap aside to look into blue.

"I'd hold you." She shrugs. "I'd let you fall apart and listen to whatever you want to say and I'd just... I'd be there for you, whatever you need. I'd reassure you that you can tell me anything."
Nodding slowly, Jules seems to contemplate if she should.
Her shoulders slouch, her gaze lowers to the concrete below their feet.
"I'm not saying I'm going to have a breakdown now." The blonde's smile is more of a grimace.
It makes Riley turn to face her better. "I can hold you anyway."
The smile that creeps onto Jules's mouth fades into a purse of her lips, tightly enough to let them turn white.
Her eyebrows furrow and she nods quietly, allowing herself to fall into Riley's open arms.
The brunette realizes then that she never closed the zipper of her coat. Jules's arms subconsciously snake around the brunette's waist, underneath her coat and it provides warmth to the both of them.
A face is buried in Riley's shoulder, her arms around Jules's back tightly.
It still amazes her how these hugs seem to be the most important things in the world lately.
Riley carefully leans her chin atop Jules's head, hearing her sniffle into the fabric of her sweater underneath.
The wind falls, the cold remains, but neither women notice. Buried in each other, buried in this small safety zone that they've created the past months.
Neither are willing to give it up just yet, as they breathe in the cold January air, on top of a high building in New York City.
The view mesmerizing, but they only have eye for each other.
That's how they spent five, ten, even twenty minutes. Riley doesn't care that her fingers are about to freeze off.
She doesn't care that Jules seems to have pressed her entire weight into Riley, making her balance them both.
She only cares for the sobbing woman in her arms, the woman that seems to fall apart once again, even though she doesn't use the words.
Riley is just there, like she told Jules she would.
Putting her own feelings aside, forgetting about her own pain, she tries to lift that heavy burden from Jules's shoulders.
They remain in that subtle bubble for a while longer. Riley doesn't even try to pull back.
But they both jump when Riley's phone rings.
It's her brother.
"Riley?" he says when she picks up, not even giving her a chance to speak.
"What's wrong?"
"It's dad."

"Remember I told you he called weeks ago?" Austin pants as he stands in front of her, as if he has been running to her apartment the entire seven blocks he lives away from her.

Jules had gone into her own apartment when she realized that this matter was really personal to Riley.

The brunette hadn't wanted to leave her on the roof, but Jules softly urged her to talk to her brother.

And here she is, in her apartment, watching her brother with wary eyes.

"Yes?" she quirks a brow when she lets him in, watching him lean on his knees when he catches his breath.

"He called me again, I didn't realize it was him. But he is in New York, and he wants to talk to us."

Her eyes grow wide when she looks at her brother, closing the door behind him. "Both of us? Just him? No mother? What did he say? Did he mention anything at all?"

"Geez, calm down with the questions." Austin lets out an amused huff before his face falls serious again. "It's just him. He sounded actually… apologetic."

"What did you say to him?" she watches her brother lean against her kitchen counter after moving further into her apartment.

She grabs two wine glasses for them.

"I didn't really say anything. He asked if I could ask you, since he doesn't have a way to contact you. He told me that he and mom got divorced."

"Divorced?" Riley lets out a hollow laugh. She remembers her parents. They have always been against divorce, always been fighting but they never actually separated because the Bible won't allow it.

"Yes. I just barely recognized his voice, Riley. He sounded old, broken." Austin shakes his head when he takes the offered wine glass.

"Do you want to meet with him?" she hops on the counter, her head spinning with the new information.

She has been given a choice and she isn't sure what she has to do with it. She wants to say no, but she fears she might regret it if she does.

"I told him I'd call him back with a decision. Riley, I won't go without you. It's us, okay? If you don't want to go, then I won't go. If you want to meet him, then we'll face him together." Brown eyes are sincere and Riley wonders what he really wants.

"Before I consider, I need to know what you want. You haven't been in touch with them, either." She bites her bottom lip.

It's just a little overwhelming. Subconsciously, she rubs the forming scar on her left palm, not quite sure what to think about the entire situation.

Taking a sip from the wine, Austin's brows furrow deeply. "I think I would want to give him a chance to say what he wants to say."

"Then we'll go."

"Riley…-"

"We'll go." She cuts in, shaking her head. Perhaps this is something they have to do.

She eyes her brother carefully, but he seems to be doing the same to her.

"No matter what he says, I'm with you." He nods then, quite seriously. A wry smile forms on her face when she takes a sip of her own wine, trying to comprehend the situation.

Her life sure hasn't been dull the past few months. As if she hasn't been through enough, her father decides to show up and she doesn't know how to feel about it.

He's always been the softer parent. He's always been sweeter, but it doesn't make anything less bad.

He screamed just as loud as her mother when she came out. He was the one to throw her out of the house and she isn't sure what will happen to her if she faces him again.

She isn't sure if she wants it, but she is willing to go with her brother, as long as they have each other's backs.

And she trusts Austin with that. He's always had her back, she knows it.

"Whoa." She sighs then, shaking her head. She can't fucking believe this.

"Whoa indeed." He agrees with a soft chuckle, shaking his head the same way she did seconds before.

They just don't have the words.

Riley remembers it, so clearly. The last time she saw her father. The fury radiating from his eyes, the fact he almost got violent.

He was the one she was supposed to be able to trust the most. He was the person she was supposed to rely on and she has never been able to do that.

She just doesn't understand what could be more important than your own child's health and happiness. She can't.

The more she thinks about what has happened, the angrier she gets. She can feel the frustration start to build when the memories become more vivid, dancing in her mind and she can't get rid of it.

"Are you absolutely sure about this, Riley?" his voice is careful when he asks her.

She leans her head back against the cupboard, letting out a shaky breath. Closing her eyes, she nods quietly. "Yes."

"Then I will call him."

"Your dad?"

"Yes."

"The one that kicked you out of the house?"

"Do I have another dad?" rolling her eyes, Riley is grateful for the way Tessa responds when they go to lunch.

"Whoa." Tessa leans back into the chair, her hazel eyes wide when she runs a hand through her controlled curls.

"Yup." Riley sips on her water, gauging the reaction of her closest colleague.

It's been two days since Austin showed up at her apartment with this information. Two days since Austin made the phone call and agreed to meet the next Saturday at a basic restaurant downtown.

Two days since Riley hasn't been able to sleep.

"I can't believe you said yes to this." The blonde then shakes her head, her nose scrunching in disgust. "From what you've told me, your father doesn't even deserve to talk to you."

"I'm not sure, Tess." Riley slips out the nickname, but neither women notice. She absentmindedly plays with the cutlery on the table, not feeling her appetite today. "Austin wanted it. He didn't want to go without me and honestly? If I wouldn't go, I think I might regret it."

"What do you think he has to say?" arching a curious brow, Tessa seems to relax slightly, but her lips are still pursed.

Shrugging, Riley sends a helpless gaze into the other lawyer's direction. "I have no fucking clue."

A silence falls between them as they wait for their orders to arrive.

"I can have a restraining order pushed through. I know a judge."

Letting out a snort, Riley relaxes subtly. "That won't be necessary."

She leans her elbows on the table. Her mind has been occupied with her father for too long now.

"I'm just hoping that... it might give me some closure, you know?"

Nodding understandingly, Tessa smiles through her frustration. "I can sit in the restaurant as back up if you need me to."

Smiling softly, Riley is grateful for this soft side of her colleague. She has definitely grown to like Tessa the past weeks.

They think alike, they have the same sense of humor, though Tessa seems more... carefree.

She doesn't give a shit about what people think of her and Riley envies that. But they're both guarded, slowly starting to trust each other and it feels good to be able to work together so well lately.

"Please tell me something other than family." She groans then, pressing her palms to her eyes in desperation of distraction.

"Uhm... I think Sean is losing his mind?" the blonde laughs. "We need more people, and all the work Sean has been doing has made him snap at Chloe so much I fear she might quit if he keeps going like that."

"He's a real grump." Riley's mouth twitches in an amused grin.

"He is. But he loves you, I think. I've never seen him yell at you."

"That's because I am the perfect employee."

Tessa's bark of laughter is a little louder than Riley expects, causing her to lift her eyebrows in surprise.

She scoffs then. "I am not that bad."

"Sure. You are very sweet." The blonde can't hold her laughter, trying to recover when she takes a sip of her own drink.

"Is that sarcasm?" Riley knows full well it is.

"Oh, Riley. My dear Riley. You have no idea, don't you?" shaking her head again, Tessa's eyes sparkle in amusement.

"Idea of what?" she growls then, absolutely not sure what the hell Tessa is talking about.

"You're just a tad arrogant, is all. Do you know that they call you the Commander behind your back?"

"Commander? Who the fuck is they?" Riley juts her bottom lip, not quite sure why she apparently seems to be the only one who doesn't notice anything around the office.

"Everyone you work with. Sean may have a soft spot for you, but the people that don't work with you directly are terrified of you. You have a reputation."

"Good. So do you, by the way. Do you know what they call you?" Riley bounces back then.

"Do tell." A grin breaks on Tessa's.

Sighing deeply, Riley shakes her head. "I have no fucking clue."

They fall into laughter together. It feels good.

"But seriously, Commander?"

"Have you seen your serious face? The face you make when you focus, or when you aren't happy with a client or a case? Or when you have to talk to the press?"

"I hate talking to the press." The brunette smirks, already knowing where this is going.

"You may be a goofball outside the office, but when you're at work, you have a true resting bitch face. You bark around orders and people listen to you because they are afraid of you."

Lifting her chin in pride, Riley laughs through all the seriousness. "That's how you gain respect."

"I'm not sure if fear is the same as respect, Riley."

Crossing her knees, Riley is thoroughly amused. "It is if it has the same result. Also, I am not a goofball outside the office."

"You totally are."

"I am not."

"You are."

She puts on her most professional outfit when she gets ready for lunch with her brother and her father.

She feels nervous. She hasn't seen him in over a decade and it scares her to no end.

What if she's weak and she'll give in to every excuse he has, only for him to hurt her more?

It's still a few hours away and she isn't sure how to feel about it. She should cancel.

Except, she can't give up on Austin. She is too curious what will happen, even though she is pretty sure it'll end in tears.

She wants to face it, though. She wants to face her past and perhaps this is a way to get over it, to get that closure she never knew she needed.

But she can't breathe, not when she looks in the mirror and sees her reflection.

She knows she has her looks from mostly her father. His green eyes, his dark curls. His sharp jawline and his nose.

She has no idea what he looks like today.

She is afraid.

She is afraid to look in those green eyes and see that plain disgust again. She lets out a few trembling breaths, steadying herself on the sink in her bathroom.

Her make-up is flawless, and she looks like she's about to go to court, but she just… as strong as she may feel in court, as weak does she feel now.

Her knees are shaking, about to give in. Her palms are sweaty, and she isn't sure what will happen today.

There is just no good outcome. Too much has happened, she won't give her father a second chance.

Which makes her think why she even wants to let him speak in the first place. If she isn't going to give him a second chance, why would she even go?

Why won't she let Austin go alone? Why won't she move on?

Deep down, she knows the answer. She knows it and she hates herself for it.

She has to know.

She has to know if her parents cared for her even remotely, she has to know if she has been worth something to them.

She has to know how he thinks of her now if he sees her as she is.

Because she still cares.

After all this time, she still cares about what they think of her, and it is too painful to even think about properly.

She isn't able to breathe, she is suffocating. She needs air, fresh air.

She escapes, taking her coat while she flees to the roof, oblivious to everything around her as she runs.

The moment the cold air hits her in the lungs, she can feel her chest expanding with each hesitating breath.

With shaky hands, she sends a certain someone a text. Because if she'd knock on that certain someone's door, she isn't sure who would answer.

She needs her, secretly hoping that the blonde is home.

She tries to breathe calmly, the cold air cutting her in her face. The wind blows through her professional updo, but she doesn't care.

For too long, she's been holding everything in the past, pushing away how it made her feel, pushing away the memories. Sure, James has been helping her with the entire process, but honestly?

She hasn't thought about it as much as she did the past two days. Not for years.

And all those painful moments, those memories constantly replaying in her head is tiring.

The pain, the loss she continuously feels doesn't lessen.

She just wishes she could let it go, that she could forget about it all.

But that loyalty is still there. That secret, hurtful loyalty that wants to give her father to opportunity to explain himself.

It feels like she's betraying herself.

Breathing in the icy air, she closes her eyes. She lets the wind cut her in her face, not even caring she never closed up her jacket.

The cold keeps her sane, it keeps her breathing.

"Are you okay?"

She jumps. Her hands instantly reach for her chest when her heart nearly thumps out of it.

"Jesus. You scared me." She breathes, turning her head to meet Jules's worried gaze.

"You texted me."

Nodding quietly, Riley's fingers wrap around Jules's wrist before she can stop herself.

The blonde doesn't flinch. Instead, she nods quietly as she steps a bit closer. The brunette finds herself wanting to tell the story. She wants to share, but she isn't sure if Jules would want to hear it.

She isn't even sure why Jules is the first person to come to mind when she panics.

"My father is back." She clenches her jaw at the thought. "My parents kicked me out when I came out as gay. I haven't seen either of them since and now my father wants to talk to me and my brother."

The blonde remains silent, but Riley can feel her stare.

The situation is just ridiculous.

"It just never seems to end, you know? First, they kick me out, then I marry the wrong woman and the moment I get divorced, my father decides to waltz back into my life and I am not sure how to feel about it all." She rambles then.

It surprises her how easy it is to let it go when Jules is around. It surprises her that she is able to form the words, how she trusts the blonde with this information.

She hasn't been able to do this with... anyone.

It's not much, but it's definitely out of her comfort zone and it scares her, but she does it anyway.

"Do you know what he wants?" Jules's voice is soft, so gentle that Riley feels like she might burst into tears, but she holds back.

She just shakes her head, staring at the ground. She sniffles a few times.

"I can't believe that people like that actually exist." There's a bite to her tone when she speaks up again. "They threw you out because of your sexuality?"

"They were religious."

"That shouldn't matter." The blonde shakes her head in disbelief. "I am so sorry that happened to you."

Vapor escapes her moving lips as she speaks. "We all have our scars, Jules."

"That we do." It's mumbled, but so, so filled with pain.

"Jules? Can I ask you something?" she turns a bit, her green eyes searching blue.

She can see the fear, the hesitation in Jules's eyes and she knows, she knows that something is up.

"Uhm, sure." Clasping her hands behind her back nervously, the blonde tries to avoid eye-contact.

"Would you come to me again if something were to be wrong? I know we got interrupted the other night, but..." she feels the desperate urge to cup Jules's chin with her hand to make eye-contact, but she won't.

The question seems to catch the blonde off guard. Her lips part in surprise, her gaze instantly finding Riley's.

"I have this strange feeling you won't do it again." Riley smiles softly.

"I don't know." her voice is weak, blue eyes just filled with grief.

Nodding, Riley can feel that Jules isn't ready. She isn't ready to share her burden and the brunette wonders what on earth can be so bad, that she can't tell.

"I won't pressure you. I just... I want you to be happy and I feel like you're not." The brunette tilts her head, carefully awaiting Jules's reaction.

She can see the subtle tremor in the blonde's lip. She can see the panic in blue eyes, watches how Jules nervously bounces her heels.

Riley reaches out, then. She places her hands on Jules's shoulders. "Don't tell me if you don't want to tell me, please. I'm just saying that... well, you listen to me. You've seen me at my worst. I am more than willing to do the same for you, if you ever need it, okay?"

Jules's nostrils flare, not in anger, but in desperation to hold back her tears. Her lips are pursed as she seems frozen in place.

"Thank you for coming here when I needed you." she admits quietly, watching those ocean blue eyes.

Riley reaches in her pocket then, grabbing her keychain. She takes off the key to the roof, taking Jules's hand in her own, carefully tucking it.

"I think you need it more than I do." Riley smiles then.

Without another word, she turns around to get back inside.

She won't pry into Jules's private life, even though she feels like the blonde was on the brink of spilling everything.

She refuses to listen now, though. Not when she knows that the blonde isn't ready.

Perhaps she never will be ready, as long as she knows that Riley would be there for her.

That is all that matters, really.

It surprises Riley, how effortlessly she is able to put aside her own feelings for Jules.

It terrifies her.

She doesn't think she's ever been able to that before, not this easily.

She groans when she makes her way back downstairs, escaping into her apartment.

She might as well go to Austin now; she was supposed to pick him up anyway.

She grabs her purse, her phone, her wallet. She still has on her coat when she steps out of her apartment.

She locks the door and the moment she turns around she's almost being tackled into one of the tightest hugs she's ever experienced.

She stumbles, but manages to keep her balance.

She doesn't have to look to know who it is, a subtle scent of coconut hitting her nostrils.

Her arms snake around Jules's shoulders instantly, feeling how a face is being nuzzled into her neck.

Then, a lingering kiss is on Riley's cheek, and she can instantly feel it burn, goosebumps forming all over her body the moment she comprehends what is happening.

She parts her lips in surprise when Jules mutters in her ear, a breath tickling Riley's neck delightfully.

"Thank you, Riley. I hope things will go well with your father."

Two hands cup her face and Riley is still too stunned to speak. They may have shared a few hugs, but this kind of physical affection is new.

"I hope so, too." She sucks in a breath, trying not to let her gaze drop lower than Jules's eyes.

They are so, so fucking blue.

It's the closest Riley has ever seen, every speck of grey, of blue.

She can see pupils dilating subtly and the touch of Jules's hands on her face is almost too much for her.

It's too intimate, she knows. She smiles then, softly reaching to take Jules's hands in her own, lowering them from her face.

"I have to go now." She murmurs apologetically. "I'll see you."

"Goodluck, Riley."
"I'm going to need it."

She puts on her stoic mask the moment she follows her brother into the restaurant. They are way too early, but it gives her some time to breathe when they sit down at the reserved table.
Austin orders a whiskey, his knee bouncing with equal nerves. Riley goes for a simple glass of tap water.
Her fingers tap on the table, her chin leaning on her other hand.
She stares out the window, probably looking like someone uninterested or impatient.
Deep inside though, her heart is beating out of her chest, her head is spinning and her stomach churning with each passing minute.
She wants to run away and hide. She wants to run away as far as possible, escape everything she's ever been and start over, but she can't.
It'll always haunt her.
It doesn't take all too long before Austin jumps out of his seat, stumbling over words Riley can't hear clearly.
She remains in her seat, completely still.
She can hear his voice. It hasn't changed a single bit in tone and shivers run down her spine.
She is afraid. She's terrified.
She doesn't look up, waits instead, until someone drops in the booth across from her.
Time seems to stand still when her gaze moves up.
He has changed.
It's the first thing she notices. He isn't the same man he used to be.
He used to be neatly shaven, short hair, always proudly walking around in a suit.
Now, he has a long beard, his hair is half-long, but waxed back. His outfit is casual, just a simple sweater and jeans.
What surprises her is the warmth in his gaze. His green eyes used to be cold, but now... there's something in them that she hasn't seen before.
He's old.
"Russell." She simply manages to say.
"Rilian." His voice lower and softer than before.
"It's Riley nowadays." She snaps instantly, feeling how Austin sits back down beside her.
Russell scrapes his throat. "Riley, sorry."
Riley can hear Austin's' heavy breathing and she can tell without looking that he's angry.
He's angry, just as Riley is and they both are on edge as they watch the man they once called their father.

Where Austin seems unable to speak, Riley can't help herself when she feels the constant need to snap at their father.

"What do you want?"

Russell seems taken aback by her cold tone, but he accepts it as he thinks about his words.

"I am not here to ask for a second chance." He starts then, green eyes darting between the siblings.

Austin scoffs. "Second chance? More like hundredth."

Riley's hand finds its way to Austin's knee to give it a reassuring squeeze. She pulls back then, leaning her forearms on the table when she folds her hands.

"What happened to mother?" Riley asks through gritted teeth.

"We separated."

"So I've heard."

"Will you let me talk?" Russell seems to lose his patience then.

Riley flares her nostrils when she looks at him, gritting her teeth. She can't bring it up to feel even remotely sorry for him.

She thought she'd be running back into his arms. She thought she'd be falling to her knees, begging him to accept her the way she is but instead of that, all she can feel is the anger burning in her veins.

It's fueling her words. "Just like you let me talk when I was a teen?"

"Did you agree to meet with me just to fight everything I say?" Russell calms down a bit, even the tiniest smile twitching on the corner of his mouth.

"You don't get to do that." Riley snarls. "You don't get to come in here and expect us to listen to every sweet word you have to say."

Russell sighs lightly. "I told you I am not here for a second chance, nor a hundredth chance."

A silence falls between them, making Riley want to roll her eyes. The initial shock of seeing him has faded completely and she's happy that she's used to arguing in court.

"Please elaborate." She almost begs him when she leans back in her seat, crossing her arms in front of her chest as she tilts her head, her eyes boring into his.

She tries to read her father, but he's always been good at hiding whatever it is he's feeling.

"Your mother and I divorced because I didn't accept the way she treated you."

"She?" Austin almost flies out of his seat in anger, but a simple hand from Riley on his arm stops him from doing anything impulsive. "I remember just fine how you were just as bad as she was."

"I know this." Russell snaps completely. "I know how I treated you. I know what I did, I am fully aware, okay? I know what a terrible father I have been and I am here to tell you that I know. I am here to tell you that I love you, both of you. I wanted to know if you were doing well. I saw you got divorced and I just… I realized how much I missed you."

Austin just scoffs again, fire in his dark eyes.

He is seriously scary like this.

"We are doing just fine. You could've just asked that over the phone. How did you even know that I got divorced?" Riley says calmly then, surprising both men.

"You've made quite the name for yourself. I saw something online. But, I wanted to see you." He seems to think about something else to say, but the brunette cuts in again.

"It'll be the last you see of us, Russell. You get to live with what you've done. We don't need you." She wants to slide out of the booth, but Austin stops her.

It is only then that she notices her father crying.

Her entire life, she has never seen him cry.

She knows he is in pain, but it doesn't give him the right to just waltz back into their lives.

"I don't expect you to forgive me." There's a tremor in his voice when he looks up. "I can't forgive myself, either. For too long, I have been living a lie. For too long, I thought I was doing the right thing."

"What made you change your mind?" Riley's tone is just as cold as it was before.

"Someone… I worked with someone. He was a kind man; I would even consider him my friend." The older man begins. "We worked together for several years, but there was always something about him that told me he was holding back. I didn't know what it was, until his husband showed up at work."

"How touching." Austin rolls his eyes.

"Apparently, he knew about you. He knew that I wouldn't accept him for who he was. But he knocked some sense into me."

"It took a stranger for you to see? Losing your kids didn't matter?"

"It mattered to me! You matter to me! Both of you do. God, Riley, I have missed you so much. I have been blind; I have done things I am not proud of. I don't deserve anything, but I want you to know."

"Know what?" she snaps again. She can't handle this. She can't handle it, despite the fact that the anger dissipates, leaving her body with several deep breaths.

"Know that I admire you." He murmurs then, defeated.

"Honestly? I don't care." She rises from her spot again slowly. This time, she isn't being pulled back into her seat. "I am glad that you see that you've been doing wrong. I hope you know that I don't ever want to see you again."

His green eyes fill with more tears as he looks up at her.

She can feel her heart aching when she realizes what she is about to do, but she has to.

Her gaze softens subtly, her voice changing. "I know that you did what you thought was best back then. For your religion. I know that you are telling me the truth right now, but it doesn't take away the fact that you damaged me. You hurt me more than anyone else will ever be able to. You were supposed to be the man I could trust the most in this world."

"I know."

"I'm not finished." She holds up her hand when his lips part to speak more. He snaps his mouth closed. "I hope you find your peace. I forgive you."

She surprises herself with her words, but she knows deep in her heart that it is the truth.

"I forgive you, but I don't ever want to see you again. I will always love you, simply because you're my biological father, and there were good things that you've done for me and my stupid heart can't let that go, but I... the thought of ever seeing you again sickens me. So yes, I hope you find your peace. I just never want to see you again."

With that, she turns on her heels, walking out of the restaurant, straight into the cold.

She quickly puts on her jacket that she snatched from the seat on her way out, turning around to see Austin still talking to Russell.

She can't make out the words, but she is shuddering, the nerves leaving her body forcefully when she feels the nausea coming up.

She holds it back, waiting for her brother to get his closure, too.

It seems like they are still in a heated argument, so she grabs her phone and dials the first number that comes to mind.

"Riley?" Jules's voice sounds after the first ring. "Is everything alright?"

"I have closure." Is all she manages to say. She closes her eyes, feeling the wind in her hair as she stands outside the restaurant.

"Yeah?"

"Yeah." It is a relief. It is such a relief, that she can't hold back her tears.

She sobs quietly, hearing something shuffle on the other end of the line, but Jules never really speaks.

She doesn't understand her friendship with Jules. She doesn't understand anything right now, but the silence the blonde offers while she cries is more than enough.

She doesn't want her father to see, but she honestly doesn't care anymore.

She doesn't care because she feels free. That heavy burden of her past is largely gone, and it is liberating in a way she never expected it to.

"Riley, I'm so sorry, but I have to go. I'm starting my shift at the hospital right now. We will talk later, okay?" Jules's voice sounds genuine.

Oh.

The disappointment Riley feels in her chest humiliates her. It hurts and stings in ways that makes Riley feel like a fool for trusting Jules, but she knows the blonde is genuine.

Yet, she feels dumb. She feels dumb for excitedly ringing the surgeon while they are barely anything, really. "Yeah, of course. Go work. Thank you, though. For listening."

"Always, Riley."

Riley hangs up the phone before she can say more.

9

The cold wraps around her like an uncomfortable blanket she can't shake off.

She waits for Austin to finish whatever he is talking about with their father, but she is staring into nothing.

Tears drying coldly on her cheeks, phone still in hand, she can't shake the embarrassment.

Should she not have called Jules? Should she even have trusted her in the first place?

She just can't shake the feeling that she made some kind of mistake, that perhaps they can't have this kind of friendship.

Realization just crashes down on her, her father completely forgotten.

She wants Jules. She wants her in ways she cannot have her, and she should stop. She should stop whatever they are having right now, because she knows that she'll be wanting more.

She has to move out, and fast. She has to let this go. Her heart is aching, and she can't handle it. Not now.

She just can't live like this, not when there is so much mystery between them, not when Riley feels like something more is going on.

"Hey." Austin's voice suddenly sounds next to her, an arm safely around her shoulder.

When she looks up, she sees a small smile on his lips, but she can tell that he's been crying, too.

"How did it go?"

"I told him exactly how I felt." Austin lets his head hang, fiddling with his free hand on his coat. "I told him what they have been missing out on. That perhaps you have forgiven him, but I can't."

"You?" Riley smiles softly then, starting to walk away from this place. "You, the man who's had infinite patience with me, not able to forgive him?"

"You don't know what he's done, Riley. You don't know what he's said after you left for good." He shakes his head, pursing his lips, but his tight grip around her shoulder makes her feel appreciated, protected even.

She leans against him, snaking her arm around his waist as they walk through the busy streets of New York, both of them trying to comprehend what is happening.

"I thought I'd be able to forgive him, you know?" he continues then. "He's done good things. He is the one who wanted to adopt me. He is the one who tried to get mom to calm down mostly, but still... he never did enough. He was the one to kick you out. He was the one to call you things, even after you left."

"Do you want to see him again?" she asks carefully, but he instantly shakes his head.

"No. He... he creeps me out, honestly. Despite the fact he seems genuine about this, I don't trust him and what he has done is unforgivable. I don't know how you are able to forgive him just like that." He shakes his head in disbelief.

"I... didn't expect to be able to forgive him. But when I saw him there... I know that he knows how wrong he has been." She thinks for a moment. "And he may not ever do it again, forgiveness is something I can give him. I want him to have peace of mind just as much as I want us to have that. There's a difference between forgiveness and a second chance."

"Yeah, I guess you're right." He murmurs to himself. "But if you think that he wouldn't do it again, why would you not give him another chance?"

"Because I can't look at him without feeling the way I always felt." She realizes how true that is. "When I look at him, all I can feel is the pain, the rejection, the fact that he wouldn't accept me for who I was and I can't live with that."

Thoughtfully, Austin's grip around her shoulder tightens. "Do you think you might be able to face him again in the future?"

"No. I don't want to. I have closure and that is enough. I can't ever look him in the eyes again and tell him that things will be okay, I can't. I can't let him into my life." She is determined. She doesn't want him back.

He has lost that right a long time ago.

No matter how much it all hurts, she has closure. She is able to forgive him for what he's done, but the fear that he'll do it again is there.

The memories are still there, the damage is done, the scars have formed, and it is too much to be able to move on like nothing happened.

She could never do that. Forgiveness must be enough.

They shiver when a cold wind hits them in the face, but they bury themselves into their thick jackets.

Winter should be over soon, but somehow it doesn't feel that way.

And Riley, she feels just as cold inside as it is out here.
Empty, even.
She may have closure, but everything that has happened with Jules is too much. She can't get it out of her head, she's retracing every step, wondering what it is that they've been building.
But the most important question is why.
Why have they been building what they have now? Why do they trust each other, but not enough to completely let go?
Why Jules?
Why?
She can't figure it out, but she thinks that space might help. She makes a mental note to speed things up with the realtor she's talking to now.
She really wants to get away.
She hates it, though.
She hates how she feels the need to run when things get hard. But space has always helped her see things more clearly.
Time to think, time to evaluate. She needs that.
"Austin?" she looks at him. His brown eyes are questioning when he looks down at her. "I am so grateful to have you. I don't think I could've done anything without you."
"Sap." He taps her nose with his free finger, but his smile is proud and his dark eyes are sparkling. "Me too, Riley. You may not think that you've done much, but knowing that you'd always have my back gave me peace of mind."
"With what?"
"With everything. With deciding to become a chef. With opening my own restaurant. I mean, you're filthy rich, so you easily could've donated something if things would've gone downhill." He teases, making her scoff and pull back.
"You golddigger." She huffs, but smiles when she hears his bright laughter. She misses this.
She knows he'd never take advantage of her.
She bumps his shoulder -or rather his upper arm- with her own, smiling when he decides to stop a cab.
"Do you want to celebrate, or do you need some time to process?" he smiles, as if he already knows the answer.
"The latter." She smiles back at him. She is about to urge him into the cab, but then she stops him. "Wait, I have something to tell you before you go. I'm planning on moving soon. I'm talking to a realtor to find myself a new apartment somewhere nearby."
Arching a brow, Austin motions for the driver to continue. "Why?"
"I just... I need a new start. I've got a new job I'm happy with, I've got you and River to spend time with but this apartment..."

"Is it because of Jules?"
She opens her mouth to speak, but the soft way he looks at her tells her that he might know more than she lets on.
"Oh, come on. I've seen the way you look at her. You know you can tell me anything." He nudges her shoulder.
Sighing deeply, she realizes that perhaps, they should talk. She needs someone to talk to, she can't hold it to herself.
But not now, not when so much has happened that she feels like they both need to process.
"It's not only because of her. But another time?" she grimaces, wondering if he's right. Wondering, if Jules is the reason she has to move away.
A part of her thinks that's true. Everything with Jules has been too much.
"Okay." He smiles then, carefully pulling her into a hug. "Get home safely, okay? And call me if you're ready to talk."
"I will."
She smiles. They manage to stop two cabs, both stepping in to get home to their respective apartments.
Riley can't think clearly. Too much is going through her head right now, she's not in the right space.
Even though she might have forgiven her father, it doesn't mean that the past doesn't hurt.
It has broken her heart, it has torn her to pieces and made her insecure and unable to love herself and she isn't sure if she can ever fully recover.
But she knows that it'll get better.
The images of her father as an older man fade completely.
She always gets back to Jules.
Always does she think about the blonde, wondering how she's doing, wondering what is happening between them.
Riley knows she wants more, and she knows it has to end.
She sighs deeply. It'll be difficult, but it'll be for the best.

She has finally found an apartment. It's not too far from here, is on a higher floor she has now, and the view is even more breathtaking.
It might be smaller, but she has plenty of space to live on her own.
One thing she's very happy with is that it has four elevators in the lobby, and they are way faster than the one in her current building.
It has a balcony, which offers her a view to the east. It's different from the roof, but it has definitely charm.
She's standing in the apartment right now, light wooden, herringbone floors in it.
"What about the floor?" Riley asks the realtor. She loves the floor, and it doesn't seem damaged.
"They left it here. You can keep it if you want to." The man smiles kindly,

but he keeps his distance as the brunette makes her way through the apartment.

It's gorgeous.

"When would I be able to move in?"

"It's available now. If we can settle with the payment, it's yours whenever you want."

"I'll take it."

She manages to get a loan, easily able to afford the mortgage each month. She won't have access to the roof, but it doesn't matter.

She's moving on.

And for the first time in a long time, she actually feels like she is. She is packing her things, making sure that things will be done in time.

She hires people to paint her new apartment within one day. She has decided not to make her apartment dark like this one, but rather white walls to make it look more spacious, matching with the lightwood floor.

She shops for curtains and a complete new set of furniture. She has more than enough savings to be able to afford it all and it feels good to leave the rest behind.

And she's excited. She is excited to move in next week when she glances around her current apartment. It feels good to be able to let it go, no matter how much she loves this place.

She has too many memories here. Not that she minds, but even after these long months, she wants to be able to get home into an apartment that she didn't once share with her wife.

She wants to get home to a place where she didn't have many emotional breakdowns. Something new, something fresh.

It feels incredibly good, and she wonders why on earth she hasn't done it sooner.

Well, perhaps that is a lie. Perhaps she knows why she hasn't done it sooner; she just isn't ready to admit it to herself.

But she is living. She is moving on, she's making peace with herself, which is more than she could've ever imagined the moment she got divorced.

She hasn't really talked to Jules. The blonde had tried to reach out, and Riley always answered, but she just refused to talk about what happened with her dad when the surgeon asked about it.

The disappointment in blue eyes had been evident and it had hurt Riley to the core. She knows that Jules knows that she's pulling away.

Not completely, but some.

Enough to have the surgeon worrying.

She's in her comfy clothes, her hair high up in a bun, glasses on top of her nose, no makeup, when there's a soft knock on her door.

There's only really one person who knocks like that.

She moves to her door, opening it quietly.
"Jules."
"Hey." The blonde looks like she's been crying. Her eyes red-trimmed, the blue so much brighter than usual. Puffy, red nose, pursed lips that still curl into a smile the moment she sees Riley.
It warms the brunette's heart.
She feels guilty for pulling back.
"Come in." she invites the blonde into her home, which is now a mess with all the boxes and the things that are just lying around.
The moment the blonde steps into the apartment, her shoulders drop a few inches and a breath hitches in her throat.
"You're moving?"
There's a subtle tremor in Jules's voice that settles deeply within Riley.
"I am." Riley is gentle when she takes Jules's hand in her own, guiding her to the couch.
The blonde is wearing a similar outfit, her long blonde hair in a messy bun as it mostly is.
She looks beautiful, even though she's been crying.
"I found an apartment not too far from here." Riley smiles as they settle on the couch. She feels the need to assure Jules that things won't have to change. "I just needed to get away. This place holds too many memories."
Nodding slowly, Jules is obviously trying to avoid eye-contact.
"What's wrong?" the brunette softly leans closer to the blonde.
When Jules doesn't speak, Riley grows bold. She has missed her neighbor.
She places Jules's chin between her thumb and index-finger, softly urging her to look into green eyes.
"Jules. Are you okay?" her eyes flicker between blue, watching how Jules's bottom lip tremble.
"I'm afraid."
Taken aback by the heavy words, Riley blinks a few times. She doesn't realize she's still holding Jules's face, not until she can feel the blonde lean into it, a quiver of a chin felt by her fingers.
"Jules?" Riley's at a loss. She quickly takes off her glasses.
"I don't… I can't…" Jules's voice cracks as she falls apart. Tears fall, her body shivering as she tries to find the words. "I'm so fucking scared."
The brunette doesn't hesitate when she pulls the blonde into her arms. She holds her tightly, feeling how Jules clings onto her, fisting the fabric of her sweater in her hands.
She sniffles, trying to hold back sobs, but she's clearly failing.
"Jules, please. You can't… you don't have to go through things alone. Isn't that what you told me a while ago?" she can't not ask.
She fears for the blonde.
"Jules, look at me." She sternly makes the blonde look at her. Cupping her

cheeks, Riley leans her forehead against hers.
It's intimate, but so, so necessary. "Jules. I know that you've been holding back whatever it is you're going through, but you can talk to me. You don't have to do it alone. You can tell me."
"No, I can't." the blonde sniffles, desperately holding on, her hands still on Riley's sweater.
"Jules." Riley can feel their breaths mingling. She closes her eyes, focused solely on the woman before her. "I care about you, okay? I need to know you're going to be okay. I want to help. Let me. Let me be here for you."
She can feel a shaky breath on her lips as she flutters open her eyes. Blue right in front of her.
Jules's tears brighten her eyes while Riley desperately tries to wipe them from her cheeks with her thumbs.
"Why?" the blonde murmurs.
"Why what?"
"Why do you want to help?"
"I want you to be happy, Jules. I've seen..." she closes her eyes again, taking a deep breath. "I've seen your pain. I don't want you to go through it alone."
"Why do you care?"
"Because I l-... because you're you." She can feel her heart thudding against her ribs. She can feel so many things right now, but this about not about her. "Because you're an amazing person and you deserve so much more."
"What if I don't? What if I'm a horrible person?" Jules's grip on her hoodie tightens.
"You're not." Riley knows this. She can feel it. She can read her. "There may have been things you have done, but you're not a terrible person, Jules. You're beautiful."
It is then, that Riley notices how Jules's breath is closer to her own. Hot, soft, shaky breath tickling her lips.
She can feel a nose bumping her own gently.
She's on fire. She can feel something running through her veins, something that makes her want to close that tiny gap between them.
But she can't. She remains in her position, slowly opening her eyes to see how Jules's have closed, thick tears still rolling down her cheeks. Her lips are parted, quivering just like the rest of her body.
And Jules's cheeks are so soft between her hands, the way she leans into Riley is making her heart jump.
She's feeling too much right now. It's overwhelming and she cannot be feeling this, she cannot be able to feel that growing desire in her entire fucking body.
She cannot be thinking about how she wants to know what those lips feel like, pressed against her own, hoping it could provide some kind of

comfort. She can't close her eyes and hope for the best.
So she doesn't. She doesn't cross a line she can't uncross. She pulls back lightly, instantly missing the warmth, the building longing between them.
"Riley…"
The way her name rolls off Jules's tongue does too many things to the brunette.
"I have done something." The blonde continues then, breathing heavily when she seems to snap out of the same daze Riley has been in the past few minutes.
"Done what?"
"I've made my decision. I have done something I should have done years ago, but…" Jules's voice isn't much more than a soft whisper. "…it could cost me a lot."
"Cost you what?"
"My life."
Riley pulls back as if she has touched fire. Blood drains from her face when she looks at Jules in plain horror. "Your life?"
"I'm afraid to lose my life because of it." Jules's voice is small and vulnerable.
The heaviness of it all falls on both of them as Riley tries to understand what Jules is talking about.
"Jules? What are you talking about?" Riley can't breathe.
She's panicking. It's rising in her chest, smothering her and she has to know. She has to help.
Riley is almost desperate when she gently wraps her fingers around one of Jules's forearms to pull her closer.
It is then, that Jules winces in pain, pulling back her arm so quickly that the brunette is staring at her.
Why would Jules…
Oh.
Oh.
"Jules." Her bottom lip trembles when she sees the blonde crumbling into herself.
She looks ashamed, embarrassed, and Riley can feel heat rise to her cheeks as she realizes just exactly what is happening. Her heart is thudding in her chest and God, she hopes she is wrong. She even prays she is.
Liam. The fucking asshole. Liam has been hurting Jules, he's been…
"Riley, I…" the blonde seems so fucking broken when Riley doesn't dare to move.
"What has he done?" her nostrils flare in pure anger and she tries not to take it out on Jules.
She can see the blonde cringe and she knows she has to pull herself together. She lets her anger fade, trying to look into clear blue eyes.

"Jules..." her voice is soft as she speaks, trying to reassure the blonde. "...I don't know what you are thinking right now, but... I'm here. I'm right here, I'm not going anywhere, I won't do anything."
Jules purses her lips tightly, her embarrassment seeming to fade as she nods quietly, humming something comforting to herself.
She rolls up one of the sleeves of her hoodie slowly.
Her skin is covered in fresh bruises, clear fingerprints almost burned into her skin.
Riley can't react. She can't.
She can't believe it is really true. She had hoped it wouldn't be, but it is.
She can't fucking believe this.
Frustration and guilt build up and Riley almost can't deal with it. She can feel how she starts to cry just like that, unable to stop when she softly takes Jules's wrist in her hand lifting up her arm to softly trace the bruises.
Her heart is fucking broken.
Jules, the most beautiful person she's ever met. Jules, the woman that carries the weight of the world on her shoulders.
This... this can't be true. She can't have been suffering for years. She can't. She doesn't deserve that.
"Jules..." Riley isn't able to breathe when she looks up. She meets a blue gaze, so vulnerable, so fragile, so much fear evident, a pool of emotions reflecting in blue.
She knows how much strength it must have taken Jules to tell her, even though Riley basically found out before she showed it. How much it has taken to be able to make the decision she has made, whatever that may be.
But Jules trusted her with this. She knows that it must've... taken everything.
"I know people. I can have an emergency restraining order pushed through. You have grounds. We... we can end this, you can't... you can't go back to him, you can't get hurt again, Jules. Fuck." Riley can't contain herself.
She can't. She is gentle when she drops Jules's arm back into her lap carefully.
She moves to take Jules' face between her hands, unable to hold back. The overwhelming adoration she feels for Jules is growing stronger with each passing second.
The need to make sure that Jules is okay is all that matters.
And the blonde doesn't speak. She cries.
She cries hard, her burden revealed and Riley thinks that it has taken all her energy, all her courage to be able to do it.
"You're so fucking brave." Riley sobs when she pulls the blonde into her arms, holding her tightly.
She's never letting go.
"Brave?" Jules lets out a hollow laugh. "It's been eight years, Riley. Eight.

Eight years."
Riley shakes her head. She has heard stories.
Just when Jules is about to answer, a knock is on Riley's door.
Instant panic flashes over Jules's face. She shoots up, panicking when she realizes who it might be.
Riley can sense it all. She quickly tells Jules to hide in her bedroom, before moving to her front door.
She lets out a sigh of relief when she sees her brother and River standing, watching them through the peephole of her door.
They are carrying bags with groceries and she facepalms when she remembers.
Their last meal. They were supposed to spend this night at her apartment as a goodbye dinner.
She opens the door with a sad smile, unable to hide her feelings.
"Hey!" River and Austin are cheery, but their happy smiles falter the moment they see her face.
"Riley? What is going on?" River's grey eyes are worried when he glances between Riley and Austin.
"Uhm… it isn't a good time, but… come in. Jules's here. I'll be right back, yeah?" she opens the door, letting her brother and best friend in before moving to her bedroom where Jules has been hiding.
She knocks softly on the door before opening it.
"Jules? It's just Austin and River." She slowly makes her way inside, watching how the blonde appears, sitting down on the bed shyly. "I can send them home."
"No, don't." the blonde sniffles a bit, wiping her tears away with her sleeve. "I'll go."
"Jules. You're not going to your house." Riley shakes her head, squatting down in front of the blonde. "If you fear for your life… if you think Liam will hurt you then you're not going there. We shouldn't risk that. Plus, I like having you around."
The tiniest huff of amusement escapes Jules's lips, before she shakes her head.
Carefully, Riley places her hands on Jules's skinny knees. She can feel every bone, realizing just how thin she is.
She's too thin. Looks too tired, too tiny.
"You can stay here, yeah? I can kick my brother out."
"No, you don't have to."
"Want to have dinner with them, then?" Riley smiles softly, trying to push away her worry.
"I have bothered you enough. I should go."
"Jules." She clicks the 'k' softly, her voice quiet. "You never bother me. Stay with us, yeah? They love you."

I love you.
The words remain unspoken, but they stay in Riley's mind.
The blonde nods quietly. "I could use the distraction."
"Good. We can tell them not to pry, I know they won't." Riley moves to stand, stretching both arms to wiggle her fingers in front of Jules.
She takes them.
They stand, in Riley's bedroom, chest to chest, their fingers laced.
The brunette is careful when she cups Jules's cheeks, smiling gently when their eyes meet. "I am here for you, Jules. Whatever you need."
The blonde nods, unable to speak.
"It'll be okay, Jules. You're not alone."
A single look of blue into green, Riley can see the pain. She can feel Jules's shivering body as she holds her steady, she can feel the exhaustion through the weak grip Jules has on her.
With that, the blonde crashes into her arms. They hold each other, not caring that the two men are waiting for them to join.
Riley buries her face in Jules's bare neck, holding her tightly. She cups the back of the blonde head to make it topple forward, against Riley's shoulder.
And Jules cries. She cries harder than Riley has ever heard before. She can feel how the blonde is unable to hold herself up, trembling on her feet while trying to hold onto Riley as if she's a lifeline.
She knows that Jules needs her, that she shouldn't give up.
She has to be here. No matter how much it hurts, how ignorant she feels for not noticing the cause of Jules's pain.
She patiently waits for the blonde, holding her, half-carrying her as they stand.
The moment Jules calms down, she pulls back. Riley's hands on her face, the brunette softly leans in to place a kiss on her cheek.
She lingers, far longer than she should, her lips ghosting over the soft skin. She flutters her eyes closed, tickling the blonde with her lashes.
She can feel the unsteady breathing turn steadier. Her lips burn as they lightly caress Jules's cheek.
She can feel a stronger grip on her arms. Not to push her away, but to keep her in place, to pull her closer. Her heart speeds up, her breathing quickens, and she feels weak.
She feels weak because this woman is able to make her lose control. This woman is able to make her feel like this, and she isn't sure if she's ever felt like this before.
This strong yearning, this feeling of being sure.
Adoration, mixed with passion, desire and so much more. It's the strong urge to make sure that Jules is safe, that Jules will be okay.
The urge to hold her when she cries, to make her laugh and make sure she enjoys things.

It's so much more than friendship, Riley knows.

She's unable to remove herself from the blonde, knowing how much she cares. She's unable to let her go, both mentally and physically.

As much as Riley wants to give in, as much as she hates Liam right now, Jules is still married.

No matter how much she wants to brush her lips over Jules's, she can't. So, she pulls back, watching Jules's flushed cheeks, her confusion, the way she must feel just as conflicted as Riley feels right now.

"Riley?" her voice is raw and lower than before.

"Yes?"

"I… I'm glad you're my neighbor. Even though you're moving, I've… I needed you. I need you." She says, quite determinedly with a strength she hasn't shown before.

It surprises the brunette when she searches blue eyes.

"I'm here for you, Jules. You have my number; I'll give you my new address. But for now, we are keeping you safe." She means every word.

Nodding silently, Jules smiles. It's filled with so many emotions, sadness, grief, but hope too.

Hope that things will work out now that she might not be alone anymore.

"You hungry?" Riley smiles as she softly tugs Jules towards the door that will guide them to her living room and kitchen.

"Actually, I am." The blonde smiles wider then, and Riley is grateful that she seems able to let go, for now.

"We should eat then. But before we go… I meant it when I said I can get a restraining order pushed through. I have connections." Riley throws Jules a questioning gaze.

"How fast can you get it?" the blonde grimaces as they stand before the door.

"I don't know. Hopefully within a few hours." Riley sighs then, pressing a soft kiss against Jules's forehead. "You'll be safe."

"Thank you."

"You, go. Just tell them not to ask and they won't. I have a phone call to make." The brunette feels the hesitation in Jules's stance.

"Riley?" blue eyes look up into green.

"Yeah?"

"Why are you doing this for me?"

There is no way to express how she feels. Not with words. She just can't.

She is so tempted to just lean in and close the gap.

For a moment, Liam just doesn't seem to exist in this room as they stand there, gazing into each other's eyes.

All Riley can do is lean forward. She presses a soft kiss on the blonde's cheek, but it's too close to her lips.

Riley can feel it. She can feel the corner of Jules's mouth under her lips and the feeling is intoxicating.

She can hear the breath hitch in the blonde's throat.

But before it can grow into something more, she pulls back, holding Jules's hands in her own.

"Because I care about you, Jules. I care about you more than I probably should, and I wish nothing but happiness for you and if I can help by doing this tiny thing, then I will." She admits quietly, watching how blue eyes seem to melt.

"You…" the blonde seems to be at a loss for words. "Riley, I… I hope you know I care just as much."

"I think I do." Riley smiles reassuringly.

She still has a call to make, and she doesn't want to waste any more time, so she softly nudges Jules into her living room, closing the door behind her as she pulls her phone from her pocket.

She dials the one number she can think of.

"Riley?"

"Tessa, I need a favor." Riley moves to stand in front of the window.

"Okay, what is it?"

"You told me you could get a restraining order pushed through because you know a judge." Riley pinches the bridge of her nose, her heart racing in her chest.

She can hear the worry in Tessa's voice. "Is your father bothering you?"

"It's not for me, Tess." Shaking her head, Riley tries to comprehend the situation as she lowers herself on the bed. "You can't ask me any more questions than needed, okay? I need you to keep this quiet."

"Riley, what is going on?"

"It's for Jules Gibson. I need a restraining order for her husband."

"On what grounds?"

The words are sour in her mouth. "Domestic violence."

She can hear the sharp inhale of a breath on the other end of the line. "Riley, are you sure? This is serious."

"I need you to do it." Riley can feel the panic rising in her chest. "Jules's life is in danger. I am not joking around; I know this is serious. When can you get it?"

"I'll make some calls. I can have it by tonight, perhaps tomorrow morning at the latest. You have to send me the details. You know what I need."

"I'll do it right now. Call me when you get it?" Riley feels pretty desperate by now.

The thought of Jules getting hurt more is something she isn't sure she can live with.

"I will. Be careful, Riley, whatever it is you're getting yourself into."

"Thank you. I will."

The moment she hangs up the phone, she sends Tessa the details she needs to file for an order.

Her hands are shaking as she puts away her phone, burying it in her pocket. She tries to breathe, tries to understand how it is possible that something like this is happening to Jules.

Jules, of all people. She doesn't deserve that.

Riley should've known. She should have known that something was so wrong about Liam, she should've, she should've… she should've seen.

She could've done something.

She tries to push away her own feelings, realizing that Jules is stuck with her brother and River in the kitchen.

She finds the courage to move, making her way into the living room as well, putting on a mask to hide what it is that is going on behind the scenes.

"I bought you guys something." Riley smiles softly when she watches the two men moving around her kitchen. She walks, grabbing the two giant aprons she bought them sometime this week.

Jules is flashing her a sad smile, which Riley returns with a knowing nod, silently telling her that the request for the restraining order has been sent.

River instantly starts smiling when the brunette hands them the aprons. They try it on and despite them being boringly black, they fit and they suit them well.

"Handsome, guys." Jules smiles from her spot at the kitchen island.

"I know." Austin wiggles his eyebrows as he spins on his heels, showing off his new apron.

The blonde giggles softly, shaking her head in amusement while she struggles to open a bottle of wine Riley handed her before.

"Since you are giving me cooking classes almost every week, I figured this is the least I can do." Riley wants to smile, but she can feel the burden of Jules's secret dawning upon her.

The moment she looks into Austin's eyes, she knows that he knows something is going on.

He just gives her a reassuring squeeze in her shoulder before continuing to move around her kitchen to prepare dinner.

When she notices Jules struggling with the bottle of wine, she carefully makes her way over to take over, their fingers brushing as they look into each other's eyes.

"It'll be fine, Jules." Riley smiles brighter now when she sees the worry on Jules's features.

"Are you two alright?" River suddenly asks then, leaning on the kitchen island as he glances between the two.

"Yes, we are." Riley feigns a grin when she takes the bottle completely, opening it with ease before filling four glasses.

"Are you sure?" the guy has a worried look in his eyes.

"Riv." Austin shakes his head softly, silently telling his friend to stay out of it.

"Oh. Sorry." River throws an awkward smile in their direction.

Surprisingly enough, it's Jules who speaks up. "No, something is going on, but I'd rather not talk about it. It's... heavy."

"Well, whatever it is, I hope that you'll figure it out." River runs a hand through his short hair, winking at the blonde sitting on the stool.

She smiles up at him, her eyes genuinely kind.

"I will." Blue eyes meet green. They have a silent conversation as Riley tries to tell her that she will be here for Jules.

And Jules smiles. She smiles, something in her eyes that Riley can only identify as hope, relief.

Eight years of suffering in her marriage. Riley can't imagine it.

It makes her wonder how Jules has been able to hide it so well when others are around.

Then, a loud bang on the door.

It startles all four of them, River even dropping a pan, thankfully empty.

"Oh my god." Jules's eyes widen in horror. "It's him."

"Who?" Austin senses the panic between the two women, but they don't have a chance to answer him when the door opens.

Riley curses herself for not locking it.

She watches in horror how Liam is stumbling into her apartment. He has an angry look on his face that tells her that he might know something.

"I knew you'd be with her." his voice is dangerously low, and the tone tells Riley he might be more aggressive than he now lets on.

"Liam." Jules's voice is shaky when she climbs off the stool, watching her husband move to threaten River, but the man won't budge.

Jules wants to move to her husband, but Riley tucks the blonde behind herself. Like hell she's going to let Jules go.

"You're not going anywhere." Riley mumbles, feeling Jules stand half behind her, their hands locked.

Liam shakes his head, his face scrunched up in disgust. "You're really leaving me for her?"

"I'm leaving you because you're a fucking asshole, Liam." Jules spits the words, and it seems to dawn upon the two other men why there had been so much tension before.

Before they know it, Liam has made his way past River, towards Jules and Riley who have backed up further into the room.

"Call the police, Austin." Riley grits her teeth, her voice icy as her gaze is focused on the furious man walking towards her.

She can feel Jules wince behind her, quiet sobs escaping the blonde's mouth but Riley remains in front of her.

"Jules, come back. Come home." Liam orders roughly, stopping in his movements.

Austin is on the phone, River seems frozen and Riley...
Riley is angry. She is ready to attack if she must, but Jules's grip around her wrists is holding her back.
"No."
"If you ever touch her again, I will end you." Riley hisses slowly, watching Liam's eyes widening in shock for a moment, seemingly taken aback by her tone and her half-hidden anger.
"You fucking dyke. You're the reason she's leaving me!" he points an aggressive finger towards her, taking a careful step closer.
In that moment, Riley's phone rings from her pocket, startling them all.
She's distracted for a moment, too late noticing that Liam is leaping forward, roughly pushing her back.
He doesn't even bother going for his wife when he pushes Riley through her apartment, until her back roughly hits the first wall they meet.
She isn't strong enough to fight back. He's towering over her, but she remains calm when her neck is trapped between the wall and his pressing forearm on her throat.
She can still breathe, she can hear several screams coming from people, but she is focused on Liam.
One wrong move and she might die. She can tell by the look in his dark eyes that he would actually be capable of doing something like that.
"Do whatever you want..." She clenches her jaw. "...but you and I both know you won't get away with this."
"I don't give a shit." He spits, his arm pressing harder on her throat.
She can't breathe properly anymore, but she won't show him that.
"I knew you were trouble the moment Jules saw you. She seems to have a thing for pretty girls like you." His voice is dangerously low.
"Anything better than you." She growls back. She has a plan.
He won't back down, he isn't intimidated by the fact it's four against one, or that Austin has called the police.
There isn't time.
So, she takes action into her own hands.
She is fast when she shoots up her knee, hitting him straight in the core.
He yells, screaming in pain as she tries to escape his grip, but he is fast when he slams her against the wall with such force that the back of her head crashes into the hard wall.
She feels a heavy flash of pain shoot through her head, instant fatigue taking over.
She can't move. She is going to pass out from the pain in her head. She can't see, her vision is black, but she can feel his hands on her.
But suddenly, those hands are gone and she slumps to the floor. She grunts in pain, pressing her palms against her eyes.
She can't hear the words that are being said to her. She can only feel soft

hands wrapping around her wrists, taking her hands from her eyes.
When she opens her eyes, she can vaguely spot Jules's silhouette, hands on her cheeks, wiping some strands of wild hair from her face.
Her head is throbbing and she can't focus on anything else.
It hurts and she groans, not wanting to deal with this. She wants to sleep.
She wants to sleep and wake up when everything is over.
That's the moment everything goes black completely.

10

The ceiling suddenly seems to be existing of much more colors than before. Riley is sure of it.
Because, the moment she opens her eyes, color swims into her vision. Bright colors that don't seem to make sense at all.
The sudden, agonizing pain changes that, though.
She can hear voices in the distance. She can feel something on her face, but she isn't sure what it is.
All she can focus on is the throbbing pain in her head, the pain the seems to get worse with each pound.
She tries to shield her eyes from whatever light there is, wants to scream just to make it stop.
A wave of nausea washes over her, making her gag before she can even comprehend what is happening to her body.
She throws up in her mouth, choking on her vomit but fast hands lie her on her side, making her able to breathe through her gags.
Something cool is on the back of her head then, somewhat relieving the pounding pain, but she can't stop herself when another heave destroys her little moment of peace.
She manages to throw up a little more gracefully now, but it awakens her further.
The most delicate voice is softly calling her name, but there's a tremor to it that sends shivers down Riley's spine.
She opens her eyes, feeling someone wipe off her mouth.
"C-Jules?" she manages to stumble over the name.
She vaguely remembers Liam, then. She almost shoots up in her position, a sudden rush of adrenaline taking over her body.
She's wide awake.
Two pairs of worried blue eyes hover over her as they support her to sit up.

"Jules, are you..." Riley stumbles over her words as her voice cracks. "...are you okay?"
The blonde looks like she's on the verge of crying, but the purse of her lips seems to be enough to hold back. She nods carefully.
River's voice cuts through, his hand on Riley's shoulder. "Riley, I am so sorry. I should've... I couldn't... I was frozen."
"I'm fine." She croaks, trying to smile.
Then, she notices her brother. Her brother, talking to the police as they take Liam away.
Has she been out that long?
"Riley, don't move too much." Jules urges her softly. It is only now that Riley realizes that the blonde's hands are cupping her face.
Those bright blue eyes are roaming over her face, searching for something.
"I'm fine, Jules."
"You're not fine. You were out for ten minutes." The blonde's chin trembles, her nostrils flare but her touch is so, so delicate.
Riley wants to lean into it, fall asleep and wake up still feeling it.
Grimacing, the brunette can feel more pain taking over once again and she slumps back to the floor, unable to find her strength.
"They took Liam." She mumbles then, closing her eyes.
"Yes, they took him. They took him and he is not coming back." River's voice is determined. "The police has seen his aggression. He's never coming back."
The moment Riley manages to open her eyes again, she sees River's comforting hand on Jules's shoulder.
She smiles through her pain.
"I don't know what would've happened if you weren't here, Riv." Riley's voice is raw as she lies on the ground, but River's eyes are sad.
"I could've prevented him from attacking you and I didn't. I'm sorry, Riley."
"Don't be." She smiles, but the stars in her vision are overwhelmingly bright.
"She's fainting again." Jules's incredibly worried voice. "I need that fucking ambulance."
Riley smiles faintly, trying to reassure the people around her that she's fine, but she knows she's failing.
It doesn't take long for her to lose consciousness again.

When she wakes up again, she's shaking.
Why is she shaking?
But then, a sound fills her ears, and she understands.
She's in an ambulance. On a stretcher that isn't comfortable at all.
Someone is holding her hand and she squeezes it because she already

knows it's Jules.
She has a brace around her neck and the headache is less than it was before. She barely notices how she's being carried out of the ambulance, into an ER.
People are talking, she's being taken into a room. She lies down on something different, into a spaceship.
No, it's a machine of some sorts. For a CT scan, perhaps?
It makes a roaming sound, but she doesn't mind. She lies completely still, until she's being taken into a hospital room. Some stranger changes her into one of those hospital gowns, lying her in the bed.
She barely registers anything as she lies in the bed, feeling something in her hand uncomfortably.
She hums something to herself when something causes her to grin.
She slides into a deep slumber, then.

The next time she wakes up, she feels a lot better. She is able to think properly and her surroundings are clearer than they were before.
She understands what happened to her, but a doctor has yet to explain how severe her head injury is.
She is bored out of her mind. She needs to talk to someone, but leaving this bed is a bad idea.
But then, a doctor walks in without knocking. He has a smile on his face, a chart in his hands.
"Good news, Miss Dunn." He checks her up, shining a light into her eyes that makes her groan.
"Good news and you shine into my eyes like that? Is that necessary?" she complains, hating how her head starts spinning the moment she lifts it.
A chuckle escapes the guy's lips.
"Just a small check-up. According to your CT scan, you have no further brain damage, nor any hemorrhages. You do have a concussion, which requires weeks of rest, and we'll prescribe you painkillers."
"And when the hell can I get out of here?" She wants her own bed. This bed sucks.
"We'd like to keep you here for another forty-eight hours for observation."
"When will I be able to go to work?" she continues asking.
"I'd say... probably eight to ten weeks? You definitely shouldn't rush it, Miss Dunn. Head injuries are serious."
"Hm, whatever." She waves him off, annoyed by his confident way of smiling at her.
He's too smug.
His grin only grows when he winks at her. She grunts in annoyance.
Is he flirting with her? She must be imagining things with all the drugs they put her on.

"Where is my brother?" she grumbles then.
"He should be here shortly." He smiles again, straightening his lab coat. When Riley doesn't speak, he nods at her and quietly leaves the room to give her time to rest.

She sighs. She's bored and her head is spinning.
She feels tired when there's a knock on her door.
But she mumbles a soft yes and the door opens again, this time quietly.
"Jules." she smiles when she watches the blonde hover in the doorway, wearing scrubs and a white lab coat.
Right, she's working. This is Jules's hospital.
Well, not Jules's, but the one she works at.
"I wasn't... sure if you'd want to see me." Jules seems insecure, avoiding looking at Riley entirely.
The surgeon wobbles on her feet, seeming to find her toes extremely interesting.
Riley swallows, trying to get the blonde to look at her, but Jules still doesn't move much. "I'm high."
That has blue eyes snapping up, an amused smile playing on the blonde's lips.
"Yeah, they drugged you up pretty bad." She softly moves closer.
Riley traces every move. The blonde seems exhausted, probably after a long night of no sleep.
The brunette has had some time to think about everything that's happened. She couldn't think too much, because that had her head spinning and she feels like she's floating.
She's been trying to process what happened.
"Are you okay?" Riley's voice is low and suddenly feels foreign on her tongue as she speaks, but it must be the drugs.
"I'm better than you." Jules shakes her head. "I shouldn't have gone to you, I should've left the moment you found out."
"Don't do that." Riley wants to shake her head, but she can't. She has to be stern. "Who knows what he would've done if you'd gone back home. We weren't alone and we made it out alive. He didn't hurt you."
"He almost killed you, Riley." Blue eyes fill with tears. They are so filled with guilt, with worry.
"Jules, please." Riley doesn't know why she's begging her. She doesn't know why she has to know what has happened. "It was worth it if it means he won't ever hurt you again."
"No, it wasn't. Riley, you could've died. If he had been any rougher on you, you'd be in a coma with a swollen brain right now." Jules seems to fall apart again, not caring that she's at work right now.
"Come here." Riley extends one hand, hoping Jules will oblige.

She does. She carefully sits on the bed, but Riley pulls her down.
Jules all but crashes into Riley's chest but the brunette doesn't mind as she snakes her arms around the woman.
She can feel Jules cry. She can feel the soft shudders, she can hear the muffled sobs as the blonde falls apart.
And Riley just lies there, holding her, trying to be there for Jules as far as she can while she's high on drugs.
It makes her smile a bit, but her arms are strong around the blonde.
It takes about fifteen minutes before Jules calms down and she sits back up with a weak smile hugging her lips.
"Is this why you couldn't completely fall apart with me? Because you feared I would find out?" Riley's voice is silent and soft as she speaks.
Jules just nods. Her eyes are so fucking blue, so desperate for something to hold onto, something like a promise. Riley isn't sure, though.
"I stopped loving him years ago, but I couldn't… I couldn't tell anyone. I couldn't go to my mom because we barely speak, I couldn't tell my best friend because she is his best friend first. I had no one."
You had me.
Riley doesn't say it, because partly it isn't true. They were never true friends. There was always something holding them back from letting go entirely.
They were never really that close, and Riley knows that you just don't go tell a stranger that your husband is fucking abusive.
The blonde looks like she's about to burst into tears again, but Riley smiles softly.
"Jules." She tries again, a little more urgent now. The moment blue eyes look into hers, Riley smiles. "I'm right here. I am so sorry you had to go through all of that."
"Yeah."
"But I'm right here and I will be just fine, okay?" She reassures the blonde.
The blonde nods weakly, trying to stop her tears from falling.
There isn't much to say.
There isn't much to do, except trying to get through this and Riley has no idea how the blonde has managed to live like that for years.
Then, Jules manages to compose herself. She's working after all. "I should go."
"Jules?" Riley watches how the blonde rises from her seat. Her heart is aching for the blonde.
"Yes?"
"I think I have to press charges." She just says.
"Are you going to do it?" Jules seems a little helpless here.
"I don't know. What are you going to do?"
The tiny chuckle Jules lets out sounds empty. "Get through with the divorce. Something I should've done years ago."

"Jules, if I press charges…"

"Do it." Jules's lips purse determinedly. "I want you to do it. I want him in jail."

Riley is grateful that she knows all about this area. "You can do it, too. He'll get more time if you want to."

"If we can prove he hurt me." Jules shakes her head.

"Can't we? What about injuries? Hospital records? Witnesses? We will make a good case, Jules. He's been aggressive towards me. Austin, River, they saw it. We can build a case here, Jules." She tries to reassure the blonde.

"How long will he go to prison?" the blonde's jaw clenches, her fists ball by her sides and Riley can tell she wants him gone.

She wonders how Jules has ever been able to put up such a big show. They seemed genuinely happy on New Year's Eve.

"Well, based on what I know…" Riley quickly calculates in her head for as far possible with the sedation and her headache. "…he will probably be charged with assault and domestic violence. I suppose that's usually somewhere between three to fifteen years in the State of New York, depending on the severity."

"Three to fifteen years?" the blonde looks like she doesn't believe Riley. "There's a big difference between three or fifteen years."

"It all depends on the lawyer, the judge and how badly injured his victims are, or were." The brunette just mumbles, biting through her pain. "How old were you when you met him? He could have had a girlfriend before that."

"He only started after…" Jules suddenly seems to give up on the fight. "…after we got married. He never laid a hand on me before that."

Riley doesn't miss how the blonde's bottom lip trembles again and she wants nothing more than to take it all away, but she can't.

"What is the difference between attempted murder and assault? Legally speaking?"

"The intent." The brunette sighs deeply, leaning into her pillow. Her head is spinning with all the information, but she wants to answer Jules's questions. "When someone attempts murder, they go there with the intention to actually kill. But it also depends on acting in the moment or not and what Liam did was quite impulsive. I don't think we can go for attempted murder. I know people, though. From my old firm."

The blonde just nods, her blue eyes searching Riley's. "I… you should get some rest. I've kept you up long enough."

The lawyer just nods quietly. Her headache is getting worse, and she knows she shouldn't talk and think this much, but she feels the need to fight and prepare for this case, despite it not being hers.

"Jules?" Riley whispers, her eyes already closing again.

"Yeah?"

"You can... talk to me if you ever need to, okay?" she offers Jules a tired, half-lidded stare and a tiny smile.
It's enough to get a twitch of lips in return, blue gaze softening when the doctor nods, turning around to leave the room quietly.

Austin takes her home, insisting that he will stay with her the night to check on her.
The moment she sets foot in her apartment, she notices a bloodstain on her wall. It's smudged almost all the way down to the floor, it must have happened when she slid down limply.
That's her blood. On her own wall.
She shivers when she remembers, how it felt.
If River and Austin hadn't been there, who knows what else would've happened. Who knows what Liam would've done to her and to Jules.
Austin notices how Riley stiffens as she stares at her wall.
"I can clean that for you." his voice is soft when he softly guides her to her bedroom, but she doesn't want to.
Her head is pounding and she hates how her wound is hurting. She is dizzy and she wishes she were able to do more.
"You don't have to, I can do it later." She mumbles, shuffling to the couch instead. "Can I ask you something?"
Her green eyes look up, but Austin carefully drops himself next to her on the couch while she lies down.
He tucks her feet into his lap, grabbing a blanket to throw over her gently.
He's a sweetheart and she is so, so grateful that he's here.
She doesn't want to be alone.
She doesn't think she can.
"Of course." He nods, leaning back with a long exhale, as if he too is relieved to know that she will truly be okay.
"What exactly happened after I hit my head? You told me some, but I want to know it all." she breathes, eying him shortly.
His smile is short lived when he rests his hands on her shins. She crawls further down the couch, awaiting his answer silently.
"Well... I was on the phone with the police when he knocked you against the wall. River was frozen in place, unable to move and Jules desperately tried to get Liam off you. But then, I hung up the phone and River and I struggled to pull Liam off you. He was already... wrapping his hands around your throat to... he didn't just give you a concussion, Riley. If we hadn't been there, I am not sure if you would've lived." He shakes his head, biting his lip as he stares into the living room, over the TV, to outside.
A few moving boxes in the way, neither of them cares.
It's dark, grey and rainy and honestly, Riley feels the exact same way inside.
"Jules desperately tried to calm him down, but Liam wouldn't listen. River

and I managed to pull him away and I just pushed him against the wall while River called an ambulance. Jules was just by your side the entire time." He keeps going, calmly, but there's just the subtlest tremor in his voice that betrays his emotions.
"Did he hurt you? Did he hurt River or Jules?" she softly asks.
Shaking his head, Austin sucks in both his lips. He seems to hesitate for a moment. "No, he didn't hurt us, but he kept yelling that he was going to kill you, even after the cops had him. Jules was probably in shock when they took you to the hospital, and River... he thought you were dead when you were out. You looked so pale and the blood on the wall, the way you just fell..."
She feels the need to comfort him. "Where's River now?"
"Working. He offered to take over my shift tonight." Austin grimaces, moving his hands to rub his face. He pinches the bridge of his nose and Riley isn't quite sure if she's ever seen him like this.
He looks tired, wearing the same outfit he did the day before.
"You can use my shower if you want to. It's a very nice one." She just smiles. "Just... let it sink in maybe?"
"I won't leave your side." He shakes his head.
"Aus." She huffs, nudging his leg with her foot. "I'm not disabled."
"You have a head wound. You have a concussion, they told me to look after you." he defends, squeezing her in the leg playfully.
"Not constantly. Are you going to bathe me, too? Take me to the toilet? Didn't think so." She smiles at him. "I can be alone for a few minutes."
"I can shower later." He shakes his head.
"Tell River he can stay here, if he wants. I have a guestroom and a very comfortable couch. And uhm..." she hesitates for a moment. "Can you let Jules know that she's welcome here, too?"
"Will do."

River joins them not all too long after that. While Riley sleeps on the couch, both Austin and River tucked on her either side, they watch movies on a low volume.
None of them actually goes to bed, but they are all just relieved to be together.
It is somewhere around nine when there is a small knock on the door, and after that instantly Jules's voice.
"Riley?"
As Austin glances at his sister, he smiles when she seems to be fast asleep for the first time that night.
"I'll go." He carefully lifts Riley's legs from his lap carefully, watching how the woman shuffles her head closer on River's lap, a pillow giving her more comfort.

He quietly moves on his socks, wanting to open the door, but he hesitates. He glances through the hole first, letting out a sigh of relief when he indeed only sees Jules standing there.

He opens the door with his index finger on his lips to indicate for the blonde to be quiet.

She gives him a small smile. She looks exhausted, still wearing her scrubs and Austin wonders just how much she cares about his sister.

"Hey." He smiles softly.

"Hey." The blonde murmurs, her blue eyes focused on Austin's gaze.

"Come in." he smiles, moving aside to let her in. He checks the hallway before closing the door behind her softly.

"Are you sure Riley would be okay with that?" the blonde seems to hesitate when she takes off her shoes, but Austin shakes his head with a small smile.

"Considering she asked you to come, I don't think it's a problem." He murmurs while he moves to the kitchen to grab the surgeon a glass of water.

He watches how Riley has pulled up her legs, how Jules sits down on the empty spot on the couch, making small talk with River softly in order not to wake the sleeping brunette.

He sighs when he looks at his sister.

She's been through so much shit already; she's seen too much and now this. He can only hope that things will get better -much better- from here on out.

He takes the glass, placing it in front of Jules while sitting down on one of the chairs Riley has near her couch.

He watches Riley. A bandage wrapped around her head, her long curls loose and messy. She looks pale, but peaceful as she sleeps, just the tiniest smile tugging on the corner of her lips, and he wonders how she has been so calm with this all.

He is shaken up. He remembers how Liam stormed in, pushing her before she even had a chance to defend herself.

How the sound of her head hitting the wall filled the house, her scream, how she instantly went completely weak and slid to the floor the moment Liam let her go.

Yeah, they are all shaken up about it, he can tell that River still is, too.

His best friend has grown close to Riley, he knows. They get along so well, and he is grateful for it.

He is just grateful to have her back in his life. She's just... an amazing person, but she keeps bringing herself down by telling herself that she's not worth it, that she can't do anything.

And meanwhile, she is one of the most caring people in the world, he knows this. He knew when they were younger when they were kids.

He knew it when she subtly looked after him when he went to college. He knew when she kept calling, even though he knew she needed time for herself.

He has always known. She could've broken contact and she never fully did. Sure, she didn't call him often at some point, but she always let him know that she'd be there for him in case he might need her.

And she's always welcomed him with open arms, accepting him the way he was. She didn't tell him that becoming a chef was probably a bad idea.

No, she encouraged him and let him know that if he ever needed anything at all, he could always knock on her door.

He wonders why she can't see that. He wonders why she kept dwelling on the past, why she kept holding on to all those negative things.

But she told him, a while ago. She told him how she had been talking to a therapist and that they had come to the discovery of how verbally abused she really was, and he had understood.

It had made sense. But he wondered, how that feeling was still lingering in her heart after all those years.

She deserved so much better. She deserves better.

She deserves better than Camilla. He knew they didn't fit together and yet, Riley thinks they once did.

He won't take that away from her because he knows she was once happy with Camilla.

He doesn't realize he's staring at his sister when River tries to get his attention, an amused smile playing his lips.

He plucks his beard, his grey eyes sparkling when he motions his head to the couch.

Jules seems to have fallen asleep as well. Riley's feet now safely tucked in the blonde's lap, the surgeon leans sideways against the backrest, her head toppled to the side.

Her lips slightly parted to allow her ragged breaths; she has her eyebrows furrowed in a way that tells Austin she might be more worried than she lets on.

Yeah, it's a mess. Riley is a mess, Jules is mess, but he thinks, that perhaps they might be perfect for each other.

He has seen the way they look at each other, how they act around each other.

He has seen the way how Jules was by her side the entire time, with such worry and care.

It's a giant mess, but he thinks they will all be okay.

Maybe, one day.

"We should get some sleep." Austin rises from his seat silently. He grabs another blanket, since Riley has about a hundred of them, tucking Jules in.

River tries to slip away from under Riley's head, making it work, but the brunette groans in her sleep.

He instantly stops moving, grinning when Austin nods to give him the okay to move again, since he knows his sister is probably not waking up any time soon.

He smiles, leaning over his sister to tuck a few strands of hair out of her delicate face.

She's always been strong. For thirty-five years, she's been so strong.

He is still surprised how long it took for her to break down.

He just... admires her. Even though she may not always have been too clever with her feelings, with her thoughts, he admires her strength. She has always managed to survive on her own.

She has come a long way.

He just prays that things will get better because she deserves the fucking world.

Riley feels a bit dazed when she opens her eyes. It's completely dark, the TV's off and there is something heavy on her legs.

Jules's head is sprawled over Riley's legs, the rest of her body covering the other side of the couch.

Riley cannot remember falling asleep. She cannot remember the fact that River and Austin may have disappeared into her rooms.

She certainly cannot remember letting Jules into her apartment, but here she is.

She is holding on to Riley's legs so tightly that Riley fears the blonde might get cramps when she wakes up.

Her lips curl slightly, she yawns, but her head is aching in the worst way possible, and she knows she has painkillers here somewhere.

Ah, they are right there on her coffee table, alongside a prepared glass of water.

She reaches with one hand, but it's a little too far for her liking. She can't reach it with Jules sleeping like that.

She can't hold back the groan escaping her mouth when she feels her head pounding, her vision blurring just slightly.

Jules is up instantly. Her hair is a mess, she looks fucking exhausted and confused as to where she is, but the moment her blue eyes connect with green, she seems to soften and calm down.

Riley's head is aching too much to be amused by it.

"Hey, are you okay?" Jules's voice is raw with sleep, lower than usual and Riley hates how attractive it is.

"Yeah." Riley tries to sit up, pressing her palms against her eyes. "Fuck."

Without asking, Jules leans forward to grab the painkillers. She pops open the orange bottle, takes two, taking Riley's hand to place them in and hands her the glass.

"Thanks." Riley mumbles, downing the two pills, before relaxing slightly.

"How did you get in here?"
"Austin let me in." Jules just mumbles, shifting uncomfortably under her blanket. "I must have fallen asleep, but he didn't wake me."
A small smile breaks on Riley's face when she softly rubs her eyes, yawning. "You must have been tired."
"I am."
"How are you doing, Jules?" Riley then asks, looking at the blonde.
She could really get lost in those blue pools. She could get lost looking at Jules forever and she wouldn't mind it, at all.
She's just so beautiful. She is so different from what Riley thought she'd be and her secret is just hurting Riley to the core.
"Weird." The surgeon admits, sighing when she leans her back against the rest, tilting her head back to stare at the ceiling. "I've been really weird. I am so, so relieved that Liam is in jail, but… the way it happened. I never meant for that to happen, Riley. If I had known…"
"Don't." the brunette murmurs. "You couldn't have known what he was going to do."
A silence falls between them. They have so much to talk about and yet, neither woman can find the words.
They can't find the words, because too much has happened.
"You've been through a lot, Jules." Riley smiles then, reaching for the blonde's hand.
It is just as soft as she remembers as she caresses her thumb over Jules's palm. "And I like you, so I hope… I hope that we can still be friends after everything that's happened. I hope you know that I want to be there for you, because I can only imagine what it must be like to go through what you went through."
"Yeah? I was hoping you'd say that."
"That I want to be your friend?" Riley raises an amused eyebrow, sinking further back into the couch.
"Yes."
"Why?"
"Because I would like that, too."

Her recovery goes too slowly. She is bored out of her mind, but Sean refuses to let her work until the hospital clears her to do paperwork.
And she's not quite there yet. She's tired all the time, her headaches don't seem to lessen, and she is dizzy when she does too much, but still.
She has nothing to do, and she hates it.
River, Austin and Jules have moved her stuff to her new apartment after the painters had finished everything up.
They forced her to sit on her new couch while the three of them asked her where they could put her things.

She told them she still had several weeks in her old apartment, that there was no rush to move, but they insisted on helping her and she's grateful that she has been able to settle into her new apartment.

It's different. It's nice to be able to have a new place, even though she has to stay all the time to recover.

She's simply too tired to go out with Austin and River. When she tries to read, she loses concentration after five minutes and it is frustrating her.

Watching Netflix on her brand-new TV all day isn't an option because it causes worse headaches, so she's just bored out of her mind.

She tries to clean her new apartment, but it has been cleaned thoroughly since she moved in.

She tries to sort out her clothes, but they are up to date since she had been sorting them out before the big move.

She strolls through her new kitchen, enjoying that it has a small bar instead of a kitchen island.

It's somehow bigger than her old kitchen, so she can easily imagine some nights here with Austin and River, hopefully Jules, too.

She sometimes takes small walks to explore her new neighborhood, but the sounds of the city are too loud.

Thankfully, she owns noise cancelling headphones. It helps, but still, she is sometimes disoriented, and she knows she shouldn't wander all too much.

Jules has insisted on doing groceries for her and checks in on Riley every day, but the brunette knows it's mostly guilt.

As for Liam, Riley has contacted Deborah. Deborah is the best criminal lawyer that Riley has ever encountered, and she refuses to take a district attorney that the state would assign if she wouldn't have the money.

They have an appointment soon, going over Liam's case, over his upcoming trial. His request for bail has been denied, thankfully.

Riley has pressed charges and she was surprised to find Jules at her doorstep one day, crying.

Jules had been wanting to press charges too, but didn't know on what grounds and Riley had happily helped her.

There is a lot happening, and she is still useless. She can't do much, she can only sit around and wait and it has her restless.

She has to do something.

Even though physically things are not quite right just yet, she's had a lot of time to think.

She has had a lot of time to go over the things she went through. The things in the past, with her parents, her dad, with Austin but also what Liam did to her.

She hates to admit to herself that whenever there is a knock on her door, she's frightened.

She uses the hole in her door to make sure it isn't Liam, even though she knows he is in jail.

She is just putting on her apron to slowly start on dinner, when there is a quiet knock on the door.

She freezes momentarily, before remembering how to breathe. She finishes tying up the apron on her back before slowly shuffling to the door.

She lets out a sigh of relief when she sees Jules through the peephole.

She opens the door with a small smile, watching the blonde snap up her blue eyes to meet Riley's. "Jules. You know you don't have to check up on me every day. It's been twenty-eight days."

The surgeon's smile is genuine when her eyes light up. "You say that every day. I just want to make sure that everything is okay."

"I'm okay, Jules. Really." She tells herself more than the blonde.

She can tell that the blonde has been... coping. Or at least, she seems to try. She's not as happy, not as talkative as she was before it all happened and Riley wonders what is going on in her head.

Jules is now fiddling with her fingers and it's the first time that the brunette notices that Jules isn't wearing her wedding ring anymore.

And even though they've barely really spoken ever since that night that Jules had fallen asleep on her couch, Riley... she wants to talk to her.

She misses her.

She wants to pop the uncomfortable bubble they've been hiding in, so she smiles when she scrapes her throat.

"Would you like to help me cook a fancy lasagna?" she notices that Jules isn't wearing scrubs, but rather comfortable sports leggings and a hoodie under her coat and she looks like she could use something to drink.

There's a small wave of relief washing over Jules's face, before the biggest smile breaks out on her lips.

Riley can only smile in return, finding strange comfort in the blonde's beauty. She lets her in, only to lock the door behind her.

"How are you doing, Jules?" Riley moves back to her kitchen, silently inviting Jules to come, too.

She hands the blonde an apron before she grabs the ingredients.

"I'm doing well." The surgeon obviously lies.

Honestly, Riley just wishes she'd open up. Even after the revelation of her relationship with Liam, what has happened, Riley barely knows anything.

She wants to. She wants to know Jules, she wants to be able to be someone that Jules can trust, but she's not sure if that is what her neighbor wants.

She afraid to ask. For a short moment, a flash of pain shoots through her skull, making her press a hand on her temple as she leans against the counter.

"Headache?"

"Hmm." Riley grimaces as she turns to lean her butt against the counter, feeling a bit dizzy.

"Why don't you sit down and let me cook for you?" the blonde offers, rubbing her chin before moving around the kitchen, helping Riley - unnecessarily so- to sit on one of the new leather stools.

The brunette just watches how the surgeon moves around her kitchen like she owns it, and it only makes Riley smile.

"I really love your new apartment." Jules smiles softly, but it falters when she sees the grimace on Riley's face. She's in pain.

But she bites through it.

"Yeah, it's pretty amazing."

A silence falls between them as Jules moves around the kitchen to prepare the lasagna.

"Jules?" she asks then, after a few moments of just sitting there, trying to overcome her headache.

"Yes?" blue eyes meet green.

"How are you, really?"

A sad smile flashes over Jules's face as she leans against the counter in the same spot Riley did moments ago.

She crosses her arms in front of her chest, looking everywhere but at Riley. She seems to be contemplating about what to say, a few times opening her mouth to speak, but no words ever form.

"Look, you don't have to talk to me, okay?" Riley's voice is softer when she smiles. "I just hope that you have someone to talk to. If not then... well, I am told I'm a good listener."

A spark of amusement twinkles in Jules's eyes briefly. "Is that so?"

Riley raises her brows confidently, smiling when she hums. "Hm-hmm. Yup."

A small snort leaves the blonde's lips then, but it falls when she pinches the bridge of her nose.

"I uhm... I am not good at sharing." Jules then reveals, making the brunette look at her. "But I haven't really been sleeping well."

Riley doesn't speak. She simply doesn't want to pressure. She knows what it feels like when people try to push you into articulating your feelings.

Jules begins to move around the kitchen again, cutting vegetables while she hums, as if she's trying to find the right words.

"I'm trying to get used to being alone." She then starts. "Even though I hated Liam, I was used to his presence. He was the only one I really spoke to every day, and it is hard to comprehend what has happened. It's hard to adjust to this feeling of not having to be afraid of getting hurt every day. I visited him in jail the other day with my lawyer and the divorce papers. I told him I insisted on the divorce and he... he freaked. He exploded."

"Did he hurt you?" Riley folds her brows, already feeling anger bubbling up her chest.

Jules is quick to shake her head. "No, he didn't have a chance. They chained him because he hasn't been very… compliant."

"I'd guess not." Riley grumbles under her breath, making Jules chuckle lightly.

"You must think I'm crazy for staying with him so long." The blonde then stops moving again, glancing at the brunette with insecurity written all over her.

Shaking her head, Riley smiles softly. "I don't think you're crazy, Jules. I cannot imagine what it must have been like, how you must have felt so I will never think something like that about you. If anything, I think that… I think I admire you."

Nodding, Jules continues to cut the vegetables, her long hair pushed back into a messy bun at the nape of her neck.

Two strands of hair cup her makeupless face and Riley tries not to stare. She tries not to figure out how the blonde is feeling, because she knows she will never be capable of understanding.

She just hopes that Jules will be okay.

Then, the blonde inhales deeply, as if she's trying to find more courage to speak. "I have no one to talk to, really. You're the first to even… ask how I'm really doing."

Jules just has a way of breaking Riley's heart.

"You mentioned your mother before. How is she?" Riley asks carefully.

"We haven't talked much but… I think she feels guilty. She feels guilty for not seeing it and being unable to protect me."

"Were you close to her, before it all started?"

The blonde shakes her head, biting her bottom lip before speaking. "No, we weren't. I was close to my dad, but my mom was usually working and when she was home, we'd often argue. After my father died, she changed. We both changed. We called once a week, checking up on each other but that was about it."

Riley rises from her seat to grab herself a glass of water and Jules a glass of wine.

"And Emma… she didn't want to believe me after Liam assaulted you. She was angry because she's known Liam all her life."

The blonde gratefully takes the glass while Riley hops on the counter smoothly, a few feet away from where Jules's working on the lasagna.

"How is Emma now?"

"I think she's coming to terms with it, but I haven't really spoken to her after the last time." The blonde shakes her head.

She's starting to cook the sauce while Riley thinks. They are both in deep thought.

"It's a shitty thing, isn't it?" the brunette then murmurs without realizing she's saying it aloud.

"What is?" curious blue eyes look up.

"Family. Relationships." Riley doesn't have much experience. Most of it is just... crap. It's hurtful and trust is a thing she doesn't find often in the people she's known.
The only family she has left is her brother and the only friendships she has are... distant enough not to need that kind of trust.
For example, how things have been with Tessa. Tessa doesn't know everything, she doesn't know how Riley is feeling and what she has done and even though it is a big relief not to have that burden around the other lawyer, Riley wishes she could trust people.
She wishes she could see the good in people, but her experience has told her that not many people are to be trusted.
"Yeah, they are." Jules nods in agreement.
"Do you have someone that you fully trust?" Riley then wonders, glancing down at Jules, leaning her palm on the counter.
Jules stops moving then, hesitating when she breathes. "Just one person."
"Hm." The brunette hums. "That's good."
"Good?" Jules scoffs. "Riley, that person is you. I don't trust my friends, I don't trust my mother. I trust nobody but you and it is ridiculous that I can't even..."
A quiet sob escapes the blonde's throat. "...I can't even trust my own people."
Riley instantly hops off the counter, putting down her glass. She watches the blonde crumble down.
She instantly moves, opening her arms. The moment Jules notices, she falls into them.
Riley has to take a step back to be able to support Jules's weight, but she holds her. She holds her closely, tightly, mumbling sweet nothings into the blonde's ear.
She cups the back of her head, feeling how Jules fists Riley's shirt, but the brunette doesn't care.
She lets the blonde cry, she lets her fall apart right here because she needs it and Riley knows it.
They hold each other tightly. They bury themselves into each other, their bodies pressing closer and Riley needs it, too.
She needs that warmth.
She needs to feel that certain... solace it gives her, that sense of hope that she's felt before when hugging the blonde.
It just makes them both cry. Riley can't contain her tears as she holds her, her arms tightly around Jules's back as they softly sway each other into comfort.
It seems like all the pain they've been experiencing, all the things that they've seen, they've felt, it's coming out all at once.
And it's relieving, at least for Riley it is. It is relieving to be able to let go

like this with Jules, to just accept that they are damaged, that they are hurting.
She can feel Jules shake so heavily, that she fears the blonde might collapse.
"Come on." She softly urges the blonde to the couch.
Jules won't let go. They all but fall into the couch so clumsily, making Riley let out a bark of laughter.
The blonde chuckles through her tears as she lands on top of Riley, almost slipping off the couch, but Riley manages to hold her by her hoodie, letting the blonde awkwardly hang somewhere in the middle.
The brunette loses more strength as she laughs, trying not to drop Jules to the floor, but the blonde manages to support herself, lifting herself on the couch.
For a moment they sit next to each other, thigh against thigh, shoulder against shoulder.
They laugh, trying to catch their breaths through their tears. The moment they look at each other, all disheveled and confused, they burst into laughter once again.
They laugh, until they cry once again and before Riley knows it, Jules is back in her arms. She is so fucking overwhelmed by everything.
So overwhelmed by Jules, by her feelings about what has happened. She worries for the blonde. She's overwhelmed by it all. Overwhelmed that she's not physically healthy.
They are both so exhausted, that they fall back into a lying position. Jules's head rests on Riley's shoulder.
The brunette's arms are wrapped around the blonde tightly as they lie. They lie, stare into nothing, quiet sobs still filling the room every now and then.
That is how they drift off to sleep.

Austin takes River to Riley's apartment. His sister has given him a key, so the two men just silently make their way up.
They knock, but nobody answers.
"Is she not home?" River raises a curious eyebrow.
"I don't think Riley has gone anywhere." Austin shakes his head in disbelief. He has seen his sister recovering.
And it didn't go as quickly as she wanted it to.
He was just grateful that she was slowly returning to being herself again, even though it was just subtle changes.
He carefully unlocks the front door, only to grin when he sees a half-cooked meal on the kitchen counter and two pairs of legs sticking off the couch.
A smile remains on his lips as he slowly steps closer. He watches his sister sleep, alongside her blonde neighbor.
He just wiggles his eyebrows at River, before grabbing Riley's favorite

blanket, draping it over the two sleeping women, before leaving a note on the kitchen counter.

He throws one last look at his sister, and then he drags River back outside.

11

Riley doesn't think she has ever slept this well. Even though her neck is hurting from the uncomfortable angle it's been in, she actually feels rested.
She is so warm and comfy; she just wants to stay like this forever.
She tightens her grip around Jules, feeling how the blonde has nuzzled her nose in Riley's neck.
It's warm, her breath tickling the brunette subtly, but Riley doesn't mind.
A certain warmth fills her chest in all the right ways, her heart speeding up just subtly.
She can feel their entangled legs, she can feel how Jules's front presses into her side.
It just feels good. Really good.
She smiles when she stares at her white, exposed ceiling, tracing each line of the pipes up there that give the apartment an industrial vibe.
It's something she loves about the apartment – it's modern, industrial and spacious, despite the fact it's smaller than her old apartment.
She is being shaken out of her trance when she can feel Jules stir, stretching her legs, groaning while an arm tightens around Riley's waist.
The blonde nuzzles her nose further into Riley's neck sleepily, probably not realizing what she is doing, but it amuses the lawyer as much as it sends shivers down her spine. A breath carefully tickling her beneath her ear, she tries not to react too much.
But then, the blonde shoots up in confusion, scrunching her nose while she rubs her eyes, trying to see clearer around her.
"Oh, shit."
"Shit?" Riley just huffs in amusement, watching how Jules finally manages to look at her.
"I'm sorry, I was cooking and I… wow. Yeah, we must have been

exhausted."

Riley grins when she sits up. She feels… lighter. Even though she hasn't really talked about what she's feeling, she doesn't always have to.

Crying has been good, despite it causing a worse headache.

She sits next to Jules, watching the blonde yawn.

"Wait, how did we even get a blanket?"

Confused, Riley rises from the couch, wondering the same thing. It's dark in the apartment, the lights in the kitchen still on, but the rest is off.

She sees a sticky note on her counter, grinning when she recognizes Austin's messy handwriting.

"My brother came by. He gave us the blanket."

"What time is it anyway?" Jules joins her in the kitchen, stretching once again and Riley likes how the blonde just feels at ease here.

She looks at her watch. "It's six in the morning. Wow. We slept all night."

"Want lasagna for breakfast?" Jules laughs softly when she sees the vegetables on the counter, still waiting to be cooked.

"Actually…" Riley grins. "…that sounds pretty good."

"It does." The blonde hums in agreement and they silently make their way through the kitchen.

Riley quickly takes some more painkillers, feeling her headache getting worse again. She hates it, but she knows she has to get through this, and she knows she will.

Riley turns on some soft music as they move around each other. They don't have much to say.

The brunette enjoys Jules's company. She likes that they don't really have to talk to understand each other while Jules stirs the sauce and Riley fills the platter with the pasta and rasped cheese.

They work as Riley preheats the oven. They silently wait after they're finished.

When Riley checks the time, she smiles.

"Hey, while we wait, can I show you something?" she looks at the blonde, who shrugs in curiosity.

She hands Jules a coat.

"You've already shown me your fancy balcony." Jules's smile grows, her blue eyes so beautiful that Riley wishes she could just look at her more often.

"Hm, but have you ever seen the sunrise from there? It's almost as good as standing on the roof of your building." she wiggles her eyebrows playfully. "We have forty-four minutes before the lasagna is done."

Jules instantly slips into the coat, not wasting time as she hurries to the balcony in Riley's study, leaving the brunette to almost run after her.

She ignores the pounding in her head when she watches the blonde excitedly bounce on her heels, waiting for Riley to open the glass doors.

Riley grins from ear to ear when they step onto the balcony, not quite sure if she's ever seen Jules this... light-hearted.
The air is fresh and cold, giving some kind of relief to her headache.
The sky is already turning all kinds of shades of pink, with purple and still the dark blue of the night on top.
Jules gasps as they walk to the edge, facing east. The wind is strong, but neither women mind as they move, watching the ocean in the distance, the Hudson on their right.
The early morning light glimmers in the water and they are both quite stunned by their view.
Buildings are lit, but nothing can compare to the colorful sky as they watch the sun appear silently.
Riley tries to ignore the little jump of her heart when Jules leans in, shivering in the cold as she snakes her arm around the lawyer's waist.
In return, Riley wraps her arm around Jules's shoulder as they watch in complete silence.
The traffic echoes, but it's barely audible with the loud wind ringing their ears.
"It is so beautiful." Jules's husky voice sounds, and all Riley can do is nod in agreement.
This view is one of the most beautiful things she's ever seen.
There are just a few white clouds up in the sky as the sun peeks over the horizon, shining in their eyes as if it's politely saying hello.
When Riley looks at Jules, she notices that the blonde has been looking at her, their noses bumping, silent breaths mingling.
In this moment, Riley wants nothing more than to lean in and just close the gap, but she doesn't.
It feels wrong. It's too soon. Too much has happened.
They aren't quite there yet, but she hopes that they will.
Maybe, one day.
The words linger in her mind, hope luring her for a brighter future.
Jules must have noticed the same thing. Blue eyes roam over Riley's face, filled with so much emotion that the brunette almost can't hold herself back.
But she does. It's for the best, really. She just smiles at Jules, tilting her head to place a gentle kiss on the surgeon's cheek.
Her lips brush the soft skin, and she can feel her eyes flutter closed as she inhales the blonde's scent.
She smells like the fucking sky.
But she pulls back, noticing the sweet, tender smile on Jules's face and Riley knows for sure that that is the most beautiful thing she's ever seen.
Not the sunrise, not the city.
Just Jules. Jules with her bright blue eyes that hold the world. Jules, with her

soft skin, those furrowed eyebrows that sometimes make her look like grumpy cat.
Jules and her smile, her cute, wrinkled nose and the dimple in her chin.
It just feels like the first time in her life that Riley is able to let go of her past.
Perhaps it's because she's tired, or because she's high from the adrenaline of being on this balcony with the city beneath her, but she feels like she can. Let go, that is.
She feels like she is stronger than her past, stronger than whatever feelings she had holding her back from living.
She knows she has a long road to go, but she will. She will fight it and she will overcome it.
"You're beautiful, have I ever told you that?" Jules just murmurs, her voice vanished, just a single breath and her eyes focused on Riley's.
"Thank you." Riley lets the smile hug her lips.
Jules is the first to look back at the sunrise, letting out a sigh that Riley thinks might just be a good type of sigh.
They watch together, until Riley's phone is ringing with the alarm for the lasagna.
They hurry back inside, opening the oven. The lasagna looks fucking perfect and Riley's mouth starts to water as she places the platter on the bar.
Then, the two women remove their jackets and Riley grabs two plates and cutlery.
They sit next to each other as they silently eat, stealing glances and smiles as they do so.
It's perfect.
It is all Riley needs, really.

Her continued weekly cooking sessions with River and Austin turn into weekly cooking classes with Jules there, too.
She invited her when they were having one and she never really left after that.
River seems quite fond of the blonde and Riley smiles each time that Jules lets out a loud bark of bright laughter when the big guy says something silly.
Austin and Riley mostly just talk together as the two blue-eyed people move together, joking about stuff that they won't let Austin and Riley hear, but the brunette never minds.
Jules looks happy in those moments.
At some point, the four of them just fall into routine together, sharing at least one meal a week together. Whether it is at Riley's place, they sometimes switch to Jules or River's apartment, on the rare occasion Austin's.

It is really good. It's a development that Riley cherishes so much that she even made a groupchat with the four of them.

She has been going back to work for two weeks and she feels good. She notices her concentration is still off sometimes, or that a headache pops up, but she controls it by always having painkillers with her.

She agreed with Sean that she won't be going to court for at least another three weeks with her condition, but she will definitely assist Tessa with everything and handle cases that can be settled without having to go to court.

Jules has told her it's completely normal to still have headaches and concentration issues, since brain injury is not something that heals in just a couple of days.

It's good to be back at work, Riley notices.

Sean and Tessa have been nothing but supportive about the entire situation and Riley just feels relieved to be able to move on from it.

Tessa knows everything. Riley had told her everything and Sean had softly pushed for an explanation as well.

And he has been really supportive, much to her surprise. He has been telling her that if there's anything she needs -more time off, another office, an assistant, or him representing her in court- all she had to do is ask.

She gratefully declined, but she smiles every time he checks up on her.

She feels good.

Energetic. Happy, even. In some moments.

She shares her lunches with Tessa, and she grows close to the woman, especially since Tessa has shown her worry for the brunette.

She's just sitting in her office, when there is a knock on her door and Sean makes his way inside with a big smile on his mouth.

"Sean." Riley grins at him, rising to greet him. He may be older and stoic on first sight, but he's smart and silly and capable of making her laugh even when he doesn't intend so.

He can often be a grump, but it amuses the brunette more than it bothers her.

"Riley, sit. I have some news for you." he seems quite happy to deliver whatever news he's talking about.

"Oh?" she saves the file she's been working on, on her pc and focuses on her boss.

"We're hiring two new attorneys. We have a few candidates." He hands her a few files then, files of potential personnel. "We want you to join Tessa on the senior staff."

"But I've only been here for... a few months." She raises a curious eyebrow.

"You were always meant to join the Senior staff as soon as possible. You seem perfectly capable of handling yourself and you have proven yourself over and over. I have to say that I am happy to see how devoted you are to the job, Riley." His smile is genuine when he crosses his knees to get comfortable.

"Well, I'm loving it." She means it. She has been loving the job, she loves her colleagues, and she loves fighting for what she actually believes in. "But are you sure? Like I said, I've only been here for a few months."

"Riley, we have wanted you in the Senior Staff from the start. You being a Junior Attorney has only been to let you get used to our ways of working, you proving to us you're capable, that you're worthy. We need you on our senior staff. We need you to guide the associates we are hiring." He motions his head to the files he just handed her. "We've decided to change the way we do things. We're hiring people now, who come straight from law school."

Riley just nods.

"Now, we have found several candidates for the jobs, people who just passed the bar. We want you and Tessa to guide them, teach them everything that you know."

Sean takes a deep breath before continuing his story. "You will get someone to work with and Tessa, too. If that program goes well and we get more clients, we will see if we can go further into expanding our staff."

"Why don't you hire more experienced people as senior staff?" Riley wonders aloud.

"Instead of you?" the bald man lets out a laugh. "Riley, you're the best lawyer I've ever seen. We'd be crazy not to put you on our Senior Staff. You are everything that we need and I need you to turn our future attorney's into yourself."

Riley hums in amusement, her eyes sparkling as she looks at her boss. She's into that. She's always loved working together with people. She's always liked teaching, but she never really had an opportunity to do so before.

"So, schedule the interviews with Tessa together. I don't care who you hire, I trust your judgement." He rises from his seat.

"I... thank you." Riley stands as well. She straightens her pencil skirt, rolling up the sleeves of her button-up.

"Don't thank me. It has always been the plan." He waves it off, but he smiles nonetheless.

"Really?"

"Yes. It was an absolute pleasure to watch you work in court. We have faith that you will be amazing with the associates."

She doesn't have the words. She knows she is a good lawyer. She has poured her heart and soul into becoming the best lawyer, and she has succeeded.

It's one of the things she's good at, but never did she expect this, not so soon.

MAYBE, ONE DAY

She's been away for more than a month after her concussion, but apparently Sean has faith in her.
She smiles widely when she watches him leave her office. She realizes just how blessed she is to work here.
She realizes that she really, really wants to stay here, probably for the rest of her life.
This is what she was always meant to do and she loses the guilt when she thinks about the fact she could've done this all along.
It doesn't matter anymore because she's here now. She smiles when she drops herself back behind her desk.
Her phone buzzes with a text message.
It's one from Jules in the groupchat with River and Austin.
Jules – Whose place tonight?
Riley – I don't mind ☐
River – Mine? I've already done groceries
Riley – I'll take the wine
Jules – Is it okay if I bring a friend?

Riley widens her eyes in surprise. Even though she has been talking more to Jules the past weeks, she has never heard the blonde talk about a friend before.
She's only heard Emma's name. Riley can only hope that Jules has been able to reconcile with her best friend.

River – Ofc! The more the merrier
Austin – No problem. See you guys tonight!

Riley grins at her phone.
"What has gotten you so mushy?" Tessa's voice suddenly sounds through her office.
Riley rolls her eyes. She should really think about just closing the door to her office, but she always leaves it open because she likes being accessible.
"I'm not mushy."
"You're staring at your phone like a goof." Tessa raises an amused eyebrow.
"It's Jules, isn't it?"
"What? No, I'm just texting with my brother." She half-lies.
"Incest is wincest." The Asian lawyer huffs, dropping herself on one of the chairs in Riley's office, propping her feet on Riley's desk.
The brunette scrunches up her nose in disgust.
"Unsanitary, Tess."
"Although would it be incest? You're not blood related." The blonde wonders aloud. "Anyway, what were you saying?"
"I wasn't saying anything."

"Ah, you were talking about Jules."
"Was not."
"Did too."
"Tessa." Riley rolls her eyes again, sighing deeply. Then, she suddenly gets an idea. "Would you consider us friends?"
A small laugh escapes the blonde's lips, her eyes amused as they look up at Riley playfully. "Riley, you're the only one I ever talk to right now, personally. I have no life."
"But are we friends?" Riley asks again.
She has started to trust Tessa, that is for sure.
"I suppose?" a curious brow is risen above Tessa's hazel eye. She crosses her arms expectantly.
"Would you like to have dinner tonight with me and… some of my friends?" Riley bites her bottom lip, not quite sure if her colleague would be up for something like that.
"Friends? You have friends?"
A huff leaves Riley's lips. "Can you be serious for just one moment? Yes, I have friends. My brother, his best friend and Jules. And one of her friends is joining, too."
"Sounds good, count me in." Tessa grins. "Your brother is a chef, right?"
Nodding, Riley isn't quite sure where this is going.
"Good. I'll bring the wine."
"I'm already bringing wine, Tessa."
"Then I'll bring the extra wine." The Asian woman rises from her seat then. "Text me the time and place, and I'll be there."
Riley just nods, an amused smile on her face.
Just when Tessa is about to leave, she turns in the doorway. Her gaze is softer than before.
"Thank you for inviting me, Riley."
Riley's smile never leaves her lips when Tessa leaves, already barking around orders in the hallway.
She shakes her head to herself, realizing that perhaps, everything will work out after all.

River fucking adores Tessa. Riley watches in sheer amusement as they move around River's kitchen, glasses of wine in their hands as they chat casually.
Riley doesn't think she's ever seen Tessa so in her element before, just chatting about everything and nothing, trying to outsmart everyone and just seeming so relaxed.
She's even wearing jeans. Tessa is wearing fucking jeans and it is a sight that Riley won't forget any time soon. Not even Riley owns jeans.
They are all still waiting for Jules and her friend to arrive, Austin and Riley relaxing on River's couch while they sip from their Italian wine.

"So you're promoted." Austin grins, his dark eyes sparkling.
"Sort of." Riley mirrors his grin, rolling up the sleeves of her thin turtleneck. It's perhaps getting too warm for turtlenecks as spring is starting to roll in, finally.
She loves it, though. She's always preferred green seasons over fall and winter.
"And Tessa was your boss."
"She was."
"And you invited her to eat with us." His gaze moves to the kitchen. Riley isn't sure if he likes her yet, but she's pretty sure that they will get along.
"Yes."
"Why?"
"Because we're friends." Riley knows it's the truth. She is starting to trust Tessa. She's starting to rely on her sometimes, not even with work related things.
"I can tell." Austin then smiles mysteriously, laughing when he sees Riley's puzzled expression.
"Are you mocking me right now?" Riley squeezes her eyelids in suspicion.
"Nope. Not at all." Her brother teases, sucking in his lips in order not to laugh.
"Why?" Riley then snaps playfully, not quite understanding where he's going.
"It's just that she hasn't said a word to you ever since you got here." He snickers then, hiding his laugh behind the glass.
She grumbles something under her breath, but her eyebrow raises arrogantly when Tessa calls out her name.
"Hey, Riley! Why haven't you taken me to them before?"
Riley sticks out her tongue to her brother, who rolls his eyes in annoyance, but the smile never really leaves his face.
"I don't know?"
"They're pretty great." Tessa laughs then and Riley watches in horror how the other lawyer throws an arm around River's shoulder.
In those few months that Riley has gotten to know her co-worker, she's never been… physically affectionate.
Not even towards Riley. She's met River once, and she's already thrown her arm around his shoulder and Riley is almost at a loss for words, but a grin breaks out on her face.
Then, there is a knock on the door and River winks at Riley before he moves to open the door to reveal Jules and a woman with Latina looks right behind her.
"Hey, guys." The blonde pecks River on his cheek. "Meet Emma. Emma, this is River."
Riley rises from the couch, watching how Jules and Emma are introduced

to Tessa.

Riley tries to hide her smile when she realizes that things indeed must be good between Jules and her friend. It is all she wants for the blonde.

The moment the brunette joins in the kitchen, Jules gives her a tight hug, and Riley smiles when she lingers at the blonde's cheek to press a soft kiss there.

"Hey." She mumbles softly, before regaining her composure as she introduces herself to Emma. "Riley."

"Ah. You're the one Jules's been pining over for months now. I can see why." Emma grins, but she stops the moment the blonde plants her elbow in the Latina's ribs.

Riley's eyes just widen as she studies Jules's friend.

Emma is pretty. She seems fit, witty and her dark eyes are mischievous as she introduces herself to the rest of the group.

She has a positive energy over her that reminds the brunette of Tessa, but then Emma seems more… childish.

"Sorry about that." Jules mumbles when she bumps her shoulder into Riley's. They remain side by side, watching how Austin seems amused with Emma and Tessa, while River starts to prepare dinner.

"Don't be." Riley just sends a warm smile towards Jules, and she gets the same kind in return.

"Hey, uhm… I was wondering." Jules then starts. "Do you maybe want to watch a movie after dinner tonight?"

"What? Just us?"

"Yeah?" blue eyes are hopeful. Riley nods. She can't say no, she really can't. She smiles vaguely when Jules beams, watching how the blonde starts helping River in the kitchen.

Riley just drops herself into a chair since she's completely useless. Austin, Tessa and Emma have occupied the couch, talking nonsense about all kinds of things and Riley doesn't bother mingling herself into the conversation.

She's always preferred listening anyway. She is grateful, really.

She is grateful that things are going well, that she has been building her relationship with Austin back to the way it once was. Perhaps it is even better than it used to be.

They are able to share things, been able to trust each other again and Riley has been enjoying it thoroughly.

She loves how alike they are, despite not sharing DNA. They have the same interest in movies, music and often share opinions.

It's refreshing to be around him frequently and she likes the man he has become. He is a hard worker and she often visits him at his work, when he's in the kitchen.

And River has proven himself to be an amazing friend, too. Even though Riley hasn't shared much personal information with him, she still trusts him

MAYBE, ONE DAY

and she knows that he can be introverted in a way that she can be, too.

Things with Tessa had always kind of been the same. Riley has always liked her, for some reason she still can't explain. Probably because she's always straight to the point, never doubting anything she says and she's confident in a way that Riley never will be.

And then there is Jules. Jules, the person who Riley can't stop stealing glances from.

The woman she has been thinking about kissing the moment they almost shared that kiss in her bedroom.

Riley often thinks about that, just like now.

She watches the blonde move around the kitchen, guarded but at ease. She loves what they are now.

They might be friends, but they are close and Riley knows that she trusts the blonde.

They haven't spoken about Liam much, but Riley knows that the guilt Jules was feeling in the beginning is starting to fade and it only makes the blonde... more lively.

Riley has noticed the subtle changes. She has noticed that Jules has been smiling more, especially after Liam eventually signed the divorce papers from his place in jail.

She noticed how Jules would share things about herself, about her childhood, about her father.

Small stories, just between the two of them and Riley loves getting to know her like this. She loves how they don't rush anything, whatever it is they are both expecting.

Riley has let go of that. Expectations.

She is just trying to get through each day, trying to get better and trying to focus on the good things she has instead of dwelling on the past and it is going pretty well.

Sometimes, she has a tiny break down. Sometimes, she feels the need to cry and she always makes sure that she does cry, because it's always a big relief.

James has given her that advice. To stop running from her feelings and facing them head on, so she does.

She feels everything. And it is amazing, even though it hurts a lot sometimes. Even though she sometimes has moments where she thinks that everything will go back to the way things were before.

That she will fall back into that emotional, depressing spiral and that she will never change.

But it never really happens. She feels strong. She feels like she will get out of this mess better than she was before and she loves how she is able to have this chance.

She will not mess it up this time.

She throws a smile at Jules when the blonde looks her way, but she's interrupted by the silent buzzing of her phone.

She makes her way to the restroom when she takes it.

"Riley Dunn." She answers quietly, not wanting others to hear.

"Riley, it's Deborah. Sorry to call you at this time of the day, but we have a date for court." Her old boss speaks. "Mr. Bennett is scheduled for his trial in three weeks."

"What's he looking at?" Riley wonders. She has had trouble to not be a lawyer around this case.

"I think I can get him around nine years, if not more." Deborah is professional as always, but Riley has been meeting with her several times.

It had been strange, sitting on the other side of the table at the deposition for once. "That's good. It's more than I could have hoped for."

"He's being represented by Grant." Deborah then speaks.

Grant Quinn. Son of Nora Quinn, founder of Quinn & Sydney, a firm that they've been rivalling ever since they were founded.

Grant is an amazing lawyer and despite that Riley has won against him more times than he has won from her, he's been the one Riley has lost most cases to.

"You don't have to worry about this, okay?"

"I'm not worried." She lies. She is worried, but Deborah is the best lawyer she has ever seen.

"Good. We will kick his ass."

Riley smiles with amusement. Deborah is never one to use language like this.

"I will send you the details per email. For now, enjoy the weekend, Riley."

Deborah hangs up before Riley can say more. She lets out a sigh. She's been worrying about the trial, even though she knows they have enough to put him away for a long time.

But it's been an emotional rollercoaster and it's just… exhausting to have to think about.

She doesn't want to go to court, she doesn't want to see him. She doesn't want to be on the other side of the witness stand, she doesn't want to be questioned by Grant, doesn't want to give her testimony.

She doesn't want to have to speak while Liam is watching.

She can feel a shiver run down her spine when she thinks about it. She's had… a few nightmares about that night.

Except, in those nightmares he actually manages to kill her.

There's a small knock on the door that gets her out of her depressing thoughts.

"Riley?" it's Jules. "Is everything okay?"

"Yeah, come in." Riley leans back against the sink, crossing her arms in front of her chest.

She watches how Jules appears, opening the door quietly, looking at Riley with curious blue eyes.

"Deborah just called. Liam's trial is in three weeks." She mumbles, carefully eying Jules's reaction.

She may have divorced the guy, but Riley never really knew how the blonde felt about it all.

Jules nods softly, her gaze gentle as she moves to stand in front of Riley.

She's beautiful. Riley has to swallow away the lump in her throat when she watches her, those blue eyes bright as she runs a hand through her loose, blonde hair.

"Can you tell me what is going to happen?" the blonde's voice is quiet and insecure and Riley knows she's out of her depth here.

"With the trial?" Riley wants to reach out, but she doesn't.

She's always been careful around Jules, often letting her initiate things or give Jules a choice if she wants to be touched or not.

She knows that if she approaches Jules unexpectedly, she will flinch.

When the blonde nods, Riley scrapes her throat. "We will be represented by Deborah."

"Your former boss." Jules understands.

"Yeah, you don't want to be against her in court." Riley hints a tiny smile, but quickly continues. "There will be a judge, there will be a jury. Liam will be represented by Grant Quinn. Deborah will provide collected evidence, for example the footage of the bodycams of the police officers that arrested Liam. There will be a lot of arguments and the both of us will be called to the stand, several other witnesses too. We will have to answer questions from Grant, questions that might steer you into another direction, questions that might throw you off your game."

"Because he will try to make it look like Liam wasn't that bad." The blonde purses her lips, crossing her arms in front of her chest defensively.

"We can practice, if you'd like." Riley tries to reassure her. "Deborah can go through probable questions to prepare you."

"What about you? Won't you have to prepare? I mean you're a lawyer, so you clearly know how things will go but have you ever been on the other side of it all?" blue eyes are subtly worried.

"I have no idea. I suppose we will meet Deborah a few times next week to talk about this, to go through the charges and what we want."

"And what do we want exactly?"

"Liam behind bars. But…" Riley bites her bottom lip, not quite sure what she was about to say.

"But?" Jules takes a step closer.

"You will have to face him again. He'll be there." She murmurs, her eyes flickering between Jules's to try and estimate how she's feeling.

The blonde just nods.

"How are you feeling about that?" Riley tries then. "I know that… I know

that we haven't talked much about him and about what has happened, but... how are you doing with all of that?"
Jules parts her lips to allow a tiny, tremored breath. She might not show much how she feels right now, but Riley can see the emotions twirl in her eyes.
"I have no idea." Jules whispers then, her arms wrapping around her own stomach protectively. "I... when I went to see him to sign the divorce papers he just... he isn't the person I married, Riley. He isn't the person I once loved, he just... he changed."
A small silence falls between them and Riley looks down, crossing her ankles while she leans against the sink. She hesitates, not quite sure what to say.
"I loved him, Riley. I loved him. He was kind, funny and he just knew me. He wanted to build a family with me." Jules's voice sounds like she's about to cry, but tears never fill her eyes when Riley looks up. "I just... it isn't hard for me to see him anymore, because I know he isn't the old Liam anymore. It hurts because of everything that has happened, but I don't give a shit about him now. I just... after what he's done to you, I want him in prison for the rest of his miserable life."
Riley just nods. She remembers him. She remembers that pure anger in his eyes. She wonders how a nice guy can change into such a violent, reckless man.
"And Emma?"
"We have talked. A lot. She visited Liam in jail and the moment she came back she told she's always known I've been telling the truth, but she just... she tends to believe in the good in people." The blonde smiles sadly.
"You two are good?"
"We are."
Riley's smile is wide. "I'm glad that you figured it out."
"Did you love your wife?" Jules suddenly changes the subject, catching Riley off guard completely.
"I did." The brunette smiles tenderly. She once loved Camilla. She once cared about her, but that is a long, long time ago.
"You never talk about her." The blonde states. It's not a judgement, not an accusation, but rather an observation.
"You never talk about Liam, either." Riley reminds the blonde.
The tiny smile on the corner of Jules's lips makes Riley's heart flutter.
The brunette can't hold back when she raises one hand slowly. She watches Jules smile wider, taking that as a silent permission.
She softly cups Jules's cheek then, her thumb slowly caressing the blonde's cheekbone.
She smiles when she feels Jules leaning into her touch, blue eyes fluttering closed as she takes a step closer.

She watches how the surgeon raises her own hand to wrap her fingers around Riley's bare wrist carefully, holding her in place as she takes another step closer.

The brunette lets Jules take the lead in this, wherever this may go. She has no expectations; she doesn't want to do anything they both aren't ready for. It's an unspoken agreement between them as they try to move forward from their pasts.

Jules widens her legs slightly as she hovers over Riley's clumsily, making the both of them chuckle when the blonde opens her eyes.

They are so, so blue.

Riley remembers that almost-kiss that they shared.

She smiles at the memory, not quite sure what Jules is about to do now, but she gets her answer when the blonde dips her head, her forehead softly resting against Riley's.

Both their eyes close as they breathe in sync, Jules's free hand moving to take Riley's other. Their fingers lace together and Riley loves the feeling, she loves how intimate this feels.

Riley has missed this. It's been too long since they've been this close, physically speaking. She has missed this.

She parts her lips to breathe properly, feeling no need to do anything else than just share this moment with Jules.

She loves these stolen moments, these small moments where they just let each other know that they still care.

No matter what their feelings are, they are just... finding that comfort in each other that they can't find with anybody else, that content feeling that makes them somewhat hopeful, happy even.

"We should get back to them." Riley smiles softly, both her hands not quite able to part from Jules's skin just yet.

"Yeah." Jules returns the smile, pulling back softly, but not before giving Riley a hug.

In those seconds, they cling onto each other, before moving back to their friends.

They can't stop looking at each other during the night. Riley can only smile whenever Jules laughs.

The brunette loves it, how blue eyes look at her every few seconds, as if they're meant to always return to each other. It's comforting, it's good and Riley enjoys the evening as it goes on.

By the end of the night, Tessa and Emma are inseparable and River is desperately trying to keep up with their humor.

Riley just watches them, watches how Austin jokes around with Jules and it feels so, so fucking good.

It is so much more than she ever could have hoped for.

She and Jules are somewhere beyond tipsy when they stumble into the blonde's apartment, laughing when Riley recites one of Emma's terrible jokes.
Riley steadies Jules by her elbow when the blonde seems a bit drunker than before.
"Want more wine?"
"Do you have anything stronger?" Riley laughs when she strolls into Jules's living room, not even registering that she's randomly dropping her coat to the floor.
It is late, it is dark and Riley has to say that so far, this has probably been one of the best nights of her life.
She has honestly never felt so complete.
She moves around the living room and for the first time, she notices all the art filling the walls. There's a sadness to them, despite being colorful.
"Can I touch them?" she grins, glancing at the blonde in the kitchen, who just nods while rummaging through her cupboards.
Riley smiles when one painting captures her attention. She can't quite see what it is supposed to be, but the gloomy shapes just... it's touching her and she has no idea why.
Bright colors fade into each other, only to part further down the painting. She traces each line with her fingers, admiring the thick strokes the painter had once used.
"You like it?" Jules's voice is suddenly closer than Riley expected, but she doesn't remove her fingers from the canvas.
"I love it." Riley murmurs, feeling the warmth of the blonde standing behind her radiate to her own body, even though they aren't even touching.
Her fingers finish each line, until she arrives at the bottom, and she sees the name signed there.
Her eyes widen in surprise.
"Jules? You made this?" she had no idea.
"I did. It's my favorite." The blonde shyly admits when Riley finally turns to face the blonde.
"What does it mean?" Riley is breathless. She really, really just wants to kiss Jules right now, but she's tipsy and Jules is drunk, and she really shouldn't, so she doesn't.
She accepts the glass of whiskey Jules hands her, instantly taking a sip to let the liquid burn down her throat.
"How does it make you feel?" the blonde doesn't really move and Riley's eyes are glued to blue.
"Sonder." Riley chokes out.
The puzzled look on Jules's face makes it almost funny, but Riley smiles.
"Uhm... you know that feeling when you are surrounded by a lot of people, or you are in the middle of a crowd, or you sit in a restaurant and

you see people pass by on the sidewalk and you wonder what their stories are, when you realize that there are billions of different stories on this planet and you are just… just as complex as they are? That they experience their own thoughts, their own feelings and might see life completely different than how you see it? I get that feeling when I'd stand on the roof, or on my balcony now." She points to the painting. "That's sonder."

Jules looks surprised, her lips parted subtly. "And that is how my painting makes you feel?"

Riley can feel her eyes sparkle when she looks at Jules, nodding when she takes a sip. "Yeah, but then… more vividly."

Riley isn't prepared when Jules reaches to push a strand of dark hair out of her face tenderly, tucking it behind her ear.

"But what does it mean, really?" Riley breathes, unable to let her voice be heard right now. She can't stop looking into Jules's eyes, can't stop wanting to know her, know everything.

"It means whatever it makes the watcher feel, Riley." The blonde seems to have lost her voice, too. "I've heard many things, but your perspective is by far the most interesting one."

Jules drops her hand, and Riley's heart starts beating again.

"And what does it mean to you?"

Jules just smiles, finally moving to sit down on her couch. Riley is fast to follow while she watches the blonde think.

"Loneliness." She then says, her voice so raw and exposed that Riley has to swallow away her feelings.

"Your loneliness or loneliness in general?"

"Mine."

Riley feels her heart ache. She wants to be able to make Jules feel okay, she wishes she had a way.

"Are you sondering over me now? Is it even a verb? It's a noun." Jules smiles amusedly, taking a sip of her own whiskey.

"It's a noun, and yes if it were a verb, I'd be sondering over you now. I want to know you, Jules." She admits to the blonde. "I just… I don't know why I feel that strong urge to know everything, but I do."

She watches Jules watch her. "You intrigue me, Riley."

"Yeah?"

"You have, from the start. I've just always wondered why you looked so distant, so sad."

Riley raises her eyebrows. "I looked sad?"

A small, cute huff leaves Jules's nose as she smiles. "You did."

"I think I was. I was sad. When you moved in, I had just separated from Camilla. I just realized that a big part of my life was just a lie."

"Was it, though? Was it a lie?" Jules asks then, making herself comfortable on the couch, her hands hugging her glass.

"Part of it." Riley nods carefully. She isn't good with sharing these kind of things, but somehow with Jules it just seems easier. "Our marriage never felt... real."
"But you said you loved her."
"I did. Even before we got engaged."
Jules's smile is soft and gentle and Riley doesn't think her heart can take more of this sweet side of the blonde.
"I don't want to intrude, but what changed?"
"Me. Us. My career. I was focused on my career, I worked too much. I was at the office all day, stayed late and left early. We barely spoke anymore. I pulled away from her and she let me. I have never been good with... expressing my feelings, my thoughts. I can talk, but when it comes to my own feelings... I just have trouble trusting people with that." She takes another sip, seeking comfort in the warmth of the buzzing alcohol in her head. Jules listens intently and it only makes the brunette smile. "I just prioritized my career over her. She was never that important to me, so just... it was a mistake to marry her."
"Then why did you marry her?"
"Because I did once think she was the one. I did want to believe that, so I'd rather lie to myself and everyone else than face the scary truth. Camilla was my safe space, my comfort zone. Until she wasn't." She realizes just how honest she is, how she is not afraid of what Jules might think, or say. She is able to express her feelings, her thoughts and it feels so incredibly good. Jules might be the first one Riley's ever been able to talk to like this.
"What happened that made you divorce?"
"I found her in bed with someone else." Riley grimaces, lowering her gaze as she toys with her glass. "For once, I decided to come home early. I found her in our bed with someone who had been our mutual friend for years. Apparently they had been sleeping together for over two years. Two years, Jules. Two years and I didn't notice. I was a horrible spouse."
"You are not a spouse anymore, Riley." Jules smiles, trying to get the brunette to smile too, but Riley doesn't feel like it.
"What kind of person doesn't talk to their wife? What kind of person does that?"
"A person who may have deep feelings she didn't quite realize until it was too late, someone who has been struggling with herself." The blonde instantly says, without hesitation. "Riley, you aren't a bad person, okay? You're such a beautiful person."
"You don't even know me." Riley shakes her head. "I hurt Camilla."
"I think you hurt each other, but you never did it intentionally. You didn't communicate, but that happens so often, Riley."
"Yeah. I realize that." Riley's voice is small.
"We've both had... bad marriages." Jules chuckles drunkenly then, shaking

her head to herself.

"What happened with Liam?" Riley knows part of the story, but she just… she wants to know it all.

"Which part do you want?" the blonde smiles, grabbing the bottle of whiskey she placed on her coffee table, refilling their glasses while she crosses her legs on the couch.

"All of it. If you want to share, that is."

The surgeon nods carefully. "We met in med school. He was the charming guy that everyone loved, but he only seemed to have eyes for me. He was the perfect gentleman, but what I loved the most was how silly he actually was. He was just not afraid to be himself, you know? I always admired that about him."

Riley listens closely, not able to look away from the blonde beauty across from her.

"He managed to woo me after half a year. It was eventually Emma who got us together."

"Emma?" Riley raises her eyebrows in surprise.

"Emma was actually Liam's best friend when we met. She was my roommate and we met through her, at this party. But she convinced me to go out with him, that he had been pining over me for a long time and I decided to give him a chance. And he proved himself. He was nice, we shared the same goals, interests." The blonde actually smiles when she thinks back.

"He was sweet, my parents loved him. He asked me to become his wife after two years and I said yes, because I thought that we were meant to be. We got married, we were happy. But, he changed after that. He lost his parents and he just changed into someone who was angry all the time. He always had a temper, but it got worse every day. And then he wanted kids."

Riley pulls her feet on the couch, suddenly aware that Scooter as settled in her lap. She didn't even realize it, but now she smiles down, pressing a few kisses on his fluffy head.

"Did you want kids?" Riley asks carefully.

"Just one or two, but not with him." She scowls, leaning forward to softly pet Scooter's tail. "We started trying to have kids when we were still in our residency, we were still young. I was afraid to tell him that I didn't want kids with him. So I pretended to try."

Riley nods quietly.

"I couldn't have his child. I couldn't live with that, I couldn't put my child in danger like that, so I kept taking birth-control secretly." Sniffing a few times, the blonde seems to be incredibly emotional as she speaks. "He found out. He found out and he almost killed me when he did. Told me I killed our chance to have kids, that I didn't deserve to live."

Riley can feel the nausea coming up. She can't believe this. She can't believe how Liam handled this all, how Jules must have felt.

"He blamed me for being unable to get pregnant and he started to get angry at everything I did or didn't do. He got angry when I wasn't able to express my feelings, when I just held everything back. We tried a few times again, but I just couldn't get pregnant. Little did he know I was still taking the pill. I couldn't stop, I couldn't bear the thought of needing to have kids with him. He was just so angry all the time and his outbursts became worse each time. He would hit me, or just push me in anger, like he did to you. The more I fought him, the more he did to me and I couldn't do anything. I was too weak."

Riley just closes her eyes, pinching the bridge of her nose. She tries not to let her anger show, but she's pretty sure that the heat is steaming off her right now.

"Jules." She just manages to say. She shakes her head, her hand cramping around her glass so tightly she wonders why it hasn't shattered yet. "Jules."

Riley has glassy eyes when she finds the courage to look at Jules. "I... I have no words."

Jules nods, a crease between her eyebrows when she seems in trance, thinking about her husband.

They just sit in silence as realization washes over them. The reality is so... difficult.

It's rough and it shapes them as how they are right now, but Riley isn't sure if that is a good thing.

"Will you let me hold you?" she then asks, her voice subdued as she seeks out those sky-blue eyes.

Jules nods then, a painful smile plastered to her face. Riley manages to scoot Scooter from her lap, leaving him to run to the other side of the apartment quietly while she opens her arms.

She can feel Jules's arms circle her waist, the blonde's head resting on her chest.

She just holds her, her chin leaning on the top of the surgeon's head, their bodies not entirely pressed together.

They remain like that, for quite some time. They don't cry, but they don't move either.

They are just trying to understand how their lives could end up in such a mess, how they allowed themselves to get into the situation they're in now.

They are wondering if it would have been better if they had made different choices, if they had only.

If only.

It's such a stupid thing to wonder how things could have been. It's no use, and yet, neither woman can't stop thinking about it.

If only they had chosen different paths, how happy would they be now?

If only they had stood up for themselves in a different way, would they still be where they are now?

If only.

If only Riley had seen. If only she had noticed Jules's silent suffering, her sorrow.

She is thinking so deeply that she doesn't notice herself drifting into a deep slumber.

12

Riley has taken a few days off work for court, for Liam's trial.
She has taken the time to prepare with Jules, River, Austin and Deborah at her old office, to try and find more witnesses, taking depositions and collecting evidence as Deborah allowed Riley to work with her, just because the managing partner knows how well Riley knows this system from being a criminal lawyer.
Most of the time, Jules seems at a loss at what is happening, but both Riley and Deborah take the time to walk her through it.
They speak to Austin and River, practicing questions and showing ways of how to answer things a certain way, not by bending the truth, but managing to tell the truth in a way that is convincing enough.
Riley misses Jules. They haven't had much time, both busy with work and stress for court.
The brunette feels like Jules is much like Riley herself – needing time for herself to process, time to think. The blonde has been quiet after since their night of intense talk about their marriages, too.
As if it had been too big of a step, too much all at once and somehow, Riley feels that way, too.
It's been hard for her to open up about that part of her life and she notices how much energy it took for her to do that, no matter how much she trusts Jules.
It's been good to be able to find someone to talk to, but if she's being honest with herself, she'd rather keep it all in. She'd rather still hide things, instead of facing her feelings head on.
It's tough for her, especially these weeks before Liam's trial.
But she misses Jules. She misses her company, even if it were only five minutes, she misses it.

Even though it's been silent and lonely, Riley feels like it's something they both needed the space.

Riley has no idea what Jules is thinking, but she just… she tries to be there, despite their silence.

She just wants to know what is going through the blonde's head. She wants to know how she can make things better for her, but she is not one to push. The last thing she wants is to make Jules feel uncomfortable or pressured into doing something she doesn't want to. But she worries for her.

Riley's mind as been with the trial, every moment. And today, it begins.

She is standing in her apartment, she dresses up as if she would be her own lawyer.

She will be sitting right beside Deborah, while Jules, Austin, Emma, River will be right behind them.

And she's nervous. She has never been more nervous. Her pencil skirt just seems too tight today, her heels giving her blisters.

Her silk blouse just feels uncomfortable, but she knows it's just psychological. She has been on the verge of another breakdown the past two weeks, awaiting the trial with fear, negative anticipation.

She knows that Deborah is the best at what she does, and she will be right there next to her.

But still, she can't shake the nerves, she can't shake that unsettling feeling in the pit of her stomach, the nausea taking over.

She pushes it aside, putting her stoic mask on as she straightens her hair, tucking it in a high ponytail, leaving two strands out to cup her face.

She has to be here for Jules today, that much is sure. She has to be here for the blonde because it's her ex-husband they're going up against.

It must be such a hell for Jules and Riley has no idea. She can't imagine how it must feel and she hates it.

It's just a giant mess and Riley has the feeling it's going to be a rough week.

There is a knock on her door when she just finishes up. It must be Jules, but she's early.

Riley opens the door nervously, trying to compose herself when she watches the blonde stand in front of her.

Jules is wearing a black, professional dress, high heels and her hair is tucked in a professional bun at the nape of her neck.

The collar of her dress is high, but it dips in the middle of her chest, revealing just a bit of skin and it has long sleeves.

She looks beautiful.

Jules throws a small smile into her direction, but the twitches at the corners of her lips betray her nerves, too.

"Are you ready?"

She shakes her head. "I don't think I'll ever be ready."

Riley just nods, opening the door further as a silent invitation for Jules to step inside.

"Are you okay?" Riley's voice is soft when she closes the door, watching how Jules remains near the brunette, as if she's afraid she'll be intruding Riley's apartment if she walks in.

"I don't know." the blonde seems to be at a loss for words, her blue eyes roaming over Riley's face as if she will find the answer there. "It's been a lot, the past weeks."

"It has been, yes." Riley nervously clasps her purse in her hands, not quite sure what to do. She doesn't know if Jules is up for more comfort. She doesn't know the boundaries anymore, not now that they are both stressed and worried.

But Jules then smiles. It's soft, it's small, but it's right there, as if she is the one comforting Riley instead of the other way around.

"What about you?"

"What about me?" Riley repeats the question, arching an eyebrow while she watches the blonde step closer. Heels click on the wooden floor softly.

"How have you been doing the past weeks?" Jules's face is closer now, blue eyes worried.

"I'm doing okay, Jules. I just... I hope you know I'm here for you." the brunette bites her lip when she watches another smile twitch on the corner of Jules's mouth.

"Riley, he assaulted you. He may have traumatized you and you are worried about me?" the blonde reaches out then, two tentative hands wrapping around Riley's forearms.

Letting out a small huff, Riley returns the smile. "But he is not my ex-husband."

"He hurt you, Riley." Jules's hands are hot around her arms. They burn their way into Riley's skin and the lawyer thinks she might be able to feel the touch forever.

"He hurt the both of us." she finally finds the courage to reach out. She drops her purse, her hands flying up to cup Jules's face carefully, hands still on her arms.

Nodding quietly, the blonde's smile turns into a sad purse of lips, a thin stripe on her face.

It's Jules, who moves her arms then to wrap around Riley's shoulders tightly. The brunette instantly reciprocates when she feels the force the blonde uses, as if she's been desperate for a hug for too long.

And she sinks into it. She sinks into Jules, carefully burying her face in blonde hair. She closes her eyes when she finds comfort in Jules's warmth, in the subtle scent of coconut that she's grown to love.

She can feel Jules's grip around her, she can feel their bodies flush, their hips locked. She can feel a soft face in her neck, lips ghosting right over her pulse point and she tries to hold back a soft moan when she feels how her body responds to the proximity.

She thinks she's imagining things when featherlight lips press to her jaw. But then Jules looks up at her, with big, sad blue eyes.

"What is going on in that head of yours, Jules?" Riley whispers, her hands in Jules's neck, thumbs right before her ears. She absentmindedly toys with the baby hairs she finds, feeling the blonde lean into her touch.

"I don't know what to expect today. I want Liam in jail for the rest of his life, but... he used to be good. He wasn't always like this. I think he... he might still be there. The old Liam." Jules sounds more broken than she shows.

Her voice cracks and she shakes her head then, a trembling chin revealing her true emotions.

"You're conflicted." Riley simply states. How could Jules not? She once cared, she once believed that he was a good person.

Hell, even Riley believes that, vaguely. She knows that he has made mistakes, that things have happened to him that turned him so... angry and frustrated.

But the way he let it all out, it was so wrong. It has been wrong of him to act so impulsive, so irrational. She can only hope that he will see this, that he will get his own redemption and that she and mostly Jules will be able to recover from this, from the damage that he has caused.

"I am." Jules's lip tremors now, too. Riley wants nothing more than to lean in further, but she doesn't.

"That makes you so beautiful." she murmurs instead. "Believing in the good in people even after what they might have done to you... you're beautiful, Jules."

Riley means it. To be able to hope, to believe that there is good left in people. She never had that. The only people she believes in are the people she cares about, not those who've grown distant, those she's never even known.

She doesn't trust humanity.

"No, it makes me naive." Jules shakes her head then, but she leans forward, softly nudging her nose to Riley's.

Their breaths mingle as a silence falls between them.

Riley smiles then. She smiles, her hands moving to Jules's cheeks.

"Well, I think you're beautiful." she mumbles then, smiling wider when she sees the blonde mirror her.

Riley can feel the rough thump of her heart against her ribs repeatedly. She can feel it in her throat, she can feel the nerves in her stomach and for once, she isn't sure if it's from the upcoming trial.

Jules simply has an affect on her that makes her feel weak. It makes her feel exposed and vulnerable, but it's somehow really comforting.

It's intoxicating, even. Different from what she's used to, it gives her courage and hope.

"We should go." Jules softly breaks the spell by pulling back slightly. Her eyes are brighter than ever before, a fire lit in them as she smiles.

"We should." Riley agrees then, dropping her hands to sink through her knees and pick up her purse again.

When she rises again, Jules has already opened her door, waiting for her to join. With one last brush of hand on Jules's cheek, the two smile quietly as they step into the elevator.

They make their way outside. The sun is shining, it's relatively warm and Riley's grateful when a car pulls up right on time. Deborah ordered it for them.

It's a luxurious, back SUV that looks intimidating.

They climb into the back together, neither woman able to speak anymore. All they need to know is written in eyes, expressed through subtle touches.

The blonde threads their fingers together, squeezing Riley's hand gently.

They remain quiet the entire way, Jules's hand slightly sweaty in Riley's dry palm, but the brunette doesn't mind.

She can feel a finger trace a pattern on her hand and realizes it's Jules tracing the scar from when she dropped the glass and fell right on it.

The gesture is sweet, it manages to calm Riley's racing heart subtly, but she can't control herself.

It just feels wrong, all of this.

Nobody should ever be in court to fight against their ex-spouse. Nobody should ever have to go through what Jules went through and yet, Riley knows it happens. Often.

Domestic violence is a real thing and she hates it, she hates every bit of violence in this world and she has experienced it more and more personally and she just...

She can't believe she was once on the sides of the guilty. She can't believe that once she did the work that Grant is doing today.

Defending a guilty person, trying to get them less time while they deserve a lifetime rotting away in jail.

She can't believe herself and she can't understand why she ever chose that side. The wrong side. Fighting for something she never believed in.

There's press waiting for them when they arrive, even Tessa is there for extra support and Riley smiles when she notices her brother, River and Emma, too.

They are all there and security scoops them through the tiny crowd of photographers and journalists.

Riley can feel the lump in her throat as she follows Deborah into court, right to their table.

She only notices that she is still holding Jules's hand the moment the blonde lets go and slips onto the wooden bench behind Riley and Deborah.

Riley takes a few deep breaths. She tries to ignore the pounding headache, but it's hard to go around when she's aware of everything that is happening to her body.
She isn't feeling good, but she pushes through.
She can feel Deborah's comforting hand on her elbow, helping her sit down while they wait for the rest to arrive.
She glances back, trying to throw a comforting smile at Jules, but she knows she's failing.
She knows that everybody can see that she's not feeling like herself today. It's more than just facing Liam.
It's the worry she has for Jules, the realization of what could have happened.
Just fucking reality in its entirety.
She hates it. She hates that she can't hide in her safe bubble at home, that she can't get back to her comfort zone on the other side of the table as a lawyer, instead of the person who pressed charges.
She feels a hand on her shoulder, when she turns around to watch she is met by Hale's brown eyes.
She can't believe that he is here, too, not really. He was her former boss but he seems to care so much more than he has always let on, just like Deborah.
It is then, that she notices that Jules has turned around, too.
She watches how the blonde hurries out of the bench, almost running towards a woman with brown hair and dark eyes. The woman seems older, and despite being a tad darker, Riley can see that it is probably Jules's mother.
It is the older woman who falls into Jules's arms. They clutch onto each other and Riley feels the need to cry when she watches the reunion from her seat.
Emma seems touched by it, too.
"Jules hasn't really spoken to her mother in… years." The Latina mumbles then, to nobody in particular.
It is emotional for them all as they watch. Even Tessa has to swallow away something as she averts her gaze, trying to focus on Riley to show her support.
And then, Liam is being brought in.
He is wearing a suit, his hair neatly done. He has big, brown puppy eyes and Riley feels her hands cramp beside her thighs.
She can feel her heart skipping a beat, fear and anger taking over and she has to look away.
She has to look away, because she knows she will snap if she looks at him for much longer.
And she can't. She can't do anything but try her best to get him into prison

for as long as possible.
Then, the jury arrives, the judge arrives and they all rise. Riley can feel her inner lawyer taking over the moment she recognizes the judge.
It starts as usual and Riley is nervous. She can feel the anxiety in her chest, her heart beating like crazy, missing half the things that are being said.
But she pulls herself together, trying to focus.
She observes, writes notes just like Deborah does.
It is their turn to show the evidence. Deborah shows a video of the bodycam of one of the cops.
Riley has to avert her gaze from the screen when she sees an aggressive Liam in her old apartment.
She can see herself unconscious on the floor, the blood on the wall. What hurts the most is Jules's worried cries.
She hates this. She can't look at it without feeling nauseous, without feeling fear and anger.
Thankfully, the video doesn't last long. The entire room is quiet the moment it ends and Riley knows the judge doesn't like Liam at all.
Deborah brings up more evidence – Jules's hospital records, the fact she's had broken bones more times than Riley can count on one hand.
Her heart is fucking bleeding.
Riley's hospital records of her concussion is also brought up, the severeness of her head injury and how long it took for her to recover from what Liam has caused.
Then, and one by one, the witnesses are being called to the stand.
It starts with Liam. He tells his story and tries to pull puppy eyes and a pout, but Riley knows this judge isn't falling for that.
Grant manages to ask all the right questions and Riley is tired of not being able to object.
Thankfully, Deborah is stronger than Grant.
Riley is being called to the stand secondly. She swears to tell the truth and sits down.
Deborah starts questioning her and Riley's green eyes search blue.
Every time.
Jules is the only person in the entire court room to be able to calm her racing heart with that tiny, encouraging smile.
Riley tells everything, answers questions. The moment Grant starts questioning her, she knows that she's won already.
He tries to throw her off her game, but she has seen him work often enough to understand the way he thinks and he doesn't manage to succeed in whatever he is trying.
She can feel Liam's dark gaze on her, that scowl that vanishes the moment the judge and jury look his way.
He's a fucking snake.

They have recess after Riley has been in the stand. She flees.
She flees before anyone can stop her, outside, trying to find a place on her own to be able to breathe.
She has no idea why it is taking such a toll on her. She has no idea why she just feels the constant need to run away as far as possible.
"You kicked Liam's ass, you know that right?" a voice suddenly sounds.
Riley inhales deeply before looking up, leaning her back against the wall of the courthouse.
Tessa is standing in front of her, a soft smile resting on her face as she crosses her arms in front of her chest.
"I know." she agrees. She knows she did. She knows she answered the questions exactly to make Liam look bad. It had only been the rough truth.
"Then why are you here?"
"Because I am weak?" she feels helpless.
A small huff leaves Tessa's nose as she smiles, moving to stand next to her. She straightens her grey suit, running a hand through her blonde curls.
Then, she grabs a pack of cigarettes from her pocket. She silently offers Riley one by holding the open package in front of her.
She takes one.
She places it between her lips, watching how Tessa lights it and she inhales deeply.
She used to smoke years ago, but she quit. But today, it's like Tessa just knows that she needs it.
She closes her eyes for a moment, secretly enjoying the cigarette just as much as Tessa seems to be enjoying it.
"I didn't know you were a smoker." Riley exhales the smoke through her nose as she watches her colleague.
"I'm not." her grin is almost mischievous and in this moment, Riley knows she is truly a good person. "Just occasionally."
"How convenient."
The sun is shining brightly and Riley appreciates that Tessa doesn't really speak much more. The sun is warm and comforting and it's working therapeutically.
"You're not weak, Riley." Tessa then shakes her head, the cigarette trapped between her tight lips. "What you did there, sitting so strong and answering those questions, it wasn't weak."
"I'm weak for running from my feelings, Tess. I always run."
She shakes her head again, taking a long drag. "That doesn't make you weak, Riley. You would've been weak if you hadn't showed. You would've been weak if you hadn't pressed charges. But instead, you are here, fighting it. You are the furthest thing from being weak."
"I highly doubt that." She mumbles, staring into nothing.
"Hey, guys." Another voice sounds hesitantly, making Riley snap her eyes

up. Jules is standing in front of them, her hands clasped behind her back while her eyes sparkle in a way that Riley never expected she'd see today. "Can I have one?"
The brunette grins, for a moment able to let go of the seriousness of the situation they're in. She watches how Jules grabs a cigarette from Tessa's offered pack, how the lawyer lights it just like she had done with Riley's.
Jules then leans against the wall, too, on Riley's other side. They silently smoke their cigarettes as they think to themselves.
It is so light-hearted that Riley almost feels like a teenager.
"You were really badass in that stand." Jules then smiles. The moment Riley looks aside, she sees how the blonde takes a drag and it only makes her smile.
"Thank you?"
"I can't do it like you did." The blonde admits quietly.
"You don't have to." Tessa interrupts, her tone friendly. "It is important to get the facts straight, Jules, it doesn't matter how stoic you look, I think it'd be good if you show your emotions. As long as you tell the truth, there will be no problem."
The brunette nods in agreement, watching how her old boss flicks away her cigarette. She hands Riley the package with the lighter before going back inside without another word.
"We have twenty minutes left." Riley checks her watch.
"Do you think that'll be enough to finish these?" Jules flicks her middle finger against the pack in Riley's hand.
The brunette lets out a small laugh, shrugging. "I think we better keep it for the other breaks."
"I didn't know you were a smoker." Jules then chuckles, shuffling closer subtly, their shoulders touching as they stare down the concrete stairs of the courthouse, watching people stroll by as they smoke.
Riley almost feels like a teenager. "I am not. I was, once."
"Me, too."
"Weren't we all?" Riley chuckles to herself then, hating how much she enjoys the smoke. Her cigarette is finished, but she places a new one between her lips to light it up.
"Is it strange that I find it sexy?" the blonde admits, a mischievous smile on her face.
Riley raises her eyebrows in surprise, the cigarette dancing between her plump lips as she speaks. "Smoking?"
Another laugh falls from Jules's mouth. "Yeah."
A comfortable silence falls between them after the lawyer shrugs with a tiny smile. Riley can feel the gentle wind in her face as she stares down the street, the little park across.
"It's so weird to think that this is your life." Jules then says, referring to the

brunette being a lawyer.

Before Riley can even look at her, she can feel the blonde's hand brush her own carefully, before threading their fingers together.

It is a sweet, comforting gesture that melts Riley's heart. "Well, I love it."

"Court?"

"Yes." Riley smiles, glancing aside. "Except for today. I suppose today is the first day of my life that I've felt so…"

"…strained? Afraid? Insecure? Hurt?" the blonde finishes, her blue eyes accentuated by subtle eyeliner.

God, she's beautiful. Her smile is soft and lingering as they keep looking at each other.

"Yes." The brunette just says again. "I've never wanted more than just to run away and never come back."

"Me, too."

"Are you sure you can do this?"

The blonde shakes her head. "No, but I have to."

"You don't have to do anything, Jules. He's your ex-husband. You loved him once." The brunette's voice only softens more when she sees the doubt in those blue orbs.

"I know, Riley. But I just… I can't forgive what he has done to you."

"And what he has done to you, Jules." Riley reminds her gently. She squeezes Jules's hand tenderly, bringing it up to her mouth to press a soft kiss on her knuckles.

"I'm sorry I keep pulling away from you." the blonde breathes then, her gaze moving between Riley's lips and her eyes. The cigarette forgotten in her other hand, Riley just smiles.

"Don't be sorry for something like that, Jules. You don't owe me anything."

"Except that I do. I owe you my life, Riley."

Riley's eyes widen. "What? Why?"

"It is my fault that Liam almost killed you." her lips are pursed when she looks away, placing the cigarette in her mouth, her cheeks hollowing when she takes a drag.

"Jules. Stop." Riley shakes her head determinedly. They only have a few minutes to get back into that courtroom, but she just has to say this. "Look at me."

She's rather stern when she makes Jules look into her eyes. "Jules, he is the one to have lost his mind. You have done nothing wrong. It's his hands that did the damage, his mind that lost control. You owe me nothing, okay? I want you to be free, I want you to be happy and not feel that kind of responsibility, that obligation to make up for something he did. I want you to see me as your friend and not see me as something that asshole has broken and you have to fix."

The blonde looks vulnerable, but her gaze never moves away from Riley's face. She nods quietly.

"I want to be around you, Riley." Jules then whispers.

"I just hope that you can let go of what has happened." Riley shakes her head, her stare moving to the ground. "I know it's hard, and that you can't just change your mind about that, but Jules, I really… I really hope that you find that. Peace of mind."

"You, too." Jules's smile is barely there, but it is more than enough for Riley to drown in.

It is more than enough for her to lose her mind completely, to feel her heart thudding against her ribs.

She watches how Jules lifts their joined hands, now she the one to place a kiss on Riley's scar. It's endearing to watch how blue eyes flutter closed the moment Riley moves her hand to cup her face.

"We have to get back inside." Riley murmurs, unable to look away, unable to pull away, not when Jules is leaning into her touch, not when Jules looks like she just has a moment of peace.

"Yeah, we do." The moment Jules's eyes open again, Riley can see the subtle tears. She instantly moves her thumb to wipe them away.

Her heart warms at the sight of Jules's careful smile.

Riley speaks before moving her hand away. "I know we can't say much in court, but… I'm right there with you, okay?"

The blonde pulls back, leaning in to press a soft kiss on Riley's cheek. "I know."

Riley can feel the pressing burn of Jules's lips on her cheek even after she has pulled away.

They tangle their hands once again before going back inside, their shoulders bumping in the process.

Riley has never felt stronger than in this moment.

Liam is sentenced to ten years, without chance of parole.

Jules cries quietly at that, while Riley sees the defeat between Liam and Grant. She should feel happy about this, but she can't.

She can only see Jules's pain as she shakes Deborah's hand, turning around to see the blonde squished between Emma and Austin as they try to hug the shit out of her.

Riley just watches how Liam is being taken away by the guards, to spend the next ten years in the New York state penitentiary.

He looks furious. He looks aggressive and the moment his dark eyes find her, he spits out a few words.

"You fucking whore!" he wants to break free from his chains, from the guards, but they just jerk his chains to drag him with them, quietly telling him to shut up.

He keeps yelling things on the way out of the court room and Riley takes it

personally. The words hit her hard, but she tries to shrug it off.
"Hey." Tessa is then in front of her, a comforting hand to be found on Riley's shoulder. "It's over."
"Yeah." The brunette nods quietly, only now noticing she hasn't been able to move, still standing by the small desk that she and Deborah had occupied during the trial. "It doesn't feel like it is."
"But it is, Riley. You can move forward." Tessa's hazel eyes are friendly and Riley allows her colleague and friend to hug her.
She allows Tessa to hold her as they try and comprehend what had just happened. She can feel how she wants to crash down, but she holds back slightly when her newfound friend holds her.
Riley has no idea how long they stand there, but when she pulls back, the entire room is empty with the exception of herself and Tessa.
"Come on, we should go." The Asian lawyer smiles, hooking her arm with Riley's.
They silently walk the aisle back to the general hall. Their heels click on the marble floors and Riley takes in the large space.
It's round, big and pillars support the roof. She's always been impressed with this building.
She's always liked coming here to do her job, but being on the other side is just... emotionally draining.
She spots the rest of their group somewhere in the middle of the floor, quietly hushing voices as they walk closer.
Riley smiles when Austin pulls her in a hug. She feels small against him, but she loves the sense of safety it gives her.
"Thank you all guys, for being here today." She muffles away her tears, smiling through them as she glances around. "Thank you for supporting us."
She watches Emma's arm snake around Jules's shoulders and she wonders how much it all bothers the Latina. She watches Jules's mother on her other side hesitantly, as if she feels uncomfortable being there.
Deborah, River, Hale and Tessa stand together, while Austin remains on Riley's side.
"We haven't properly introduced." Jules's mother then steps forward, her voice just as deep as her daughters'. "Mary Gibson."
Riley takes the offered hand. "Riley Dunn."
The rest remains silent, but Mary seems more confident when she asks Riley to come with her to speak privately.
Riley has no idea what Jules's mother would want to discuss with her as they make their way outside, almost to the same spot where Riley had been smoking before.
"How is Jules doing?" Mary then asks, her brown eyes big. Despite the different color, Riley can just see the same type of vulnerability in them as

she can see in Jules's sometimes.

"I think she can answer that question best, Mrs. Gibson." The brunette replies in all honesty. "We haven't talked much lately."

Mary nods quietly. "I just wanted to thank you."

Green eyes snap up to meet brown. "What for?"

"For being there for Jules. She may not say it, but she... I think she trusts you the most out of all of us. I am sorry what has happened with Liam, what he did to you. I should have known." Mary tries to compose herself.

Riley's smile is small, but genuine. "We all make mistakes, Mrs. Gibson. We can't change what we've done, or haven't done. The only thing we can do is move forward and try to be better. Learn from our mistakes."

Mary just nods to that, nervously playing with the buttons of her dark blouse. "I don't think Jules can forgive me for being so unavailable, so distant."

"I can't answer that, Mrs. Gibson." Riley clasps her hands behind her back.

"Please, call me Mary, Riley." The woman almost pleads.

"Mary, I think that Jules needs time to recover from all of this. It's not nothing, she's had a rough time. I can't speak for her, but I think she's loyal and forgiving, so perhaps just... allow her that time. Give her what she needs, but remind her that you're there for her." Riley just advices. She doesn't know what else to say.

The older woman nods with a grimace on her face. "You're very smart."

Riley just shakes her head. "No, I'm not smart. If I were truly smart, I could have prevented a lot of things, but I didn't. The road to redemption is long, Mary."

"But we'll get there. You, too."

"You don't even know what has happened." The brunette shakes her head, not trying to be disrespectful.

"I don't have to, Riley. The reason I wanted to talk to you is because I... I wanted to ask you if you could keep an eye on Jules where I can't. She doesn't want me around, but she trusts you."

"I will, if she'll let me." She says from the bottom of her heart and she knows that Mary knows that, too.

"You're a good person, Riley. I hope you know that." Mary doesn't give her time to respond, already turning around to get back inside.

Riley just stands there, a little flabbergasted with everything that has happened.

It takes her a few seconds to follow Mary back inside, where the group is waiting for her.

"How about we grab dinner?" Austin proposes then.

The brunette shakes her head. "I think it's time for me to get home."

A few tired chuckles sound around the courthouse, but most people agree. They all say their goodbyes and it feels strange to have so many people supporting her.

"Want to order food?" Jules then pops up, mumbling in Riley's ear.

"Yeah." Riley smiles as the two take a cab to Jules's building in silence. She feels like they have a lot to talk about.

Their hands automatically find each other's as they stare into the city, the sun slowly lowering in the west.

It's quiet again when they move into Jules's building, up to her apartment.

Riley softly smiles the moment she realizes that there are boxes. Everywhere. Decorations are gone, there's just furniture and moving boxes.

"You're leaving, too?" Riley murmurs, trying to hope the blonde will stay close enough.

"I couldn't stay here." The blonde nods then, softly nudging the brunette to sit on her couch. "I found an apartment not too far from here."

A sense of relief washes over Riley. She has no idea why she was so afraid to think that Jules might move out of the city.

"Pizza?" Riley already grabs her phone, not really wanting to talk about it, but Jules's soft fingers around her wrist make her stop in her motions.

"What are we doing here, Riley?" she murmurs, sitting close enough for Riley to feel her body warmth, but they're not quite touching yet.

"You tell me, Jules." Riley's voice is barely a whisper.

Shaking her head, Jules runs a hand through her now loose blonde hair. Her blue eyes look away and Riley tries not to reach out and kiss her.

She wants to, but she refuses to. She just can't.

"I feel like too much has happened."

"Too much has happened to what? Be friends?" Riley can't help but feel a bit... frustrated.

"I think you and I both know that we don't want to be friends." The blonde bounces back then, but her hand is still around Riley's wrist, her thumb on the brunette's pulse point.

"Then what are we doing?" Riley repeats Jules's words, trying not to drop her gaze to those sharp shaped lips that she vaguely remembers almost kissing.

She tries not to remember what it felt like to have Jules's body pressed into her own, but at this point, it is getting difficult.

Riley reaches up, running her fingers up the strong line of Jules's jaw, tucking a tiny strand of hair behind her small ear. Her thumb can't resist moving back down, slowly tracing each curve of her jaw, to her dimpled chin.

The moment is delicate, intimate.

She brushes Jules's lips with her thumb, feeling soft, shaky breath tickling her fingers.

"You don't know me, Riley. You don't know me." The blonde then speaks, so softly, her voice trembling when Riley realizes she has started crying.

"You don't know who I am, you don't know what I like."

"I know more than you think I do." She whispers, her breath shaky when she moves to dry Jules's cheeks.

"I'm… I'm not ready to be with anyone…" The blonde shakes her head then, pulling back from Riley's touches and the brunette instantly snatches her hands back, landing them in her own lap. "…not yet."

Nodding, Riley rises from the couch. "I should go."

"Riley, wait." Jules follows her, but Riley turns around at the door, waiting for Jules to speak, but no words ever leave the blonde's parted lips.

"Jules… I care about you." Riley murmurs, her green eyes glancing between blue. "I care about you and I wish nothing more than for you to be happy. I… I'm quite tired so I'm just going to go home."

"Riley…" Jules's voice is almost pleading, but Riley's hand is on the button of the elevator to escape to her own apartment. "Riley, please."

The brunette wants to run, but she stays. There's something in Jules's voice that just has her listening.

"Riley, I… we are both a mess. I think we just… we have to find out what we want, who we are without each other." Jules swallows a lump in her throat. "I am so grateful for everything that you've done for me and I care about you, too."

"You don't trust me." Riley figures.

"I do trust you, Riley. It's myself I don't trust." The blonde shakes her head. "I just… I want you to be happy, too. I just need time."

"Time for what? What do you want, Jules? What do you expect from me? To be your friend? An acquaintance?" Riley almost snaps. She just can't bear to think that Jules is leaving, that Jules might be pulling away for good. It breaks her fucking heart.

"No, Riley, please listen to what I'm saying here. I told you I wasn't ready yet. I want to be. I care about you and I want you in my life, I want to be able to talk to you about things, but right now I am in no such state to do so." The blonde elaborates. "I can't think past today. I can't think past the fact I just helped putting my ex-husband in jail."

Riley just nods. She knows Jules's right. Too much has happened. Too many things that they both have to process, alone.

Too much baggage.

"Okay." She replies then, finally looking up to meet those blue eyes again. "I'll be here. Whatever you decide, Jules."

Her heart is aching when she watches how small Jules is, how much weight she's lost and just how fragile she is looking right now.

Her eyes are big and blue, her bottom lip jutted out to try and stop her tears, but Riley knows she won't be able to.

Riley's already in the hallway, but she moves back to Jules suddenly.

She moves back to fall in her arms, not quite sure how Jules has always

been able to pull so many emotions out of her.
They hold onto each other tightly, their tears flowing freely as they take each other in.
But Riley is the first to pull back. If she stays in Jules's arms a second longer, she won't be able to leave anymore.
So she pulls back, her vision blurry. She tries to smile when she presses her lips against Jules's forehead.
"You have my number and address." She mumbles, her lips brushing over Jules's face, to her cheek.
They share one last hug, before Riley turns around to the elevator.
She doesn't look back.

Riley falls back into her routine. Or rather, she's creating a new one.
She has to adjust to the fact that right now, she doesn't have anything to worry about, nothing other than work and her brother.
But those worries aren't anything major.
She creates a routine for herself, adjusting to the fact that Jules is gone from her life and they haven't seen each other in weeks.
Work is going well for Riley. She's been guiding Aurelia Brooks, attorney, freshly passed the bar exam.
Tessa is having fun with her own 'personal assistant' as she calls Luna. The four of them work together closely, but Riley's sole focus is Aurelia.
They share their cases and Riley tries to let Aurelia do her own thing, but it is still her who has to present their clients in court, to be the ultimate responsible person for it all and she's not about to risk that to someone who just came out of university.
But Aurelia is good. Really fucking good and Riley knows she'll be ready soon.
She's driven, she doesn't show it when she's nervous and it reminds Riley of herself not all too long ago.
She's having fun. She's enjoying her job, every day she goes to the office with a smile.
She grows closer to Tessa, sharing lunch together every day as they talk.
Sometimes, Liam is brought up.
Sometimes, they talk about the trial and Riley finds that she can talk about it with ease more and more.
It doesn't bother her as much as it did when it had just ended, but the nightmares are still there.
The fear hasn't left, even though she knows Liam is behind bars permanently.
She's moving on.
She's been seeing James, still. She's been talking to him a lot, that burden of being unable to talk about her feelings suddenly gone.

Ever since her divorce, she's been able to form her words better and better and she is getting there.

James has been an amazing help. He's been giving her tips, he's been showing her things she could do if she'd ever have a break down again, but honestly?

She's never felt stronger in her life.

Even though a part of her seems missing, she feels strong, as she stands on her balcony, inhaling the early morning air that isn't stained by smog yet.

It's fresh, the sky is breathtaking, and she doesn't think she'll ever get enough of it.

She just feels so… alive.

She's been getting more and more energy.

She goes for a run each morning before work, showers, taking a cab to the office.

She goes through her cases, guides Aurelia where she can, goes to court, has lunch with Tessa.

She often dines at Austin and River's restaurant, with either Tessa, Austin or River themselves.

Tessa has slipped her way into their little family. Not that Riley minds – she's actually one of the best friends she's ever had, understanding her on a level not everyone gets her.

They're both pretty closed off, but once they open up they have much to share, many things in common that makes Riley feel… safe.

They still keep their cooking sessions every weekend, but it is different without Jules.

Tessa often joins them, too and Riley enjoys it thoroughly.

But she misses Jules.

She misses the blonde's presence. She misses their hugs, that strange connection they shared.

Often, when she's home alone she just stares at the painting that Jules had sent her, a note attached.

It's the painting they talked about, the colorful painting that expresses so much sadness, so much loneliness.

Riley finds herself staring at it more often than not when she's home.

The fact that Jules gifted it to her before she left means a lot. It means everything. She knows it was the blonde's favorite.

The fact that she left it, is just… it gives Riley a strange sense of comfort.

As if it is a silent promise that Jules will be back, or that things will be okay in the end, no matter what happens, no matter the outcome.

It soothes the brunette.

She does still have a lot to think about. She does still wonder what she could have done differently.

She does still feel guilty, over a lot of things but she knows she's changed.

She knows that things will get better, but it doesn't stop her heart from aching.
It doesn't stop her from standing on her balcony, thinking about Camilla, about her parents.
About Liam and Jules. About what impact it has on her, that it's all taken its toll on her and she wishes she could let it all go.
She wishes she didn't wonder what could have happened if she had just been more honest, if she'd made better decisions.
She still regrets many things, even though it doesn't hurt as much as it used to when she thinks about it.
Summer is around the corner when she stands on her balcony once again, no jacket on.
She's made it a habit to come up here every weekend, in good or bad weather. She needs to remind herself of a few things, and she does that whenever she sees the sun peek over the horizon.
She is reminded by the good things in life.
And often, while she stands there, she goes back to her relationship with Jules, whatever that was.
She thinks back about the fact that Jules made her feel things she has never felt before.
And the strange part about those feelings is that Riley has never been afraid of them.
She's never feared anything, not even when she knew that whatever it was she felt was more than just friendship.
She doesn't know why Jules is the only she's felt so incredibly safe with, despite the secrecy, despite the strange things happening between them, that certain mystery she couldn't quite put her finger on.
Despite the fact that Jules could be closed off and Riley has been guarded, too. They trust each other.
It is something Riley has been thinking about often. How easy it was for the blonde to break down Riley's walls, walls that have been there her entire life.
Walls that nobody has ever been able to break before, not even herself.
And the more she asks herself why that is, the more complicated it gets. There isn't a real answer to that question and she knows it.
The only thing she knows is how she feels about Jules. She knows that, that connection that they share, that deep-rooted care... it is just there.
It wasn't something that they acknowledged, but it has always kind of been there. From the moment Riley started talking to Jules, it was there and she keeps thinking if it was... just chemistry or something more.
But, as she stands today, she feels more sadness in her heart. It's been too long since she's heard Jules's comforting voice.
It's been too long since they shared a hug that made Riley feel like

everything was going to be okay.

She's watching the sunrise at an ungodly hour, remembering that one morning she had shared here with Jules.

She cherishes that memory.

It's just... it's been a month.

It's been one month and she hasn't heard from Jules and she worries. She worries about how Jules is doing.

She just wishes she could be there for her, like Mary had asked her that day in court.

She feels like she failed that, but she didn't have much of a choice. Jules wanted to leave.

Jules needed to be on her own and Riley will never blame her for that. She understands.

She gets it.

Perhaps, she needed it, too. She needed to calm down from it all. She needed to be able to let it all sink in.

Jules has given her that and Riley is grateful for that, because she doesn't think she would ever be able to take that kind of time for herself, not after everything that had happened.

But all of this, how right it is, it doesn't stop her from missing her.

It doesn't stop her from thinking about Jules every single second she isn't doing anything.

It doesn't stop her from remembering those blue eyes, that smile filled with sadness, grief, but also the moments her laughter would be bright, real and so, so beautiful. It doesn't stop her from longing to just hold her.

She's been thinking a lot about what Jules means to her, exactly. She doesn't think she's ever felt for Camilla what she's feeling for Jules, whatever that means.

It's just a feeling that Riley knows will never leave. It is a certain admiration, a longing, the urge to make sure that Jules is okay, that she's happy.

The need to hold her and check up on her, the feeling that Jules gave her whenever she'd make a terrible joke.

That feeling that filled Riley's chest whenever she saw Jules interact with her brother and his best friend.

She just can't explain what it is, but she knows it'll never leave. She knows it has settled in her heart, in her head, just... in her entire being.

If that makes sense.

To her it does.

The view is still taking her breath away. It is so beautiful, the colors of the sky, the ocean in the distance, the Hudson on her other side.

The high buildings.

Yeah, she feels like she's on top of the world and yet, something is missing.

And she knows exactly what it is.

MAYBE, ONE DAY

13

"So... she left six weeks ago-"
"-seven-"
"-seven weeks ago, and you haven't heard a single word from her?" Tessa's eyebrows are high while she sits across from the desk, annoying Riley to no end.
"I'm trying to work here." Riley has her focus on her monitor, busy with a case she had just gotten handed to her from Tessa.
"Just give it to Aurelia. She can do all the research for you." the other woman props her feet on Riley's desk, causing the brunette to scrunch up her nose in disgust.
"Aurelia is my associate, not my slave."
"She's gotta learn, Riles."
"Don't call me Riles." The brunette grumbles. She's grumpy. It's Friday afternoon, she should be almost done with work, but Tessa came in barging, plopping herself down in the seat and bothering Riley.
A chuckle escapes Tessa's lips. "This is a perfect example of one your commander moments."
"Zip it." Riley rises a warning index finger, throwing a stern look at Tessa.
The way the blonde then bursts into laughter, has Riley huffing through her nose, but a secret smile toys on the corner of her lips.
Tessa always manages to cheer her up. Even when Riley doesn't show, it does something to her.
She cherishes this friendship.
"Come on. Talk to me. I know you have been closed off the past weeks, but come on. Jules?"
"There is nothing to talk about." The brunette shrugs then, sighing when she leans back into her chair, her arms lazily on the rests.

"You have been grumpy the past weeks." Tessa states simply, wiggling her feet much to Riley's annoyance.
"Get your feet off my desk, will you?"
"You're avoiding the question."
"You didn't ask me anything."
"Fine. How are you doing?"
"I'm fine. Can you leave now? I have to finish this." Riley has a stare down with the blonde.
She watches Tessa's facial expressions change, but the blonde doesn't budge.
"Come on. Talk."
Riley clenches her jaw. "There isn't much to talk about."
"You are pining, Rilesie."
"I'm not pining. And, don't fucking call me Rilesie." Riley rolls her eyes.
"It's Riley. R-I-L-E-Y. Riley. Rileeey." She exaggerates, tired of being cranky.
It earns her a chuckle from her colleague. She can't help herself anymore, shaking her head at herself and chuckling along.
A deep sigh, exhaled through her nose. She plays with her fingers, crossing her knees.
"I miss her, Tess." She admits then, smiling when Tessa is fast to close the door for some privacy. "I just... I hope she's doing okay. I want to make sure that she's okay, and the fact that I don't know how she is doing, is just... frustrating."
Tessa's face softens, her smile still present. "She'll be back, you know that right? That girl loves you."
Riley's eyebrows shoot up when she tilts her head in surprise. "What?"
"I am not blind, Dunn." Tessa leans her forearms on her knees then. "She looks at you with love-sick puppy eyes."
"That was weeks ago. Months, even." Riley juts her lower lip forward, for once allowing herself to feel pity.
"I'm sure her feelings for you haven't changed, just like yours haven't for her. You know she needs time, right? Seven weeks to process the trauma she went through... it's nothing. She has seen years of shit."
She has a point and Riley knows it.
Spending time alone after years of an abusive relationship is healthy. It's good that Jules takes her time to get to herself again.
Riley knows this.
"But you miss her." Tessa says then with a soft smile.
"Yeah." Riley's smile is sad, twitching at the corner of her lips before it falters. "I just... I depended on her more than I thought I did, you know? I thought that I was supposed to be there for her, but I didn't think that I'd need her just as much."

"In what way?" Tessa takes all the time in the world to talk to Riley and she smiles at her friend.
Sometimes, Riley is grateful that Tessa knows when to push and when not to. She just needs to get this off her chest.
"I don't know. We never spoke that much, but... her presence was enough. The fact that we just didn't need many words to communicate was nice. That we didn't need to talk to be comfortable around each other. And I miss her hugs. She's an amazing hugger." Riley smiles shyly at that, watching Tessa grin.
"Hm, sure she is. I'm just surprised that you haven't done it yet."
"Done what?"
"It, Riley. It. You know, the do? The big thing? Intercourse? Sex? The do, it." Tessa laughs at Riley's oblivion, making the brunette groan and lean her head back against her chair.
"I respect her, Tessa. I'm not trying to get into her pants."
"Well, I'm just saying. You're both hot for your age."
"For our age? Really? Like we're what... fifty? Do I really have to remind you that you're older than me?" rolling her eyes, Riley decides it's enough.
She gives up, throwing her feet on her desk for the first time in her life and it feels... exhilarating.
"Wow. Did you just..." hazel eyes grow wide.
"I have these alcohol wipes; I'll clean it later. Fuck it." She grins then, leaning back.
"Okay, who are you and what have you done with Rilesie?"
"Tess." A warning glare from green eyes to hazel.
"Okay, okay, geez. Anyway. You were saying how you were getting it on with your hot ex-neighbor."
"Tess!" Riley growls, watching how her friend throws her head back to start laughing like a freaking maniac. "You are so... weird."
"That's your way of insulting me? Saying that I'm weird?" Tessa chokes on air as she tries to catch her breath laughing, bending forward while she gasps for breath.
"You're such a drama queen."
"Says you! You're the one pining."
"Not pining!"
"You are. Anyway. So, you haven't had sex with her. Did you even kiss her?"
"No."
"You are the biggest useless lesbian I know." Tessa bites her lips in a failed attempt to hold back her laugh. Her eyes are teary, and she looks like she's about to explode.
"Are you only here to offend me?" the brunette scoffs, but she is past caring. Secretly, she enjoys this banter. Not that she wants to show Tessa

that, but it's just funny.
Tessa is funny.
"Of course, what else do you think I'm doing here? Kiss you?"
"Gross." Riley scrunches up her nose, crossing her ankles. "Anyway… no I haven't kissed Jules. I wanted her to make the first move since… you know… she came out of a crappy relationship."
"Okay, so you're a useless lesbian and a gentlewoman. It has its charms." Tessa finally calms a bit, but the teasing grin never leaves her face. But then, in all seriousness, she continues. "She'll be back, okay? Just have a little faith."
"I ju-"
They are interrupted by the loud ring of Riley's personal phone. Without checking who it is, the brunette answers with her lawyer voice.
"This is Riley Dunn."
"Well hello, Miss Dunn. It's Dr. Gibson." A playful, familiar voice sounds.
Her heart flops. Her jaw drops and her eyes grow wide when she jumps from her chair, the phone plastered to her ear.
She motions random things to Tessa, who knits her eyebrows together in thorough confusion.
"Jules." Riley mouths, watching how Tessa's eyes grow equally wide.
"What is she saying?"
Shaking her head, Riley smiles when she hears Jules's worried tone.
"Riley? Are you okay? What are you doing?"
"Nothing, I was just… I am at work." Riley drops herself back into her chair, but the smile on her face grows when she hears that voice that she has been missing so much the past weeks.
"Oh, I can call you back if you want."
"No, no, I'll just kick Tessa out of my office and then we can talk." Riley motions to the door, but Tessa makes no indication of moving.
A giggle on the other side of the line. "Is Tessa teasing you? Say hi to her for me."
"Jules says hi. Now scoot!" Riley moves to open the door, her heart thumping in her chest in excitement.
Tessa finally moves then, leaning into Riley's personal space.
"Hello, Gibson. You have no idea how glad I am that you're calling."
"Why is that?" Jules's voice sounds playful, and Riley closes her eyes, not even caring that Tessa is making fun of her.
She has missed Jules so fucking much.
"Riley's been cranky all week. You, apparently, are the only one able to cheer her up."
"Okay, that is enough." Riley laughs, shoving Tessa out of her office, closing the door and leaning against it, taking a deep breath.
She closes her eyes again, her head back against the door when she smiles.

"Hi."

"Hey."

A small silence on the other end of the line has Riley smiling even wider. "How have you been?"

"I'm good, I have been doing okay. Uhm... I'm not really good at talking over the phone, because it makes me awkward and all... but sending a text just seemed lame." Jules chuckles lightly, the sound sending stupid butterflies through Riley's stomach.

"It's fine, Jules. You could've texted, I would've loved hearing from you either way." She says in all honesty.

"Can we meet? Tonight, maybe? If you have no plans."

"I have no plans." Riley is quick, smiling when she realizes just how badly she would like to see Jules. "When and where?"

"Grounders? It's a little café not too far from your office, I think." Jules sounds hesitant.

"I've heard of it."

"Maybe we can go there, you know, take a bite to eat?"

"That sounds lovely, Jules." Riley smiles, just grateful to be able to hear from Jules again.

"I know you're at work, so uhm.. you tell me the time?"

"I can be there in ten." The brunette blurts out before she can stop herself.

"Are you sure?"

"If you can make it."

"Actually, I am already there." Jules's chuckle is shy. The brunette smiles to herself, trying to picture Jules at the café.

"I'll grab my things. I'll see you soon, Jules."

"Okay. Bye, Riley."

"Bye."

The moment Riley hangs up the phone, her smile grows wider. She doesn't even care what will happen next. She is just grateful to know that Jules is okay, that she sounds good and that she wants to meet.

Riley doesn't have any expectations, but just being able to see Jules again is more than enough for her.

She then moves quickly out of her office, to the restrooms. She has her hair in a casual bun at the nape of her neck. A navy suit with a white button-up underneath, she tucks open the top two buttons to make it less professional.

Her tight slacks stop right above the ankle, showing her feet and her high heels. She looks just fine, right?

"You look lovely, Dunn." Tessa suddenly shows when Riley is about to check her make up. "So, you're meeting her?"

"Yeah, in about ten minutes."

"Couldn't wait?" Tessa smiles, throwing her arm around Riley's shoulder.

"Not really." Riley shakes her head in all seriousness. "She said she was already there."
"Where are you meeting her?"
"Not telling you." the brunette grins, checking her make up while Tessa still has her arm around her shoulder.
Her eyeliner is still intact, but she needs a little more lipstick. She applies the subtle color, before smacking her lips together.
"Is it a date?"
"I don't know what it is, Tess, but I just…"
"…you want to look good for her. Trust me, Riley. You could wear a plastic bag and you'd still look good."
Furrowing her eyebrows, Riley isn't sure if Tessa is serious. "Sarcasm?"
"You'd know if it were. It was not. You're hot." Tessa's grin is growing when she pulls Riley into a hug. "Let me know how it went?"
"Sure." Riley leans into it, smiling when she wraps her arms around Tessa's waist.
Even though she's not a fan of talking personal things at work, she needs it now. She needs the support, and she is grateful that Tessa seems to understand.
"Go get her then, tiger."
"Oh, please." Riley rolls her eyes, pulling back with a grin. "We're just going to talk."
"Right." Tessa wiggles her eyebrows. "Have fun."
Before Riley can say more, the blonde leaves the restroom. Riley is quick to move back to her office, grabbing her things.
She checks the watch on her wrist, realizing she might be a little later than she promised Jules.
She hurries to grab the files, moving to Aurelia's cubicle. "Can you look at these before you leave?"
"Sure."
"No hurry though if you don't have the time just pick it up on Monday. We have a deposition scheduled on Tuesday." Riley smiles at the black-haired girl she's grown quite fond of. "I have to go, I have an appointment. Have a good weekend, Aurelia."
"You, too." Aurelia grins, clearly feeling at ease with her boss.
Riley then escapes the building, her heels clicking on the pavement as she walks to the café not too far from here.
Her briefcase in hand, her coat tucked over the other, she arrives, walking inside.
She scans the room, trying to hide her nerves when she spots a familiar figure sitting at a booth near the window.
The smile is instantly on Riley's face.
Jules.

The blonde has cut her hair to right above the shoulders, curlier than ever and it looks amazing on her.

It gives her maturity that she may not have radiated before, but suits her perfectly. She seems to have tanned and gained a bit of healthy weight and she looks happy while she looks outside, sipping on a glass of wine.

Riley didn't realize that she was standing near the entrance, frozen while her gaze focused on Jules.

"Can I help you?" a waiter smiles when he makes his way over to her.

"Oh, I'm meeting a friend." Riley motions to Jules's booth before finally feeling her legs move.

At the sound of Riley's clicking heels, the blonde looks up.

Her eyes are bright blue, a huge smile on her face as she puts down the wine rather clumsily, hurrying out of her seat to make her way over. The brunette can feel her heart ache in a good way the moment she realizes that sadness in Jules's eyes has gone.

Riley's heart skips a beat at that. She drops her stuff in the booth, stopping until she stands in Jules's personal space.

Riley's got at least a few inches on her now, Jules without heels. She wears a simple blue t-shirt, lowcut, showing off her cleavage. Her jeans is dark and tight and she looks really good, fit even.

Jules's smile grows when her hands grip around Riley's forearms, holding her close.

A whisper. "Hi."

"Jules." Riley's breath hitches in her throat when the blonde pulls her into a hug, then.

She can feel arms snake around her waist, a head tucked beneath her chin as her own arms slip around Jules's shoulders.

She holds her tightly. Really tightly. She smiles when she inhales the familiar scent of coconut, something that she has missed so fucking much.

She can feel Jules's warm body against her own, loving the way Jules holds onto her just as tightly.

They stand there, probably longer than would be normal, but they don't care.

Riley's skin is on fire with Jules's warmth. Her heart is racing, her breathing intensifying when she realizes the physical affect Jules has on her.

She smiles when she presses a soft kiss on Jules's temple, both of them pulling back.

"You cut your hair."

"You are freakishly tall like this."

They say at the same time, making them chuckle as they part completely. Jules slides back into her side of the booth, while Riley sits down across from her.

The table isn't big, leaving them close enough to be able to whisper.

"You look good, Jules." Riley smiles widely. "Really good."
"I feel good." The blonde smiles back, her blue eyes sparkling, looking straight into Riley's. "How have you been?"
"Well, my life has been rather dull the past weeks, can you believe it?"
"Not really." Jules grins, grabbing her glass of wine. The way she leans forward just slightly gives Riley a generous view of her cleavage.
She tries not to lower her eyes, not wanting to be that kind of person.
"Well, it's the truth. Nothing much has happened, it's just… it's been calm. It's been good. Lot of therapy sessions on my balcony." She smiles softly.
The waiter interrupts them. Riley orders a red wine, too, before the waiter hands them a small menu.
"Kitchen is open until eight." He smiles, before turning around to leave.
"Does your balcony ever talk back?" Jules continues the conversation.
"No, but the sun does." The brunette rolls her eyes at her lame joke, but Jules's smile is worth it.
A comfortable silence falls between them as they glance over the menu. Riley realizes that this must be the first time that she's seeing Jules outside of one of their apartments.
They've never really been out, and it feels good. It's new, it's refreshing and she likes it.
"I recommend the lasagna here. It might sound lame, but it's really good." Jules's voice is soft.
"I trust your judgement." Riley folds the menu, lying it on the side of the table.
She leans back, just quietly observing the blonde across from her.
"How have you been doing, Jules? With Liam? With everything that's happened?" she asks carefully then, not wanting to cross a line.
But the way Jules smiles reassuringly tells Riley that she didn't cross a line.
"I've been processing. It's been difficult at first, but uhm…" the blonde seems to search the words. "…I've been seeing a therapist about it all. It's been quite helpful, and even though I'm not quite there yet I feel like…"
Jules's blue eyes look down at the table shyly.
"…I've missed you." Jules says instead, before looking back up. She runs a hand through her hair, smiling more confidently then.
"I have missed you, too." Riley murmurs, not sure what to make of this all.
"I've been thinking a lot. I'd taken some time off work, just so I could adjust to my new apartment, the new situation. It's been strange to not have to constantly worry about a husband, or a trial. I visited him in prison a few times."
"How did he react?"
"He's been more compliant. He's been… he apologized. I think he never truly realized what he has done."
Tilting her head slightly, Riley crosses her arms in front of her chest,

gauzing Jules's reactions. "Do you believe him?"

"I do. But it doesn't mean I forgive him." The blonde sighs deeply, finally putting away the menu as well. She never even looked at it. "I suppose I was seeking closure. I wanted to know why."

"Did he tell you why?"

"Not specifically. He was too wrapped up in his head, his emotions. Too angry at everything and everyone and he lost control."

Riley shakes her head bitterly. "And it almost cost you your life."

"And yours." Jules instantly adds, making Riley lean forward on the table slightly.

She slowly reaches out then, her hands sliding over to Jules's side.

The blonde doesn't hesitate to take them in her own.

The touch may be small, but to Riley it means everything. The way Jules starts playing with her fingers, tracing patterns in her palms.

It makes them both smile.

As the waiter returns with Riley's wine, they both order the lasagna.

"So, how's your new apartment?" Riley smiles then, loving the way Jules won't stop playing with her hands.

"It's good, actually. It's not far from yours, just a few blocks away. It's smaller, but I love it." The blonde smiles. "I have my own studio room, to paint."

"Yeah?" Riley's smile grows. "Did you have time to make new works of art?"

"Just one, actually. It had been a while." Jules's fingertips brush over Riley's scar.

She tries not to shudder under the gentle touch, biting her bottom lip.

"Maybe you can show me sometime." She hints softly, smiling further when a small blush creeps on Jules's cheeks.

"Yeah, I think I would like for you to see it."

Jules has never looked this carefree. It's something that Riley realizes, something that settles within her, something that makes her regret the past, even though it wasn't up to her.

It hurts her to think that Jules has spent years stuck, unhappy, terrified and just... in pain.

It hurts her.

"Hey, where did you go?" Jules's soft voice pulls her out of her daze, blue eyes softly urging Riley to speak.

"Uhm..." Riley doesn't really have the words. When it comes to her feelings, she just can't find a way to express herself. "I was just thinking about how unfair it is that you had to go through everything that's happened. Right now, you look like the weight of the world is finally off your shoulders and I didn't think how much of a difference it would be for you."

Jules's eyebrows rise in surprise, but she doesn't really speak.
"It makes you beautiful, Jules. I mean, you were beautiful before, but seeing you like this... it's a relief. It's all I've ever wanted for you and I just... I sometimes can't wrap my head around it." She tries to say.
"Wrap your head around what?"
"About everything that you've been through. You're just... you've had to be so strong, for years, and you came out of it. You came out of it and I admire you for that. I guess what I'm trying to say is... I'm happy that you're doing better. I really am." Riley nods quietly, smiling when she takes over the play of fingers, watching how Jules's fingers are slightly shorter than her own.
She threads their fingers together, feeling how Jules holds onto her tightly.
"Me, too." Blue eyes are filled with tears, but her smile is genuine. Her smile is everything. "I don't think I could've done what I did without you, Riley."
"You did it all on your own, Jules. I was just there, watching from the sidelines."
"No, you weren't. You gave me strength. You made me see the important things in life, even if you might not be aware of that." Jules retrieves one hand to wipe tears from her rosy cheeks.
The waiter interrupts them, handing them two plates of lasagna.
They fall into a comfortable silence as they start eating.
"Hm, you were right. This is delicious." Riley smiles when she digs in.
"It is."
They eat quite fast. They don't speak, but Riley is eager to continue their talk, wherever it may take them.
Her mind is working over-hours, though. It's overwhelming to see Jules again, to know that she's doing well.
As she finishes her meal, she smiles brightly. "How's Scooter?"
"I think he's missing you." Jules huffs then. "He never loved me the way he loves you."
"Is that so?" Riley wiggles her eyebrows playfully. "Well, I've missed him, too."
"Maybe you would like to see him tonight?" Jules finishes her piece as well.
"I think I would like that, yeah."
As they wrap up their dinner, Riley excuses herself to get to the restroom, but she secretly pays at the bar.
Then, she returns to a confused Jules.
When Riley nudges her towards the exit, the blonde turns around. "I have to pay, Riley."
"It's been taken care of." Riley smiles, putting on her coat while she opens the door for Jules, letting the blonde walk out first.
"I was the one asking you for dinner." Jules pouts.

"And I paid." She offers her elbow to the blonde, smiling when an arm slips through. They walk down the street to catch a cab.

Jules's quiet smile is beautiful as the brunette motions her arm for a cab, stopping one.

Riley lets Jules slip in first, before following right after. Riley vaguely registers Jules giving her address to the driver, but all she can focus on is the way the blonde absentmindedly laces their fingers together, as if she's unable to separate.

Riley feels overwhelmed. She didn't think she'd actually see Jules again, especially not this soon. She has gotten used to the waiting, the thoughts that went through her head. The worry.

But Jules looks amazing. The smile barely leaves her lips, she has more color in her face and she looks so healthy that reality comes crashing down on Riley hard.

She realizes how Jules looked before, how she had her shoulders slouched, not always smiling, that sadness pooling in her eyes.

The mystery behind blue orbs, the flinching. How incredibly skinny she had been, unhappy.

Riley can only be grateful to see how well the blonde is doing now. She may still be healing, but at least that burden, that responsibility of keeping her private life a secret... it's gone.

The brunette can only wonder how hard it must have been for Jules, how strong she has to be to overcome her pain.

The drive is silent as Riley subconsciously takes Jules's hand into her lap to play with small fingers. The blonde's hand is warm and soft.

Riley cannot help herself when she brings it up to her lips to press the tiniest kiss on those knuckles.

What she doesn't expect is those fingers to stretch, reaching out to trace each line of Riley's face with such tenderness that the brunette's heart feels like it's about to explode.

She snaps up her eyes, watching Jules look at her with such adoration written in her features she almost can't take it. She leans her head into Jules's hand, closing her eyes, just enjoying the simple touch.

She can feel fingertips brushing her lips, tickling her. They move down to ghost over Riley's jawline, before cupping her cheek and stroking her thumb over Riley's cheekbone.

This is what she has missed. This is what she has been needing all this time, just a simple touch that makes her feel like anything is possible.

The moment she opens her eyes, Jules's blue gaze is still on her face, the softest smile on sharp-shaped lips. Riley cups Jules's hand with her own, before taking it and threading their fingers together once again.

She isn't sure if she's ready for more touches now, her heart simply aching with care for this woman.

"You're beautiful." Jules mouths then, a loving smile hugging her lips as she leans in slightly.

Riley is quick when she wraps her arms around Jules's shoulders, pulling her closer as the blonde topples into her embrace, a head buried in the crook Riley's neck.

They hold onto each other. They ignore the driver, they ignore the awkward position they're in on the backseat, they just feel each other.

Riley cannot comprehend her feelings. She cannot identify what it is that fills her chest, making her feel so full, so ready to pour it all out.

She can only press her lips on top of Jules's head, finding comfort in her scent, her warmth.

"God, I have missed you." the words slip from her lips before she can swallow them back. She can feel Jules's arm snake beneath her blazer, around her waist to pull her closer.

The blonde then rises her head, her lips brushing over Riley's jaw. The brunette is frozen at that, feeling the softness against her skin.

Right now, she wants nothing more than to lean down and press her smile against Jules's, but it's not the time, nor the place.

She can hear the tremor in Jules's breath when the blonde nudges her nose into Riley's cheek, smiling when she pulls back then.

"Almost there."

The moment Jules lets go of Riley, she feels cold and empty, almost instantly wanting to reach out to pull her back, but she doesn't.

Instead, she observes the cab driver slowing to a stop in front of a high apartment building and Jules hands him a few bills before dragging Riley out of the cab.

The lawyer laughs when the blonde guides her inside, into the lobby, towards the elevators.

"This is an upgrade." Riley grins when she notices two elevators, one already opening for them to step in.

"It is." Jules smiles then, her hand still tangled with Riley's, while the brunette struggles with her briefcase and her coat.

It doesn't take long for them to arrive on Jules's floor, and Riley follows with a small smile, watching the blonde bounce on her heels while she grabs her keys, opening a door.

The moment Riley sets foot in the apartment, she grins. It's not as large as the previous one, but it is spacious. The living room is L-shaped, separated from the kitchen by a wall and a glass door.

The dining table is against the wall to the kitchen, the couch in the larger area.

It's messy.

There are things everywhere, lying around. Art is on the walls and the walls itself are art, too.

It's as if Jules took all the time in the world to decorate her walls with different, but calming colors.
The furniture is neutral, but the creative walls make up for that.
"Wow, this is so…"
"Messy? Full?"
"…you." Riley smiles warmly, feeling free enough to hang up her coat on the rack near the front door. She takes off her heels and places her briefcase there, too. "I love it, Jules. It feels really homey."
"It's a mess." Jules sighs then, smiling when she makes her way into the kitchen, only to come back with two glasses of wine. "Did you want wine?"
"Yes." The brunette smiles when she watches the blonde placing the two glasses on the coffee table.
Riley takes the liberty to dispose herself from her blazer too, finding it warm enough to just be in her button up.
She follows Jules then, joining her on the couch. "So where is my beloved Scooter?"
"Ah, I see, you only came here for him."
"Well, if I remember correctly, you were the one to ask if I wanted to see him tonight. I came here for him only indeed." Riley's green eyes sparkle when she sits on the couch sideways, able to face Jules.
"Hmm, I see. Let's see if I can find him." The blonde grins, already rising from her spot, but Riley's fingers around her wrist softly nudge her back onto the couch.
The brunette can't stop herself when she pulls Jules into another embrace. She has been… sleepless. Exhausted. Worried.
Having Jules in her arms safe and soundly, makes her heart warm, makes her head calm. It's something she needs for a moment and she can feel by the way Jules reciprocates the hug, that she knows it too.
"I am sorry for staying away for as long as I did." A muffled voice comes from Riley's shoulder as they softly sink onto the couch in a lying position.
"Don't. Don't do that, Jules." Riley closes her eyes, tangling her hand into Jules's short hair, gently massaging her scalp as they lie.
Staring up at the ceiling, the brunette can feel Jules's body curl around her, a face buried in her neck, arms around her waist and legs entwined.
The brunette smoothly moves to take out her bun, displaying her hair all over the pillows that Jules has stuffed into the corner of her sofa.
"You needed time. I know what that feels like." Riley grimaces. Perhaps now, she can understand Austin.
She has never seen it from the other side, but she knows she'd wait for Jules forever, however much time she'd need.
And she knows Austin would have done the same thing. She realizes that now.
She smiles softly when she can feel Jules's grip tighten. Riley rests her cheek

on top of the blonde's head, sighing in simple contentment.
She has missed this.
But then, she can feel the soft shudders in Jules's body, passing it onto her own as the blonde cries softly.
All Riley can do is hold her closer, hold her harder, let her know silently that she's here.
She murmurs quiet, meaningless words into Jules's hair, closing her eyes when she can feel the pain in her own heart.
She thinks that maybe now, Jules is able to let things go. Even if it's only partly, or just a start, it's something.
Riley just makes sure she's there, holding her, talking to her softly, her hands on Jules's back to run soothing circles.
After a while, the sobs subside, and Jules is sniffling into her neck.
"I ruined your shirt."
"It's okay, I have like thousand of 'm." Riley admits with a press of lips on Jules's forehead.
A tiny giggle from the blonde, she lifts her head to look at Riley.
Her eyes are bluer than ever, red-trimmed and her cheeks are damp.
Riley instantly reaches to clean it carefully, her thumbs working on the subtle smudges of mascara, her palms covering the cheeks.
"Why are you like this?" Jules then blurts, her voice raw from the crying.
"Like what?" Riley's eyes widen in surprise, her hands dropping back to tuck Jules back into her side.
"So fucking adorable."
A snort leaves Riley's nose. She smiles when she can feel the flutter in her heart. "I'm adorable?"
"No, I meant... sweet. Kind."
"I care about you, Jules. Just making sure that you're okay."
A soft yawn comes from the blonde. "I am okay. More than okay now that you're here."
The honest confession makes the lawyer smile widely. She's grateful that Jules can't see her blush from her position on Riley's chest.
"I'm always here if you need me, Jules." It's a promise. Something she may have promised before, but she wants to remind Jules that she is not alone in this.
"I know." a sharp inhale of breath, quivering voice and Jules's hand resting softly on Riley's sternum is enough for the brunette to nearly fall apart. "Riley, I... you've been there for me. I am here for you too, okay? I know that you've... we've both have had things to deal with, our marriages, our pasts. I want you to know that you don't have to do it alone, either."
"I know, Jules. I know." Riley closes her eyes. She can feel exhaustion taking over.
The way Jules lies against her somehow manages to relax her in a way she

hasn't been able to the past seven weeks.
She leans her cheek onto Jules's head, her free hand reaching up to wrap around the one Jules had resting on her chest.
It feels a whole lot like home.

She wakes of wetness in her face.
Is Jules licking her? She opens her eyes, not having a hard time to adjust to the light since it's completely dark in the room.
But then, something is licking her cheek again.
"Scooter?" Riley smiles, feeling fur in her neck, paws in her shoulder. Scooter has managed to roll himself into her neck, licking her face while he purrs quietly. "Hey, buddy."
"He's been lying there ever since I woke." Jules's raspy voice is soft, but startling Riley anyway.
"How long have you been awake?" Riley is wrapped between Scooter and Jules.
The blonde is pressed between the brunette and the backrest of the couch. Their limbs still entangled; Riley's eyes widen when she can feel fingers brush on her hipbone.
Her bare hipbone. Her button up must have slipped out of her slacks while sleeping and Jules's thumb is absentmindedly burning its way into Riley's skin.
The brunette is over-aware of each touch, but fairly unable to move.
Her heart swells the moment she meets playful blue eyes.
"Just about half an hour, I suppose."
"Why didn't you wake me?" Riley's eyes grow wider when she manages to scratch Scooter on his head, making him lick her even harder.
She scrunches up her nose in disgust, but she has missed him, so she'll allow this unsanitary licking.
"You looked exhausted."
"You could've just woken me. What time is it anyway?" she tries to stretch, but it's still impossible.
It secretly feels like a tiny little family, having Scooter there with her, Jules on her other side.
"I don't know what time it is. Scooter never lies with me like that." The blonde pouts adorably, her head propped onto a hand.
Her other hand moves to pet Scooter, tickling him under his chin.
"Oh, you like that, huh?" Riley grins when he purrs even louder. "He is so cute. What breed is he, anyway?"
"He's a British Shorthair. Lazy and chubby, my spirit animal."
"You're not chubby." Riley rolls her eyes playfully. "Not sure about the lazy part, though."
"Oh, so you're calling me lazy?"

"I think that technically, you hinted that you're lazy." Riley's grin only grows, but it falters when she notices the proximity of Jules's face near her own.
Her breath hitches in her throat, feeling Jules's legs move against her own to readjust position.
Jules's hand then moves from Scooters chin to Riley's cheek.
The emotions are evident in cerulean eyes, so raw and bare that Riley has to swallow a lump in her throat.
Her lips are parted to allow hesitant breaths. Is Jules leaning closer? Or is Riley imagining things?
"Riley?" Jules's breath isn't even remotely more controlled than Riley's is.
"Yeah?"
"Can I kiss you?"
Riley's gaze instantly drops to pink, freshly wetted lips. She has been imagining for so long, how they would feel like pressed against her own.
What they would taste like, how they'd move against her own.
She nods breathlessly, feeling her cheek tingle under Jules's tender touches.
The moment she can feel a shaky breath on her waiting lips, her eyes flutter closed. She can feel a nose bump her own, the warmth emanating to her own skin.
Their bodies pressed together, Riley's can feel her breath quicken, her heart speeding up, too.
She swallows deeply when she can feel Jules's lips ghosting over her own, making it impossible not to shiver.
She trembles when she closes the remaining gap, just unable to stay away, their lips meeting in a soft, unrushed kiss.
It's not heated. It's tender and slow.
Jules's lips are even softer than they look, moving with careful purpose against Riley.
Riley's simply intoxicated by the feeling of those pink lips on her own, unable to move, unable to process the flaming tingle on her mouth.
Hands cup Riley's cheeks when the blonde's mouth softly slides against her own in the most addictive of ways.
All Riley can do is happily sigh into her, hoping that this moment will last forever.
Their lips move in sync, until Riley grows impatient. She wants more. She deepens it gently when she changes angles, meeting Jules's parted lips with her own, her tongue searching for more.
And Jules moans. She fucking moans in a way that has Riley's head spin, that has her heart jumping in her chest, her hands roaming over Jules's hips to pull her on top of her.
Scooter meows loudly, but Jules giggles when she softly nudges him off, leaving the two women flustered. But it's Riley, who places her hand in

Jules's neck to pull her in.

Now that she's tasted heaven, she isn't sure if she's ready to let that go yet.

Jules straddles her, deepening the kiss immediately, their tongues colliding wonderfully.

Riley holds her tightly as their kiss grows desperate, as if they're trying to make up for the lost time, as if they're trying to tell each other how much they've missed each other, how much they care.

"Jules." Riley lets the name escape through her swollen lips in a whisper.

She's tingling in her entire body, her eyes half-lidded when she looks up to watch Jules glance down on her.

The way the blonde's blue eyes are turning black, the way she allows those ragged breaths between kiss-bruised lips is a sight that Riley wants to remember forever.

Jules is fucking stunning. Addictive.

There's a spark between them the moment their lips touch again. There's a hunger building within Riley when she feels again just how soft, how hot Jules is.

Jules's hand flies up to cup Riley's jaw as she changes angles, her lips already parting mid-air.

And Riley catches her.

She catches her, feeling teeth sink into her bottom lip shortly before a tongue runs over it to soothe the subtle sting.

Fuck.

She digs her fingers into Jules's hips. She pulls her closer on instinct, even though it's quite impossible with their lying position.

She breathes deeply when she feels the blonde's tongue softly asking permission to enter and Riley is foolish enough to let her, again.

The moment their tongues collide, Riley knows she's in too deep. She feels too much, it's something that she feels with every fiber of her being, everything that she is.

Her entire body is aching for Jules, for more.

Riley can feel the moan bubbling up in her throat as she hungrily moves against Jules's hot mouth, feeling a leg slip between her own.

A throbbing heat forms between her legs, something she'd rather ignore, but it's impossible when a thigh is pressing against it deliciously. She's barely able to stop herself from rolling her hips into it.

She is unable to think rationally when her hands move around Jules's waist, pulling the blonde impossibly close as their lips slide together heatedly.

But then, the blonde pulls back just slightly, resting her forehead against Riley's.

"You have no idea how long I've been wanting to do that."

"How long?" Riley gasps for air, her hands reaching up to Jules's face, tucking blonde hair behind small, adorable ears.

She can't stop touching Jules. She doesn't want to stop touching her.
"Uhm... ever since you first started talking to me."
"That is months ago, Jules." Riley's eyes widen in realization.
Jules groans then, dropping her head on Riley's shoulder. "I know. But you have no idea just how sexy you are, do you?"
Instant heat rises to Riley's cheeks, a crimson color on the tips of her ears.
"It's not like I'm looking in the mirror each day and think – damn, I am hot." Riley rolls her eyes at herself, but she smiles when Jules's giggle sounds softly in her ear.
Jules's breath tickles her. The moment that chuckle disappears, lips attach right beneath the skin of Riley's ear.
The brunette inhales sharply, feeling goosebumps spread over her skin. It tickles, it sends tiny jolts of pleasure to inappropriate places, but she loves it.
Jules's lips are magical.
"Jules." She breathes then, hearing a low hum in her ear that drives her insane. "Fuck."
The moment Jules pulls back, Riley whimpers from the lack of lips on her skin.
Those blue eyes hover above her, that bite of bottom lip too much for her to see.
She has missed it all and she realizes just how badly her heart has been aching for this woman.
Riley can't help herself when she bites her lip, moaning softly when she lowers her hands to press Jules's hips into her own just a little more.
A hitch of breath has the blonde's throat bob in a dry swallow.
Their fronts pressed together, Riley's can feel her breath quicken, her heart speeding up again, rapidly.
"Riley, I want you." A shaky breath escapes Jules's parted lips, her blue eyes open again and the moment they meet green, neither woman is able to stop themselves from leaning in once again.
Riley's heart is in her throat when she tastes Jules again. She's so soft, so wet and wanting.
Her tongue twirls around Riley's with skill and the brunette doesn't think she'll ever feel anything better than this.
The kiss is filled with desperation on both ends, both women so eager to show their mutual affection, their attraction and their care.
They pour everything in that kiss and they can both feel it.
It's fucking home, to Riley.
It's exactly what she missed with Camilla.
It's everything

14

"Stay with me tonight."

Riley flutters her eyes open, meeting blue right above, a choky breath against her lips. She can't hold back anymore, but she has to be sure.

"Are you sure, Jules?" she hesitates.

"I am if you are." A shaky smile. Jules's voice is low and raw and Riley can feel the growing heat between her legs.

"Okay." She smiles back. She can feel the body weight of Jules on her own and it feels amazing.

It feels good to be able to show her affection, but she can't help herself when she's being careful in her every movement.

But Jules is bold when she leans back down, her lips parting halfway there and Riley catches her.

She catches her with her tongue, her teeth. She moans into the blonde's mouth, feeling Jules's hips start a soft grinding rhythm.

Fuck.

Riley's fucked. She is so, so fucked. She kisses Jules deeper, harder, with desperation that she has been feeling for several minutes now.

Her hands roam over the blonde's back, slowly trying to slide under a shirt. Riley pulls back though, wanting to watch Jules's reaction to her touches.

"You don't have to walk on eggshells around me, Riley." The blonde smiles, but her breathing is heavy.

Biting her bottom lip, Riley knows she's been caught. "I don't want to make you feel uncomfortable."

"You don't." blue eyes are soft, but Jules leans down to nudge Riley's face aside with her nose.

Breath tickles her neck. "Riley, you… I want you. I want to feel you and I want you to feel me, too."

Riley swallows away the lump in her throat when she can feel Jules's lips connect with the skin in her neck again.

"Isn't it too soon, though?"

That has Jules pulling back from her. Riley automatically whimpers at the loss of contact, making the blonde grin lightly as she sits up, straddling Riley's hips.

Riley sits up too, leaning on her hands while Jules cups her face.

Blue eyes search her face carefully. "You're not ready."

"I am." Riley smiles. She smiles brightly because she is ready. She wants this. "But we've only… it's only been a few hours since you're back and I think we should maybe talk first?"

Soft lips claim her own in an unrushed kiss.

Riley loses herself, though. She loses herself when she can feel the press of Jules's front against her own, those soft lips sliding with hers in a delicious rhythm.

Tongues starting to explore mouths more hungrily and Riley isn't sure if talking is entirely necessary anymore.

They part with a pop, their pupils blown.

"You're right." Jules admits in a whisper then, smiling softly when she pulls back. "We should talk."

Riley presses one last kiss against those addictive lips, before gently nudging Jules to sit on the couch, off her lap.

They sit, side by side, trying to catch their breaths, their lips bruised.

"I am not ready to be… anything." Riley admits then quietly, fumbling with her hands in her lap. "I want to be with you, physically and mentally, but I can't… I don't want to label anything."

Blue eyes are bright and understanding when they look into green. "I don't think I'd be ready for that, either."

"I don't want to rush it." Riley is grateful that Jules seems to understand. "But I know that… I care about you, Jules. I care and I want more, eventually."

A hand slides in Riley's own, squeezing softly in reassurance. Riley finds only then, that she's shaking.

Her body is trembling with nerves, and she knows she is afraid. She is afraid to start something, she is afraid of rejection and so much more. She's afraid that Jules won't agree and will fight her.

She hates that.

She still has a long road to go, but the soft way Jules's hand is in hers, is a reassurance that she didn't know she needed that desperately.

"Right before we broke contact…" Jules's voice is low, but soft. "…you asked me what I expected of you. I told you that I wanted you in my life, but that I didn't really know how."

Nodding carefully, Riley tries to stop her knee from bouncing, but she fails.

When Jules's thin thigh presses against her own, the warmth gives her enough comfort to stop.
"You did." Riley adds. "You told me you weren't ready yet."
"I wasn't ready then. The past weeks, I haven't only been processing my marriage with Liam. I haven't only been trying to recover from him, but I've been thinking about you." the honesty in Jules's voice is vulnerable, making Riley look at her. "I knew it the moment I saw you disappear into the elevator after Liam's trial – I want you to be more than a friend. But it scares me, Riley. You scare me."
A silence falls between them, but Riley manages to push away her nerves, tilting her head to the side to press her nose into Jules's cheek, softly asking for her attention.
When the blonde turns her head, their breaths mingle. "You don't have to do anything you don't want to, Jules. I… I want to be with you. But if you're not ready, then you're not ready."
"I am so ridiculously attracted to you." Jules's small laugh is low, but it falters when she leans in to slowly press her lips against Riley's. It's brief, their mouths barely moving, but it is enough to make Riley drop all her worries. But Jules continues. "I want you, too, but I think I agree with you. I am not ready to label anything. I think we both have to come to terms with what we have dealt with in the past."
"I am scared too, Jules." Riley's tremored breath escapes her parted lips when she hides her face in the crook of the blonde's neck.
She feels like she is about to cry, but the way Jules's arms snake around her shoulders and hold her close, it makes her feel stronger.
"I am scared because I… I am afraid I will fuck it up again." Riley murmurs. "I am afraid that I'm not able to change who I am. I'm afraid I will hurt you, that I'll leave you behind just like I did with Camilla."
An understanding hum comes from the other woman. Once again, they settle on the couch more comfortably, tangled in each other.
"If you keep talking to me the way you do, I think we'll be okay." Jules smiles then. She smiles and she lights up Riley's world with that.
The brunette isn't able to stop herself from smiling back, still stunned with the way Jules makes her feel.
She knows she hasn't felt this way before. It scares her, but she knows she can do it.
She knows she wants to.
"I just… I need to ask you something." Riley mumbles then. It has been on her mind the entire night.
"What is it?"
"Do you trust me enough to know I won't be another Liam?" she knows the question is rough.
Jules parts her lips to speak, but no words come out. Blue eyes turn sad

when Riley looks up.
She is gentle when she places her palm on Jules's soft cheek, thumb wiping away fresh tears.
"It's okay if you don't, I hope you know this, Jules." Riley assures her. "A spouse is someone you're supposed to trust the most. I can imagine that if that trust is broken the way it was with Liam, that it's hard to find again, even though if it isn't necessarily in marriage."
"I trust you." Jules blurts out.
"Do you say that because you want to trust me or because it's the truth?" green eyes search Jules's face for doubt, but the blonde shakes her head.
"I trust you, Riley. I am scared, because what I feel for you seems to be... so much stronger than whatever it was that I felt for Liam, and I don't trust myself with that." Jules whispers, reaching to tuck some loose strands of hair behind Riley's ear.
The blonde sighs deeply before she continues. "I don't trust myself, because I haven't been able to be myself for the past eight years, Riley. I am afraid that I will eventually trick myself into thinking that you're no different from Liam and that is not because I don't trust you. I... I don't really know how to explain it."
Taking in the words, it does make sense to Riley. "I think that I feel the same way. I have always had trust issues with everyone around me, even with Austin. I've always trusted you, though. I think it'd be wise to take things slow. If you want to be with me, that is."
"I want that." Jules cuts in before Riley has time to doubt it. "I want to be with you. Like I said, I feel strongly about you. You make me feel safe and alive and I want that. Being around you is... I don't know. It's really good."
They both smile when they lie further down, this time Riley being the one curled around Jules as she presses a soft kiss on the blonde's clothed shoulder.
She closes her eyes, lingering for a moment. She simply takes it in, slowly coming to terms that they're deciding to try and date. She inhales Jules's scent, smiling when she realizes it hasn't changed.
An arm around her shoulder presses her closer, lips on her forehead warm and soft.
Riley knows that what Jules has said, applies to her too. Even though she is afraid, she has never felt as safe with anyone as she has with Jules.
Some things just don't seem to matter as much when the blonde is near her, and no matter how terrifying this can be, Riley knows she wants it.
She wants Jules, as long as Jules wants her too.
The need to make sure that the blonde is okay is still there, and that is exactly why Riley tucks her arm around Jules's waist to press them closer together.
She brushes her hand over the blonde's stomach, slowly gauging Jules's

reaction when she slides a few fingers under her shirt near the hem of her jeans.

She can hear the sharp inhale; she can feel the grip around her shoulders tighten when she softly nudges on Jules's bare ribs to roll her on her side so that they are face to face.

Riley tries not to get lost in the feeling of that soft skin beneath her palm, her fingers.

"So, I think this is the right moment to ask you out on a date." Riley smiles softly when Jules's blue eyes sparkle.

"A date." Jules's smile grows.

"If you want to."

"I do."

"Good." She smiles.

Riley can't get enough. Their faces are so close, their breathing synchronized. Green eyes trace a wide jaw, sharp lips. The blush on Jules's cheeks, up to those blue eyes that Riley loves so much.

"Do you think... that over time, you'll be able to be yourself completely again?" Riley asks then.

"I am on my way, Riley. I am coming to terms with myself. And you... you help with that. You have never judged me, you've always been there." Jules whispers, almost playfully as if they're sharing a secret, just between the two of them. "You're you and you're amazing."

"And I think you're beautiful the way you are." She smiles. She knows it's cheesy, but she means every damn word.

She loves how Jules reaches for her face. She loves the softness she feels on her cheek as the blonde tucks brown baby hairs away.

"So, dating without labels then?" the blonde smiles.

"If it is up to me, then yes." Riley smiles right back. She loves how Jules leans in.

Their smiles meld together then in a pool of softness, hotness. They mingle together, sliding their lips together with more hunger every second.

Riley's hand is still beneath Jules's shirt, moving slowly to the blonde's back to press their bodies flush.

The brunette moans when their tongues fight softly, as she tries to explore Jules's mouth more thoroughly.

A leg is thrown over her hip and she lifts her thigh dangerously close against Jules's core.

The moan that comes up from the blonde's throat is doing too much to Riley. The heat between her legs begins to ache, her lips more desperate to find domination.

She moves, until Jules is tucked beneath her. She rolls her hips into Jules, unable to stop moaning when the blonde's hands grip on her ass to support her, to pull her closer.

Her breathing is heavy when she traces her lips along Jules's jaw, down to the delicious column of her throat. One hand frees dark curls before tangling into them.

"Fuck, Riley." Jules's voice is so low, so deep that Riley groans hearing it, feeling the vibrations beneath her lips as she works her way back up.

She recaptures the blonde's mouth with her own, their tongues tangling in a heated kiss.

Riley's grinds intensify, her hand beneath Jules's shirt searching for more.

But then, she pulls back.

"We should stop." She pants, trying to hold herself together. She doesn't think she's ever been this out of control, unable to stop.

"Should we, though?" Jules's pupils are blown when she opens her eyes. Her cheeks are flushed, her lips pink and so, so kissable.

"If we want to take it slow, then yes. I won't be able to stop if we go on now." It takes everything in Riley not to continue.

She wants more. She wants to explore Jules's body, she wants to know every wrinkle, every scar, every curve. She wants to make her feel good, she wants to worship her.

This desire within her, it's new. It makes her hungry and desperate and it scares her as much as it turns her on.

The feeling of Jules's hand in her hair is so fucking good, to be pressed against her is just... it's overwhelming and beautiful and Riley wants it more.

But not now.

She bites her lip, trying to hide her smile when she smoothly removes herself from Jules.

The blonde whines softly, trying to chase after her subconsciously, but holds back a chuckle when she sits up, too.

"You're beautiful." Jules murmurs then, pressing her lips to Riley's cheek when the brunette is about to get up from the couch.

She remains seated, though, smiling when she crashes her lips against Jules's one last time.

It's brief, but it's hot enough for Riley to feel it in her entire being.

Her lips remain parted when she pulls back, her gaze plastered to Jules's mouth. "You take my breath away. Quite literally, actually."

Another chuckle from Jules, two arms around Riley's shoulders and they hug.

They hug, holding each other close for a moment, before the brunette pulls away.

"I'll text you?"

"Yeah." Blue eyes twinkle.

Riley smiles when she rises from the couch, searching her blazer. She tucks her button up into her slacks.

She checks the watch on her wrist, snorting to herself when she realizes it's in the middle of the night.

"Do you have to work tomorrow?" the brunette asks when she grabs her things, smiling when Jules hesitantly follows her to the front door.

"Yes. Noon till midnight."

Riley hesitates, too. She watches Jules walk closer to her, smiling when she realizes that she now finally knows what it feels like to have those lips on her own.

It's the best feeling in the world, really.

"Okay. I hope you have a good day tomorrow, Jules. We'll be in touch." The brunette leans in softly.

She can't wipe the dopey smile from her face when Jules's hands fly up to hold her head close to the blonde's as their lips connect in the softest kiss so far.

It's delicate, it's a silent goodbye for the day.

When they part, their foreheads lean together.

"Bye, Riley." Jules's breath is warm.

"Bye, Jules." Riley pulls away, opening the door.

She doesn't really look back when she makes her way to the elevator, but once there, she can see Jules standing in the doorway, leaning against the wall casually, her arms crossed.

The smile on the blonde's face makes Riley's heart topple in her chest. She's so... overflowing with admiration and more, she can't even describe it to herself what it is that she's feeling.

She's just intensely happy with the way things are going so far. She realizes how good it is to have Jules back in her life, now seeming to be more permanent than ever before.

And it feels good.

One of the first new things that Riley learns about Jules, is that she is a childlike, free and open-minded spirit.

To think that Jules has been trapped inside an abusive relationship, stuck for more than eight years... it breaks Riley's heart all over again.

That Jules hasn't been able to be her dorky self, her happy self. Riley almost can't take that thought as she looks at the blonde in the kitchen of Austin's apartment, laughing at her own joke while Austin shakes his head in subtle amusement.

Jules is beautiful. It is amazing to be around, because Jules is so much more than Riley thought she'd be.

And even though she might have not seen Jules in her element like this before, it warms her heart to think that the surgeon feels comfortable enough around them now.

That she's comfortable enough to joke around, to tell some lame college stories. To try and get River to talk about his past, too, to share stories that'll entertain them.

That she isn't able to stop laughing, to stop smiling. It looks so incredibly good on her and Riley wonders how much happiness the blonde has to make up for.

The brunette's heart simply does flips in her chest when she hears that bark of laughter, when she sees the blonde hide a chuckle behind her hand or when Jules manages to make River grin like a fool.

It is amazing, and Riley simply can't stop observing, wanting to make sure that Jules keeps that smile on her face, that playfulness in twinkling cerulean eyes.

And Riley feels pretty happy, too. It does good things to her to know that they have become closer, that they have been able to show their mutual feelings.

Riley can only hope that Jules knows how much she means to the brunette.

One of the best parts is that Jules trusts them. She trusts Riley, and the fact that the brunette gets to see it like this, it makes her heart flutter.

"You are so fucking smitten." Austin joins her on his couch while River takes over the work in the kitchen.

Riley snaps her eyes to look into brown, watching the amused grin on her brother's face grow.

"What?"

"You are smitten. So is she." He winks then, his hand on Riley's shoulder to give it a subtle squeeze. "How are the two of you?"

"We're good." The smile on Riley's lips refuses to leave, the warmth settling in her stomach lowly, and she knows it'll probably never leave.

Ever since that first night Jules returned, they haven't done much more than just kissing. Riley has yet to take the blonde on the date she asked, because they both have chaotic schedules.

Tonight though, it is nice for them to be around familiar people, people that they're both comfortable around.

They need the time to adjust to the fact that they both know how attracted they are to each other, how much they care. They have seen too much to simply jump in quickly and Riley wants to make sure that she won't make the same mistakes she has before.

The lawyer catches Jules's curious gaze from Austin's kitchen, blue and big, accentuated by that radiant and happy smile that Riley lives for.

"Are you official yet?"

"No." Riley shakes her head, pulling one leg underneath her other knee, slouching a bit when she focuses on her brother. "We have decided to take things slow. You know, since we've both come out of crappy marriages and we just don't want to jump in too soon."

"Smart." Austin smiles then. "I am happy for you, Riley. I don't think I've ever seen you like this before."

"Like what?" she raises a curious eyebrow, running a hand through her straightened hair.

"Happy. You are smiling like a dork and you can't keep your eyes off her. You look really happy and… I can't remember you ever looking like that. Not even with Camilla."

For a moment, Riley's heart drops to her stomach at the mention of her ex-wife. She bites her lip, starts fumbling with her hands in her lap.

It's been a while since she's really thought about Camilla, about their relationship. She knows for sure that whatever it is she's feeling for Jules is so much stronger than what it ever was with Camilla.

She knows this.

But still, she's afraid. She's afraid that this will end up in heartbreak, that she will make the same mistakes she has made in the past.

She doesn't want to break Jules's heart. She's trying so hard, not to become the person she once was.

She doesn't trust herself when it comes to close relationships, not fully able to pour her soul into it. Not yet.

She will get there, she is sure of it, but until she can't, she wants to make sure that she and Jules are on the same page.

"Don't worry about it, Riley." His hand squeezes her again. "I know that history won't repeat itself."

"How would you know that, Aus?" she looks at him, quite helplessly. She has been too afraid to talk to Jules about this, especially since they aren't officially anything just yet.

"Because I know you. I see you. I have eyes, you know." he grins. "You have changed. Ever since you met Jules, I think that you've grown into a wonderful person, that you've started to see your own limits and that you're working on yourself."

"Yeah?"

"Yes. And I think you and I both know you'd go to the ends of the earth for this woman." He subtly motions his head towards where Jules is now focused on cooking, her eyebrows furrowed, her tongue peeking out in concentration.

With a sigh, Riley runs her hand over her face, before leaning her chin on her hand, elbow on the back of the couch as she looks at the woman she can't get out of her mind.

"Look, Riley. Jules isn't Camilla, okay? I think Jules is more important to you already that Camilla ever was. The fact you are taking things slow, trying to communicate, that's good, right?"

Nodding quietly, Riley smiles when she receives a playful wink from River.

"Yeah, I think it's good. But what if that changes? What if I just… fall back into old habits?"

"Riley, tell Jules what is going on, you know? You don't have to tell her how you feel instantly, as long as you tell her what is going on, whenever you need time. Talking about feelings isn't easy, and if you need time, then you need time. Remember to tell her that if it ever comes to that, yeah? Communication like that is important in relationships." He softly nudges her shoulder, making her look at him.
She knows he's right. He's always right.
"Just keep talking to her and you will be fine. If you ever need time, she'll give that to you. If she needs time, you'll give that to her, too." He says easily.
His brown eyes are sparkling when she looks into them with a soft smile.
"Thank you. How's your dating life?"
"I'm too busy with our restaurant to start dating." He huffs then, making Riley chuckle to herself.
"But you do have time to spend with us?"
"That's different." Another huff. He rolls his eyes when Riley wiggles her eyebrows.
"How is that different?" she teases him, loving the way a subtle blush creeps onto his cheeks. "You met someone."
"I didn't!" his eyes grow wide, but Riley can tell that he's lying.
She grins widely. "I hope you know I won't judge."
"I know." his sigh is small, but a small smile hugs his lips then. "I've been dating this girl."
"Yeah? How is she?"
"She's good. She's really good." His smile only grows.
Riley can only mirror his happy expression. She knows that this look means that he might be in deeper than he realizes.
"You know her."
Choking on air, Riley's eyes grow wide. "Uhm, what? Who is it?"
"Aurelia Brooks."
For a moment, Riley stops in her motions. Austin, dating her associate?
"We met on Tinder." He continues then, looking insecure about the entire thing.
Scraping her throat, Riley smiles then. "Well, I like her. You knew that Aurelia and I work together?"
"Yeah, the moment she knew my last name, something clicked." He still eyes Riley like he's doubting if he did the right thing by telling her.
"That is… major coincidence. In a city filled with millions of women, you choose her?" she teases then, feeling her skin wrinkle beside her eyes in amusement.
The relief washing over Austin's face then is adorable.
"Don't worry about it, okay? I am happy for you as long as you're happy with her." She encourages him more. "She's a good person."

A mean grin then forms on Austin's lips. "She is. She told me that you have quite the reputation at the office."

Rolling her eyes, Riley groans while she slouches further into the couch.

"What's going on?" Jules suddenly plops down beside Riley, her hand dropping on the brunette's thigh casually.

"Nothing at all." Riley leans her head back, still groaning because she knows what is coming next. This will haunt her for the rest of her days.

"We were just talking about how Riley's being called 'Commander' at her office." Austin leans closer to Jules then, completely ignoring Riley sitting in the middle.

"Guys, I'm right here." She pushes them aside, loving the way both Jules and Austin have playful twinkles in their eyes.

"Do tell?" Jules laughs, her thumb softly caresses Riley's clothed knee.

"She's a hardass."

"I have to be, I'm a boss." Riley fights them. "Can we please talk about something else?"

"Oh no, I am interested." Jules leans back, subtly placing herself against Riley's side.

The small gesture sends chills down Riley's spine while she watches Austin sit up to start talking.

But Riley throws her head back on the rest of the couch, grinning when she feels Jules's hand tuck a strand of hair away from her face.

"There is nothing to tell, guys."

"She commands everyone at work. Like she owns the place."

"This is extremely exaggerated." She whines, trying to push Austin away.

"And do tell Austin, how would you even know this?"

"From a secret source." His eyebrows wiggle.

"Oh, come on guys, this is not a surprise." River suddenly cuts in, laughing when he hears Riley's loud groan.

"It is, actually." Jules's deep voice is close to Riley's ear. "You're all soft with us, but not at the office - so it seems. I am very curious."

"It's necessary in our line of work, Gibson." Riley lifts her head from the couch, glancing between her family. "Please. Drop it?"

"Fine, fine." Austin raises his hands in amusement.

"Aus, I need your help." River grins then, motioning to the kitchen.

Riley watches as they make their way back to work on dessert, preparing it while they make small talk, leaving the two women on the couch.

"Hey." Jules smiles then, her elbow leaning on the rest as she faces the brunette.

"Hi." Riley's smile grows. She can feel a hand tangle in her hair softly, making her lean into it. "They missed you."

"I missed them, too." Jules smiles, pressing herself just a little closer. Then, she tilts her head to whisper in Riley's ear. "Not as much as I missed you, though."

The brunette tries to hold back a shudder, but she fails miserably when Jules's lips wrap around her tiny earlobe, a breath tickling her in her neck.

"Jules." Riley warns slowly, not daring to move even an inch.

When the blonde pulls back, a grin is on her face. "Commander mode?"

"Oh, stop it." Riley hides her face behind her hands, leaning into Jules, only to feel arms wrap around her and a press of soft lips against her temple.

She smiles then, looking up to meet blue eyes close to her own.

Jules's smile is just as wide, a gaze flickering between Riley's eyes and her lips.

"Guys, dinner is ready!" Austin calls then, grinning when he notices the two women on the couch.

"Right." Riley can't tear her gaze away from Jules's face, her eyes tracing the wide cheekbones, her jaw, to the dimple in her chin. Then, to those soft lips she remembers kissing, tasting like heaven.

She doesn't notice Jules doing the exact same thing, not until pink lips briefly press on her own before the blonde pulls back with a mixture of mischief and darkness in her eyes.

Riley breathes then, abruptly rising from the couch to join her brother and her best friend at the dining table.

This is going to be a long night.

She's been a nervous wreck all fucking day. She had no court, she's just at the office and she just… she is losing her mind.

She can't fucking date.

She hasn't dated in… ever.

She didn't even date Camilla, they were just friends that turned into more and she never asked her out, she never reserved dinner at a silly restaurant before.

And yet, she asked Jules on a date.

So. Fucking. Stupid.

It feels stupid. She doesn't even know if Jules would like what she has chosen for them and she hates that she has let it occupy her mind all fucking day.

"You have to stop that." Aurelia grunts as they work on a case together, doing mostly paperwork and some research.

They are in the small library of the building and Riley's knees have been bouncing ever since she sat down.

"I don't have to do anything. You, however, have to prepare this case." Riley mumbles when she watches Aurelia's piercing green eyes.

"Seriously, Dunn, what the hell is going on with you?" Aurelia tucks her black hair in a ponytail, an amused grin on her face.

"Nothing." Riley shakes her head, shoving her glasses further up her nose as she tries to focus on the file she has in front of her.

"She's going on a date tonight, that is what is going on." Tessa suddenly pops up from behind, placing her hands on Riley's shoulder to annoyingly lean over the brunette.

"Fuck you, Tessa." Riley grunts. She hates this. She hasn't felt like this in ages.

"She's a nervous wreck because she's taking a pretty girl out to have dinner with her tonight." The Asian lawyer continues when she sees the satisfied smirk on Aurelia's face.

Riley tries to shrug off Tessa's hands. "I hate you."

"Nah, you love me. Your brother loves me, too. Everyone loves me." She laughs then. "Seriously, it's been a while since we've all been together. You should invite them to the gala."

"Gala?" Riley looks puzzled.

"Yes, Dunn. The annual beneficial gala? You know, the yearly event that we hold to raise awareness? To raise money and meet sponsors? It's in… a month, give or take." Tessa sits down next to Aurelia and the two share a high five.

"Seriously, are you guys twelve?" Riley rolls her eyes, crossing her knees.

"You're avoiding the subject." The Asian blonde rolls her eyes, while Aurelia tries to hide a chuckle behind her hand.

Riley just sends a stern glare at the younger lawyer, instantly making her shut up.

"Whoa commander, calm down, Brooks did nothing wrong." Tessa grins, way too satisfied with the look of horror on Riley's face.

She snickers, throwing her head back and Riley sometimes wonders how on earth Tessa can be such an amazing lawyer while she's really just a childish person, taking nothing too seriously.

"Commander?" Riley asks carefully. "You're really using that?"

Aurelia raises her eyebrows, quickly taking a sip of her bottle of water to avoid Riley's stern gaze.

"Yeah, did you really think I was joking about that?" The blonde shrugs, leaning her forearm on the backrest of Aurelia's chair.

"Aurelia?" Riley seeks confirmation.

"Well, it's true. You can… look quite commanding when you're focused. You order everyone around you, you command in court and it's… intimidating. So yeah, we call you commander."

Riley can feel a proud grin creep up her lips. She then lets out a satisfied hum. "Good."

Aurelia almost chokes on air, probably not having expected such a response.

"Good? Riley, people fear you."

"So Tessa has told me." She laughs then, grateful for the distraction of her

date tonight.
"Everyone would do everything for you around here. With the exception of Sean and maybe Tessa. Although I'm pretty sure she'd run for you, too." Aurelia reasons then and Riley is amused to see that the black-haired girl seems comfortable enough around them.
Tessa lets out a huff at that, rolling her eyes when she drops herself on the chair beside Riley.
"Exactly. I have minions." Riley jokes with a steel face, making Tessa snort until she's trying to hide the laughter that sounds like a bloody seal.
Riley lets out a snort of laughter as well, making Aurelia chuckle, too.
It's good, to have a connection like this.
It's light, it's not too personal, but personal enough to be comfortable around each other. Exactly what they need on a Friday afternoon.
The three women laugh for a moment, until Tessa's teasing face is back on.
"So, shouldn't you go home and get ready for that hot chick of yours?"
"Firstly, Jules isn't just a 'hot chick'." Riley huffs in annoyance. "Secondly, she isn't mine and thirdly; I'd prefer to keep things… private."
"Oh, lighten up commander. It's not like this is a fancy firm like the one you once worked for. We're family here. Plus, isn't lovely Brooks here dating your brother?" Tessa rolls her eyes.
At that, Aurelia's cheeks turn pink, making Riley hide a smile.
When she checks the time on her watch, she realizes that it is indeed time to go home and get ready.
Tessa's gaze softens when they meet green eyes. "I hope that things work out for you this time, Dunn."
Riley grabs her things, smiling hopefully towards her colleagues.
"Me, too."

She thinks she's going to throw up. Why the fuck does she have such a weak stomach when it comes to her own feelings? Why is she feeling this nervous when they already shared a few kisses, intimate moments? When they've talked?
Why does a date feel so much differently from just hanging out? She is losing her mind.
She is insecure, worrying that Jules will change her mind about liking Riley. What if she turns out to find her annoying? Or too quiet? Too introverted?
She just showered, she is wearing the towel around her hair and she has a bathrobe on and she just… she's panicking.
She is panicking because how could she ever be good enough for Jules? How could she ever live up to the blonde's expectations?
She isn't Liam, but she's never dated before and the only relationship she did have turned out to be one, big, giant fiasco.
She tries to talk to herself in the mirror, but she can't take herself seriously.

She watches herself.
She's thirty-five. She's had her best years. Is she still beautiful? Would Jules still find her attractive?
She doesn't have much wrinkles, just a bit around her eyes, but nothing more than that. Her skin is still pretty glowy for her age and she's tanned up a bit.
Her green eyes are still bright as they used to be, her lips still full. She still looks the same as she did ten years ago.
Right?
Her nose is still small and long, her ears haven't dropped half an inch.
She rolls her eyes at herself. She's thirty-five, not fucking seventy.
She just hopes that Jules will find her at least attractive.
Because Jules is… she's out of Riley's league, the brunette is pretty sure about that.
Jules is beautiful, she doesn't look like she is turning thirty-five soon.
She still has a young skin and a good body. Riley scolds herself for being able to remember the blonde's body. She has been checking her out like a horny teenager.
Fuck.
She doesn't even know what to wear. She doesn't even know what make up and… shoes…
She's just a fucking mess.
She calls her brother.
"Riley? Aren't you on your date with Jules?" his voice is just as mischievous as Tessa's had been before and she rolls her eyes.
"I need your help."
"With what?"
"I don't have an outfit!"
"You'll be fine, Riley." Austin sounds amused. "She's been sending heart-eyes your way too much now, so I think that it wouldn't matter at all what you're wearing."
"Aus." Riley sighs. "I am freaking out."
"Hey, I am not the person you should call, okay? I'm a dude. Call River."
"But River's a dude, too." She whines, not understanding why he won't help her.
"But he's into that stuff. Call him, he isn't working tonight. And Riley?"
"Hmm?"
"You'll be fine. I've seen the way she looks at you. Goodluck. I love you!" he hangs up before she has a chance to say more.
She calls River, after contemplating if she should really do it or not. But he seems really happy that she called him and tells her that he is on his way.
She quickly dries her body further, putting on her underwear. She isn't ashamed of her body, she takes runs each morning since a couple of

months and she doesn't eat excessively.

She wouldn't mind River seeing her like this, but she still wraps the robe around her body, drying her hair while she waits for him to arrive.

Her curls are wild and natural when she finishes to blow it dry.

River arrives then and she hurries to open the door for him. He grins like a proud father when he sees her, leaning in to give her a chaste kiss on her cheek.

"Let me see that wardrobe." He keeps grinning as he follows her to her closet. "Anything you had in mind?"

"Uhm, just not too professional but not too casual either. I just... I want to look pretty." She admits, enjoying the way River goes through her closet.

Sometimes, she wonders how he and Austin are best friends. River looks like a tough guy, but he's such a sweetheart and yes, sometimes he can be... so obviously gay. And Austin is quite the opposite.

But then again, they match pretty well and they always joke around like they're long lost brothers and she just loves that.

River doesn't speak. Instead, he throws a few pieces of clothing her way, ordering her to try it on.

She obliges easily, slipping on the broken white, soft slacks that have wide pipes. She tucks in the navy blouse he has given her, rolling up the sleeves until right under her elbows.

"And these shoes." He gives her a pair of navy high heels.

"That's it?" her eyes grow wide when she looks at herself in the mirror. She still has to do her make up, but River has managed to give her a combination of clothes she never even considered before.

She looks good.

"Yup. Oh, go for subtle eyeliner. Your green eyes will pop that way." His eyes sparkle then as he moves to stand behind her to look into her eyes through the mirror. "You're a beautiful woman, Riley. I may be gay, but I'm not blind. Jules will love whatever it is you're wearing."

"That might be, but I'm hiring you to be my personal advisor from now on." She laughs, quickly moving to the bathroom to apply her make up.

She has half an hour left before she has to go and pick up Jules from her apartment a few blocks away.

"What do I do with my hair?" she questions when she's done with her make up.

"Leave it like this."

"Like this? But I never wear it... naturally." Riley scrunches up her nose in disgust when she realizes her messy, heavy curls, but River shakes his head.

"You have amazing hair, Riley. Just listen to me."

Once again, she obliges. She does add a little oil to make it smoother, but she doesn't change a thing.

She grabs simple, golden jewelry and then she's ready to go.

She is almost as tall as River with these heels.

"Thank you for your help." She smiles at him, pulling him into a hug. "Thank you for being there, for me, for Aus. It means a lot."

"Oh, but Austin is family, Riley. He's always been there. And you are my family, too. I hope you know that." He holds her tightly, before smiling proudly.

He ruffles her hair teasingly, making her squeal in surprise. "My hair!"

His laugh is loud and bright as they make their way out of Riley's apartment, on their way down.

They part ways, River taking a cab to his own place, but not after Riley hugs him again, thanking him for showing up.

She feels confident in her outfit, she feels convinced that Jules will like it. She just has to face it.

So, she takes her own cab, on her way to the apartment.

She rings the bell, only to be buzzed into the building, taking the elevator up.

She breathes deeply. She still isn't sure if this is the right thing to do, but she wants it.

She knows she wants it.

She remembers Camilla's words, from the day of their divorce months ago. She remembers how Camilla pointed out that she would find it.

Love.

Riley can only pray that perhaps… she can find it with Jules. She wants to.

She knows she already feels stronger for Jules than she ever has for Camilla. But, she doesn't know how Jules feels, she doesn't know what the future holds.

She hopes it can grow into something amazing, something that will make them both better people.

But for now, she can't think past today.

She trembles when she reaches Jules's door. She knocks quietly, only to panic after because she didn't bring fucking flowers.

She forgot flowers. It is fucking dating 101, knowing to take flowers and she didn't and she is such an inconsiderate idiot.

She didn't bring flowers and Jules might think that… oh.

Oh.

The door opens. Riley's eyes widen, her jaw drops and she just mesmerized. Hypnotized, even. For a moment she is frozen, her heart beating rapidly in her chest.

She allows herself to breathe then, hoping she doesn't come across as a stupidly staring moron.

It's almost unfair how beautiful the blonde is right now.

She realizes that she has never seen Jules in anything other than scrubs or relaxed at-home outfits. The only exception had been her dress in court, but it's nothing compared to now.

Jules looks fucking stunning. She's wearing a simple, navy dress, matching Riley's outfit. It has long sleeves, and it drapes loosely around her body.

Her toned legs are revealed until about halfway up her thighs and she's wearing heels that make her just as tall as Riley is right now.

But what captures Riley the most is just her smile. Her smile so bright, so wide, Riley doesn't think she's seen it like this before.

She is so, so fucking beautiful.

"Wow, I…" Riley bites her bottom lip, almost shyly. "Jules, you look… my god, you look so beautiful. But I didn't bring flowers."

Jules grins then amusedly, taking one step closer. "Why would you bring me flowers?"

"Because that is what… well, isn't that the… cliché?" Riley really has to hold herself together as she watches Jules step closer.

She can't move, her eyes glued to blue.

"You look amazing, Riley." The blonde then breathes. Before Riley knows it, their fronts are pressed together and Riley doesn't think she's ever felt this high.

"Jules." She swallows away her name, unable to move, still.

"Are you going to kiss me, now?" the blonde teases, her hands moving up to rest on Riley's hips, softly pulling their bodies closer together.

Riley can feel the blonde's breath teasing her lips. She can feel every fucking thing.

She's intoxicated.

"Am I not supposed to kiss you after the date?" oh, so she can talk properly after all.

Jules's hands burn on her hips and Riley isn't sure what to do with her own. She's never felt like this. She's never been so fascinated by someone before. She's never been able to feel like fire is fueling her veins before.

She's never felt this kind of connection, this kind of chemistry and it is fucking with her head.

She can't think. She can only allow herself to push oxygen into her lungs, her hands shaking when she reaches up to cup Jules's face.

She's terrified.

But the way those blue eyes stare into her own, the way Jules wets her lips, she can't hold back.

She can't stop herself when she lets their shaky breaths mingle, when she can feel the warmth of the blonde on her face.

Their noses bump. Riley lets out another tremored breath, but this time she finds the courage to close the remaining distance between them.

The moment their mouths connect, Riley can literally feel her legs go numb. She can feel the burn of those soft, hot lips on her own.

This is all she's ever wanted. Needed.

It feels like she's kissing her for the first time all over again, except this is different, somehow.

She can't stop her subtle smile as she softly opens her mouth, allowing Jules in and it's the best feeling she's ever had the privilege of having.

It's slow, it's soft and the feeling of Jules's tongue in her own mouth is almost too much.

She tastes like mint, like strawberry chap stick. She tastes like Jules and Riley can't stop herself when she deepens the kiss, changing angles more desperately, the need to be closer growing with every heartbeat.

Their teeth clash, but neither woman minds. Their tongues crash together, their lips move hotly, it's pure and passionate.

It leaves them breathless. Riley can feel Jules's fingers dig into her hips. She can feel hands lift her blouse from her slacks.

She can feel fingers brushing her bare skin, slowly teasing her right under her ribcage.

She can't breathe when the kiss turns hot and they stumble into Jules's apartment, unable to disconnect from each other.

Her heart is fucking racing and she just needs to feel Jules everywhere. She needs her pressed against her.

It's like Jules can read her mind as Riley is being pushed against the closed door with a thud and their bodies connect, as close as possible.

The blonde lets out a moan when Riley sucks Jules's bottom lip between her own, before meeting parted lips again, a soft tongue ready to catch hers. It's messy, it's hot but it's perfect.

But then, Jules pulls back, her breaths heavy. She leans her forehead against Riley's, their noses touching.

"If we don't stop now, I don't think we'll ever get to our date." Jules breathes then, her voice raspy and an octave lower than Riley is used to and it fucks with her.

She's just on fire, really.

"I wouldn't mind." Riley whispers in return, making sure that the blonde is okay.

She tucks some hair behind Jules's ears, only now realizing that her hands have been tangled in short, blonde hair, making it messier than it was before.

Riley moves her hands to Jules's cheeks and the brunette is gentle when she caresses the skin.

Her cheeks flush at her desperation to have Jules close.

"You're... fuck, you are so beautiful." The blonde's pupils are blown. She doesn't seem to know where she has to look, her eyes roaming Riley's face.

"Yeah?" Riley smiles shyly, still enjoying the feeling of Jules's body against her own.

The playful scoff Jules lets out is unexpected. "Have you seen you, Riley?

I'm just surprised you don't make a living out of being so gorgeous."
Riley lets out a nervous laugh, biting her bottom lip. "We should go."
The lawyer misses her warmth the moment the blonde steps away from her. She is just... unable to look away. Unable to stop herself from admiring Jules.
Yeah, okay, she might already feel way more than she thought she did.
She loves her.
She loves Jules.
And she isn't afraid to show it.

Jules is... funny. She is actually a very funny and bright person when she feels safe, Riley finds out.
All those burdens, those times Jules looked like she carried so much with her, it has disappeared completely and it makes her so stunning.
Riley can feel her cheeks ache because she seems unable to stop smiling at Jules's childlike enthusiasm.
It's amazing. They are seated at a French restaurant not all too far from the blonde's apartment and Riley isn't able to look away from the beauty across from her.
She barely cares about what she picks for dinner, she just leans her chin on her hand, looking at the woman across from her, listening to some of her stories.
Jules is open.
She's free.
That realization hits Riley hard as they talk, trying to discover each other.
And Riley wants to know it all. She learns that Jules loves food and hates exercising.
She learns that Jules would've preferred to become an artist, but being a surgeon is something she would never give up. She gets to save lives and she tells Riley how much that means to her.
And Riley admires her for that.
She discovers that Jules is just an amazing person. Her favorite color seems to change every day, she doesn't have a favorite dish, that also changes regularly.
She's openminded, hectic and refreshing and Riley loves it all.
The blonde is caring and selfless and she doesn't seem to think she is. But Riley can see it.
She can hear it in the stories Jules tells her. Stories about her childhood, about how she met Emma in college.
About her father's death and how it changed her.
About the newfound relationship she has with her mother, much like Riley is rebuilding hers with Austin.
And Jules asks Riley, too.

The brunette finds herself talking more than she ever has. She loves the way Jules's eyes light up when she tells her stories about college, about how she'd sneak Austin into night-clubs, how they'd do things together – sometimes illegal, sometimes not.

How things changed after her parents permanently kicked her out and how it affected her. How it felt when her dad returned and she told him she forgave him.

She tells Jules how she got into law in the first place – the need to be able to stand up for people without a voice large, but fading once she found out the temptations of career and money.

How she stopped caring about her job along the way and found that passion again after her divorce.

Riley tells Jules that her favorite color is the subtle orange mixed with pink that often appears in the sky during sunrises.

She tells her that her favorite dish is pancakes with half a bottle of syrup and the blonde laughs at her.

And it is good. It is amazing to share and to feel so appreciated. She has never felt this way.

She feels shy when somewhere during dinner, she reaches over the table to thread her fingers through Jules's and the blonde starts playing with her fingers, as she had done that night at Grounders.

She feels shyer when the blonde sends a confident smile her way, a smile that is almost seductive and causes something to stir in her lower stomach.

She's so weak for this woman and she loves it.

They forget about the time.

"I can't believe that Austin made you do that." Jules holds her stomach in laughter when Riley tells her another college story with Austin.

"Well, he was too shy to do it." Riley hides a grin behind her glass, loving how Jules's laugh settles in her heart.

"And then she kissed you. That's amazing." The blonde shakes her head, trying to hide her giggles.

"I thought he'd be furious, but he laughed instead. Told me he couldn't believe that my gaydar was so terribly bad I couldn't even notice that girl being obviously gay. Then I told him the same thing." Riley chuckle along.

Those were really good times.

They fall quiet for a bit, both too much in thought.

"Uhm, excuse me? I don't want to bother you two lovely ladies, but we are soon closing." Their waiter of the nightstands beside their table, hands clasped behind his back.

"Oh, of course. Can I get the check?" Riley instantly sits up, reaching into her purse to grab her wallet.

"I got this." Jules shakes her head, but Riley insists.

"I was the one to ask you on a date. It's only fair that I pay."

"But you paid at Grounders, too." Jules pouts, looking adorable as ever.
"But this is an official date." She insists.
The blonde's eyes sparkle when she obliges.
Riley quickly pays, before rising from her seat. "Need to go to the restroom before we go?"
"I'm good." Jules shakes her head, smiling when she softly bumps her hip with Riley's.
Their hands find each other's the moment they step outside, their fingers lacing together.
"Hey, can I show you something?" Riley asks then, almost shyly. She isn't quite ready to go home yet, she's enjoying this way too much.
"Always." Jules's free hand wraps around Riley's bicep and she holds the grip the blonde has on her now, holding her close.
The brunette stops a cab then, letting Jules go in first.
The blonde remains in the middle to make sure they're pressed up together. Riley is smooth when she slides her arm around Jules's shoulder, loving how they lean into each other instantly.
"Roosevelt Island, please. South side." She tells the driver.
"Roosevelt Island? Isn't that very touristy?" the blonde smiles.
"Have you ever been?"
"No."
"Then it isn't touristy enough." Riley smiles, placing a kiss on Jules's temple.
It feels good to be able to do this. For so long, even before Jules left, she's been holding back.
She has been wanting to touch her, to be able to show her how much she cares and the fact she gets to do that now is amazing.
"The view from there is amazing, especially now that it's getting dark." Riley smiles while she nudges her nose against Jules's cheek, her head tilted to the side.
The surgeon turns her head then, softly pressing her lips to Riley's.
She can never get used to this feeling. The kiss is soft and innocent, but it has both women smiling like mushy teenage girls in love.
The ride isn't all too long. Before they know it, they're dropped on the south side of the island and Riley guides the blonde to a bench near the edge, offering them an amazing view over the skyline across the river.
The wind is warm enough for them to still be out here, even though the sun has set.
Jules buries herself into Riley's side as they sit, both quite stunned by the view they have.
"It's different from the roof." The blonde mumbles, one arm around Riley's waist.
"It is." She hums in agreement.

The blonde bites her bottom lip then, as if she's collecting the courage to say something. "I… I had a thing for you the moment I saw you, Riley. You made me feel things I hadn't felt in a long time."

"Is that a good thing?"

"God, yes. You gave me hope when I thought there wasn't any. You gave me courage to make a decision and leave Liam a letter to tell him I was leaving him." Jules's voice is lower than usual in its vulnerability. "You made me feel like I was more important that I thought I was."

"You are important, Jules." Riley adds quickly. Her voice is soft, her fingers underneath Jules's chin to make sure the blonde hears this. "I'm so happy that you chose to get away from him because you deserve so much better. You're amazing and I… I feel so strongly for you."

The sad smile on Jules's face means everything. "I know I just came waltzing back into your life… but I want to stay, if you'll let me."

"You needed that time, Jules. I would wait for you forever if I had to." She admits quietly.

"You're amazing."

Sighing with a smile, Riley looks back at Jules. Her eyes trace the column of her neck, up to her wide jaw, the dimple in her chin. Her wide cheekbones, that tiny nose and those big, sky-blue eyes. "God, I wish I could look at you forever. You're so beautiful."

"Flatter." Jules softly leans in to press her smile against Riley's.

She could get lost in this woman. She wants to get lost in Jules.

"It's true, you are beautiful, Jules. Sometimes I can't explain the way I feel, the way I'm wired, but you make things seem so clear." She knows she's being sappy.

She knows she is. But the way Jules's smile fades, the way her eyes lower to Riley's lips tells the brunette that the other woman might not mind at all.

A mouth crashes against her own before she knows it, but she smoothly catches it. She can feel Jules's emotions.

She can sense it behind those quivering lips, that hesitating tongue that demands access.

She can feel it in the way Jules grips onto her face, holding her in place as if she's afraid Riley will leave.

Like she would.

And Riley reciprocates with just as much. She wants Jules to know how much she cares, she wants to know how important the blonde is to her.

When Jules pulls back, they part with a soft pop, their breaths heavy, their foreheads pressed together.

Jules's soft hands on her cheeks are comforting her in ways she didn't know Jules could.

She didn't even know she needed comfort. Perhaps she's been trying to show Jules she wouldn't leave, that she wouldn't hurt her but maybe, just maybe, she's been seeking the same thing.

Because she doesn't want this to end. Not now and not ever, not when Jules feels like home.

"I should take you home." Riley smiles softly, feeling a hot breath on her lips.

Jules leans in again, this time a lingering peck.

How good it feels to know how Jules tastes, how she smells, how she feels... Riley wants to remember this forever.

"Yeah." The blonde pulls back then.

They rise from the bench they had been occupying, slowly making their way to the road, their heels clicking in sync.

Riley's arm around Jules's waist, she holds her close. As if she's unable to let go now that she knows how it feels to have this woman by her side.

They are able to stop a cab, leading them back to Jules's apartment building. It's quiet, as they lean against each other. They glance outside, smiling to themselves.

When they arrive at Jules's building, Riley pays the driver and guides Jules outside, into her building and up to her floor.

"Do you want to come in?" the blonde asks then softly, her free hand fiddling with her keys, her other in Riley's.

"I'm not sure if that would be a smart move." Riley bites her bottom lip.

The attraction between them is there and the way they kissed before... she isn't sure if they'd be able to hold back.

"I want to show you something, but... you don't have to stay." Jules just smiles and it's innocent. It doesn't hold secrets, it doesn't hold silent promises of something more and Riley instantly caves.

"Okay."

She lets the blonde guide her in the apartment. Once again, Riley notices the colors, how different this place is from her own.

"I really love those colors. It makes it so lively." Riley smiles then, squeezing Jules's hand before moving to stand before the window, glancing outside.

Even though it's the tenth floor, the view is amazing. She can feel the heat of Jules's body behind her, arms snake around her waist and she happily leans back when she feels a chin on her shoulder.

"I didn't know your hair was this curly. It's sexy." The blonde murmurs in her ear, sending goosebumps all over her body.

Jules's voice has always been attractive but now, it's low and raspy, seductive in a way the blonde probably isn't even trying.

Riley can't help herself when she presses herself further back into Jules, her ass meeting hips. She can hear the sharp intake of breath beside her ear, smiling when she covers Jules's hands with her own.

"It's messy."

"It's hot." Jules insists then, softly spinning Riley around in her arms. Then, her voice turns more serious. "You have a way with words and you manage to tell me such beautiful truths I can't even think of. I just... I trust you, okay? I really do."

Riley can feel Jules fiddling with folded fingers behind the brunette's back.

The lawyer slides her arms around Jules's neck. "I know how hard that is for you."

Swallowing away something, Jules's throat bobs, her blue eyes puppy-like when she awaits more reactions from Riley.

"I know how hard that is and I get it. I... it frightens me to think that this might become more. And what do we do when it gets serious? Do we take the leap? I am scared and I don't want to move too fast. But I want this. You make me feel alive, Jules." She smiles softly, hoping that she doesn't scare her away.

But she has to make things clear between them, before they even start being... something.

But Jules nods. "It's really fucking terrifying."

"I hope it's not, with the right person. Perhaps we'll be able to let go of our fears. Maybe, one day." Riley smiles with small encouragement.

A brighter smile forms on Jules's lips as she leans in, gentle when their lips connect. "Stay with me tonight?"

"Jules..."

"Not for that. I just... I need you to hold me." The blonde breathes heavily as she pulls back.

"I'll stay, Jules." It's a promise, Riley knows this. She hopes that Jules knows, too.

They quietly make their way to Jules's bedroom.

Riley drops her jaw in awe when she sees the wall behind the headboard of the bed. It's a large mural. It's the view from the building they both used to live in. The view they had when they were talking lightly about embarrassing stories.

The colors are dark, blue and black, but the horizon hidden behind the buildings still seems somewhat pink and purple.

"Did you paint this yourself?" Riley's eyes nearly pop out of her head when she notices every detail, all so on point.

It's realistic enough, but it has Jules's signature wild strokes, making it livelier than it had been in real life.

"I did." The blonde smiles while Riley moves closer.

"How did you even... remember this?"

"Photographic memory comes in handy sometimes." She smiles shyly. "Do you like it?"

"Yes, it's amazing, Jules. It really is amazing. Could you... do you maybe want to paint a mural at my apartment, too?" Riley smiles widely, turning around to watch Jules stand there, hands nervously clasped behind her back, biting her bottom lip shyly.

"Of course." The blonde's smile is adorable.

She carefully makes her way over, reaching up to push a strand of blonde hair out of Jules's face before cupping it completely.

"You're amazing." Riley is slow when she presses her smile against Jules's mouth.

"You still don't know me." She fights weakly, but the smile never leaves her lips.

"Would you say you would not know me?"

"No…"

"My point exactly." Riley smiles then, loving how a small blush creeps up on Jules's cheeks. "We may not know everything there is to know, but don't we know enough? For now? Getting to know each other takes time, Jules."

"You told me once you wanted to get to know me." The blonde presses her forehead against Riley's, something they've been doing a lot lately, but god, does it feel good. "You're the only person to tell me that. And when you did, I realized just how much I want to get to know you, too."

Before Riley can say more, those soft, pink lips are on her own. She can't help herself when she lets out the smallest moan at the feeling.

She wants to deepen the kiss, but Jules pulls back with a trembling breath. "Riley, are you sure that you are okay with me disappearing for two months?"

"I am." Her bottom lip is quivering, the yearning to hold this woman growing every minute. "We both needed time, Jules."

"My feelings for you haven't changed over the past weeks. I hope you know this." Jules admits quietly, her voice low and soft as she speaks, her body pressed against Riley's.

"You have feelings for me?" a goofy, crooked smile forms on Riley's lips and she knows for sure her eyes are sparkling with mischief.

The way Jules lets out a huff is cute. "Yes, you idiot. Like I told you, I have from the start."

"What start exactly?"

"The first time I saw you, I told you." Jules bites her bottom lip.

"And I ignored you for several months." Riley chuckles softly. "I barely noticed you."

A silence falls between them when Riley places one hand in the nape of Jules's neck. "But I see you now. I see you."

When Jules opens her mouth to speak, no words come out.

"Come on, let's get you into bed." Riley smiles softly, silently urging the blonde to move and get ready for bed.

The blonde smiles weakly, nodding when she reaches into her closet for some sleepwear for them both.

"The bathroom is just around the corner. There's a spare toothbrush in the cabinet under the sink." Jules smiles wider then. "You can change there if you'd like."

Riley smiles softly at Jules's gentleness, pressing a kiss against her cheek. "Okay, I'll be right back."

She quickly moves to change into the t-shirt and shorts Jules gave her, brushes her teeth with said toothbrush before tucking her hair in a bun.

Then, she makes her way back to Jules's bedroom, smiling when the blonde is sitting on the edge of the bed.

"Are you sure you want to stay?" she bites her bottom lip, blue eyes glancing up into green.

"Why wouldn't I be?"

"I have nightmares sometimes." Jules shrugs, as if it doesn't mean anything, but Riley can feel that it bothers her.

"I'm sure, Jules." She moves to stand between Jules's legs, softly leaning down to take the blonde's face between her hands, pressing a kiss on a warm forehead.

Somehow, Jules manages to pull them into the bed clumsily, making them laugh as they struggle with the duvet.

But once in position, Riley feels Jules nuzzling herself into her side. Like she's seeking safety.

The brunette is more than willing to give her that, a happy sigh escaping her lips when she lies with the most beautiful woman in the world in her arms.

"G'night, Riley." Jules yawns then, her arms across Riley's stomach.

"Goodnight, Jules."

Riley wakes to several whimpers, eventually a yell. She sits up hurriedly, watching the blonde squirm in the bed, as if she's trying to fight something, or someone.

"Jules, hey." Riley sleepily reaches for Jules's wrists, trying to carefully stop the blonde from moving so frantically.

But, the moment their skin connects, Jules seems to wake from her nightmare. Her eyes are wide.

"Don't fucking touch me!" she yells. Riley pulls back as if she touched fire, her eyes wide in shock.

"Jules, I..."

An elbow to the nose is something Riley doesn't see coming at all. She groans in pain, falling back onto the mattrass while she holds her now bleeding nose.

"Riley! Oh my god." The blonde seems to have realized what she's done the moment she puts her hand over her mouth.

"I'm fine, I'm fine." Riley groans softly, but tears sting her eyes. The hit has awoken some kind of headache that Riley hasn't had in a while, but now that it has reappeared it's quite ruthless.

"Can I... can I look at it?" Jules's voice is incredibly soft and vulnerable.

Riley can only imagine how the blonde must feel. She tries to sit up and leave the bed, not wanting to leave any bloodstains.

She moves to the bathroom without another word, reaching for toilet paper to try and clean herself up, but blood is still gushing out.

"Riley?"

"Yeah. I didn't want to stain your bed." Riley looks at herself in the mirror. Blood streams down her chin, her throat and into the t-shirt Jules had given her to wear.

"Will you let me clean you up? I made this mess, it's only fair." The blonde looks like she's about to cry, but pushes away her feelings when Riley nods with a careful smile.

"You have a strong left hook." She smiles then, making Jules chuckle lightly.

"Sit." The blonde urges Riley to sit on the edge of the bathtub, grabbing a wet cloth.

She tilts Riley's head back with soft care, standing between her legs while she moves to clean the blood from Riley's face.

"Does it look badass?" Riley smiles when Jules starts on her chest.

"Sure, Riley." The subtle sparkle in blue eyes is mixed with a silent apology.

Riley winces at the cold towel on her sternum, but she allows it to happen. The way Jules handles it with such gentle care is warming her heart.

She doesn't care that Jules may have broken her nose. She knows where it came from and she knows that perhaps she has made a mistake by touching her.

Her headache doesn't feel that way, though. She closes her eyes to avoid the light, feeling the tender touches in her face.

"I'm going to feel if it's broken, okay?" Jules murmurs.

Without opening her eyes, Riley nods. She can feel Jules's bare legs between her own and she realizes it's the first time so much skin must be revealed between the two of them.

It makes her smile while she feels careful fingers touching her nose.

"Does it hurt?"

"No."

"It's not broken." A sigh of relief escapes Jules's lips. "Wouldn't want to break this beautiful nose."

Riley's eyes are still closed when she feels soft fingertips brush away the baby hairs from her forehead.

Before she knows it, her head is being tilted back subtly and soft lips are on her own.

"I'm sorry." Jules's whisper tickles Riley's mouth. "I... I thought you were Liam."

She steadies her hands on Jules's hips when she opens her eyes, meeting a blue gaze that's filled with regret. "I should've thought about that. It's my fault, Jules."

"No, it's not. It's been months since... and I still..."

"Jules, trauma stays." Riley shakes her head then, moving to stand on her feet. She's slightly taller than Jules this way, but she smiles when she cups the blonde's cheeks softly. "It will probably stay for a while."

"I don't want to hurt you."

"You won't. Okay, you did today, but I understand. We'll just have to find a way to compromise."

Shaking her head, the blonde steps out of Riley's grip. "I don't want you to have to walk on eggshells around me, Riley. I trust you. I trust you, and I still do something like this."

There's a bite to Jules's tone that Riley knows isn't directed towards her, but it stings nonetheless.

"Then what do you suggest, Jules?" the brunette doesn't move, wanting Jules to have space. "I can go home. We don't have to sleep together, not when you're not ready."

"What if I'll never be ready?"

Riley bites her bottom lip. "I want you to feel safe, Jules. I want you to be happy. I can live with whatever you need, okay? Even if that means you are punching me again, or if you'll always want to sleep separately."

The blonde nods thoughtfully, before her lips curl into the tiniest of smiles. It's enough, though.

"It may not be broken, but let's get you some ice." She is sweet when she tugs the brunette with her, into her dark kitchen.

She rummages through her freezer before handing Riley a towel and an icepack.

"I'm really sorry."

"Stop apologizing." Riley smiles, but winces when she places the pack against her nose. "Do you want me to go home?"

"No!" Jules is fast when she reaches out, a hand softly playing with Riley's free fingers. "No, I'm not sending you home now."

"I can sleep on the couch." She offers then.

When the blonde purses her lips, it is clear to Riley that she's conflicted about the entire situation.

"Hey, come here." Riley removes the pack, leaning against the counter. She pulls Jules into her arms, pressing their bodies close.

It's one of those hugs that they've shared before.

It's tight, it's intimate and Riley can feel the way Jules is holding onto her shirt.

"It'll be okay, Jules." She mumbles in blonde hair, ignoring the flash of pain in her nose.

That is how Riley softly takes Jules back to her bedroom. The blonde is asleep with exhaustion the moment Riley lies her down.
For a moment, the brunette takes her time to look at the girl. She seems innocent, happy even in her deep slumber.
"You'll be okay." She whispers, before moving out the room to fall asleep on the couch.

Dating Jules has been... exhilarating. It's been refreshing and new and fragile, but Riley loves every single moment.
They take it slow, though.
After Jules had punched her in the face, the blonde had been hesitant about sleeping together, but a week ago they had tried again. And it had worked.
They found out that they have to learn how to deal with certain things. The next morning, Jules had been emotional when she had woken up in Riley's arms.
Then, Riley had never felt safer in her life than right there with that woman in her arms, able to wake up next to her is something she wants more.
But the sexual tension between them is palpable. Often, when they kiss, it quickly grows into something more and the brunette cannot remember ever being so attracted to someone before.
Not even Camilla. She just wants to make Jules feel good, she wants to be able to show her just how much she cares and kissing, sex... it may be a tiny part of affection, but she just wants to be able to show the blonde, for some stupid reason.
But Riley is patient. She has been.
She is enjoying the small moments she has with Jules, the kisses that they share, but they've never gone more physical than they have on the night of their first date.
She can feel something pool between her legs because now she knows what it feels like to have Jules against her.
She knows what Jules's moans sound like and she knows what kind of reactions she can draw out of the blonde when they kiss.
Riley just wants to worship her.
But she's patient.
She wants to be sure that they're both ready for whatever it is that's coming. And she gets to know Jules. She gets to know little facts about her that the blonde has admitted not many other people know.
She knows that Jules prefers to eat cold pizza, after its been in the fridge overnight.
She learns that Jules prefers beer over wine, no matter how fancy the wine may be.
She starts to see that Jules can be quite neurotic and energetic. It comes with waves, really, but Riley enjoys every minute of it.

She enjoys the fact that Jules can ramble about a random fact about the constellations for minutes, only to continue about a subject they left an hour before.

She learns a lot of things about Jules and she can't deny that she loves every single thing about them. She just does.

She loves Jules's grumpy cat face, she loves it when the blonde pulls back because she's thinking about the things she's been through.

She loves it when Jules opens up about her marriage, how that affected her.

And Riley can only imagine. She can only imagine what it must have been like to think you marry the right person, only to end up with an abusive husband.

Sometimes, reality hits them hard. Sometimes, they just need to be alone and that is okay.

Sometimes, they pull away from each other to try and process what is truly happening, but they always tell each other when they need the time, it's just an unspoken agreement between the two of them.

It's also why they're taking things slow. They still haven't labelled what they are and Riley likes it that way, even though she's been thinking about asking Jules to be her official girlfriend for some days now.

She just... she needs to breathe sometimes. She needs to breathe, to take her time and tell herself that things will be okay, that her relationship with Jules will work out if it's meant to be.

And she believes it is. She doesn't think that she'd feel so strongly for someone if it wasn't meant to be.

But they need their time. They need to come to terms with their pasts that somehow entangled together at some point.

"What has gotten you all goofy?" Austin laughs, snapping Riley out of her daze.

She is sitting at the bar in his restaurant, Tessa next to her and River in the kitchen grabbing something.

But Tessa is calling with a client and Riley has used that time to zone out completely.

"I'm not goofy." She smiles goofily.

"You are. You're mushy and goofy and sappy and I don't think I've ever seen you like this before." He grins.

"Get used to it." Tessa drops, before continuing her call.

Riley rolls her eyes, leaning on the bar heavily.

"You were thinking about Jules, weren't you?" his grin turns softer.

"Perhaps." She grins, but her teeth pull her bottom lip into her mouth shyly.

"Are you official yet?"

"It's been barely a month, Austin." Riley runs a hand through her curls.

He winks.

"You guys really have to let go that Jules and I are dating." She huffs, hating how they all seem to notice every little detail.

"Kinda hard when it's all you ever talk about." Tessa finishes her call, laughing when she sees the look on Riley's face. "I bet you're already thinking about your next date."

Riley drops her forehead on the bar, groaning unnecessarily loud. She has no idea when she turned into such a... sap.

The hearty laughs that escape Austin and Tessa's throats is enough for Riley to rise from her seat. "I can't listen to this today. I'm gonna go."

"Say hi to her for me!" Tessa calls out when the brunette makes her way out of the restaurant.

She groans when she makes her way to the nearest Starbucks, buying the coffee that she knows Jules likes.

She may perhaps be... smitten. She may be thinking about Jules all the time and it is annoying her.

It's annoying her how much she almost always wants to be with her, and hold her and kiss her.

It's really started to work on her nerves, especially when they are all teasing her with it.

So what if she's happy? Why does it have to be mentioned all the time?

She straightens her pencil skirt, completely oblivious when the barista is flirting with her.

She takes off her blazer, since it's comfortable outside as she walks to the hospital, that isn't all too far from the restaurant.

She walks in, goes up to the surgical wing. She is smiling when the nurses recognize her.

"Is Dr. Gibson in?"

"She's in her office." Harper smiles.

"She has an office?" Quirking a brow, Riley realizes that there are a lot of things that she doesn't know yet about the blonde.

"Every attending has an office here." Harper winks then, grinning when she points Riley into the direction of Jules's office.

The brunette doesn't know why she feels nervous when she stands in front of the closed door, only now seeing Jules's name on it.

She feels a certain pride when she realizes the work that the blonde does. She's a trauma surgeon, she saves lives every day.

She is so fucking smart and selfless and Riley just loves it all.

She quietly knocks on the door, holding the coffee cup in her hand. She can vaguely hear Jules's voice telling her to come in, so she does.

She watches Jules sit behind a wooden desk, not looking up while she seems to be catching up on paperwork.

Riley's heels click on the hospital floor when she walks in and it makes the blonde look up with a smile.

"Did you just know it was me just by the sound of my shoes?" Riley arches an amused eyebrow, setting the cup down in front of the surgeon.

Jules looks beautiful, her hair loose, wearing scrubs covered by her signature lab coat. She is even wearing glasses and Riley is once again reminded with how lucky she actually is.

"Well, no doctor here bothers to wear those heels like you do, so I could only presume it was you." the blonde grins in amusement, happily taking the cup Riley put down in front of her, but the lawyer stops her.

She leans over the desk, down to capture Jules's addictive lips with her own. She never meant to deepen the kiss, but the moment their mouths connect, neither woman seems able to pull back.

She can feel how Jules fists the fabric of her blouse near her cleavage, pulling her slightly closer.

Riley moans when she can feel the blonde's tongue, their kisses growing heated.

"Hmm, what was that for?" Riley brushes her lips over Jules's, before opening her eyes to pull back slightly.

She drops herself into one of the chairs that stand opposite the surgeons desk.

"I just missed you." Jules smiles, rising from her chair to sit in the seat next to Riley. "You look hot today."

"Well, it's pretty warm outside. Wait, do I really look that bad?" Riley wants to smell her armpits, but Jules lets out a laugh that somewhat startles her.

"Riley. You're sexy. Hot. Sexy-hot." The blonde giggles while Riley's cheeks burn.

The brunette groans, throwing her head back while pressing her palm against her forehead. "I'm a disaster."

"You're adorable." The blonde huffs, her hand resting on Riley's thigh.

"I am not adorable." Riley says sternly, throwing a glare in Jules's direction, but she fails miserably.

"You are." The blonde leans in to peck the brunette's lips shortly, but Riley places her hand in Jules's neck to hold her close.

She moans softly when she parts her lips to enter Jules's mouth with her tongue.

She grows hungry when she explores every single corner, feeling some pressure building between her legs as she does so.

"Riley." Jules then breathes, her lips swollen and red when she pulls back. "I'm at work."

Riley just winks at her, rising from her seat. "Still on for Saturday?"

"Why would I ever miss your fancy gala?"

"Because it's a lame work-thing. I wouldn't blame you if you didn't want to come." Riley smiles, taking Jules's face between her hands to kiss her one last time.

It's deeper than before and Riley grins when she nips her way down Jules's jaw, softly sinking her teeth in the skin of her neck.

Jules's throaty moan is louder than she probably means it to be, two hands on Riley's face to guide her back to Jules's lips.

The blonde kisses her with desperate hunger, hands trailing down to feel Riley, but the brunette teasingly pulls back before Jules has a chance to do more.

"I'll see you Saturday then, Dr. Gibson. Enjoy your cold coffee."

Before Jules can say more, Riley laughs when she escapes the office. The blonde had looked a bit flabbergasted and Riley loves teasing her.

It doesn't take long for her phone to buzz with a text.

Jules – You're such a tease
Riley – You love it.
Jules – You wish

Riley only laughs louder when she makes her way back to her own office.

Since Riley is going to the gala with Sean, Tessa, Aurelia, Chloe and Luna in a fancy limousine, she'll meet Jules, Emma, Austin and River there later.

She had taken Tessa's advice and invited them all. It's big.

It's huge, even.

Riley has been asked to prepare a speech and she never minds standing in front of crowds, but this is bigger than she's ever seen.

She had no idea that it was such a big event. But there are countless of people and the building they're in is just as huge.

The ballroom is spacious and there's a live band somewhere. Riley is just grateful for the open bar as she manages to grab a glass of champagne.

She still hasn't seen Jules. She checks the watch on her wrist, smoothing out the fabric of her dress.

It's a navy, glittery dress with small straps and a deep dip to show subtle cleavage. The skirt is long and loose, elegantly draping behind her as she walks and she just loves it.

Jules will wear a matching color, she told Riley a few days ago.

The brunette just can't wait to see... Jules. She misses her more and more every day they aren't together.

She hovers at the bar, not quite in the mood to talk to people just yet, silently sipping on her champagne.

"Come here often?" Jules's husky voice suddenly sounds in her ear and the brunette startles at that, goosebumps forming on her skin.

"Hey." Her smile is soft, her gaze focused on Jules's twinkling blue eyes. "Not really. You?"

"Hmm, only when there are pretty girls at the bar."

Riley grins in amusement, only now noticing the dress Jules is wearing. It is indeed the same color as her own, but the fabric is smooth.

The straps are thick, starting at the outer ends of Jules's clavicles, dipping deeply to show the perfect amount of cleavage, the side swell of her breasts visible. A long necklace falls between her breasts in a way that has Riley's eyes linger there for longer than necessary.

Riley downs her drink. She doesn't think she can handle an entire night with Jules near her, not when the blonde is looking like that.

Then, the brunette leans in to whisper in Jules's ear. "Want to leave after my speech?"

The moment she pulls back, Jules's hand is around her wrist to hold her close. Blue eyes dark, lips pulled back between teeth, Riley knows that Jules is thinking the same thing.

The surgeon nods then, grinning when she softly leans in to place a kiss on Riley's lips. "Hi."

"Hey." A smile forms on Riley's lips as their lips connect tenderly. "I've missed you."

"I've missed you, too." The blonde admits then. "You look really beautiful, Riley. I love your dress."

The lawyer rests her forehead against Jules's, lacing their hands together. "You never cease to mesmerize me, Jules."

"You're such a charmer." The blonde smiles, but her breath hitches in her throat.

"I mean every word."

Before they have a chance to say anything more, Riley's name echoes through the room and she's being called onto the stage.

She's been asked to say a few words in the name of the LGBTQ+ community, so she does.

Her speech isn't long, it isn't special, she just wants to get it over with.

She quickly climbs off the stage once it's done, making her way back to Jules, who is now joined by Austin, River, Tessa, Emma and Aurelia.

Much to Riley's amusement, Austin and Aurelia seem completely oblivious to the rest of them, so busy talking together that Riley playfully nudges Jules and motions her head in their direction.

Everyone notices how obviously happy they are.

They stay for an hour or so, softly speaking to Sean, to a few clients that Riley's had the honor of defending in the past.

They make use of the open bar, but not once do they leave each other's sides.

Riley loves this. She loves feeling Jules's arm around her waist while she sips on the champagne, walking around the room to make small talk with past clients and donors.

It's quite amazing, actually.

But, Jules is subtle when she pulls Riley away from the rest after subtly saying goodbye, away to walk outside.

Their hands tangle together when they wordlessly step into a cab, only for Jules to give the driver her own address.

Riley is nervous. She has no idea what is going to happen when they get there. She has no idea what Jules is thinking.

The brunette has just been... she's been wanting to tell Jules something, but she fears it might be too soon.

She fears that it might ruin what they have, so she just holds it in.

She lets Jules hold her hand. She lets Jules guide her out of the cab, into her building.

In the elevator, Riley is being pushed against its wall.

They are not burdened by their pasts anymore, so it seems.

Riley can feel it.

With Jules is where she should be. But then, Jules's lips are on her own and she just lets go.

She lets everything go, pouring her heart and her soul into that kiss. She changes angles, presses herself into the blonde, because that is where she belongs.

This elevator is faster than the one in Riley's building, but Jules is smooth when she drags the brunette to her apartment, fiddling with the keys as if she's nervous.

"Jules." Riley's swollen lips move, her hand one top of Jules's. "We don't have to do anything you don't want, okay?"

The blonde nods, smiling so beautifully that Riley lets out a happy sigh, watching how Jules manages to put in the key to open the door.

The door closes. Before Riley can move inside though, the blonde cups her face so tenderly that she can't help but look into those blue orbs.

Yeah, blue is her new favorite color. Jules is her favorite person and she knows it.

Jules looks desperate to say something, but it's as if she can't find the words.

Riley just pulls her closer, her arms around the blonde's waist, patiently waiting for her to find the right thing to so.

"Riley, I..." she breathes, her thumbs on Riley's cheekbones softly. "I love you."

The lawyer blinks a few times, taken aback by the sudden revelation. "What?"

"You don't have to say it back, but I... I think I lied when I told you that I loved Liam. I thought I loved him once, but it's nothing compared to what I feel for you, okay? And you really don't have to say it back..."

"Jules."

"...you don't have to say it back because I know it's soon and we aren't even officially a thing yet, but I love you. God, I love you. I love you so much."

"Jules." Riley can't help the smile curling her lips.

"You're just amazing, you are so patient with me, so understanding and you have never blamed me for anything. You've never laid a hand on me and you give me all the time and space I need and you're so, so fucking adorable when you don't think anyone is paying attention to you. You're a giant nerd, you are so smart, you are so fucking beautiful that I can't stop thinking about you." Jules finally breathes, her face close, a lost tear flowing somewhere down her cheek.

"Jules." Riley tries to get her attention again, but she only tries to hide her overjoyed chuckle when Jules only rambles on.

"You make me feel things that I've never felt before and you scare me. You scare me because I don't know what the future brings for us, but I know that I want you. You make me happy, you make me believe in the good things again. You make me want to live, Riley. I love you."

"Jules." Riley kisses the tip of her nose.

"Yeah?" Jules bites her lip in insecurity and Riley wants nothing more than to kiss it away, but she has to say it.

"I love you."

She feels lighter now that she's said it.

"I love you and I am not afraid to say it anymore. I was waiting for you, because I had no idea what you wanted, if you were ready for any of that, but I love you. I want to be with you. I want to call you my girlfriend. I want to be able to kiss you and hold you and I want to be patient for you, because Jules, you make me feel all those things, too. You make me... you make me... I don't even know the fucking word." Riley laughs shortly, before focusing her gaze back on Jules's surprised face.

She topples her head forward, their foreheads touching as she whispers. "I love you, Jules. Be my girlfriend?"

"Yes." The blonde smiles. Her smile is what lights up everything inside of Riley. It's cliché, it's stupid, but it is the plain truth.

As long as Jules smiles, Riley doesn't care what happens.

Their hands entangle when the blonde starts to guide them to her bedroom.

"Jules, are you sure?" the brunette hesitates in the doorway, but the blonde nods.

"I am sure if you are." She breathes, closing the door behind them.

"I am." Riley can't stop looking at her. She can't stop thinking how the hell they got here, but she is so grateful, just so happy that things worked out the way they did.

Even though they haven't been... dating long, she has never seen a brighter future for herself.

And she doesn't think she's ever seen the emotions in Jules's eyes as she sees it now.

She can't even begin to describe what she thinks she sees, because Jules is pulling her in, their lips connecting lusciously, and all is forgotten.

All she just knows is Jules.

There is a certain desperation growing between them as they kiss. The need to feel each other, to hold each other closer.

To kiss just a little deeper, their hunger, their longing growing with each passing second.

It's Riley who softly pushes the blonde towards the bed. She gives the blonde all the time in the world to change her mind, but Jules's lips are demanding, they're strong when they move down to trail kisses down Riley's jaw.

The brunette throws her head back when she can feel the hot softness of Jules's mouth lower down her neck, to nibble on her pulse point that leaves her trembling.

Her breathing intensifies as she guides Jules's face back up by her chin, eagerly exploring her mouth with tongue and lips and teeth.

Riley can't stop her hands from roaming over the blonde's torso, moving to try and get the zipper of her dress on her back, but she fails because Jules is doing this certain thing with her tongue that drives her crazy.

She can only smile into the kiss, making it unable to deepen it. But then, Jules's gaze is soft as she pulls back.

The blonde's hands move to lower the straps from Riley's shoulders, her own dress sliding down her body easily, until it's pooling around her feet.

"You're smooth." Riley smiles cheekily, her voice lower than before. Jules arches a teasing brow, before grinning to place a few kisses on the brunette's bare shoulder.

It's tender and intimate and Riley loves it.

Then, Jules turns around for Riley to open the zipper of her dress. The lawyer's hands are shaky when they fly up to pull down the tiny piece of metal, more and more skin revealed.

She can hear the blonde's breath hitch in her throat, she can feel the slight tremor as she moves up her hands, to Jules's shoulders, smoothly under the fabric of her dress to be able to slide it down.

And then, Jules's bare back is against her front, her skin silky. The brunette's lips instantly move, placing the softest kisses on Jules's shoulder, up her neck after brushing away blonde hair.

The blonde tilts her head to give her more access and Riley grows braver when she lets her hands trail patterns on Jules's stomach, trying to memorize each line, each curve as they move.

She is already so addicted to the way the blonde softly whimpers when she gently sinks her teeth in the soft flesh of Jules's shoulder.

Intoxicated by the way her skin is on fire wherever Jules is connecting with her. She slowly turns the blonde around, silently asking if it'd be okay to remove the lacy bra.

Jules's only answer is a deep, open-mouthed kiss that makes Riley forget what she wanted to do in the first place.

Because Jules's hands are on her, Jules's tongue is in her mouth and she wants it all.

She is finally able to reach behind the blonde's back to smoothly unclasp her bra, sliding the straps off her shoulders to let it drop to the floor, forgotten the moment green eyes meet blue.

Jules is so beautiful. Her skin pale, every shape, every curve so perfect. Each birthmark, every scar, Riley just wants to remember it all.

She wants to worship her, to remind her that she's worth everything.

She wants to take away the burden of the past.

"Riley." Two delicate hands cup her face, wiping away tears that Riley had no idea she was crying. "Riley, what's wrong?"

Shaking her head, Riley tries to compose herself but she has no idea what has gotten into her. She doesn't know what possesses her to cry when they're about to make love.

"Thank you, Jules." She manages to crack out, feeling how the blonde presses their bodies flush.

"What for?" blue eyes roam over her face, a worried look in them and Riley shakes her head, not wanting the blonde to think the worst.

"For being you. For caring about me. For showing me the important things in life." She breathes then. She's unable to stop her tears, but she isn't sobbing.

The tears flow freely, her bottom lip is trembling but she leans in anyway. She leans in, her mouth connecting with Jules's in the best way possible.

She can feel the blonde press into her at every point possible, before they shuffle to the bed, unable to break their connection.

It's Riley, who softly manages to lie Jules down, feeling hands on her sides to tuck her close.

The brunette explores the blonde's mouth with a newfound hunger, loving how their bodies slide together perfectly.

She moves lower, kissing and nibbling on pale skin. She traces the blonde's jaw, the single muscle in her neck that leads to her pulse point.

She presses open mouthed kisses there, while her leg makes its way between Jules's in a way that has both their cores aching for more friction.

As she moves further down, she's still careful when she takes a hardened nipple between her lips, sucking softly. But, the way Jules moans beneath her, the way those hands thread in Riley's wild curls, tells the brunette that perhaps she wants more.

She grinds down, her skin is on fire and she wants more.

"Riley..." Jules's voice has dropped at least an octave when she moans, softly urging the brunette back up for a searing kiss, leaving both women aching.

"What do you want, Jules?" Riley nudges her nose to the blonde's cheek, moving her lips to curl around an earlobe.

"I want you inside me." The blonde moans deeply when Riley's teeth bury into the skin underneath Jules's ear. "I want your tongue on me. I want to feel you."

The brunette can only oblige when she lowers herself, softly nudging the blonde to lift her hips so her underwear can be removed. They rid themselves any leftover clothing, the need to feel each other bigger than ever.

The way Jules spreads her legs for Riley to settle between, makes the brunette drip. The sight is something she won't forget anytime soon, not when she leans up to kiss Jules's lips desperately, her desire growing when they are completely bare.

The gasp the blonde lets out when they separate is hot, but Riley lowers herself once more.

She pays attention to every inch of Jules's skin, making sure to map it all, to remember it. She wants to know every reaction, every spot that Jules likes to be touched.

She's careful in her movements, though. She fears that she might do something that will trigger Jules.

"Riley." The blonde's voice is raw when she tugs on Riley's hair to make her look into blue eyes.

"Yes?"

"I'm not fragile." The smile is small while Jules reads Riley's mind. "Sex is not an issue."

"Are you sure?" Riley leans down to kiss a hipbone, loving the soft warmth radiating from her skin.

"I'm sure."

With that, Riley places Jules's legs over her shoulders, her lips ghosting over the skin of the blonde's inner thighs.

She's gorgeous.

Hands tangle in dark curls. Liquid arousal is awaiting Riley as she lowers herself, dipping her head to carefully test Jules's reaction while she drags her tongue through glistening folds.

Hips buck roughly, curses filling the room as Riley takes it as encouragement, savoring everything she can find.

She moans against Jules when she can feel more wetness pouring out with each lick, each kiss.

She finds a rhythm that has the blonde's hips roll into her face with each flick of her tongue, but it's not enough.

Two fingers tease the blonde at her entrance and the way she writhes tells

Riley she needs it.

She slides into her, walls instantly trapping her fingers in a way that has Riley moaning.

She feels good. She feels so fucking good.

"C'mere." Jules scratches at Riley's scalp in an attempt to get the brunette up.

Her chin is covered in Jules's fluids when she kisses her way up a stomach, slowly pumping into her with her fingers.

The way Jules pulls her in to crash their lips together with hunger encourages the brunette to place one leg over Jules's so she can grind down to still her own aching core.

As tongues collapse together, Riley misses a hand sliding down between their bodies. She jerks her head up when she can feel two fingers slide into her unexpectedly.

Her lips part as she moans at the sensation, only causing her to plunge into Jules with purpose harder.

She curls her fingers, her thrusts increasing as the blonde moans into their heated kiss.

But pleasure is building, it's aching in their veins as they move together. Riley riding Jules's fingers while she pumps into the blonde, feeling muscles clench.

"Fuck, Riley." Jules pants frantically as they move in a synchronized rhythm.

They are both reaching their orgasm, together. Their lips connected, their thrusts equally delicious, their get to their highest point only to crash together.

Riley can feel Jules's arousal pour over her hand, moaning when they ride out their high.

Then, the brunette gently falls on Jules, feeling a hand at the nape of her neck to scratch her head gently.

"I love you." Riley murmurs, nudging the blonde's cheek with her nose.

"Stay with me? Tonight?" Jules's lips are glued to Riley's forehead, their gasping breaths slowly evening out.

"I will." She promises, smiling into the crook of Jules's neck.

They are a sweaty, sticky mess, but it's perfect.

Riley hums happily with the way that Jules's hand keeps massaging her scalp at the nape of her neck.

But then, she is being flipped on her back and Jules's mouth is ruthless when she lowers down Riley's body.

Letting out a moan the moment the blonde nips on her thigh, Riley can feel the heat between her legs throbbing again, aching more than before.

"I want to taste you."

"Please do." Riley's gasps are short-lived when she can feel a teasing breath on her core.

She squirms, but Jules's grip on her hips is firm.

But then, a hot tongue slides through her folds so pleasantly, Riley can't hold back a high-pitched moan, her hands shooting to thread in short, blonde hair.

Jules is skilled as she moves around Riley's clit, dipping a few hesitating fingers inside.

"Fuck. More." Riley begs, her thighs trapping the blonde's head when she can feel her orgasm build quicker than the last one.

The way Jules's fingers curl inside of her has her vision blurring. She moans, feeling how her orgasm ripples through her body, leaving her to shudder uncontrollably while the blonde's tongue soothes it out between her folds, allowing her to shake in the after waves.

"Fuck. Fuck." Riley tries to breathe as she moves to sit up against the headboard, her chest rising and falling while she watches Jules straddle her hips. "Where did you learn that?"

"Before Liam." Jules just smiles with arched eyebrows, but it turns hotly smug when she lifts her left hand to suck her fingers dry from Riley's liquids.

Riley smiles, lifting a hand to tuck Jules's sex-hair behind her ear. "You're beautiful."

Her hand traces a jaw, a neck. Softly, moving to her clavicle, down her shoulder. Jules's skin is soft when she moves to softly massage a perfect breast, her head dipping down to suck on the other.

She can feel Jules's body arch into her touches, Riley's free arm sliding around her back to press her closer.

Like that, the blonde starts to grind on Riley's thighs, eager to find more friction.

While Riley takes her time to mark the woman in her arms, her right hand moves down. She finds Jules hot and ready for her when she slides in.

She just has to keep her fingers bent as the blonde rides her, rolling her hips so smoothly that Riley is pretty sure she will never recover from the sight.

Jules is sexy. Her breasts bouncing, her head thrown back, Riley can't ignore the column of her neck as she leans in to dig her teeth in skin, soothing it with her lips and tongue.

It earns her a low moan and two hands in her hair to hold her there.

"More." Jules breathes, her eyes half-lidded when she dips her head to steal a hot, open-mouthed kiss.

Riley moans right into it when she slides another finger in, already feeling how Jules's softness is capturing her inside.

She loves the feeling.

"Come for me." Riley begs her as she curls her fingers tighter, feeling how her fingers are unable to move the moment Jules comes undone on top of her.

Her hips buck feverishly, her arms tight around Riley's shoulders when she collapses.

And she holds her. She holds her tightly, listening to Jules's ragged breaths, feeling her tremble in her grip.

Riley is gentle when she moves them both to lie down, the blonde curling into Riley's side.

They are quiet as they bury themselves into each other, their limbs tangling, their bodies pressed together as tightly as possible.

All Riley knows is that she wants to marry Jules one day. She never thought that she would want marriage again, but with Jules it feels so fucking right.

She doesn't know what their future holds, but it has her praying. She wants to be with Jules.

She wants to marry her, she wants to promise her everything. She wants to prove, not only to herself but to Jules too, that marriage can be beautiful.

She whispers then, her nose buried in the crook of the blonde's neck to inhale her scent.

"Maybe, one day."

15

One and a half years later

Riley terrifies her.
It frightens her, that she feels so happy with Riley. It petrifies her that this seems real, that this deep-rooted love still seems to grow every day.
She knows Riley wouldn't lay a hand on her.
She knows this, but she's terrified to the core when she stands in front of a door, ready to knock.
But she's frozen, something clasped in her palm, trapped by her fingers. Her knuckles are white, her hand is cramping but she won't let go.
It's a ring.
An engagement ring.
She has been carrying this with her for the past months, unable to pop the question, unable to put her fears aside and take the leap.
She wants it. She wants a life with Riley. She wants more than that if it would be possible.
She manages to smile when she thinks of the woman that has been in her life for the past two years.
Jules doesn't really believe in coincidence. She doesn't think it was by chance that she and Liam moved into the building Riley lived.
She truly believes that it somehow was destiny, however cheesy it may sound. Without Riley she would have never had the courage to leave Liam.
Without Riley she never would've realized that she could truly love. Her smile grows slightly when she thinks of the brunette.
One of her favorite things about Riley is her eyes. Those green eyes that are so telling, expressive, always filled with warmth that only seems reserved for the blonde.

Those eyes are so honest, so bare and Jules knows that often words aren't needed when she loses herself in them.

Another favorite thing about Riley is the way her hand always finds Jules whenever they are in the same room.

Even if they have separate conversations at a party, or someplace public, Riley's hand is always there to reassure Jules she won't leave.

Whether it's on the small of her back, or their fingers laced, Jules always loves Riley's hand.

And then there is her smile.

That bright smile, that cute lip that scrunches up under her regal nose. Her big, pearly teeth that are revealed each time, stretching those thick lips.

The way skin wrinkles around green eyes, sparkling when they meet blue.

It's Jules's favorite thing. Riley's smile can light up a room, an entire building.

The lawyer doesn't smile often in public, but at home, it's almost all she does when she's not working, or not focusing on one of her nerdy books.

Even when watching a documentary, there's always the tiniest curl of her mouth that lets Jules know that she's happy. And it makes her stunning.

That happiness radiating from Riley, that simple contentment with their life, their relationship, it makes Jules want to marry her.

Simply because she can tell the difference between Riley and Liam. Riley is always genuine.

Always.

Where Liam had been faking most of his attitude, hiding his true self, Riley has never hidden anything. It's something Jules admires, it takes true courage to be yourself and even after everything Riley has told the blonde about her life, she is able to be herself.

And Jules loves it. She loves to be able to read Riley's eyes. She loves that she can tell by the subtlest slouch of Riley's shoulders when she's tired or frustrated.

Riley never hides it. She never tries to push things away – she faces it head on and she is one of the strongest people the surgeon has ever met, that is for sure.

She loves that woman so much. She is so sure and yet, she doubts it all. She doubts if she wants to get married again.

Even though she trusts Riley through and through, that fear in her mind won't leave her. It is bothering her, keeping her up at night while she tries to convince herself that Riley is the one for her.

She knows it.

She really does.

But.

But, she is terrified. But, she keeps giving herself reasons not to ask. She's being weak.

The blonde has been trying to be as strong as Riley is, but she can't bring it up, she can't be as courageous, she can't put her heart out on the line like that. Not even when she loves and trusts Riley the most.

She is so torn, so conflicted between what her head is telling her and what her heart is trying to convince her of. It is exhausting.

She tries to change her own mind by remembering all the things she's learned about Riley the past two years.

Jules has discovered all these tiny things about the brunette that only make her love more.

The fact that Riley drinks that disgustingly bitter Campari on weekends like it's water. The fact that she can get really nerdy about the things she loves.

Rambling on and off topic, her voice silent but confident in a cute way that has Jules listen even though it may not interest her at all.

Like the documentary Riley watched recently. A documentary about space that had Riley drag Jules to the balcony in the middle of the night to point out stars and recite fun facts.

The way she listens whenever Jules has one of her chaotic rambling episodes, or when she cleans up after the blonde, not minding tidying up at all.

She loves how invested Riley is in her family – in Tessa, Austin, River, Aurelia and even Emma and Mary regularly receive a phone call from the brunette.

She has changed her priorities since they first met and it is so, so incredibly admirable how Riley has been able to become such a beautiful version of herself.

Jules is pretty sure that the brunette has always had that care in herself. It is what she learned first about the lawyer when they started their friendship.

The fallout Riley had with her brother, when she fell apart in her own bathroom and Jules had to fix her up. She had been so raw, pouring out her heart and the blonde often thinks of that day.

She often thinks back on how Riley had just been there for her, without question. So fucking loyal, so loving.

Even though Riley may not often talk about her feelings or her parents, Jules knows. She knows what happened, she knows how her girlfriend feels. The only thing she has to do is pay close attention.

Riley's body language is really subtle. She may seem stoic, but she's so telling to Jules. She can sense everything by the brunette's body language, by the look in her eyes and the way she speaks.

The blonde knows they've done an excellent job at getting to know each other. They took it slow, carefully exploring these feelings between them. But.

There is this tiny voice in the back of the blonde's head. What if Riley alters? What if she changes for the worst?

It is this stupid question, lingering in her mind and she hates it with everything she has. Her heart trusts Riley completely.
Her head doesn't. And this battle between her head and heart seems never-ending. It is simply because she has trusted her heart before and that didn't turn out well.
She wishes she could turn off those thoughts. She wishes she could pour all her love and trust into their relationship, but she is not sure if she can.
This is a part of her that she hasn't told Riley. She thinks that the brunette might know, though. Riley has always been good at reading people, especially when it comes to Jules.
But the blonde shrugs off her train of thoughts, or at least, she's trying. She thinks of all the good things happening between them, because she is happy.
Really.
Jules can never get used to a life with Riley. She doesn't even think she wants to.
She doesn't want to get used to the way Riley always seeks physical contact. She doesn't want to get used to the way Jules's name rolls off her tongue delicately every time like she is saying it for the very first time.
She doesn't want to get used to sleeping with Riley in her arms.
The only thing she wants to get used to is the fact that she doesn't have to worry for her safety around the lawyer.
Jules has never met anyone so gentle with her the way Riley is. Every touch, every kiss. Even the way she speaks, it's gentle and tender and not once has Riley lashed out to her, or anyone around her.
The brunette has never raised her voice, not to Jules and not to her friends or family. Jules doesn't even know if Riley has ever even been angry.
But Riley has never been frustrated at her, never lifted a hand.
Not when Jules basically, very unofficially started living at Riley's apartment and made a mess out of it. Not when Jules used Riley's study as a studio and accidentally spilled paint on the floor. Not when Jules dropped a two-hundred-dollar bottle of wine while trying to open it for them and Austin and River.
Not when she asked if Scooter was allowed to live with Riley because Jules was barely home anyway.
Not once has Riley raised her voice, or a hand.
She is patient and her composure is needed. Jules needs that. She needs that reminder that Riley isn't Liam.
And yet, she stands in front of the door in the cold of the New York winter, unable to knock. She is frightened because she doesn't know what to do.
Even though she doesn't know if she'll get an answer, she knocks anyway.
She waits.

One, two seconds. Even five pass before the door is opened.
"Jules."
"Hey, mom." The smile is real, but it falters.
They have never been close.
Something changed, though. It's probably when Riley entered her life and changed it for good, that she saw the opportunity to put their differences aside and reconcile.
They used to clash in ways that made them fight horribly, never able to calm down. In those moments, Jules would miss her father, the voice of reason.
But lately, things have been well between her and her mother.
Mary's brown eyes are filled with worry when she looks at her daughter. She opens her arms without another word, waiting for Jules to step into them.
Jules has never been good at crashing into someone's arms, but the past two years, she has.
The past two years, those arms have been Riley's. But today, it's the first time since Liam's trial that Jules allows herself to crash into her mother.
"Oh, baby." Mary wraps her arms around Jules tightly, softly nudging her inside to close the door.
The blonde holds on tightly. Her fist clenched, because she can't lose the ring, she buries her face in her mother's shoulder.
Mary sits them down on the couch, before pulling back and cupping her daughter's face.
"Is there something wrong with Riley?"
"God, no." Jules smiles through her tears, shaking her head. "I love her, mom."
"I know you do." Mary smiles, taking away the tears from Jules's cheeks.
"I'm scared." Jules's voice is small when she speaks, looking up to meet sympathetic brown eyes.
"Why?"
"You know why." The blonde sniffs a few times, afraid to lose the ring in her hand. She stretches her fingers, holding the diamond ring in front of her mom.
"You want to marry her." Realization dawns upon Mary as she looks at her daughter. "What are you afraid of, Jules? That she'll turn out to be another Liam?"
Pursing her lips, the blonde shakes her head. "No. Yes. No, I don't know. I'm just… what if this goes wrong, too? Marriage is a big deal."
"It is." Mary nods.
"And I think Riley is just as afraid of marriage as I am, but she never told me that." Jules quietly continues. "I want to spend the rest of my life with her."

"You don't have to get married to do that, Jules. You know this."
"I don't know why I came here." Jules shakes her head then, attempting to smile at her mother but she still fails.
"I think Riley would marry you in a heartbeat, Jules." Mary smiles then, knowing full well how much these two women love each other. "Even though she may be afraid, I think that she knows it'll be worth it."
"What about me? If I am too afraid to marry her, am I selfish? Will I think it's not worth it?" Jules shakes her head then, not sure what to do.
"I think your idea of marriage is that it's a prison, Jules. That you're stuck and that you can't get out, not until it's too late. But with the right person, it isn't." she starts slowly, unsure of what to say. "You two… you love like I've never seen before. Not even me and your dad were as close as the two of you are. Perhaps you bonded over heartbreak, over trauma. Bonds like that are hard to be broken, Jules."
Jules nods quietly, listening to what her mother has to say. Something she hasn't done in ages.
"You two make each other happy, Jules. You two understand each other without words and that is rare. Marriage doesn't have to be like it was for you, like it was for Riley. But, spending a lifetime together doesn't have to be in marriage. So don't pressure yourself into doing something you're not ready for."
Taking Jules's chin between her fingers, brown meets blue.
"Just follow your heart, Jules."

Emma had forced them to celebrate New Year's Eve with them, but Jules has other plans. She did promise her best friend to attend the after party at some fancy club downtown, but only after midnight.
She has other plans with Riley. It is their second New Years together and she wants to spend it alone with her girlfriend, for the first time.
She has been thinking about her mother's words the past few weeks. She has been thinking about marriage, about how she had been sure when she married Liam. She had been sure about him, but it was different.
She thinks she settled for him, perhaps afraid she'd end up alone if she didn't stay with him. And marrying him came with that, so she did.
She had been pretty sure.
But she hadn't been confident the way she feels with Riley. Riley is… home. Whenever something happens at work, or with Emma, Riley is her go-to person. She wants to talk to her, she wants to cuddle with her and come home to her, Jules knows this.
Riley is her best friend.
She wants that for the rest of her life.
"Good morning." A sleepy, raspy voice sounds then.
A hand slides around Jules's bare stomach, a warm, naked body pressing

into her side and long curly hair tickles the blonde's shoulder.
She smiles when she looks down, seeing Riley's lethargic eyes. "Hey, baby." Green eyes light up at the endearment in the blonde's voice. A smile on a gorgeous face and Jules is a goner.
Her heart flutters when Riley leans up, pressing her thick lips on Jules's jaw in a featherlight kiss.
She loves waking up like this. It doesn't happen often enough.
"Happy last day of the year." Jules moans quietly when Riley does that thing with her teeth, scraping right below the blonde's ear.
"Old years day?" Riley's voice is sexy when she moves to throw one leg over Jules's, half sliding on top when she drags her tongue down the blonde's neck softly.
Jules can't stop herself from arching into her, loving how her body doesn't hesitate to revel in Riley.
"Hmm, yeah. Gotta spend it well." Jules's voice is lost when a hand is on her breast, softly kneading the flesh.
"It is a miracle that you even have time off."
"Perks of being Chief of Trauma surgery." The blonde grins then, trying to control herself when she moves her hands over Riley's spine, tracing the strong muscles down to her girlfriend's ass.
She cups her bum, pushing her girlfriend further into herself.
The blonde rolls her eyes back when she can feel Riley's wetness already on her thigh, a strong leg pressing against her own core pleasantly.
It has never taken much for Jules to get wet. Not when it involves Riley.
The sight alone of the woman on top of her does many things to her. And then the press of that soft, tanned skin on her own and those green eyes with blown pupils.
The bite of Riley's bottom lip and her soft moans are almost enough to send Jules over the edge.
"I have morning breath." Jules scrunches up her nose when Riley wants to kiss her.
Riley just smiles, shaking her head when she leans in to capture Jules's lips anyway.
And it is amazing. Riley is all softness, hot and demanding when the blonde manages to plunge her tongue into the brunette's mouth after being convinced that the lawyer doesn't mind her morning breath.
Their struggle for dominance is turning her on even more, but Jules lets Riley win this round, feeling how Riley's teeth scrape her bottom lip, licking it before changing angles.
"Riley." Jules moans when the brunette once again goes down her neck, probably marking her.
"Hmm?"
"I need you to fuck me." The blonde tangles her hands in Riley's gorgeous

wild curls, loving the scrape of the brunette's boobs over her stomach as her girlfriend lowers herself slowly.

"Last night wasn't enough?" green eyes sparkle when Riley's tongue teases Jules near her navel.

She's already writhing beneath Riley. She gasps. "You're never enough."

Something Jules has always loved about Riley is her fingers. Long, thin fingers. Fingers that know the exact spot to curl inside Jules to make her come hard.

Those same fingers are now sliding through the blonde's wet folds, making her buck up her hips, so desperate for more.

Her body is craving Riley.

Jules's eyes follow the brunette, loving how Riley's eyes are fixated on her face when she softly dips into her, spreading the slick heat between her legs.

"Riley. Stop teasing." Jules's voice is low.

The grin stretching Riley's lips is smug, but it falters when she suddenly pushes into Jules.

"Fuck." The blonde closes her eyes, her hands reaching for Riley, pulling her down to press those lips against her breast.

The sensation of a tongue teasing her nipple sends extra stimulation to her core as Riley starts an annoyingly slow pace, two fingers trapped inside Jules.

"More."

But Riley pulls away. The blonde widens her legs further, so fucking desperate for more touches, but the lawyer sits up.

Jules gulps when she sees the brunette look at her, all bare and wanting before her.

"Can I fuck you with a toy?" Riley's words barely register when her fingers slowly massage Jules's clit.

She's fucking pulsating.

"Fuck me however you want." The blonde breathes. She just wants Riley.

She is yearning to be touched, to be kissed by this woman.

She whines when Riley pulls away, leaning down to the nightstand to grab the strap-on they bought a while ago.

Jules bites her lips when her eyes trace Riley's body. She is so beautiful.

Even at thirty-seven, she doesn't look her age. Sure, she is mature, really mature and aging like a goddamn fine wine, but still. She's gorgeous. She looks a few years younger, but Jules doesn't think she'd mind to witness Riley grow older.

The tattoo on her spine accentuated by the muscles that fRiles with each movement. The softness that is her tanned skin, the incredibly long curls that nearly reach Riley's ass.

Ever since they had gotten to know each other, Riley never cut her hair. Jules has no idea why, but the only thing she ever did was trimming the ends just to make it healthy again, but no length has ever gotten lost.

That wild mane is really something Jules envies, even though Riley complains about its thickness and its weight.

"You're staring." Riley's lopsided smile is warm when she looks down on Jules. She is struggling with the strap-on, but manages to wrap it around her hips.

"I can't help it that you are so gorgeous." Jules blushes furiously when Riley raises one cocky eyebrow and her crooked grin grows.

The brunette settles between Jules's spread legs, both hands beside the blonde's head as she dips her head to whisper against lips.

"Have I ever told you that I get wet just looking at you?" the brunette teases her.

Riley is barely touching Jules, but the blonde moans when the brunette's mouth slowly moves to her ear, her hot breath sending shivers down her body.

"Jules…" Riley moans softly in her ear, driving her insane.

The blonde wraps her arms around her girlfriend's waist, wanting to pull her close but Riley won't budge.

"Wrap your legs around me." Riley buries her face in the crook of Jules's neck, nipping on the skin there while the blonde obliges.

She can feel the tip of the dildo already teasing her near her entrance, making her moan when she can hear the hitch in Riley's throat.

But the brunette doesn't really move, other than softly testing the waters, her lips wrapping around Jules's earlobe.

The blonde gets impatient. She unwraps her legs from around Riley, smoothly turning them around so that the brunette lies on her back.

But Riley sits up in protest. "Jules."

"I can't help it that you're teasing me." Jules moans softly, grabbing the dildo with her hand while she guides it to her entrance.

Riley's eyes are focused on her face the moment Jules sinks onto it, letting it fill her inside.

Her mouth falls open, her eyes close shut.

She has always loved this position. She's always loved riding Riley, being in her arms, able to see her and to feel her.

She rocks her hips into her girlfriend, loving how Riley's hand steadies itself on the small of her back to support her motions.

Then, the brunette's mouth is plastered to Jules's skin. She moans when she throws her head back, feeling the shivers down her spine when Riley's tongue shamelessly drags over the column of her neck, licking her up and down before dipping lower, circling around her hardened nipple.

Her hips roll more frantically when the heat between her legs grows, making her tremble.

She dips her head down, though, one hand roughly tangling in dark curls to guide Riley's head up.

The brunette's lips are bruised when she crashes her mouth on them. She loves how their bodies sensually move together in practiced sync, how Riley's tongue catches her own when she licks the roof of Riley's mouth.

Her girlfriend is an amazing lover. Especially when two arms wrap around her waist to hold her closer, hips thrust into Jules from underneath and the dildo reaches deeper.

"Fuck." the blonde can't help but throw her head back when she increases the speed of her moving hips, feeling Riley's mouth on her chest while she bounces, the pleasure building intensely between her legs.

It grows with each thrust, with each throb of her clit and she can't stop the moans escaping her opened mouth.

Her hands tangle rougher into Riley's hair, needing something to hold onto when she almost reaches her high, the pressure building so much that she can't move anymore.

She can't move and Riley knows exactly how to make her explode when she thrusts up her hips hard, hands on Jules's ass to push her down.

The high-pitched moan that escapes Jules's mouth has Riley moaning, too. She finally manages to move again, feeling the pleasure maximize between her legs, thrilling her body so wonderfully, she collapses while Riley remains inside of her.

She spasms, feeling the hot liquid seep between her legs. She tries to catch her breath, feeling soft fingers wipe her hair from her sticky forehead.

"I love it when you do that." Riley bites her bottom lip, her green eyes roaming Jules's face.

The blonde can't stop the fluttering in her chest, so filled with affection for this woman that she cups Riley's face softly. "Do what?"

"Take control and ride me like that." The brunette's grin barely reaches her lust-filled eyes.

Jules already opens her mouth when she leans down. She meets those plump lips in a heated kiss. It is dirty, moans fill the room as they explore each other.

The blonde can feel how sensitive she is down there, but she starts grinding again anyway.

Riley however, has other plans when she turns them around in one, swift move. Jules lands on her back, her legs wrapped around the brunette as Riley starts pounding into her.

She reaches less deep, but the intensity of the second orgasm already forming is more than enough when Riley leans down to pull Jules's bottom lip between her teeth.

"Fuck." The blonde can feel her body move with each rough thrust. She cups Riley's ass with her hands, pulling her deeper, closer, encouraging her to go faster because she's nearly there and she is ready.

She comes with a scream of Riley's name toppling off her lips, arching her hips up to find that right angle to ride out her high, frantically moving as the heat turns unbearable, her entire core pulsating with fucking pleasure.
"Oh my god." Jules's eyes are wide when Riley's mouth is back on her chest lazily, softly pulling out of her once her movements have stilled.
"You are so sexy." Riley moans, sitting up to take off the strap-on.
Jules tugs on her thighs to hint something. Green eyes look at her curiously, before realization dawns upon the brunette.
"Are you sure?"
"Right now I don't have the energy to do anything else." The blonde grins, smiling when Riley listens and moves to steady herself with her hands on the headboard, carefully placing her knees on either side of Jules's head.
"Are you really sure?"
"I want to taste you." Jules is pretty sure that her eyes are black when Riley lowers herself.
She is dripping. Riley is dripping. Fluids of arousal ooze on Jules's chin the moment she runs her tongue up through folds.
Her hands move up to steady Riley on top of her, loving how the brunette throws her head back while she bucks into the blonde's face.
Jules moans when she tastes Riley's salty bitterness, devouring her when she starts thrusting her tongue into the opening, her nose teasing Riley's clit.
"Fuck, Jules. Fuck."
As Jules changes between circling her tongue around the pulsing bundle of nerves and dipping inside, she can tell that Riley is close by the uncontrolled moans she lets out, the spasms in her muscles as she rides her face.
It doesn't take long before more slick arousal pours down Jules's chin, even into her neck as Riley comes. And she comes hard.
She cries out Jules's name, her knees digging into the mattress beside the blonde's head.
She rocks her hips onto Jules's face without holding back, the tremor in her muscles evident when she slows to a stop.
When Jules is sure that she's ridden out her high, she is smooth when she makes Riley lie down beside her, still trembling from her orgasm.
The brunette lies on her stomach and Jules is fast when she dips her fingers between Riley's legs from behind.
"Oh, fuck." Riley stifles her moans in the pillow when Jules sits up, trailing wet kisses down a spine when she softly slides into the brunette.
Her walls are already clenching, trapping her inside and the feeling is nearly enough for Jules to come herself.
Riley spreads her legs while Jules lowers her torso, paying full attention to the brunette's spine and her shoulder blades with her mouth, smiling when she feels the tiniest goosebumps beneath her lips as she ghosts over skin.
She doesn't move much when she curls her fingers downwards, feeling the

ribbed spot behind Riley's pubic bone.
The brunette's hips instantly press against the mattrass in a failed grind, seeking more friction as she writhers underneath the blonde.
But Jules smiles when she lowers herself further, her boobs against Riley's smooth back as she nips on the crook of the lawyer's neck, sucking hard.
She soothes the flesh with her tongue, smiling smugly when Riley is panting hard, shaking beneath her.
"What do you want me to do, Riley?" Jules rasps lowly when she can feel walls clench around her fingers again.
"Jesus... Just fuck me. Hard." Riley's voice is barely audible when she gasps for air. "I need you."
And Jules finally obliges. She positions herself for better access, sitting on her knees behind the brunette.
She tugs on Riley's hip, pulling it up to give her a better angle and she knows what Riley is about to feel is much more intense than it was when she rode her face.
The blonde pulls out her fingers, before pushing them back in. She's testing Riley's reaction, but the brunette seems eager for more, so she starts a calm pace, bending her fingers each time.
"Fuck. Oh, Jules. Please." A high-pitched whimper sounds and Jules loses her mind.
Before she knows it, she is fully pounding into Riley with everything that she has. It only takes seconds before Riley comes undone, roughly spasming into the bed as the orgasm ripples through her, her arms reaching back to hold onto something.
One, loud moan and a gasp of air, before Riley collapses on the bed, a little pool of sweat resting in the two little dimples on her lower back.
Jules is still inside her when she allows the brunette to rock it out, clearly still feeling something as she softly moves her hips up and down.
The blonde's hand softly roams over a muscled back, tracing the geometric tattoo that Jules loves so much.
But then, Riley's hand is around her wrist and she pulls out, placing her hands beside the brunette's head to press kisses everywhere, before gently moving to lie beside the woman.
"I am getting too old for this." Riley murmurs, before letting out an exhausted laugh.
The blonde chuckles along, watching how hooded green eyes try to stay open, bruised lips parted to try and allow oxygen into the brunette's lungs.
"You're not old." Jules smiles softly, lying on her side. With one hand, she reaches up to Riley's face, brushing the dark hair away.
Riley's eyes flutter open, her smile is tired but so, so beautiful. "Hi."
"Hey." The blonde reaches to press a tiny kiss on Riley's nose. She smiles when she notices the little freckles sprawled over it, over cheeks. "Have I

ever told you how beautiful you are?"

"Just about every day." Riley's smile grows, but her eyes close again.

Jules's finger starts to trace that sharp, small jawline, hovering over thick lips.

The blonde has always thought Riley was a work of art. She's flawless. Really.

Impeccable. Even though she has a few wrinkles in her forehead, some playful permanent lines beside her eyes, Riley is flawless.

Blue eyes are plastered to full lips, watching how a bottom lip has the tiniest crease in the middle. They flicker up, to the tiny nose, the dark, long eyelashes.

High eyebrows, high hairline. Jules watches it all.

Right now, she doesn't feel scared. Right now, she believes in them. It is as real as it gets.

She knows this.

"You have given me so much." She whispers quietly, but she then realizes that Riley has fallen asleep.

She can't stop her smile from growing as she watches this woman beside her. Riley's hand reaches up then, tucked under her chin in her sleep.

It is endearing. The soft sighs that escape the brunette has Jules's heart filled with admiration and she feels sappy for it.

But she can't help herself. She is going to marry this woman, if Riley wants it too.

"I want to show you something." Jules smiles, tipsy from the wine that they've consumed the past hours.

Riley seems hardly affected, but by the way her eyes linger on everything longer, Jules can tell that she's intoxicated, too.

"I thought we were going to stay in until we had the after party?" Riley's speech is still perfect.

Jules smiles softly when she leans into the woman she loves, half-lying on the couch in their after-dinner dip.

Well, it's late and they should go, but still. They just finished dinner. Jules has braided Riley's endless hair, just the tiniest braids to keep her hair out of her face.

They mingle at the back of Riley's head, disappearing into thick, leftover chestnut waves.

"Yes, but I want to show you something first." The blonde smiles, finally managing to stumble up from the couch.

The pout on Riley's lips is too adorable, but the blonde just giggles when she pulls the older woman from the couch. "Come with me?"

"Hm, I'd like that very much." Riley licks her lips, her eyes already darkening and Jules sometimes wonders how they can still have the libido of freaking teens.

"Riley, not that." Blue eyes roll teasingly. "I've had enough orgasms for the day."

"Have you, though?"

"Yes. Twenty-three must be a record." Jules giggles, putting on the white, silk blouse that Riley picked out for her. "I don't think my cooch could take more than that."

"I'd like to try, though." Riley looks so fucking smug, it makes the blonde laugh softly. But it falters when she realizes just how lucky she is.

She finishes buttoning up her blouse, her tongue poked out in drunken concentration.

Her entire outfit is picked out by Riley. From the loose blonde curls to her blouse, to the dark slacks with wide pipes (seriously, Riley has an unhealthy obsession for slacks with wide pipes) and high heels.

But Jules has picked out Riley's outfit as well. And she had gone all out. It's a silver dress, entirely covered with glitters.

Riley hates it, but Jules hasn't been able to stop touching her girlfriend ever since she put on that damned dress.

It is wrapped around her body tightly, revealing her cleavage, her hips. It does have long sleeves, but the collar is wide, showing off her collarbones, sternum and the perfect swell of her breasts.

The back dips even lower, allowing Jules to take peeks at the gorgeous tattoo despite Riley wearing her hair mostly loose, aside from the occasional tiny braid.

Not to mention those legs. Riley's toned, long legs, her calves fRilesing with every step in those high heels.

Jules could go on forever. She could look at Riley forever, except that they have to go.

"Riley?"

"Hm?"

Riley's hands are on Jules's back and their bodies are pressed flush.

"I'm a bit tipsy." The blonde reveals. The brunette raises an eyebrow in amusement.

"I know."

"Riley?"

"Hm?"

"I don't think I've ever been as attracted to someone as I am to you right now." Goddamn stupid alcohol makes her say silly things.

Gorgeous green eyes darken. "I wanted to say the same thing, actually."

"No, you didn't."

"No, I didn't, but I do feel that way."

Jules can feel her body respond to the tone in Riley's voice, the subtle press of their bodies together.

"We should go."

"Or we could stay. New Year's Eve is overrated anyway."

Two hands slide into Jules's curls, thumbs caressing her cheeks. Riley leans in, closing the gap between them.

It is softer than Jules thought it'd be. It's delicate, tender, no tongue. Just lips pressed together, softly sliding against the other in order to enjoy the proximity.

"You think all holidays are overrated." Jules then puffs out a breath against thick lips.

"Because they are." Riley's tone grows more playful, but Jules pulls her back by her hips, trying so badly to stop herself from groping Riley's ass.

"You are so sexy." The blonde moans, already tilting her head to drape kisses down Riley's neck.

"We should go."

"You just tried to keep me here a minute ago."

A tiny laugh. "True. But we should go, Jules. No matter how much I love showing you how much I love you, there's a social event we should go to."

"But not before I show you the thing." Jules wiggles her eyebrows when she is finally able to put some distance between herself and the goddess in front of her.

They both smile dopily, before grabbing their thick coats and their purses. Jules takes Riley's hand in her own, lacing their fingers.

She can feel the lines of Riley's scar against her own palm as they make their way into the elevator.

The brunette melts Jules's heart when she wraps her arms around the blonde's shoulder, briefly holding her.

"I love you, Jules." The softest voice in her ear.

The blonde leans against her heavily, her heart thudding rapidly in her chest. She can feel something pool in the pit of her stomach and she knows it is love and affection.

She knows it is a longing for a life with Riley.

"I think I love you more." She admits tipsily, her arms around Riley's waist. She fists the fabric of the lawyer's fancy coat in her hands, not quite ready to let go, even when the elevator announces it presence on the ground floor.

They don't even notice. Jules feels so safe when she inhales Riley's familiar scent. She feels safe with those arms around her, that nose pressed into her hair.

Soft lips that brush over her cheek, a hand that tilts her chin so those lips can claim her own.

She loses herself in it. She always does. She's never really paid attention to details before, not until Riley came into her life. But now, she's reveling in it.

"We're down." Riley's smile is cute when she tries to hide it, two hands cupping Jules's face.
The blonde knows that her girlfriend wants to deepen the kiss, but she won't allow it just yet.
"We should go." The blonde murmurs against addictive lips, before tugging the brunette out of the elevator.
New York during New Year's Eve is something else entirely. Really.
Streets are half-empty; Times Square is closed for traffic and it is chaotic in a different way than it usually is.
It is cold but beautiful, as the sky appears completely void of clouds. It is freezing, but Jules doesn't care when Riley is tucked into her side as they hail a cab.
"Where are we going?" Riley is curious when she slides into the cab, pulling the blonde against her the moment her ass hits the leather.
"It is a secret."
"You have to tell me where we're going though, sweetheart." The cabdriver turns around.
Jules grins when Riley throws her a smug, confident look, but the blonde reaches in her pocket to reveal a piece of paper with the address.
"Dammit." Riley mutters, but the playful twinkle in her eyes doesn't leave.
"I am smarter than I look, babe." Jules pecks the brunette's lips with a proud smile, grinning wider when the cabdriver chuckles and starts driving.
She hopes that it's okay, where they're going. She's been hiding it for a while, that she still has access to this place.
She hopes that Riley doesn't mind, bringing up pieces of the past. To her, though, the place is perfect.
It holds memories she often thinks about. Jules holds it close to her heart and she is pretty sure she'd be devastated if she wouldn't be able to go back anymore.
"Wait." Riley's eyes grow wide when the cab stops in front of a familiar building. "Jules?"
Green eyes are glancing between Jules and the building. The blonde pays, before sliding out the car to take Riley with her.
But a tug at her wrist stops her from moving.
"Jules, are we going where I think we're going?" Riley's eyes roll up to look at the top of the high building.
"Yes." The blonde reaches in her bag, that she secretly took. She pulls out a set of keys and a tag, buzzing them into the building.
"How did you even… Jules, it's been what, a year and a half?" Riley's voice becomes more playful when they enter the building, the lobby empty.
"I happen to have a colleague living in this building. I convinced him to lend me his spare tag and I've had it for a long time." Jules smiles when they walk to the elevator that they haven't been to in years.

"You…"

"I kept it." Jules then reveals the one key Riley once gave her, a long time ago. "I kept it, because I… call it sentiment or nostalgia, I was just never able to give up on it."

"Have you ever visited on your own after you moved out?" Riley's hand is wrapped tightly around Jules's own, soft and warm and squeezing in subtle excitement.

"I haven't." Jules shakes her head, grinning when she realizes just how long the elevator takes to come down. "They should really program this one to go to the ground floor when it isn't in use."

"Jules." There's a soft tremor in Riley's voice as it cracks.

"Is it too much? I am sure it's too much. But you told me once you can see the ball drop from there and it is almost midnight and I thought it'd be a perfect moment to… I don't know…-"

Lips crash against her own before she knows it. She instantly answers, cupping Riley's face with the keys still in hand, holding her close as her breathing stops.

They part with a soft sound, Riley's shaky breath telling her that the brunette doesn't seem to mind at all.

"I've always wanted to go back, even if it'd just be once." The lawyer admits quietly then, smiling when the metal doors finally open.

They step in and automatically reach for the button to the top floor.

"Yeah?" a hesitant smile hugs Jules's lips then, closing her eyes when Riley's hand reaches up to tuck some blonde hair behind her ear tenderly.

"Yeah."

"I brought champagne to keep us warm and… muffins. I know you like muffins."

"You mean you like muffins."

"You like them too, Dunn." Jules grins, feeling how Riley bends forward. The brunette scrunches up her nose teasingly, before pecking Jules's lips briefly. "You're cute."

"Whatever." The blonde can't stop her smile when she can feel Riley's hand sneak underneath her coat, wanting to take the blouse from her slacks, but Jules won't allow it. "You've had enough."

"Jules." A whine.

"Riley, you're tipsy. I am tipsy. It's almost midnight and I want to watch the fireworks with you and not have sex in the elevator."

"Fine." A huff when Riley pulls back, crossing her arms in front of her chest childishly, an adorable pout on her lips that Jules is quick to kiss away. When they finally arrive, Jules smiles as they walk up the final stairs. "I hope they haven't changed locks while we were gone."

"They'd be about six years late if they had." Riley laughs softly, standing right behind the blonde.

She tucks in the key, turning it. She sighs in relief when the door opens and instant cool air hits her in the face.

They are both quiet when they walk onto the roof.

It's been... almost two years since they've last been here.

"Truth be told, I never came here after you gave me the key. It felt wrong to be here without you." Jules admits quietly as she walks to the edge that offers them the view of the ball on Times Square in the distance.

"Truth be told, I spent New Year's here alone those two years ago, before I found you and Liam in the hallway." Riley bites her bottom lip, moving to stand beside Jules.

"I know."

With their heels, they're the same height. Their breaths disappear in vapor as they stand, side by side, taking in the view that only they know.

The blonde leans her head down on Riley's shoulder, sighing happily.

She is getting there. She can feel it. She wants this woman, she wants the woman that puts Jules before herself.

She always has, even from the start. It's so admirable.

Riley's arm finds home around Jules's shoulders as they stand wordlessly, watching how the ball isn't moving yet, but quite colorful as the lights change.

The small, irregular tremble in Riley's stance tells Jules that she might be crying.

"Riley?" she looks up, wrapping her cold fingers around Riley's clothed forearms, making them stand face to face.

Riley's indeed letting out soft sobs, but a smile shines through.

"Baby, what is wrong?" Jules places her palms on Riley's cheeks, hoping that the brunette will look at her.

"Nothing, I'm just tipsy and..."

"And?" blue eyes search the lawyer's face.

"Last time I was here, I wasn't sure about how my life would turn out." Riley topples her head, leaning into Jules's touches.

The brunette is fiddling with her fingers, playing with an imaginal wedding band. Jules's heart pangs strangely when she sees that.

It's been more than two years since Riley has worn a ring on that finger.

"I felt miserable because my marriage had fallen apart and I wasn't sure if I'd ever find love, Jules. I wasn't sure if I was worthy of it."

Jules's heart aches. Riley doesn't talk like this often.

"I loved you soon, I think. The moment we shared our first hug. It felt like... it felt like everything I'd ever missed." The brunette shakes her head to herself, clearly emotional when her green eyes finally meet blue.

And Jules can feel the tears sting her own eyes as she watches every speck of gold, of blue and grey in those green orbs that she knows by heart.

She remembers their first hug. She remembers it so well – how she had felt that pain in her heart, realizing that she never felt as safe in her husband's arms as she had in Riley's – even though Jules was the one comforting Riley and not the other way around.

"The second time we shared dinner. When Camilla showed up at your doorstep." Jules nods carefully.

"Yeah. I may not have realized it then, but looking back I think that's the moment."

"You know what I love about you? Something I loved about you from the start? In that moment we first hugged?" Jules murmurs into Riley's ear when she presses her closer. "The fact you let yourself be that vulnerable around me."

"I don't know why I've never been able to hold back when you were around." Arms slide around Jules's waist.

"Probably the same reason I eventually allowed myself to fall apart around you. I never fall apart around people." Jules smiles when she buries her face in the crook of Riley's neck, tugging down the collar of her coat in the process.

A shaky breath in Jules's neck allows her to relax further into her girlfriend.

"I love you, Jules. I wish I had a word for it, but what you make me feel, it's indescribable." Riley's voice is so soft and raw in her ear as she admits her feelings.

When Jules pulls back slightly, she smiles when she meets Riley's eyes. She smiles when she holds her close, pressing her lips to Riley's mouth.

The wind is cold in her hair, seeping through her coat. Her nose is freezing off, just like her fingers and her toes and yet, she doesn't feel it.

She is so focused on the soft lips against her own, the tiniest breaths escaping Riley's nostrils. She can feel the tremor in the brunette's lips as she quietly changes the angle.

"I love you." locking her hands behind the lawyer's head, Jules sighs, her heart leaping out of her chest.

And then: "I trust you." and myself.

As they stand, entangled, they slightly move their heads to look at the ball. It has started to drop.

Cheek against cheek, front against front, Riley's body radiates the heat that Jules lacks.

Then, the ball has dropped completely, and fireworks start. It echoes through the city, just like the distant cheers from Times Square.

"Happy New Year, Riley." Jules focuses back on her girlfriend, smiling when the glow on her skin changes color with each different fireworks.

"Happy New Year, Jules."

She feels heavy when she stands in front of Riley's apartment, not more than a week after the new year has begun.

Or well, it is the apartment they share but they never officially moved in together.

She knows Riley won't be back from work yet when she opens the door, Scooter greeting her with a purr and a lick to her bare ankle, right above her sneaker.

She moves to the bedroom, smiling when she sees how neat everything is. No matter the time of the day, Riley always finds time to tidy up.

Jules removes the scrubs from her body, sighing deeply when she steps into the shower.

She's just had a fourteen-hour shift at the hospital. She has gone all those hours without seeing Riley, which only occurs when her girlfriend has court. Usually, Riley manages to squeeze in the time to bring Jules's coffee, breakfast or lunch. They would make out, or even have sex in Jules's office for as long as they could before Riley would disappear back to work.

But she hasn't seen her girlfriend today and she aches to just lie on the couch and cuddle.

Or watch Riley work at the dining table whenever Jules is home, because Riley's study has been forgotten the past months.

Deep in thought, she finishes the shower, subconsciously using Riley's vanilla shampoo because it smells so good.

She tucks herself into one of Riley's hoodies, burying herself to inhale her girlfriend's scent.

She grabs sweatpants and furry socks. The weather is calling for it.

Taking her sketchpad, she makes sure to take a blanket to the couch where she settles in the corner, her feet tucked up.

Wearing her glasses, she smiles when Scooter joins her, purring softly as he lies in her lap.

She starts drawing. Doodling, really.

Her mind is elsewhere.

She is so deep in her thoughts, she almost misses the front door opening.

"Jules?" Riley's soft, angelic voice calls out, making the blonde look up.

A smile is on her face instantly. Riley has that effect on her, whenever she enters a room.

Tucked in a thick trench coat, the brunette sets down her leather briefcase near the coat rack, shrugging off her jacket to reveal a tailored grey suit.

It's wrapped tightly around Riley's body, hugging her in all the right places. Heels click when her girlfriend walks up to Jules and the blonde doesn't think she'll ever get enough of Riley's professional wardrobe.

"Hey, babe." Jules smiles when Riley leans down to press a soft kiss on her lips. As always, the brunette is unable to pull back, deepening the kiss while Jules's hands tangle in those delightfully long curls.

"Hi." Riley breathes, her green eyes bright today.

"You're beautiful." Jules murmurs, her hand in the nape of Riley's neck to

pull her closer.
Gently, Riley takes the sketchbook out of her hands before straddling Jules's hips.
She takes off her heels, allowing Jules to open her blazer and slide it off her shoulders.
A basic, white button up revealed, two buttons popped open at the top. Riley is wearing a small, golden necklace to accentuate her neck in the best way possible.
Jules grins when she pops open another button, able to see Riley's cleavage.
"Miss me much?" Riley murmurs hotly in the blonde's ear, instantly driving her crazy.
She doesn't know why Riley's voice does many, many things to her.
"Hm, a bit. You?"
"I missed me lots." Riley teases then, cupping Jules's face gently.
"Dork."
For a moment, foreheads are pressed together. "I did miss you, actually. I hate court."
"No, you don't."
"I do, now that I know that it makes me lose time to spend with you." Riley's words are truthfully beautiful, as always.
Jules can't help the growing smile on her lips when she pulls Riley closer by her hips. "You are such a sap."
A kiss on her nose. "You love it."
"Sometimes."
"It always has you grinning like a goof, so don't try and tell me you don't love it." Riley warns, a chuckle behind her voice as she speaks.
"I never grin like a goof." She grins, nudging Riley's nose with her own.
She knows that she has never felt like this before. This kind of love, the way that even a single smile of Riley has her knees weak.
The way her skin tingles whenever Riley touches her, or the way she is unable to sleep whenever the brunette isn't beside her in bed.
"I love you, Jules." Riley always has a way of saying it like she says it the first time. Like it's something delicate, something that has to be cherished deeply.
Something that might be a secret she's revealing to Jules, except she knows. Riley doesn't even have to tell her.
She knows in the way green eyes look at her. She knows in the way Riley's hands touch her, in the way Riley seeks contact whenever they are apart for longer than an hour.
It's in everything.
"I want to ask you something, though." Riley always articulates her words with such care.
She bites her full bottom lip, her teeth sinking in the flesh. It has Jules

distracted for a moment, before soft fingers are under her chin to make her look up.

She meets playful green eyes, amused raised eyebrows.

"Hm, yes?"

"I uhm… I was wondering how I missed the fact that you moved in with me. When did this happen?" Riley is adorably cute when she blushes, the tips of her ears pink, her lips sucked between teeth in insecurity.

"Riley." There's amusement in Jules's voice when she looks into her girlfriends' gorgeous eyes.

"Yeah?" her breath is shaky and Jules knows how much courage it must have taken her to even ask.

"It happened months ago."

Riley's eyebrows furrow in confusion, her eyes searching Jules's face to find the answer to the joke, but when she doesn't find any, her lips shape into a quiet oh.

"I mean… I can't remember the last time I went to my apartment and even Scooter moved in." Jules smiles when she pets Scooter, who has moved to lie beside them on the couch.

Riley's bottom lip juts forward in the cutest pout ever. "But your stuff?"

"Everything I need is right here, Riley." Jules smiles softly, gauging Riley's reaction.

The moment the brunette looks around her, she notices.

Jules's favorite chair is sitting in the corner near the window, for whenever the blonde feels like sketching the sunset.

Jules's paintings are spread over the walls. Her laptop and its charger permanently sit on the coffee table and her clothes have moved into Riley's closet a long time ago.

Her art supplies are tucked in a closet in Riley's study, her easel has replaced the desk there, and her medical journals lie around everywhere.

"Oh." Realization seems to seep into Riley's mind, a crooked smile appearing on her face. "Well… I talked to Tessa today and she said… she asked when you had moved in, and I told her we hadn't. She laughed and said we had."

"It took Tessa telling you for you to see?" Jules teases her, placing a soft kiss on the brunette's strong jaw.

"Well… yeah. I have no idea when this happened." Riley huffs cutely, before snaking her arms around Jules's neck.

The blonde can't hold back her smile. She tries, but she can't. "But I'm still paying rent. I can ask Emma if she'd like to move in the apartment. She always loved it."

"I think Emma has moved in with Tessa by now." Riley reasons, thinking deeply.

Ever since Emma and Tessa have been introduced, those two have been inseparable. They started dating not long after Jules and Riley officially got together.

"They are disgusting." The lawyer wrinkles her nose, but smiles when Jules presses her lips there, peppering Riley's face with kisses.

"Riley."

"Yes, Jules?" green eyes are endearing.

"Do you mind that I moved in with you? I didn't even ask." Jules bites her lip, loving how Riley instantly shuffles closer.

"I don't mind, Jules. I love having you here." Her smile is small, but so, so beautiful. It takes Jules's breath away. "Anyway, do you want to go out for dinner tonight? You're free tomorrow, right?"

"I am."

"Or are you too tired? You look tired. I can cook you something and we can watch a movie." Riley rambles, subconsciously toying with the hairs in Jules's neck.

"I would love to get out to dinner. Where did you have in mind?" the blonde smiles, pressing her face in the crook of Riley's neck.

"Well, I was thinking maybe Aus- ah."

Jules can't help herself when she nips on the skin right below the hook of Riley's jaw, that place she knows drives the brunette insane if she keeps going long enough.

"Sounds good." The blonde husks, brushing her lips down the tanned skin of her girlfriends chest.

She moans when she arrives at the swell of Riley's breast, eagerly pressing open-mouthed kisses there.

"Fuck, Jules. Don't start anything you can't finish."

"Who says I can't finish?" she grins against the crook of Riley's neck.

"I made reservations."

"You just said we could stay in if we wanted." Jules pulls her head back.

"I would've cancelled if you were too tired. I know what fourteen-hour shifts do to my girlfriend." Riley smiles, cupping Jules's face affectionately before she leans in to kiss her.

"I love you." The blonde manages to breathe, their smiles pressed together. She never grows tired of this.

Domestic bliss.

Riley being thoughtful. Riley being sweet and tender. Riley in general.

"I have to take a shower and change." The brunette smiles widely. "If you're sure you want to go."

"I'm sure, Riley."

Jules wants to look pretty again for Riley. She doesn't even really know what a gorgeous woman like Riley sees in her, but she tries her best anyway. She puts on a black dress, one of which she knows will have Riley drooling.

It shows just enough cleavage, hugs her tightly around her hips.
She has been doubting about how she should be asking Riley to marry her. She wants to, she really does, but she is so anxious, afraid that Riley might not want it.
She bites her lip in insecurity while she puts on her heels, waiting for Riley to emerge from the bathroom.
She can hear the brunette hum a song to herself, smiling when she imagines Riley in front of the mirror to apply her make-up, her lips smacked together and her eyes wide while she attempts to apply mascara.
"Almost ready!" Riley yells then, making Jules smile while she fills her purse with her wallet, her phone and keys.
"Hey, baby." Jules grins when Scooter makes his way into the bedroom, jumping on the bed. "You know Riley doesn't like it when you're on the bed."
She goes to mimic Riley's tone. "Scooter, so… unsanitary."
"But I know Jules has been allowing you to sleep on the bed while I'm not home." Riley's voice is suddenly closer.
"Uhm… oops?" Jules offers as an apology, watching the corners of Riley's eyes crinkle playfully.
"Never one with many words, Jules." Riley snorts, pulling Jules closer.
She leans in for a searing kiss that leaves Jules completely breathless.
"What was that for?" she pants, searching Riley's face.
"For the fact you've been secretly moving in with me, being all domestic with Scooter and you turning my study into your studio." Riley grins, tapping Jules's nose with one hand. "Don't think I didn't notice."
"You didn't. Not until today." Jules laughs, pecking Riley's lips once more before parting from her girlfriend, taking Scooter off the bed to usher him to the living room.
"I did notice you turning my study into your painting space, Jules." Pouting, Riley looks like she's asking Jules to pet her shoulder for noticing at least one thing.
All the blonde does is let out a cackle at her girlfriend's childish acts.
"Didn't you have dinner reservations?"
"Not until later."
Feigning a gasp, Jules places her hand over her heart. "You lied."
"I didn't tell you what time those reservations were. But I'm hungry, Jules. Like really, really hungry."
"Why do you always forget to eat when you have court?" rolling her eyes, Jules grabs her jacket to slide it on, only to grab Riley's and tuck her girlfriend into her coat like she's a kid who can't do it herself.
Riley rolls her eyes. "Because court is chaotic and there's not decent place nearby where I can buy lunch."
"I could've brought you something, you know."

"No, you couldn't, because you're a busy surgeon and your schedule is even more hectic than mine." Riley's grin is smug when she tucks Jules out of the apartment, into the elevator.

As they make their way down, Riley's hand is on the small of her back, her nose nudged into Jules's cheek.

She sighs happily, leaning into her girlfriend.

Riley manages to stop a cab, letting them drive to Austin's restaurant.

"Are they working tonight?" Jules smiles while she rests her head on Riley's shoulder.

Their fingers thread, their thighs pressed together, they have never been able to separate when they are in the same space.

"Austin? Not sure. I think it's River's night." Riley presses a kiss on Jules's forehead.

A silence falls between them as they watch the city darken.

Winter has always been beautiful in New York, despite the cold, the dreariness. Jules sees the beauty in that.

"Riley?"

"Hm?"

"I'm happy." Jules hasn't said these words in years. Perhaps college was the last time she has said it and after that, she never felt like it.

She has never been happy, but the past year she has.

When she glances up, she can see the surprise on Riley's face turn into the sweetest smile ever.

"Yeah?" Riley's voice is hopeful when she nudges her fingers under the surgeon's chin to lift her head, thick lips claiming Jules's.

Addicted is the right word.

She's addicted to Riley's full lips on her own. She's addicted to Riley's skilled tongue fighting her own, exploring her mouth like she's never had the chance before.

"Yeah."

It seems to be the right thing to say when the cutest smile breaks out on Riley's face, pulling back as if she's the happiest woman in the world.

"I never thought I'd hear you say that, Jules." She then murmurs in all honesty. "But it's all I've ever wanted for you."

"Are you happy, Riley? Are you happy, too?" she breathes, not even caring if the cabdriver can hear.

"Happier than I've ever been."

A thumb caresses Jules's cheek, green eyes are sparkling with so much hope that Jules almost can't take it.

Riley is beautiful. So, so beautiful.

Jules can't wipe the smile from her face when she pulls back subtly when they arrive at the restaurant.

They silently make their way out the cab, into the restaurant to sit at the bar.

"Hey, guys." Ilian, the bartender, grins at them in recognition.

"River around?" Riley smiles, leaning one of her forearms on the bar, her other wrapped around Jules's waist.

"Yes, Austin, too." Ilian's dark eyes sparkle in amusement when Riley grins. "Do you have a table for two?" the brunette asks then.

"Take whichever is free, Riley." Ilian smiles at them, throwing a towel over his shoulder. "I'll let them know you're here."

"Thank you." Riley smiles, moving her hand to the small of Jules's back in order to guide her to an empty table.

"Riley?"

Jules hears a vaguely familiar voice then, feeling Riley freeze beside her. It doesn't register yet, who it is.

She knows when she and Riley turns around in sync, and a gorgeous woman stands in front of them.

A woman, looking like a goddess, with blue eyes and half-dark curls dancing around her shoulders.

"Camilla?" Jules offers a small smile. She remembers her old neighbor. She remembers bumping into the woman a few times before she moved out permanently.

Camilla had always been kind.

"Jules. Riley." Camilla's smile is wide when she glances between the two girlfriends.

"Cam." Riley's voice is painfully soft, making the surgeon look at her.

Green eyes are wide with shock, but Jules can feel Riley's arm around her waist pulling her closer into the brunette's side.

"How have you been?" Jules asks with a smile on her face, knowing Riley might be too startled to speak.

"I'm good. I'm really good, actually." Camilla's smile is genuine as she steps closer, reaching out to softly nudge both Jules and Riley in the arm. "What about you, guys? Are you together?"

"Yeah. Yeah, we are." Riley seems to have pulled herself together, her smile tiny when she briefly glances at Jules.

The blonde's heart warms when she notices the happy sparkle in Riley's eyes.

"I thought you were married?" Riley's ex-wife seems surprised when she looks at Jules.

"Oh, I was. It's uhm… complicated." Jules grins then. "But hey, it is really good to see you, Camilla. It's been… over two years?"

"Something like that." The other woman smiles, still unable to stop glancing between the two. "Riley… you look really happy."

Jules's heart warms when Riley's ex-wife observes. She smiles when she can feel the soft press of Riley's lips on her cheek shortly.

"I am."
"We are." Jules leans further into her girlfriend, loving her warmth.
"I told you." Camilla's deep blue eyes then twinkle. "I told you you'd find it."
"Yeah, yeah." Riley rolls her eyes playfully, letting out a small laugh. "Did you?"
"I did." Camilla's smile is equally as happy as Riley's is.
"With her?" Riley doesn't sound like she's judging her ex-wife.
Camilla shakes her head. "No, she was never the one for me. I don't think you'd know her, but she's…"
The woman glances into the restaurant, pointing at a woman sitting in the corner, alone at a table. "…right there. I can introduce you if you'd like."
"Oh, no. We don't want to intrude." Riley is fast when she shakes her head, but the smile remains. "I'm happy for you, Cam."
Camilla's smile lingers in lost sadness. "Yeah. I'm happy for you too, Riles."
Jules smiles when she watches them interact. They have a certain softness for each other that Jules wishes she could have with her ex.
But as nice as it may seem, she knows it still hurts Riley in ways the brunette would never tell her with words.
She can see it now, though, in the small twitch of the corner of Riley's mouth. She can see it in the soft green gaze that lingers on the floor longer than necessary.
It is then, that Camilla leans in to press a kiss against Jules's cheek. "Take care of her."
It's a whisper and Jules is pretty sure that Riley hasn't heard it. But when Camilla pulls back, the blonde gives her a reassuring nod, watching her lean in to give Riley a kiss on the cheek, too.
"Good to see you." Jules smiles.
"You, too. I'll see you around." Camilla dips her head in a small nod, before smiling one last time and disappearing to her date.
Jules squeezes Riley's waist to offer some kind of comfort, watching her girlfriend stand there, just frozen.
"Hey. We can go home if you want." Jules offers quietly, leaning into the brunette.
"No, I'm good." Riley's smile is shaky, but genuine.
"Riley." Jules smiles. Hearing Camilla call Riley 'Riles' is strange to Jules. The nickname doesn't fit her girlfriend at all. "Baby, if you don't want to stay, we can just go home, okay?"
She can tell that even though Riley might be happy, she's visibly uncomfortable.
"I don't want to ruin our date." Riley almost pouts when her green eyes search blue, but Jules smiles.
She then turns back to the bar, watching River emerge from the kitchen.

"Jules, hey babe." He winks at her, a big smile on his face, but it falls when he watches Riley's stiff composure.

"We have some change of plans." She smiles at him, feeling Riley's hand slip into her own.

"Are you okay?" River's grey gaze is worried, but Riley straightens her stance beside her.

"Yeah. I just... I need a breather." Riley smiles, squeezing Jules's hand in the process. "Raincheck?"

"Of course." River winks again, grinning when Jules moves to lean over the bar to press a kiss against his bearded cheek. "Ah, I never say no to a kiss from a gorgeous woman."

"I think we all know that is a lie." Austin suddenly appears beside him, slapping him on the shoulder. "Can I get one, too?"

Jules can hear Riley's small laugh when she leans over the bar to press a kiss against Austin's freshly shaved cheek, too. "Don't let Aurelia see that."

"No worries, she knows you're gay as fuck for that lawyer of yours." Austin laughs.

Both men are tucked in their chef's wear, looking like quite the pair. Austin throws his arm around River's shoulder.

"Are you guys leaving?" he has a puzzled look on his face while he glances between his sister and Jules.

"Yes." Jules doesn't wait for Riley's answer, she can feel that the brunette wants to leave. "But we will see you guys soon. Dinner tomorrow?"

"Of course."

"And bring your significant others!" Jules smiles. "Bye, guys."

"Bye!"

The blonde is careful when she tucks Riley out of the restaurant they often visit, until they stand on the sidewalk in the middle of New York City.

Riley stops her from walking, taking both Jules's hands into her own.

"Hey." The blonde smiles, watching Riley bite her bottom lip.

"Hi." Riley smiles shyly then, finally looking up. "I'm sorry about that, I just... I wasn't prepared to ever see her again."

"I know." Jules loosens one hand, moving up to tuck a strand of Riley's wild curls behind her ear.

She can feel the brunette lean into her touch.

"We could go somewhere else." Riley smiles then, softly leaning forward to press a kiss against Jules's lips.

The blonde tries not to get lost in them, but as usual she fails miserably. She can feel Riley's subtle desperation as she deepens the kiss, not even caring that they are standing in the middle of a sidewalk with people walking around them.

But nobody seems to care.

Jules is out of breath when she pulls back, smiling when she presses a small kiss on the tip of Riley's nose.

"Let's get home." She offers, but Riley shakes her head.

"I have an idea." She smiles, taking Jules's hand in her own.

They walk around the block, the sun lowering over the city. It's chilly, but perfect and Jules waits curiously until Riley will reveal what they are going to do.

Riley then drags Jules into a random hardware store, leaving the blonde to look at her girlfriend like she's completely crazy.

"I thought you were hungry." She laughs in amusement when Riley grins, wiggling her eyebrows.

"We'll just buy some chocolate. Change of plans, right?"

"And what exactly are those new plans?" Jules glances down at her dress, feeling overdressed for the fact they just walked into a random hardware store.

It isn't big at all, but Riley makes her way to the paint section. She grabs big brushes, three cans of paint and puffs when she carries them to the counter. Jules looks baffled when she follows her.

"Jules, can you get... blue, white and black?" Riley asks over her shoulder. The blonde nods, her lips parted in surprise when she listens to her girlfriend, grabbing one-liter cans of paint.

"And what are we painting tonight?" Jules raises an eyebrow in amusement when she watches her girlfriend move back to grab protective plastic.

"It's a surprise." Green eyes sparkle and that is all Jules needs.

She watches Riley pay at the counter, watching her girlfriend smile at the foreign man behind it.

"Goodluck, ladies." He grins in amusement when Riley huffs and puffs when she grabs the cans, brushes and the plastic, before moving outside.

She stops a cab and Jules struggles behind her with her own cans, falling into the cab with a sigh.

"Riley, what the fuck?" she laughs when she sees her flustered girlfriend.

"Well, I remember you promising me a mural in my apartment years ago and we still haven't done that. I figured we could start on that now." The brunette grins then, biting her bottom lip while she does so.

"A mural with crappy paint?" Jules grins when she watches the cheap brand of paint, sitting by their feet.

"You're an artist, Jules. You can paint with whatever." Her smile is so beautiful and happy, that Jules can't say no.

She really can't.

She is beaming when she watches her girlfriend smile, leaning into her to give a chaste kiss on the lips.

"Uhm, could you stop around the corner?" Riley asks the driver.

"Sure thing, love." He smiles at them in the rear view mirror.

When he stops, Riley jumps out. "I'll be right back."

"I have no idea what she's doing." Jules shrugs then at the guy in the front. He looks like he might be Indian, but his smile is mischievous in a way that amuses the blonde to no end.
"You make a lovely couple."
"Thank you." she smiles at him, patiently waiting for her girlfriend to return. "She usually isn't this impulsive."
"It's a good thing." He opts.
"How so?" she arches a curious brow.
"Means she's happy. I saw her smile just now." He grins, looking at her over his shoulder. "Whenever my wife is happy, she randomly thinks of things to do. It comes in waves, really. Sometimes, she just drags me to the other side of town to watch a damn cheap musical, or forces me to go out paintballing. Paintballing. She hates guns."
"That's… interesting." Jules smiles at him, looking at him in sheer amusement when she listens to him speak.
"Yeah. Your wife probably has the same."
"Oh, we're not married." Jules is quick to correct him, but his assumption gives her butterflies. "I hope we will, though. Soon."
"Good luck." He winks, before turning back to look forward when he spots Riley before Jules does.
The blonde can't shake the feeling. She can't shake her thoughts, that warmth in her chest when she watches Riley with several bags, struggling to open the door with her full hands.
But she manages to collapse into the cab, her grin wide, but tired. "I got us something from everything. Gatorade, booze, chocolate, white chocolate with those weird thingies that you like, uhm…" she rummages through the bag. "…I got some of those disgusting sugary bagels you love, too and these."
She pulls out big muffins and doughnuts.
"I know you like those and…" she reaches in the bag again, wiggling her eyebrows while her tongue pokes out. "…last, but not least… cheesecake."
"And they had it all in that store?" Jules tries to hold back a laugh, watching Riley shake her head.
"I ran to that bakery next to the store. They had some left and I figured I'd take some because I know how much you like it."
"Marry me." Jules mumbles then, too soft for Riley to hear.
"What?" the brunette seems confused.
"I said, you're adorable." Jules quickly corrects herself, leaning in to peck her girlfriends' lips while the driver continues their journey home.
"I figured we deserve unhealthy dinner. Did you know that my college dinners were usually muffins?" Riley grins cutely, so filled with energy all the sudden that Jules is a bit overwhelmed.
"You didn't tell me, but Austin did." Jules smiles at her girlfriend, laughing

when Riley's cheeks turn a shade pinker.
"What else did he tell you?"
"Hm, not much." She lies, grinning widely while they arrive at their place.
Jules reaches into her purse, handing the driver a hundred-dollar bill. "Keep the change."
"Thank you."
"Take care." Jules smiles at him while Riley already escaped the cab, her arms completely full with everything they've bought.
"You, too." His smile is genuine when he patiently waits for Jules to retrieve their supplies.
They struggle into the building, up in the elevator. Jules groans when she finally releases it all, placing it in the living room where Riley put her things, too.
"Come on, let's have dinner." She drags Jules to the bedroom, because logically, that is not where they're going to eat dinner.
"You are acting weird, Riley." Jules teases when she watches her girlfriend change into something easier.
Jules is fast when she steals Riley's old NYU hoodie, throwing it on without a bra underneath.
"Hey, that's mine." Riley laughs while she steals one of Jules's old hoodies.
"I know. But I always paint in this one." Jules grins at the paint stains on the sleeves.
Riley's jaw drops. "Have you been ruining my hoodie?"
"Maybe? Oops?" Jules laughs when Riley almost runs to her, leaving the blonde to squeal and escape to the living room.
But Riley is fast when she catches her and they fall onto the ground, while Riley starts tickling the blonde.
Jules can't stop laughing as she fails to fight back.
"Riley, stop!" the blonde pants, laughing louder when Riley's flustered face hovers above her own.
"You're lucky I love you." Riley grabs Jules's wrists gently, placing them above the blonde's head while she leans in to capture Jules's lips with her own.
The blonde instantly moans into it, feeling Riley's desire already grow with each thrust of her tongue.
Riley moves to nip on her jaw, her neck, before licking her way back up, leaving Jules to shudder beneath her.
The brunette gives an experimental grind down on Jules's hips, before crashing her mouth back on Jules's.
The kiss is heated and the blonde can't hold back her moans when Riley's hip roll into her with a newfound rhythm, smooth and hot against her lower abs.
"Riley." Jules breathes, trying to wriggle her hands out of Riley's strong

grip. "Let me touch you."

The brunette instantly lets go, but her kisses grow frenzied, desperate. As she straddles Jules's hips, she sits up for a moment, only to remove the hoodie she just put on.

Jules gasps at the sight of Riley sitting on top of her, shirtless. Her small breasts perfect, her abs so strongly evident.

Her sun-kissed skin (seriously, even during the winter Riley is tanned) is smooth and Jules can't get enough of this beauty that is her girlfriend.

She lets her hands roam over Riley's torso as the brunette leans back to kiss her again, nipping on Jules's skin as they lie on the floor in the middle of the living room.

Jules can feel her tug on her own hoodie, easily obliging to let Riley slide it off her body.

A mouth wraps around her nipple and her back arches of the floor when she can feel the sensation shoot from her breast, straight to her core.

She needs more.

Moaning, she tangles her hands in Riley's long curls, pressing her closer, urging her to be rougher.

Riley's teeth sink into her skin and she lets out a groan at the feeling, loving to feel her girlfriend on top of her, half naked.

Brown hair tickles her skin as the lawyer moves lower, pressing lingering, open-mouthed kisses all over Jules's stomach, moving down to tuck down her sweats.

"Fuck." The growing heat between her legs feels amazing, but it leaves her wanting more and more.

When she lifts her head, she can see Riley's mouth kissing and nibbling on her hipbone, but her green eyes never leave Jules's face.

Jules knows how wet she is for her girlfriend, the pleasure already sending tiny shocks through her body and Riley hasn't even touched her there yet.

That is the effect she has on Jules. It's ridiculous.

She can feel Riley's thick lips lowering further down there, but she needs them on her own.

Sometimes, she just needs Riley close. So, she softly tugs on Riley's hair, watching the knowing smile on the brunette's face as she kisses her way back up, but not before spending a generous amount of time on Jules's breasts, her hand softly palming Jules's core in the process.

The blonde moans when she can feel their skins together, tugging on Riley's own leggings to encourage her to take them off.

Riley is smooth when she does so, their naked bodies pressed together.

"You're so lovely." Riley's voice is soft, but low in Jules's ear, her long fingers teasing the blonde near her entrance.

"Hm." Jules has her hand in the nape of Riley's neck, needing her close, needing that mouth on her as much as possible. "Fuck me, Riley."

She doesn't have to say more, as two long fingers fill her in the best way possible. She can feel her pleasure growing the moment Riley starts pulling out and pushing back in, creating a tempo that is too slow for her liking. She's always been impatient when it involves Riley's touches.

But, this way, Jules can take her time by thoroughly licking Riley in her mouth, loving those lips on her own, bruising and clashing, but she needs it. She needs to be able to express how much she loves this woman on top of her. She moans into her when Riley picks up her speed, loving how their stomachs slide together, their breasts pressed together in the best way imaginable.

She loves how Riley takes her time to roam her torso with her free hand, her thumb brushing over delicate skin, sending goosebumps down Jules's spine.

But Riley grows brasher when she thrusts harder, adding a finger. The blonde can't stop her moans from filling the room, her pleasure building, higher and higher.

The floor isn't comfortable, but she doesn't even notice. She only sees Riley. She only feels Riley.

She can only focus on the brunette on top of her, moving with lust in her green eyes, her mouth relentless on Jules's.

The blonde wraps her legs around Riley's waist, needing her closer, deeper.

"Fuck, Riley." Jules closes her eyes, holding her breath when her orgasm starts.

It starts, it makes her arch her body off the floor, into Riley. The pleasure implodes between her legs, making her grind into Riley's fingers for more, more release, more friction, more of that addictive feeling that topples her over the edge.

And Riley keeps going. She doesn't stop. She doesn't stop while Jules shudders beneath her, a second orgasm already rippling through the blonde's body.

It's rough, it has her crying Riley's name, tugging on chestnut hair while she so desperately rides it out, her hips rocking into Riley, breathing heavily while her body jolts in the after waves that Riley keeps causing with her long, curled fingers inside of her.

"Enough." Jules pants heavily, feeling Riley then collapse on top of her, their bodies close.

The blonde can't help herself when her arms wrap around the woman she loves so much.

"Fuck, you are so sexy." Riley murmurs in her ear, nibbling on a lobe before kissing her way back to Jules's mouth.

The blonde can feel how Riley moves to straddle her hips again.

Jules grins when she watches the brunette sit on top of her, already grinding into her, but the blonde knows it isn't enough.

She can feel Riley's arousal on her lower stomach.

As Jules attempts to sit up, Riley is smooth when she sits in Jules's lap, the blonde's hand sliding down between their bodies.

"What do you want?" she leans forward, smiling when Riley shudders under her lips as she ghosts over her neck.

"I want you to fuck me with…"

"You want to use the toy on you?" Jules grins then, loving it when Riley gets shy. Usually, it is Riley using the toy on Jules, not the other way around.

"Hmm."

Hands tangle in blonde hair while Jules takes her time to kiss the brunette in her neck.

This is something that Jules has always loved to do. Kissing Riley right below her jaw, because she knows what kind of reaction she gets when she does so.

It's Riley's most sensitive spot above the belt.

Jules wants to do this, often. Whenever she is free from work and goes to court to watch one of Riley's public cases, she wants to do it.

When she sees her girlfriend in her professional wear, she wants to drag her tongue in Riley's neck to taste her, making her shiver, making her moan Jules's name until she can't do it anymore.

Just like now. The way Riley almost tumbles out of Jules's lap when the blonde sinks her teeth in soft skin, she knows Riley is a goner.

But, she softly urges the brunette up to take to the bedroom.

She grabs the strap-on Riley was referring to earlier, making sure its harness is tightly around her hips when she watches her girlfriend lie on the bed.

"How do you want me to fuck you?" Jules smiles, admiring Riley's beauty when she crawls onto the bed, settling between Riley's legs.

"However you want." Riley's voice is trembling, her eyes are wide, pupils blown and her lips are thick and bruised, inviting Jules for more.

The blonde leans down to kiss her, roughly. Her tongue is demanding access in Riley's mouth, moaning at the brunette's hot, wanting lips.

"Inside." Riley moans loudly when Jules's hand teases her near her entrance.

The blonde listens, feeling wet folds ready and wanting for her. She bites her lip when she softly pushes the dildo inside, feeling Riley slowly.

"Oh, fuck." The brunette instantly wraps her legs around Jules's back, pulling her as close as possible.

Slowly, but surely, Jules leans down to take a perky breast in her mouth, nipping and sucking while she thrusts her hips into Riley.

She grows rougher every time, feeling Riley crumble beneath her as she pumps into her, their bodies moving together smoothly.

"Fuck. Jules, please. Harder." Riley begs her, pulling her close to press their lips together, their teeth clashing, their tongues messily fighting, but Jules doesn't mind.

She pulls back, burying her face in Riley's neck when she relentlessly pounds into her girlfriend, unable to stop marking her girlfriend in her neck.

She licks, she nips, she thrusts and she moans, hearing Riley's pleasure build.

But she sits up, able to thrust deeper this way. She loves the sight of Riley beneath her, her breasts moving with each pump, every movement. Riley's eyes closed, mouth wide open when she is about to come.

Arms pull Jules down the moment Riley's orgasm shocks through her body and the blonde collapses, trying to give the brunette some kind of stimulation to ride out her orgasm.

Riley rolls her hips into Jules while she pulls down her girlfriend on top of her, needing to feel her close as she comes to a still, panting heavily when her green eyes open to look up at the blonde.

"Hey, beautiful." Jules grins, her hands moving to stroke away Riley's wild sex hair, smiling when Riley attempts to speak, but she's out of breath and completely motionless. "Still hungry?"

"God, yes." Riley lets out a short laugh, moving her hands to tangle in blonde hair. "But kiss me before we go."

Jules smiles when she nudges Riley's cheek with her nose, loving the way Riley can't seem to stop smiling whenever they are physically close.

She loves the warmth, their soft skins connected at so many points between them. Riley's legs still around her, Jules softly pulls out.

"I love you." the blonde admits from the bottom of her heart, placing a kiss on Riley's jawline, smiling when she feels a head turn to capture her lips.

She moans softly, never getting enough of her girlfriend.

"Hm, as much as I love kissing you, I am starting to get hungry too." Jules grins when she pecks Riley's lips one last time, before softly pulling away.

She takes off the strap-on, watching her girlfriend collect herself before removing from the bed.

"Short shower?" Riley grimaces when she feels herself down there.

"Good idea." Jules grins as they silently move to rinse themselves off quickly, before moving to the living room and putting on their relaxed wear. They sit on the floor, their backs against the couch as they start digging into all the food that Riley bought.

"Riley?" Jules asks then.

"Yes, Jules?"

"Do you want me to call you Riles?" she can see the amusement flash over Riley's features.

"I hate that nickname." The brunette admits then, smiling when she takes a bite and kisses Jules with her mouth full of muffin.

"It doesn't suit you."
"It should've been a sign." Riley still has a shimmer of amusement in her eyes when she glances at Jules.
"With Camilla?"
"She called me Riles from the start. I never dared to tell her that I didn't like it, though." The brunette chews, licking her fingers before grabbing a bottle of Gatorade, taking large gulps.
Riley could do literally anything and she'd still be adorable.
"Do you still regret it?"
"Marrying her?" Riley's green eyes are a little wider than before.
Jules bites her lip, nodding softly. They don't often talk about their marriages, but when they do, it often turns serious.
"I don't know. I think I learned a lot from it, but it will probably never stop feeling like a mistake."
Jules munches on a bagel, leaning her head on Riley's shoulder.
"Why did it take you so long to notice I had moved in with you?" she continues her questions, suddenly feeling nervous when she thinks about the questions she has been meaning to ask for a few months.
She knows that they haven't been together long, but they've known each other for two years and not once, did Jules doubt what they have.
Not once.
Her feelings grow stronger every day, her confidence conquering her fear.
She wants Riley. She has known this for a long time and it hasn't changed. In fact, she thinks her mind is finally catching up with her heart.
"Uhm…" Riley seems to be at a loss, her green eyes searching Jules's face the moment the blonde looks back up. "…I don't know. Perhaps because I didn't want to pressure you."
"You waited for so long because you didn't want to pressure me? While I basically already moved in?" Jules smiles when she softly kisses Riley's cheek, feeling the brunette lean into her lips.
"Yeah. I wanted you to set the pace."
"So, are you going to wait forever until you propose then, too?" the blonde asks the question.
She knows she's catching Riley off guard. She knows that the brunette has thought about it, though.
She could sense it every time they'd walk past a jewelry store, she could see it whenever they spotted someone in a wedding dress.
"Jules, I… I don't know. I didn't think you'd ever want to get married again." Riley admits then, the last bite of her muffin somewhere in the air, waiting to be eaten.
"What if I want to?"
"Then… I don't know." Riley smiles shyly, but her eyes tell Jules so much more.

She can see the want in those green eyes, she can see the hope, the happiness sparkling subtly.

It's barely there, but it's obvious to Jules.

"We will see." The blonde offers then, shrugging it off like it's nothing.

But, her heart is racing.

They continue eating, both seem to be lost in thought.

"So, what did you want to paint? Which wall?" Jules asks then, watching Riley's gaze move to the biggest wall in the living room.

"Our old view? You inspired me at New Year's Eve." Riley smiles then, leaning in to press a kiss against Jules's lips.

The blonde smiles into it. "Okay."

They finish up their food, starting on their booze as Riley puts on some music in the background.

They move away the furniture that occupied the wall, placing the plastic in front of it while they both sing along with the music.

"Wait, can we paint some stupid stuff before we really make the final thing?" Riley's soft chuckle is adorable when she moves the cans onto the plastic, opening them and stirring them with the brushes.

"Hm, okay." Jules grins mischievously. "I'll paint something for you. But don't look!"

As they both move to the white wall, Jules watches Riley concentrate to put something on the wall. The brunette's tongue pokes out, her eyes narrowed as she works.

Jules smiles to herself. She reaches in her pocket. She was so close to being busted when Riley lowered her sweats when they were having sex on the ground.

She has the tiniest box in her pocket. She somehow wants to carry it with her the whole time.

They work quietly, for about ten minutes, when they both pull back.

"I'm done." Riley smiles so proudly, that Jules can't hold back a snort when she moves to see Riley's piece of art.

Her heart drops when she sees three stick figures, one with blonde hair, one with brown hair and a tinier one with blonde hair.

She can feel her stomach churn, in a good way, butterflies all over when she realizes what it means.

"Riley?"

"I want a family with you." she blurts out then, not so tactical. "I love you."

When Jules doesn't speak, panic is visible in green eyes, but Jules is fast to tug Riley to her own side of the wall.

She can hear the hitch of a breath when they both look at what Jules painted. Or rather, what the blonde wrote.

On the white wall, in small, graceful black calligraphy, it says: 'Riley, marry me?'

MAYBE, ONE DAY

Underneath, there's two words. Yes and No. Beneath that, two empty squares.
"Jules." Riley's eyes are as wide as Jules has ever seen them; plump lips parted in surprise.
"Go write your answer." The blonde nervously urges the brunette to do so.
"I think my painting is pretty clear, isn't it?" Riley manages to pull herself together, brush still in hand when she moves to the wall, filling the square underneath the word 'yes'.
Jules reaches in her pocket then, but she is stopped by Riley scooping her up in her arms, twirling her around before putting her back down, peppering Jules's face with kisses.
"Yes. I want to marry you. I've been wanting to marry you for a while, now." Riley's smile is so wide, so sweet and so, so Riley.
It warms Jules's heart when she snakes her arms around Riley's neck, pulling her in for a searing kiss, feeling her girlfriend pressed up to her, their lips moving together as their tongues fight.
"I love you, I love you." Jules repeats the words, hugging Riley so tightly she knows might knock the wind out of her.
"I love you more, Jules. I love you so much." Riley holds on just as tightly.
And so they stand, in their living room, a proposal written on the wall. They clutch onto each other, buried in each other, knowing that they are able to put aside their fears to love each other.
They still hold their brushes, but they breathe each other in.
"I trust you." Jules then murmurs into Riley's ear.
"I trust you, too." Riley smiles then, pulling back subtly.
Despite it being a serious conversation, Jules pulls back with a mischievous smile on her face.
"Be careful with what you say, Dunn." Jules then laughs, pulling up her brush to dip it into Riley's face, leaving a dark, big stroke on her face.
"Oh, no. Oh, no, no." Riley barks out a laugh, trying to wipe it off, but she only makes things worse.
Before Jules knows it, something is in her face, too and they struggle to get as much paint on the other as they can.
They are laughing when Jules's hair is completely yellow and Riley's face is completely black, their hoodies and sweats ruined.
Then, a familiar song comes up.
"May I have this dance, to make it up to you?" Riley drops her brush, laughing and stumbling over her feet as she sings along the lines, grabbing Jules's hand to pull her into a clumsy ballroom dancing position.
Jules wants to collapse in laughter, unable to breathe normally when Riley marches them through the room on the beat of the song.
"Can I say something crazy, I love youuuu." Riley sings, burying her wet painted face in Jules's neck to leave a huge stain.

Jules shrieks with laughter, holding onto her fiancée tightly.

"Gimme both your hands, to make it up to youuu. Let me spin and excite youuu." Riley laughs with the blonde as they stumble through their room, not noticing them leaving paint stains on the floor.

"You must have been booorn with two right feet!" Jules laughs then when Riley stumbles over her feet, dragging them both down to the floor, a rolling mess of painted limbs.

"I love you more than your mooother, more than you love yourself. May I have this dance?" Riley laugh falls quiet as they lie, breathing heavily, Jules on top.

The blonde fills in. "Can I say something crazy? I love you."

Before Riley can continue singing, Jules leans down. Riley's lips are soft. Painted, but soft.

She leans into it, her eyes closed when she feels those lips move against her own in a silent promise.

It's a yes.

Jules knows this as they lie there, Scooter jumping on Jules's back but she doesn't notice.

All she notices is the brunette beneath her.

Her future.

Her love.

As it was always meant to be, to be each other's home.

And she wants it.

She wants Riley.

"Hey, Riles?" Jules teases her then, pulling back with extra paint on her face.

"Yes, Julesie?" Riley's hands are on her face, tucking short blonde hair behind Jules's ears.

"I have a ring for you."

"You do?"

"Wanna see?"

"Hell, yes."